CHARLES SHEFFIELD

THE MIND POOL

Free
Read and pass
along

"Opening a
Sheffield book
is like turning on
a mind link."
—Robert L. Forward,
author of *Rocheworld*

72165-8 (CAN. $9.99) U.S. $6.99

© MATTINGLY '92

$6.99 U.S.
$9.99 CAN.

ISBN 0-671-72165-8

50699>

S

EAN

PRAISE FOR CHARLES SHEFFIELD

"[*Brother to Dragons*] is a compulsive read . . . a pageturner. . . . Why did I find it so riveting? It could be because Sheffield has constructed a background that is absolutely convincing, and set against it a walloping good story."

—Baird Searles, *Asimov's*

"One of the most imaginative, exciting talents to appear on the SF scene in recent years." —*Publishers Weekly*

"The best modern examples of 'hard' science fiction . . . not only genuine but up to date . . . a talent to be reckoned with."

—*New Scientist*

"Charles is one of those SF writers who makes the rest of us think seriously about a career in retail sales. . . . He has the scientific grounding of a Clarke, the storytelling skills of a Heinlein, the dry wit of a Pohl or a Kornbluth, and the universe-building prowess of a Niven." —**Spider Robinson**

"Sheffield is a master of the hard science story . . . the Asimov or Clarke of the future." —*Noumenon*

"Comparable to some of Arthur C. Clarke's fiction in its concepts . . . one of the best." —*Science Fiction Review*

"A treat for readers who like their science fiction loaded with intelligent scientific extrapolation." —*Chicago Sun-Times*

"A creator of far future romances with all the sweep and grandeur of the best Arthur C. Clarke. . . . an original and even unique voice." —Dan Chow, *Locus*

"Opening a Sheffield book is like switching on a mind link."

—**Robert L. Forward**

"One of the field's most successful new science fiction writers."

—*Washington Book Review*

BAEN BOOKS by CHARLES SHEFFIELD:

CHARLES SHEFFIELD

THE MIND POOL

This is a work of fiction. All the characters and events portrayed in this book are fictional, and any resemblance to real people or incidents is purely coincidental.

Copyright © 1993 by Charles Sheffield

All rights reserved, including the right to reproduce this book or portions thereof in any form.

A Baen Books Original

Baen Publishing Enterprises
P.O. Box 1403
Riverdale, NY 10471
www.baen.com

ISBN: 0-671-72165-8

Cover art by David Mattingly

First printing, April 1993
Sixth printing, November 2001

Distributed by Simon & Schuster
1230 Avenue of the Americas
New York, NY 10020

Printed in the United States of America

To Dan Chow,
who said why it should be done,

and to Algis Budrys and Charles N. Brown,
who said how it could be done.

in the United States of America

Introduction

The Mind Pool, the volume you are now holding in your hand, was originally a somewhat different and rather shorter book, *The Nimrod Hunt*.

Writing a book is hard work. Writing a book *twice*, the same book, sounds like masochism. I want to explain why I did it.

Before *The Nimrod Hunt* was published, I knew three things. First, the book was the longest and most complex science fiction novel that I had ever written. Second, because of my own worries over that length and complexity, I omitted a substantial subplot that I was very fond of, but which was not an absolute essential. That did allow the book to be a good deal shorter, although at the cost of an ending different from the one that I had originally intended. (I have put that subplot back in. It first enters in Chapter Three. Although the beginning of *The Mind Pool* is like the start of *The Nimrod Hunt*, the ending is radically different.)

Third, and less obviously relevant, in writing *The Nimrod Hunt* I had been greatly influenced by a classic novel by Alfred Bester, *The Stars My Destination*. I've loved that book since I first read it. I had no thought of imitating Bester's style, which although marvelous is uniquely his and quite unlike my way of telling stories. But I wanted to emulate the multitude of ideas, the diverse backgrounds, and the blowzy rococo decadence of his future society. I also wanted to put in a good deal more science, an interstellar landscape, and some rather odd aliens. That told me I was going to write a pretty long novel.

My admiration of Bester was not particularly hidden. How could it be, when his book had a major character named Regis Sheffield, and mine had one called King Bester?

But soon after publication, I learned two things that I had not known before it. First, the influence of Bester was direct enough to upset some reviewers, particularly in the way that *The Nimrod Hunt* ended. Dan Chow told me as much and said it marred the novel for anyone familiar with Bester's works.

Second, and perhaps more important, I had committed a basic sin of story-telling. At the beginning of the book I set up a red herring, an expectation in the reader's mind which was never fulfilled. Algis Budrys told me just what I had done, and how to correct it.

All these things would normally be irrelevant. The moving word processor writes, and having writ, moves on. A book, once published, cannot be unwritten, and even if rewritten it will not normally be seen in print.

Enter Jim Baen, publisher of *The Nimrod Hunt*. In August of 1991, Jim called to say that he was going to reissue the book, with a new cover. Was I interested in changing, deleting, or adding anything?

Was I! Of course I was, and my task sounded easy: remove the red herring, restore the original subplot, and make the homage to Alfred Bester less intrusive.

Naturally, it didn't work out like that. I am not the same writer I was six years ago. I finished by rewriting the whole novel to match my present tastes. Some passages grew, others shrank or disappeared, many became unrecognizable. I don't think any page was left untouched. The one-week easy fix became the two-month concentrated effort. I found that I had produced a different book.

The Mind Pool is that book. If you have read *The Nimrod Hunt*, I invite you to compare the two. If you have not, I invite you to read the book that you are holding.

I hope the story is a success. If not, I'm not sure I want to know about it. It would be a real pain to have to write everything a third time.

Prologue:
Cobweb Station

The first warning was no more than a glimmer of light. In the array of twenty-two thousand monitors that showed the energy balance of the solar system, one miniature diode had flicked on to register a demand overload.

To say that the signal was neglected by the crew at the Vulcan Nexus would be untrue and unfair. It was simply never seen. The whole display array had been installed in the main control room of the Nexus for the benefit of visiting dignitaries and the media. "There!"— a wave of the hand—"The power equation of the whole system at a glance. Left side, energy supply. Each light shows energy collection from a solar panel. The individual demands are on the right."

The visitors took a moment or two to examine the array of gently winking lights, and the tour went on. The impressive part was still to come, with the powered swoop past four hundred million square kilometers of collectors, each sucking in Sol's radiance. The array orbited only two million kilometers above the photosphere, where Sol's flaming disk filled thirty degrees of the sky. It was an unusual visitor who gave the display room a second thought after a roller-coaster ride to the solar furnace, skimming over vast hydrogen flares and the Earth-size-swallowing whirlpools of the sunspots.

So the overload signal was seen by no one. But human ignorance of minor energy fluctuations was no cause for concern. Supply and demand had long been monitored by an agent far more efficient and conscientious than unreliable *homo sapiens*. The distributed computing network of *Dominus* at once noted the source of the energy drain. It was coming from Cobweb Station, twelve billion kilometers from the Sun. In less than one hour, energy demand at Cobweb had increased by a factor of one hundred. Even as that information came through the computer network, a second light went on in the displays. Energy use had increased again, by another factor of a hundred.

Dominus switched in an additional power supply from the orbiting fusion plants out near Persephone. Reserve supply was more than adequate. There was no sign of emergency, no thought of disaster. But *Dominus* initiated a routine inquiry as to the cause of the increased energy demand and its projected future profile.

When there was no reply from Cobweb, *Dominus* brought new data on-line. A communications silence for the past twenty-four hours was noted for Cobweb Station. That was correlated in turn with the pattern of energy use, and a signal showing that the Mattin Link system at Cobweb Station had been activated, although not yet used for either matter or signal transmission.

Dominus flashed an attention alert to the main control displays at Ceres headquarters and scanned all probes beyond Neptune. The nearest high-acceleration needle was nearly a billion kilometers away from Cobweb—seventeen hours at a routine hundred gee.

Dominus dispatched the needle probe just a few seconds before the problem first came to human attention. The technician on duty at Ceres checked the status flags, noted the time, and approved both the increased energy drain and the use of the needle probe. She did not, however, call for a report on the reason for the energy use on Cobweb Station. The anomaly appeared minor, and her mind was elsewhere. The end of the shift was just a few minutes away, and she had an after-work date with a new possible partner. She was looking forward to that. Staying overtime to study minor power fluctuations, far away in the Outer System, formed no part of her evening plans.

Her actions were quite consistent with her responsibilities. That she would later become the first scapegoat was merely evidence of the need for scapegoats.

When the needle probe was halfway to Cobweb Station, energy demand flared higher. That surging rise by another two orders of magnitude finally pushed the problem to a high-priority level. *Dominus* signalled for an immediate increase to emergency probe acceleration and began the transfer to probe memory of all structural details of Cobweb Station.

The racing probe was less than two years old. As a class-T device it contained the new *pan inorganica* logic circuits and a full array of sensors. It could comprehend as much of what it saw as most human observers, and it was eager to show its powers. It waited impatiently, until at five million kilometers from Cobweb Station it could finally pick up the first image on its radar. The hulking station showed as a grainy globe, pocked by entry ports and knobby with communications equipment. The probe's data bank now included a full description of the station's purpose and presumed contents. It had started all-channel signalling even at extreme range, with no reply.

Cobweb Station's silence continued. The probe was closing fast, and it was puzzled to observe that all the station's entry ports appeared open to space. It sent a Mattin Link message back to *Dominus*, reporting that peculiarity, and decelerated hard until it was within a hundred kilometers. The high-resolution sensors were now able to pick up images of small, irregular objects floating close to the station. Some of them gave off the bright radar reflection of hard metal, but others were more difficult to analyze. The probe launched two of its small bristle explorers, one to inspect the space flotsam, the other to enter and examine the interior of the station.

If the second bristle explorer's task was ever completed, the results were not recorded. Long before that, every message circuit on the probe had hit full capacity. A blast of emergency signals deluged through the Mattin

Link to *Dominus*, while rarely-used indicators sprang to life on every control board from the Vulcan Nexus to the Oort Harvester.

The first bristle explorer had encountered the debris outside Cobweb Station. Some of it was strange fragments, mixtures of organic and inorganic matter blown to shapelessness by the weapons of station guards. But next to those twisted remnants, sometimes mixed inextricably with them, there floated the bloated, frozen bodies of the guards themselves. In shredded uniforms, cold fingers still on triggers, the dead hung gutted and stiff-limbed in the endless sarcophagus of open space.

Throughout the solar system, alarm bells sounded their requiems.

Chapter 1

LINK NETWORK COMPLETE. STAND BY FOR CONFERENCE CONNECT.

The musical disembodied voice sounded from all sides. In the last few seconds before final Link Connection, Dougal MacDougal turned to the two men standing next to him in the domed hall.

"I want to emphasize it one more time. This is strictly a *briefing* for the Ambassadors. Although the hearing takes place in the Star Chamber, there's currently no criminal charge at issue. I'm sure you want to keep it that way. That means your testimonies have to be as accurate and complete as possible. No concealing of information, even if it makes you look bad. Understood?"

Ambassador Dougal MacDougal was a tall, imposing figure. The traditional robes of office were handed down from one Terran Ambassador to the next, but on him they sat as though made for his shoulders alone.

The other two men exchanged the briefest of glances before they nodded.

"And be *consistent*," went on MacDougal. "You are in enough trouble already. You don't want to add to it by *contradicting* each other."

"I understand perfectly." Luther Brachis was a match for MacDougal in height, and massively broader. Even in the low gravity of the Ceres' Star Chamber, his booted tread shook the gold and white floor. He was in full uniform. On his left breast sat a phalanx of military decorations, and the swirling Starburst of Solar Security was

5

blazoned across his right sleeve. No matter that those meant less than nothing to the alien ambassadors. They mattered to *him*.

His eyes, a weary grey-blue, were unreadable as they met Dougal MacDougal's. "I will describe everything, and conceal nothing."

"Very good." The Ambassador turned at once to the other man. "I know you two never stop bickering. I just want to tell you, this isn't the time and place for it. If you have anything to disagree on, do it *now*. The Link will close in a few seconds."

Esro Mondrian had to look up to meet MacDougal's glare. Both MacDougal and Brachis towered over him by a full head, and in contrast to them his build was slender, even frail. Unlike them, he was also wearing the plainest of costumes. The severe black uniform of Boundary Security, precisely tailored and meticulously clean, stood unadorned by medals or insignia of office. Only the single fire opal at his left collar served as his identification badge—and concealed its other multiple functions as communicator, computer, warning system, and weapon.

Mondrian shrugged. "I'm not in the habit of concealing information from anyone who legitimately has a need to know it. As soon as we have full identification for the parties tapping in to the Link, and a secure line, I'll give them all the information that I believe appropriate."

His voice was agreeable and low in volume, but it was not offering the commitment that Dougal MacDougal was asking. Before MacDougal could reply, the lights for full Mattin Link operation began to blink. The Terran Ambassador gave Mondrian one unsatisfied scowl and turned to face the sunken well of the room. In front of them, the hemisphere of the Star Chamber's central atrium had been empty. Now three oval patterns of light were flickering into existence within it. As the men watched, the lights gradually solidified to reveal the three-dimensional images of the Ambassadors.

On the far left hung a shrouded, pulsing mass of dark purple. The image steadied, and the shape became the swarming aggregate of a Tinker Composite, imaging in from Mercantor in the Fomalhaut system. The Tinker had clustered to form a symmetrical ovoid with appendages of roughly human proportions. Next to it (but fifty-plus lightyears away in real space, halfway across the domain of the Stellar Group) loomed the dark green bulk of an Angel. And far off to the right, beyond a vacant spot in the assembly and still showing the margin of rainbow fringes that marked signal transients, hovered the lanky tubular assembly of a Pipe-Rilla. It was linking in from its home planet around Eta Cassiopeiae, a mere eighteen lightyears away.

MATTIN LINK NETWORK COMPLETE, said the same pleasant human voice. *THE CONFERENCE MAY NOW PROCEED.*

It was a historic moment. The representatives of the Stellar Group were in simultaneous full audio and visual contact for the first time in twenty-two Earth years. Dougal MacDougal, conscious that he was about to take part in a singular event of Stellar Group history, adjusted his already-perfect robes and stepped forward to fill the one remaining spot in the tableau of ambassadors. "Greetings. I am Dougal MacDougal, Solar Ambassador to the Stellar Group. Welcome to the Ceres' Star Chamber. Can you all see and hear me, and each other?"

The question was pure diplomatic formality. The Link computers would have confirmed full audio and visuals before permitting any of the participants to enter link mode. "Yes," said the Pipe-Rilla, in a fair approximation to human speech. "Yes," echoed the Tinker, and, after a few seconds, the computer-generated response of the Angel Ambassador.

"As you know," went on MacDougal, "we have called this special meeting to discuss a difficult situation. A recent event here in the Sol system is cause for grave concern, and it could be a problem affecting the whole Stellar Group. We may have to consider unusual—maybe unprecedented—control measures. Naturally, any such decision must involve all members of the Stellar Group. But first, you need to know the background of the problem. For that purpose, I have arranged for you to receive a briefing from two of the principals involved in this matter from the beginning,"

"Preparing to pass the buck." Luther Brachis spoke with an impassive face and without moving his lips.

"Naturally." Both men had learned the parade ground knack of invisible speech long ago, but the trick could still come in useful. "Did you ever doubt it?" went on Mondrian softly. "Mac's a good bureaucrat, if he's nothing else. He decided long ago where he was going to place the blame."

"First, a statement from Commander Luther Brachis," said MacDougal, as though he had managed to intercept Mondrian's last remark. "Commander Brachis is the Chief of Solar System Security. As such, he is responsible for monitoring all anomalous events that occur within half a lightyear of Sol." MacDougal turned away from the other Ambassadors, and moved so that all four were in line facing the witnesses. Hidden lamps came on to frame Brachis in a crossfire of illumination.

"You may begin," said MacDougal.

Brachis nodded to the four shapes in their cocoons of light. His thoughts, whatever they were, would not be read from his blunt lion's face.

"The Ambassador correctly stated my duties. Security is my job, from Apollo Station and the Vulcan Nexus, out to the edge of the Oort Cloud and the Dry Tortugas. I have held that position for five years.

"Two years ago, I received a request for a development project on Cobweb Station. That station is a research facility about twelve billion kilometers from Sol. It is a free orbiting artificial structure, in the ecliptic, and roughly halfway between the orbits of Neptune and Persephone. Cobweb Station has served as a research center for more than seventy Earth years. The proposed project was a secret one, but that is not unusual for the facility. I approved the request, and the project began under the code name, *Operation Morgan*. With your permission, we will defer description of the nature of the project itself until Commander Mondrian's testimony." Brachis paused, and waited for the four stylized gestures of assent.

"Then I will say no more than this: From my point of view, Operation Morgan was conducted with the highest level of security. Twenty of my department's most experienced and valued guards were assigned to the project. They took up residence on Cobweb Station for the duration of the project. General supplies of volatiles were dropped in from the Oort Cloud, and energy came through the solar system's supply grid. That power was controlled from the Vulcan Nexus, with the master boards here on Ceres. In two years of operation, no anomaly of any kind was ever noted. All progress reports on Operation Morgan indicated excellent results, with no substantial difficulties experienced or projected.

"That situation ended twenty days ago. On that date, an anomalous energy demand triggered a flag in our general power monitoring system.

"This concludes the first part of my testimony." Brachis glanced from one Ambassador to the next. "Are there questions?"

The four figures facing him were silent. There was only the usual faint hiss of the Mattin Link connection. The Angel was restlessly waving its upper lobes, while Dougal MacDougal was glancing from side to side. Brachis knew better than to expect support from the Solar Ambassador.

"With your permission, then, I will continue. The changed energy requirement that I referred to came directly from Cobweb Station. Unfortunately it happened during a quiet period, very near to a change of shift. The evidence of increased load was not at first noticed by my staff. I take full responsibility for that operational failure. However, the demand change was registered by our automatic monitoring system, together with a lengthy communications silence. A probe was dispatched to Cobweb Station.

"It arrived too late. All my staff were dead. The station was empty of human life. The Mattin Link had been operated. And I finally learned things about the nature of Operation Morgan that I should have taken the time to learn long ago. All activities at Cobweb Station are under my jurisdiction. I take full responsibility for what happened there."

He had finished his testimony and was ready to stand down, but now there was a stir from the ranks of the Ambassadors. "You said that the Mattin Link was activated." It was the Pipe-Rilla, gently vibrating her thorax plates. "For transmission of objects, or for signals only?"

"For objects."

"Then, to what destinations?"

"I do not know. But the energy drain says that it must have been many lightyears."

As Brachis was giving his testimony, new individual components had flown in silently to join the Tinker Composite. Now it bulked much larger than a human. There was a fluttering of tiny purple-black wings, and then a sibilant facsimile of human speech came again through the Link. "We would like the records, if you please. We wish to attempt our own analysis of possible destinations. And we wish to know more about the nature of the project you term *Operation Morgan*."

"Very well. But for that, I will with your permission defer to Commander Mondrian. My own records will be sent to you at once, and I will of course be available to answer any further questions." Luther Brachis stepped back, ceding the spotlight to Esro Mondrian.

His companion had been performing his own close inspection of the Ambassadors. There was no chance of recognizing any particular assembly of Tinker Composites, but the Angels and Pipe-Rillas both had stability of structure. It was possible that he had met one of them before, on their own home worlds. In any case, he knew he would have to talk right past Dougal MacDougal if he hoped for any kind of sympathetic response from the alien Ambassadors.

"My name is Esro Mondrian. I am Chief of Boundary Survey security. My territory *begins* half a lightyear from Sol, where it meets the region controlled by Commander Brachis. It extends all the way out to, and includes, the Perimeter. Between us, Commander Brachis and I divide the responsibility for human species security. However,

Operation Morgan was my initiative and its failure is my responsibility, not his.

"I have worked in the past with each of your own local monitoring groups, and I have visited your home systems. We are fortunate, all our species, in that we live in stable, civilized regions, where there are few unknown dangers. But out on the Perimeter, fifty lightyears and more from Sol, there are no such guarantees."

Down in the sunken atrium in front of Mondrian there was an odd grunting sound. It was Dougal MacDougal, clearing his throat. He did not speak, but he did not need to. Mondrian understood the message. *Get on with it, man. The Ambassadors didn't link in from halfway to the Perimeter just to hear platitudes from you.*

And yet they had to hear this, whether MacDougal liked it or not. Esro Mondrian hurried on.

"Out on the Perimeter, distances are enormous. But our resources to monitor what is happening out there are limited, and operating uncertainties are large. A few years ago I realized that we were losing ground. The Perimeter constantly increases in size, but our capability was not growing with it. We had to have some new type of monitoring instrument—one that could function with minimal support from the home bases, and also one that was tougher and more flexible than anything that we could make with the *pan inorganica* brains. It was while I was wrestling with that problem, and evaluating alternatives—none of them satisfactory—that I was approached by a scientist, Livia Morgan. She offered an intriguing prospect. She could, she claimed, develop symbiotic forms that combined organic and inorganic components. By the end of our first meeting, I was convinced that what she had might be perfect for our needs." Mondrian nodded at one of the figures in front of him. "I also knew of at least one example, sufficient to prove that such a blend of organic with inorganic was not impossible."

The Angel acknowledged the reference with a wave of blue-green fronds. It was itself a symbiotic life-form, discovered a century and a half earlier when the expanding wavefront of the Perimeter had reached the star Capella and the planets around it. The visible part of the Angel was the Chassel-Rose, slow-moving, mindless, and wholly vegetable. Shielded within the bulbous central section lived the sentient crystalline Singer, relying upon the Chassel-Rose for habitat, transportation, and communication with the external world.

"Imitation is the sincerest form of flattery," said the computerized voice of the Angel.

Mondrian stared back at the gently waving fronds. The Angels had that disconcerting habit of employing human cliches and proverbs at every opportunity. No one was ever sure if it represented the symbiote's perverse ideas of racial politeness, or served some wild sense of humor.

"Regarding the entities that Livia Morgan proposed to create." Mondrian had realized after a few seconds that the Angel intended to offer no further comment. "I will from this point term them the *Morgan Constructs*. They were designed specifically to patrol the Perimeter. Their performance specifications were drawn very precisely. Each unit had to be mobile, durable, and highly intelligent. Livia Morgan told me once that they would be—I quote—'indestructible.' Fortunately, she was exaggerating. However, they were designed to be very tough, since they would cruise the unexplored regions of the Perimeter, and perhaps there encounter life forms inimical to them and to everyone in the Stellar Group. However, I intended that they should serve a reporting function only. They would be able to protect themselves from attack, but they would not, under any circumstances, harm a known intelligent life form, or any life form that might possibly have intelligence.

"I was present at every initial demonstration of the Morgan Constructs. They were exposed to each of our four species, and to the seven other possibly intelligent organisms within the Perimeter. They were also allowed to interact with a variety of Artefacts, simulacra of differing degrees of apparent intelligence. The Constructs recognized each known form. The unknown ones, they responded to in a friendly and harmless manner. They treated the Artefacts with caution and respect. When attacked themselves, they did no more than remove themselves from harm's way. However, they did so too reluctantly, and would have been destroyed in any real attack. I therefore authorized the next stage of the work, to raise the Constructs to a higher level of sophistication. Livia Morgan began that program. But somehow, out on Cobweb Station, a crucial design blunder must have been made." Mondrian faced Dougal MacDougal. "May I show the images obtained by the probe?"

"Carry on. But hurry. We can't hold the Link indefinitely."

"I want to warn you all, these scenes are deeply disturbing." As Mondrian spoke, a sphere of darkness was forming behind him. Within it glowed the rough-textured ovoid of Cobweb Station as it had been seen by one of the bristle probes. At first the whole station sat in the field of view. It grew in size, and increased steadily in resolution. Soon dozens of flattened and twisted objects could be seen, floating outside the airlocks. Many of them were quite unrecognizable, little more than fused fragments of metal and plastic. The camera ignored those. It closed remorselessly on a score of space suits. Each one was filled, but if their occupants had been alive when they were expelled from the locks, they would not have survived for long. The detailed images showed missing limbs, disemboweled trunks, and headless torsoes. The camera locked on one figure, a turning eyeless corpse that lacked feet and hands.

"That is the mortal remains of Dr. Livia Morgan." Mondrian's voice was unnaturally calm. "Although neither she nor the guards were able to send distress signals from Cobweb Station, the monitors preserved a complete record of their last few hours. Based on that evidence, Morgan Constructs are cunning, and deadly, and utterly inimical to human life. I would like to express my admiration for the performance of the guards assigned to Cobweb Station by Commander Brachis. Although they had no warning when the Constructs ran wild, they did not give up or panic. There were seventeen Morgan Constructs on Cobweb Station, each at a different stage of development, and each designed with a different level of sophistication. The guards were able to destroy fourteen of them completely, inside or outside the station, but with great loss of life. Dr. Morgan and four surviving guards attempted to negotiate with the remaining three. She was seized and systematically dismembered. Unless you insist, I do not propose to show you details of those scenes.

"The remaining guards were hounded through the station interior. They managed to destroy two more Morgan Constructs before they were killed themselves. By the time that the bristle probes reached Cobweb Station, it was empty of all life."

"Seventeen Constructs." The whistling voice of the Tinker Composite spoke at once. "Fourteen died, and later two more . . ."

"You are quite correct." The images behind Mondrian were fading. "As Commander Brachis told you, the Mattin Link had been operated. That should have been impossible for a Construct which had received no assistance or training. It is a further proof of extraordinary intelligence. The seventeenth Morgan Construct—the most recently developed, and the most sophisticated—has disappeared. We are doing our best to trace it, but our working assumption must be a pessimistic one. Somewhere within the fifty-eight lightyear radius of the Known Sphere—close to the Perimeter, we hope, rather than near one of our home worlds—there is a formidable threat, of unknown magnitude. I do not believe that any of our races is in immediate danger, particularly since the Constructs were designed and trained to work out on the Perimeter, and it is likely that the escaped one will have chosen to flee there. But we cannot guarantee that, or that the Construct will stay in one place. The purpose of today's meeting was to inform you of these unfortunate facts; and to hear your suggestions as to ways of dealing with the situation. That is the end of my official statement. Are there questions?"

Mondrian waited, glancing from one oval pool of light to the next. The Tinker, Angel, and Pipe-Rilla were too alien for him to be able to read their feelings. Dougal MacDougal merely seemed irritable and decidedly uneasy.

"Then, your Excellencies." Mondrian took a step

backwards, intending to align himself with Luther Brachis. "With your permission—"

"Questions!" The fourteen-foot figure of the Pipe-Rilla was unfolding, rising high on its stick-thin legs. The forelimbs were clutching the tubular trunk, and the long antennas were waving. "I have questions."

Mondrian stepped forward again and waited, while the Pipe-Rilla went through a writhing of limbs and a preliminary buzzing.

"Tell us more about the *capability* of the Morgan Constructs. A being, designed for defense but turned against its makers, sounds unpleasant. But it does not sound like a great threat, or a cosmic issue. Presumably you designed these Constructs without major means of aggression?"

"They were designed that way, true enough." Mondrian glanced around, to see if Luther Brachis wanted to make any comment. The other man seemed more than ready to stay in the background. "However, as I mentioned, the Constructs were all equipped with considerable powers of self-defense, to protect them from possible enemies of unknown strength. Remember, they were supposed to operate alone, far from any support, against any dangers. Unfortunately, their defensive powers can also be used offensively. Their power plants can produce small fusion weapons. Their power lasers and shearing cones are enough to destroy any ship. They contained the best detection equipment that we could produce, since we wanted them to be able to find other life forms at the longest possible range. I could give you full details, but perhaps a single example is more informative: any single Morgan Construct could destroy a city, or lay waste a fair-sized planetoid. The surviving Construct, unfortunately, was the best equipped of the seventeen that were made."

Throughout Mondrian's reply there had been a slow stirring within the Tinker Composite. As he ended there came a burst of speech, so fast that the computers cut in to decipher and re-translate it.

"Why?" gabbled the Tinker. "Why, why, *why*? In the name of Security, you humans have produced a danger to yourselves and to all the other species of the Stellar

Group. Why does anyone *need* a Morgan Construct? Consider yourselves. You have been exploring the region around your Sun for six hundred of your years. We have watched that exploration for more than three centuries, ever since humans discovered our world and offered us space travel. And what have we seen? The Perimeter now encloses a region one hundred and sixteen lightyears in diameter, with more than two thousand star systems and a hundred and forty-three life-supporting planets. And *nowhere*, at any place within that vast region, has any species been found that is in any way murderous or aggressive—except your own. You humans are lifting a mirror to the universe, seeing your own faces within it, and declaring the cosmos terrifying. We, the Tinkers, say two things: first, until you *created* your Morgan Constructs there was no danger anywhere. Second, tell us why you continue this insane rush to expand the Perimeter. It now ends fifty-eight lightyears away from Sol. Will you humans be satisfied when it has reached eighty lightyears? Or one hundred lightyears? Will you stop *then?* When *will* you stop?"

Esro Mondrian looked to MacDougal. He saw no support there. "I cannot answer your general questions, Ambassador. However, I can make a relevant point. I have long suggested that the Perimeter be frozen, or at least the expansion slowed. You say that the region within the Perimeter has no dangers to any of us—"

"*Had* none." The Tinker was a blizzard of components, flying furiously about the central cluster. "Had none until your species created one."

"—but the region *outside* the Perimeter may contain absolutely anything. Who knows how dangerous it might be, to all of us?" Mondrian turned to face the Terran area of the atrium. "With all respect, Ambassador Mac-Dougal, I must say that I agree completely with the Tinker Ambassador. I know that such decisions are made at levels well above mine, but as long as expansion *does* proceed, something like the Morgan Constructs is essential. We must take measures to protect ourselves against whatever lies—"

"That's enough." Dougal MacDougal moved one hand,

and the lights illuminating Esro Mondrian were instantly extinguished. "Commander, you are removed from the witness stand. You were brought here to present a statement of a situation, not to offer your personal—and unsound—views on human exploration." MacDougal moved out of the atrium, and turned so that he could be seen by the other three ambassadors of the Stellar Group. "Fellow Ambassadors, my apologies to all of you. As you have heard, both these men bear fault in permitting this serious problem to arise. Their own words convict them of error and of negligence. As soon as this meeting is over, you have my word that I will move at once to have them removed from office. They will never again be in a position to—"

"No-o-o." The word came rolling from the Angel, delivered slowly and heavily through its computer link. "We will not permit such action."

Rarely for him, MacDougal was caught off balance. "You mean—you do not want me to dismiss Commander Mondrian and Commander Brachis?"

"No indeed." The topmost frond of the Angel went into slow but wide-ranging oscillation. "That cannot be. *The punishment must fit the crime.* We, the Angels of Sellora, request a move at once to Closed Hearing. We request full closure, without staff. There should be no one but Ambassadors present."

"But then the record—"

"There must be no record. The subject for discussion is a question so serious that it can be pursued only in full closed hearing. For this, we invoke our ultimate Ambassadorial privilege."

Even as the Angel spoke, an opaque screen was flickering into existence around the atrium. The lighted areas around the four Ambassadors were visible for a few seconds more, then there was nothing in the center of the Star Chamber but a ball of scintillating darkness.

Luther Brachis stepped forward to stand next to Esro Mondrian. The two men were alone, outside the dark sphere. Within it sat the four Ambassadors of the Stellar Group. Their earlier meeting had been the first full audio and visual meeting in twenty-two years. Now came the first Closed Hearing in more than a century.

Chapter 2

Mondrian and Brachis had clearly been excluded from the Ambassadorial meeting. Just as clearly, they had not been given permission to leave the Star Chamber. There was nowhere to go, nothing to do.

That should have been no problem. With overlapping areas of jurisdiction, the two men had a thousand points of shared responsibility and a hundred disputes to settle.

But not today. They remained speechless, Brachis pacing and Mondrian sitting in brooding silence, until after two long hours the opaque screen shivered away. The atrium that it revealed had only two places occupied. The Pipe-Rilla and Dougal MacDougal were still in position, but the Angel and the Tinker Composite had vanished. Even MacDougal's presence was debatable. He sat crumpled in his seat, like an empty bag of clothes from which the occupant had been spirited away.

The Pipe-Rilla gestured to Brachis and Mondrian to step forward. "We have reached agreement." The high-pitched voice was as cheerful as ever, but that was no more than an accident of the production mechanism. The Pipe-Rillas always sounded cheerful. The nervous rubbing of forelimbs told a different story. "And since the others are gone, and your own Ambassador appears to be indisposed, it is left to me to tell you the results of our discussions." The Pipe-Rilla gestured around her, at the two empty places and then at the shrunken, miserable figure of Dougal MacDougal.

"What happened to him?" asked Brachis.

18

"There was a point of dispute between your Ambassador and the Ambassador for the Angels. The Angel has forceful means of persuasion, even from a distance of many lightyears. I do not understand them, but Ambassador MacDougal will—I trust—recover in just a few of your hours." The Pipe-Rilla waved a clawed forelimb to dismiss the subject. "Commanders Brachis and Mondrian, please give me your closest attention. I must summarize our deliberations, and our conclusions. First, on the subject of your own blame . . ."

Mondrian and Brachis froze while the Pipe-Rilla stood, head bowed, for an interminable period. If a human had done such a thing, it would have been by design. But with a Pipe-Rilla . . .

"All the Ambassadors agree," said the Pipe-Rilla at last. "You are *both* responsible in this matter. Commander Mondrian for initiating a project with such enormous potential for danger. Commander Brachis, for failing to make sure that the monitoring for which he had responsibility was suitably carried out. You, and Livia Morgan herself, are culpable in high degree. The willingness of both of you to accept responsibility does you credit, but it is not ultimately relevant. You are guilty. The suggestion of your own Ambassador was that you should be relieved of all duties, dismissed from security service, and stripped of all privileges."

Brachis glanced at Mondrian. *Their* Ambassador! He held up his hand, palm outward. "If I could be permitted a comment—"

"*No.*" There was a barely discernible tremor in the Pipe-Rilla's voice. "I must proceed, and as rapidly as p-possible. If this discussion was *impossible* for the others, can you not see that it is far from easy for me? Ambassador MacDougal's proposal was of course unacceptable. As the Angel Ambassador pointed out to him, we hold you, Commander Mondrian, more to blame than Commander Brachis, since you initiated the project, but it would be preposterous to dismiss either of you, or relieve either of you of your duties. In any civilized society, it is the individual or group who *creates* a problem that must have responsibility for solving it. *The cause*

must become the cure. The creation of the Morgan Constructs, and the subsequent escape of one of them, came
from your actions and inactions. Livia Morgan, who made
the Constructs, is d-dead. And therefore the seeking out
and d-disposal of that escaped Morgan Construct must
be in your hands. We recognize that humans follow codes
of behavior quite different from the rest of the Stellar
Group, but in this case there is n-nothing to d-discuss.
We are . . . *adamant.*"

There had been a shift in the Pipe-Rilla's posture, and
its voice reflected the change. It was too gabbling and
jerky to be understood without translation, and *Dominus*
had cut in to provide computer support.

"Ambassador MacDougal has agreed," went on the
Pipe-Rilla. "B-beginning at once, there will be created a
new group within the department of Human System
Security. It will be of a form peculiar to human history
. . . a *military expedition* . . . what your species knows
as"—there was an infinitesimal pause, while *Dominus*
selected and offered for Pipe-Rilla approval a variety of
words—"as an Anabasis."

"As a *what*?" The grunted question from Brachis to
Mondrian was nothing like a whisper. "What's she
mean?"

"Anabasis," said Mondrian softly. "We need to review
our translation boxes. I don't know what she means, but
I'll bet that's not it—the original Anabasis was a military
expedition, one that turned into defeat and retreat. Not
a good omen."

The Pipe-Rilla took no notice of their exchange. She
was in serious trouble of her own, limbs moving spas-
tically and her narrow thorax fluttering. "The Anabasis,"
she whistled, on a rising note. "It will be headed by
Commander Mondrian, who has principal responsibility
for the problem, assisted by Commander Brachis. Your
t-task will be simple. You will s-select and t-train Pursuit
Teams, to find the—location of—the Morgan Con-struct.
You will follow it to—wherever it is hi—ding." Now
even *Dominus* could not help. The speech pattern of the
Pipe-Rilla was becoming more and more disorganized as
its voice rose past the range of human ears. It became a

great, shivering whistle, matching the shake of the giant body. "Each pursuit team must contain one—trained—member of—each intelligent species. Tinker—Angel—Human—and . . . and *Pipe-Rilla*." The voice became a supersonic shriek. *"The Pursuit Teams will find the Morgan Construct and—they will—destroy it. DESTROY IT!"*

The Pipe-Rilla was gone. The Link was broken, the Star Chamber atrium empty except for the huddled form of Dougal MacDougal.

Brachis turned to Esro Mondrian. "What in the name of living hell was all that about?"

Mondrian was rubbing his cheek and staring at the chromatic flicker of the dying Link connection. "I guess she couldn't stand it. None of them can. No wonder they had to have a Closed Session, and a secret vote."

"Couldn't stand *what*?" Brachis was scowling. It had just occurred to him that according to the Pipe-Rilla's edict, he now reported to Mondrian. "You're as bad as they are."

"Come on, Brachis. You know the prime rule of the rest of the Stellar Group as well as I do. *Intelligent life must be preserved.* It's not to be destroyed *ever*, for any reason."

"Yeah. As stupid a damned rule as I ever heard."

"Maybe. But that's the way they think of it—true at the individual level, and even more true at the species level."

"So?"

"So they want us to find the Morgan Construct—and *destroy it*. Suppose it's really an intelligent living form?"

"Tough. Happens all the time. Hell, I just lost twenty of my best guards."

"That's *individuals*. This Construct is the only one of its kind in the whole universe. Livia Morgan is dead, and we didn't find her records. Without them we don't know how to make a Construct. The ambassadors must have gone through agony to make that ruling—you saw them when they were looking at the images from the Cobweb Station probe. They told us we're the most aggressive species they know—but they must be afraid that the Construct is a lot worse than us."

"But if they can't stand the thought of violence, why did they come up with that dumb idea about a member of each Stellar Group on every Pursuit Team? You can see what will happen when a Pursuit Team gets to the Construct and has to wipe it out. The other species will just fall apart."

"Maybe they will. But that's consistent, too, with their way of thinking. It's the old idea of the firing squad, where one man gets a blank instead of a live bullet. Each species won't know *for sure* that it was the one responsible for the death of the Morgan Construct."

"Big deal." Brachis stared down at the zombie figure of Dougal MacDougal. "I guess we're dismissed. I don't see *him* giving us orders for a while. If I'd been in that meeting, I'd have told us humans to go ahead and catch the Construct for ourselves. I care about intelligent species, too, but I'd blow away a thousand of 'em, and not think twice about it, for solar system security."

"You're proving the ambassadors' point."

"So what? Even *you've* got more in common with me than any one of them. They're all less human than a damned jellyfish." Brachis frowned. "Know what really pisses me off about this whole thing, apart from losing my guards? You screw up a lot *worse* than me, so the bug puts you *in charge* of me. Did you ever run across a more ass-backwards logic in your life? You've come out a *winner*! You ought to be in the worst trouble, instead you can sit there grinning all over your face. Though I must say, I don't see you smiling much."

"You know me, Luther. I could be laughing my head off inside, and you'd never know it. Come on, let's go before the ambassador wakes up."

He led the way out of the Star Chamber.

Esro Mondrian was not laughing, inside or out. He needed to track down the last surviving Morgan Construct. And when he met that Construct, the last thing he wanted around him was members of the other Stellar Groups.

TO: Anabasis (Office of the Director).
FROM: Dougal MacDougal, Solar Ambassador to the Stellar Group.
SUBJECT: Pursuit Team selection and assembly.

Item one: Pursuit Teams, General. As agreed in the ambassadorial meeting of 6/7/38, redundancy of Pursuit Teams may be essential. Therefore, a total of ten (10) Pursuit Teams will be established. The final composition of each team will be determined by the Anabasis in consultation with ambassadorial representatives.

Item two: Pursuit Teams, Composition. As agreed in the above meeting, each Pursuit Team must consist of four members: One Human, one Tinker Composite, one Pipe-Rilla, and one Angel. Team members from each species will be proposed by that species. The Anabasis will have the authority to reject candidate team members on the grounds of incompatibility and performance. Any rejection by the Anabasis must be confirmed and approved through the office of the Solar Ambassador.

Captain Kubo Flammarion frowned, reamed at his left ear with the untrimmed nail of a grubby pinkie, and laid down the written document. He ran his right index finger over the last sentence he had read. There it was, Dougal MacDougal pushing into the middle of things. Why should rejections have to go through the Ambassador's office?

Flammarion sniffed, attacked his waxy left ear again, this time with the point of a writing stylus, and read on.

Item three: Pursuit Teams, General Requirements for Human candidates. Candidates must be unaltered *homo sapiens*, male or female. Synthetic forms, *pan sapiens*, *delphinus sapiens*, and Capman modulations are excluded.

Item four: Pursuit Teams, Selection of Human candidates. Candidates must be less than twenty-four

Earth years of age, in excellent physical condition, and unbound by contract commitments. Candidates must also have at least a Class Four education (which may be achieved during training with Anabasis approval).

Item five: Pursuit Teams, Restrictions. Candidates will be excluded if they have military associations, or if they fail standard psychological tests for interaction with aliens.

Item six: Training programs.

Flammarion did a double-take and his eyes skipped back to the previous item. *Impossible.* What was Mac-Dougal trying to do to him? He jammed his uniform cap onto his bald head and hurried next door to Esro Mondrian's office. The door received a flat-palmed bang as he went through, but he did not wait for permission to enter.

"Did you see this, sir?" He slapped the sheet on the desk in front of his superior, with the assurance of long familiarity. "Come through less than an hour ago. See what it says about Pursuit Team candidates? That's my job, but there's so many conditions tied on to it I bet I won't find one acceptable candidate in the whole system."

The road map of wrinkles on his forehead disguised his worried look. A long stint of security service out near the Perimeter had produced three permanent results on Kubo Flammarion: premature aging, a total lack of interest in personal hygiene, and a permanent rage against bureaucratic procedures of all kinds. For the past four years he had been Esro Mondrian's personal assistant. Others wondered why Mondrian tolerated the scruffy appearance, insubordinate manner, and periodic outbursts, but Mondrian had his reasons. Kubo Flammarion was totally dedicated to his work—and to Esro Mondrian. Best of all, he had a unique knowledge of where the bodies were buried. Flammarion kept no written records, but when Mondrian needed a lever to pry from Transportation a special permit, or force a fast response from Quarantine, Flammarion could invariably deliver the dirt.

Some deputy administrator would receive a quiet, damning call, and the permit magically appeared.

Mondrian sometimes wondered what facts about *him* were tucked away in Kubo Flammarion's scurvy, stragglyhaired skull. He was too wise to ask, and on the whole he preferred not to know.

"I saw this," he said quietly. "Commander Brachis already ran a check. As it happens, it's not MacDougal's fault at all. Those conditions were imposed by the other Stellar Group members."

"Yeah—but did MacDougal *protest?*" Flammarion jabbed at one point on the page. "There's the killer. We're supposed to find Pursuit Team members with no military training. That excludes *everybody.*"

"Everybody over sixteen years old, Captain."

"All right. But *before* they're sixteen, they're all protected by parental statute." Flammarion was angrier by the minute. "We're scuppered. We can't touch 'em *before* they're sixteen. And *at* sixteen they go straight to military service. Those instructions make the whole damn thing impossible."

"We'll find the candidates. Trust me." Mondrian was leaning back in his chair, staring across the room at a three-dimensional model of known space and the Perimeter. The display showed the location and identification of every star, color-coded as to spectral type. Colonies were magenta, stations of the security network highlighted as bright points of blue.

The Perimeter did not form the surface of a true sphere, but for most purposes it was close enough to be treated as one. Its bulges and indents showed where probes had been slowed down in their progress, or had managed to expand the frontier exceptionally fast. Beyond the Perimeter lay the unknown and the inaccessible. Within it, instantaneous transmission of messages and materials could be accomplished. The probes contained their own Mattin Links, and through them more equipment, including Links, could be transferred.

Every century the probes, creeping out at a fraction of light speed, extended the Perimeter by a few lightyears. And somewhere near its extreme edge, in the three-lightyears-thick shell that comprised the little-explored Boundary Layer, lurked almost certainly the fugitive Morgan Construct.

"But *where*, for Shannon's sake?" Flammarion had followed Mondrian's look, and thought he understood it. "Maybe we'll find the Construct out there—but where will we find the *candidates*? If you're thinking, the Colonies, I don't believe it. I've tried them before. They need every pair of hands they can get for their own projects."

"Quite true. I don't look for assistance from the Colonies."

"There's nowhere else." Flammarion scratched his unshaven chin. "You're saying what I thought when I read the directive—we'll *never* staff the Pursuit Teams. It's an impossible job."

But Mondrian had turned to face another wall of his office, where a display showed a view from Ceres looking inward towards Sol. "Not impossible, Captain—just tricky. We tend to forget that one planet of the solar system still refuses to be part of the Federation. And people there seem ready for anything, including trading their offspring . . . if the price is right." He pressed a control on his desk, and the display went into high speed zoom.

"Sir!" Kubo Flammarion knew that only one planet lay in that direction. "You don't really mean it, do you?"

"Why don't I? Have you ever been there, Captain?"

"Yessir. But it was a long time ago, before I was with the service. Everything I hear, it's got even worse now than it was. And it was crazy *then*. You know what Commander Brachis says? He says it's the world of madmen."

"Indeed?" Mondrian smiled at Flammarion, but his voice took on a cold, bitter tone. "The world of madmen, eh? That's the way the Stellar Group views all humans. To them every human world is a world of madmen. And what about you? Do you agree with Commander Brachis?"

"Well, I don't know. From all I've seen—"

"Of course you do. Don't start being polite to me now, Captain—you never have before. Now listen closely. You have the memorandum from the Ambassador. I want you to review it in detail, and think about it hard. Then if you can bring me within forty-eight hours a proposal that will provide the necessary human members of the Pursuit Teams, I will consider it. But *unless* that happens, you will—within seventy-two hours—begin making arrangements for a visit. *A visit to Earth*. For you, me, and Commander Brachis. We'll all see his 'madworld' at firsthand."

He turned away, with a gesture of dismissal.

"Yes, sir. As you say, sir." Kubo Flammarion rubbed his sleeve across his nose and tiptoed from the room. At the door he turned and took a long look at the display, now glowing with the cloudy blue-white ball of Earth at its center.

"Madworld," he muttered to himself. "We're going to madworld, are we? God help us all if it comes to that."

Chapter 3

"No. Phoebe Willard. That's who I want. Not the inventory. See, I already looked at that. *Phoebe Willard*. Where is she? Can you take me to her?"

The guard stared, first at Luther Brachis and then at the screen showing a segment of the dump contents. His eyes were puzzled.

Brachis sighed, and waited again for a reply. Patiently, although through the solar system he was not known as a patient man; because if there was one place where patience was a necessity, it was the Dump. Brachis knew that he was the cause of his own problem. He, *personally*, had made all the Dump's staff assignments.

And now here he was himself, in the Dump.

Sargasso Dump.

The Sun and planets are the deep gravity wells of the solar system. Once a spacecraft—or a piece of space junk—has been parked around a planet, it can remain in stable orbit as long as the human species endures.

But space around the planets is valuable. No one wants it filled with floating garbage, or cares to have random hazards in orbit around the Sun.

Not when there are other options.

The Lagrange points are local minima of the gravitational potential. They are places where no planet is present, but a body may still remain in stable orbit. Their positions were plotted centuries before humanity went to space. Within the solar system, the deepest and best-defined of them are the Trojan positions, trailing and

leading Jupiter in its orbit by a sixth of a revolution.
Space flotsam drifts here naturally, and stays for millennia.

What Nature can do, Human can copy.

Three hundred years before the visit of Luther Brachis,
the trailing Jupiter Lagrange point had been designated
by the United Space Federation as a system "indefinite
storage facility." For that, read "garbage dump." Everything from spent reactors to disabled Von Neumanns had
been towed there, to float slowly (but stably) around the
slopes of the shallow gravitational valley.

The Dump was computer-controlled. It had been that
way for centuries, unattended by humans—until Luther
Brachis took over as head of System Security, and began
to lose men and women. To death, inevitably; murder
and greed and sabotage still inhabited the system, and
security work always carried risk. The incident on Cobweb Station was only the most recent. Brachis hated to
lose his trained and dedicated guards. But it was part of
the job. For the dead he could do nothing, and they
could feel nothing.

And for the living? The pain of injury was temporary.
Limbs could be re-grown, hearts and eyes and livers
replaced. It was done, routinely.

But *mental damage* was another matter. Toxins and
bullets and air loss could leave a body with normal function, and a ruined mind that hovered somewhere beyond
the brink of humanity.

Brachis had seen a dozen human wrecks in his first
year as head of Security. He made a personal decision.
The guards would remain on Security payroll—for life.
They could not be long hidden from the accountants on
any inhabited body, but no accountant had ever, in
Brachis' experience, paid a visit to the wasteland of the
Sargasso Dump. He saw a melancholy symmetry in his
act: the throwaway material of the system, forgotten by
humanity, would be guarded by the throwaway people.

The staff at Sargasso were Luther's big secret. He
could not protect them past the time of his own death,
but they would be shielded until then. And he had never
regretted the decision—although now, trying to coax the
guard to rational response, he came close.

"*Phoebe Willard.*" He tried again. "Remember her? Brown hair, not very tall, very pretty. She came here two days ago." Brachis went to the control desk, and called another part of the Dump inventory to the screen. "These. See? She was working on these."

The guard stared. There was a slow dawning of *something* behind those troubled eyes. He nodded. Without speaking he closed his suit helmet, turned and left the control room. Brachis followed in his own suit, still unsure. In any other situation he would have been furious at the waste of time. Here anger was futile, except perhaps to focus his own concentration.

Soon they were outside, twisting their way through a topsy-turvy array of debris. Brachis stared at the flotsam on all sides and re-evaluated the guard ahead of him. If the man knew where he was going, through such a tangled wilderness, then his mind was far from gone. Perhaps it was only that he could not speak, or interact with people.

The guard halted and pointed. Brachis saw a huge green balloon, blotting out the stars ahead. It might be an air-bulb. where he would find Phoebe Willard working inside. Or it could be that the brain-damaged guard was offering random responses to questions.

There was one way to find out. Brachis nodded his thanks and headed for the green sphere. Somewhere in that featureless facade there had to be an entry point. He found a layered sequence of four flexible flaps, and squeezed through into a lighted enclosure.

Phoebe Willard had been at the Sargasso Dump for two days. Typically, in that time she had turned a house-sized open space into a working laboratory. A lattice of interlocking beams ran from one side of the air-bulb to the other. Fixed to lattice nodes, neat as any museum collection of butterflies, hung sixteen fused and shattered objects: the Morgan Constructs.

It was possible to deduce their original shapes only by comparison of the whole set. This one had wing panels intact, but a head that was fused to a melted blob of grey. Another, two farther over, had no wings and no legs, but the upper half of the rounded top was intact. Not one was more than a third complete.

Phoebe was working on a well-defined compound eye, removing it from a blunt head. She saw Brachis and nodded to him.

He floated across to her side and opened his suit. "Any hope?"

"Are you kidding?" She gestured around her at the fragments. "The Cobweb Station guards should have posthumous medals. They blew this lot to hell and gone—except for the one you say got away."

"Nothing to be salvaged?"

"I didn't say that. This one"—Willard pointed the tool to the burnt mass she was working on—"doesn't have weapons, or limbs, or working eyes. But I think there's a fair sized chunk of brain intact. Maybe even most of it."

"Could it ever function again?"

"Nope. Not in the way you were hoping."

"Then maybe we ought to quit."

"Don't say that. I haven't had so much fun in years. Livia Morgan was a genius. Half the time I can't tell what her circuits are trying to accomplish. But it's a hell of a game *trying*."

"Phoebe, we're not doing this for pleasure. Can you tell me one reason why we ought to go on?"

"Because I'm getting *results*, Commander-man. I can't build you one of these, now or ever. But give me another week in this hell-hole, and I'll tell you a whole lot about how they work. That ought to be valuable when you people start chasing around the Perimeter."

"What you just said is secret information."

"Nuts. Everyone back at the shop knows it. Why do you think I agreed to come?"

"To build me a detailed model of a Construct. One that functions and is safe to be around. That's what I had in mind when I asked you."

"Bricks without straw, eh? Well, tough on you. It can't be done." Phoebe picked up a tiny fiber bundle inspection tube. "Give me a week, though, and if the half-wit zombies around here don't get me I'll have something close to a general schematic for this Construct. It's the only one with any working brain functions, and it's one of the more sophisticated. But we won't have details. Will that do you?"

"It will have to."

"Then go away, and let me work."

Brachis reached out and took the inspection unit from Phoebe Willard's hand. "I will. But not right now. You and I have an assignation."

"Why Luther! I thought that was all over long ago."

"Not that, Phoebe. More fun than that. We're going to sit down at a formal dinner, you and me and the staff of the Dump—every last half-wit zombie of them. I promised. They've not had visitors for years. So we're going. And we—you and me both—are going to sit, and smile, and pretend we enjoy it."

"Nuts! I'm not going *near* those brain-dead buzzards."

"Look at the date on your orders. It expires tonight. You want to stay and play games? You go to dinner with us."

"Blackmail!"

"And you *smile*, Phoebe. Like this." Luther Brachis grinned wide and hideous. "You can do it. Just imagine you're the belle of the ball, all dressed up in a long gown, looking beautiful, and dancing . . ."

"Bastard!"

". . . on my grave."

Chapter 4

Earth was served by a single Link Exit point. Travelers stepped into the Link Chamber at the center of Ceres, and were at once spat out by the transfer system at a point close to Earth's equator. When Mondrian, Brachis, and Flammarion left the terminal they found themselves standing at the foot of a gigantic dilapidated tower, reaching up to the sullen overcast of a tropical afternoon.

Brachis craned his head back, following the silver-grey column until it vanished into the haze. "What the devil is that?"

"Don't you recognize it?" Mondrian was for some reason in excellent spirits. "This is the foot of the old Beanstalk. Everything between Earth and space went up and down that for over two hundred years."

Luther Brachis stared at the ancient, beetle-backed cars, nestling in their cradles along the hundred-meter lower perimeter. "People, too? If they rode those things all the way to geosynch, the first spacers had real guts. But why do they still leave it around on Earth? It must mass a billion tons, and it looks like useless dead weight."

"It is—but don't even suggest getting rid of it, not to people down here. They think it's a precious historic relic, one of their most valued ancient monuments." Mondrian spoke casually, but he was gazing off to the west with an experienced eye and an air of anticipation. There were woods a few hundred meters away, and he was watching the fronded crowns of individual trees. It was coming . . . coming . . . *Now*.

A blustery equatorial breeze ruffled their hair and tugged at their clothing. Brachis and Flammarion gasped, while Flammarion glared wildly around him. "Lock failure! Where—where's—" He slowly subsided.

Mondrian was watching with quiet satisfaction. "Calm down, both of you. And you, Captain Flammarion, you ought to be ashamed of yourself. You told me you'd been on Earth before."

"I have, sir. Sir, I thought—"

"I know what you thought. But it's not a pressure failure, or a collapsed lock. It's just wind—natural air movements. It happens all the time on Earth, so you'd better get used to it before the natives die laughing at you."

"Winds!" Luther Brachis' broad face had turned rosy with fear or anger, but he had recovered much quicker than Kubo Flammarion. "Damn it, Mondrian. You *planned* that. You could have warned us easy enough—but you wanted your fun."

"No. I wanted to make a point. You can look down your nose at Earth and its people as much as you want to, but we have to watch out for surprises here—and that applies to me as well as you."

Mondrian was stepping forward, away from the Link terminal towards an odd-looking throng of people clustered not far from the exit. The other two men followed him hesitantly. He was heading for a long covered ramp that led below ground. As they approached the crowd there was an urgent babble of voices. "Hottest little nippers on Earth" . . . "Need a Fropper? Get you the best, at a good price" . . . "Trade crystals, high rate and no questions asked" . . . "Want to see a coronation—genuine royal family, forty-second generation" . . . "Like to visit a Needler lab? Top line products, never see them anywhere else." They all spoke standard Solar, poorly pronounced.

Most of the crowd, men and women, were half a head shorter even than Kubo Flammarion. Mondrian strode through them, scanning from side to side. The people he pushed out of the way wore brightly colored clothes, their purples, scarlets and pinks in striking contrast to the quiet black of Security uniforms. Mondrian brushed aside the grasping hands. He paid no attention to anyone, until he caught sight of a grinning, skeleton-thin man in a patchwork jacket of green and gold. He plowed through to the man's side.

"You a busker?"

The skinny man grinned. "That's me, squire, at your service. Welcome to the Big Marble. You want it, I got it. Tobacco, roley-poley, lulu juice. You name it, I'll take you to it."

"Cut it, shut it. You know Tatty Snipes?" Mondrian's question in low Earth-tongue interrupted the sales pitch.

"Certainly do." The busker faltered for a moment, taken aback by Mondrian's use of his own argot. He began again, half-heartedly. "Paradox, slither, velocil—I can get 'em all. Want a guided tour of the Shambles? Never mind what the rule books say, I can find you—"

"Slot the chops. You find the Tat, bring her to me, right now. Cotton? And more of this when you got her." Mondrian reached out his hand. There was the dull glow of a trade crystal before dirty fingers closed on it. The man looked at Mondrian respectfully.

"Yessir. Right away, squire. Be back." The skinny figure started to push off through the crowd, then checked himself and turned back. "Name's Bester, sir—King Bester. I'll be here with Tatty in half an hour. She's just a couple of Links away."

Mondrian nodded. As Bester vanished along the below-ground ramp, he sauntered towards a solid bench planted a hundred yards away. A Sun-simulator stood just above it. After a look at each other, his two companions started after him.

"He's right at home here." Flammarion's voice and manner made it clear that he wasn't. "Did you hear him chit-chat in their lingo? Earth-gobble—I couldn't understand half of it."

Brachis nodded. He was staring around inquisitively. "I ought to have anticipated this. It's my own fault. I had all the information, and I didn't use it."

"You *knew* Commander Mondrian spoke Earth-talk? How could you?"

"Not exactly that." Brachis brushed away the admiring hands that were trying to touch the glittering decorations on his chest. "But I could have guessed that he might. Use your common sense, Captain. I've tracked Commander Mondrian's movements for the past four years—just the way you've tracked mine. That's what a Security department is for. And Mondrian's records show that he's been coming to Earth an average of five times a year, ever since we started tracking. He knows this place well."

"But what's he do down here?"

Brachis shook his head. "I don't know—and if I did, I'm not sure I'd tell you. Not unless you've decided you want to work for me, instead of him. Come on."

When they reached Mondrian he was already sitting quietly on the bench, staring thoughtfully around him at the surrounding group of Madworlders. Once King Bester had been picked out by Mondrian, the rest of them had given up their importuning. Now they stood a few yards away, watching the three visitors with frank curiosity. They were nudging each other, grinning, and whispering comments in the old Earth languages.

Flammarion sat down on the bench next to Mondrian. He stared suspiciously at the wooden seat, and at the flat surface beneath his feet. It was old, weathered brick, with half-inch spaces between the worn blocks. Tiny ants were hurrying out of the open cracks to explore the sides of the men's boots. They showed most interest in Kubo Flammarion, drawn by the interesting smell of unwashed flesh. He shuffled his feet from side to side, keeping a wary eye on the energetic insects.

Luther Brachis remained standing, his attention on the crowd. "This is all quite futile, Esro," he said after another half-minute. "Just look at them. Can you really see any one of those cretins being accepted into a Stellar Group pursuit team? I mean, would you even *consider* one for your own security staff? We're wasting our time."

Mondrian recognized the beginning of another skirmish. So far as the ambassadors were concerned it was all decided, with Luther Brachis reporting to Mondrian for everything that concerned the Anabasis. But the two men had not yet settled into their new relationship. Brachis was still responsible for Solar Security, and he had retained full control of that department. His power was undiminished.

The two men had been equals and rivals for years. There had been a mutual understanding that one day there would be a final piece of infighting, in which one or the other would gain overall authority. Both Brachis and Mondrian had accepted that. What Mondrian knew Brachis would *not* accept, any more than he would have accepted it himself, was victory by arbitrary *fiat*—victory unrelated to (or *inversely* related to) performance.

He listened quietly as Brachis continued: "Just look at them. *Earthlings*. No wonder Captain Flammarion is worried. Would *you* take responsibility for making something out of one of those idiots? I wouldn't. They're dirty, and ignorant, and *inferior*."

"Why don't you come out and say it, Luther? That you think my decision to bring us to Earth was crazy."

"Those are your words, not mine."

"But you think them. You underestimate the potentials of Earth. You forget that this was the stock of your own ancestors."

"Sure it was—half a millennium ago. And half a billion years before that, it was fishes. I'm talking about *now*. This is the dregs. That's what you have left when the top quarter of each generation is skimmed off for seven hundred years and goes into space. It's a flawed gene pool here. Look back over the past century. You won't find any worthwhile talent that came from Earth."

"Have you attempted that exercise?"

"I don't need to." Brachis nodded at the crowd, who were watching open-mouthed. "Look at them. They don't even know they're being insulted. We're wasting our time. I think we ought to get out of here right now."

He was needling hard—and finally he could see signs that it was working. Mondrian was staring away from him, over the heads of the crowd.

"You underestimate the potential of the people of Earth, Luther. And you overestimate what's needed for the Pursuit Teams. Not to mention the training programs that I've developed for Perimeter work over the past decade. If I didn't think I could find what we need here, do you think I'd have brought you?" Mondrian turned at last to face Luther Brachis. "You could pick one of those—*any* one of those." He pointed to the crowd. "And I could train your choice to be a successful Pursuit Team candidate."

"Would you wager on it?"

"Certainly. Name the stakes."

"Nah." Brachis snorted. "You're stringing me along. You know you're not risking anything, because not one of that lot would be eligible for training. They're too old, or they're bonded in some sort of contract, or they'd never pass the physical. See their hair and teeth. Show me somebody in the right age group, and healthy, and *then* tell me you'll make the same wager."

"Here we are, squire!" The argument was interrupted by the sudden return of King Bester. The thin man called out from the edge of the crowd and began to push his way rapidly towards them. He was followed by a tall woman, easily visible above the other people. As they arrived at the bench Bester gave a grinning nod and held out his hand.

Mondrian ignored him. He stood up. "Hello, Tatty." He had switched again to Earth argot. "How's the hustling?"

"Hello, Essy. It's good. Or it was, until he interrupted me. I was working a deal up in Delmarva. I told the King to go to hell."

"She sure did, squire. But I told her I wouldn't hear no for an answer."

Mondrian took the hint. Another packet of trade crystals went quietly into Bester's open hand, then Mondrian patted the bench to indicate that Tatty should sit down next to him.

She remained standing, examining the other two Security men. After a few moments she nodded to them. "Hello, I don't think that we've met," she said in excellent standard Solar. "I'm Tatiana Sinai-Peres."

She held out a hand to Luther Brachis. Tatty was tall, slim, and spectacular. She stood eye to eye with Brachis, who openly gawked at her. She stared right back at him. Her gaze was direct and bold, with bright brown eyes.

But there were tired smudges of darkness underneath them, and the grey tone of Paradox addiction marred her complexion. The skin of her face and neck was clear and unblemished, but it was the skin of one who never saw sunlight. Her dark green dress was loose sleeved, revealing an array of tiny purple-black dots along her thin arms. In contrast to King Bester and the rest of the crowd Tatty was spotlessly clean, with neat attire, carefully groomed dark hair, and well-kept fingernails.

"I assume that it's a first-time visit," she went on to Brachis. "What can I do for you?"

Mondrian squinted at her in the strong light of the Sun-simulator. "It's not what you think." He reached up to touch her bare arm. "Sit down, Princess, and let me tell you what's going on."

"I'll sit down, Essy. But not here. There's too much light—it would fry me. Let's Link back north to my place, and I'll introduce your friends to some genuine Earth food." She smiled at the uncertain look on Kubo Flammarion's face. "Don't worry, Soldier. I'll make sure it's not too rich for Commoners."

Rank Has Its Privileges. That had never been more true than during the first decades of space development. One odd and predictable—yet unexpected—consequence of automation and excess productive capacity had been the re-emergence of the class system. The old aristocracy, diminished (but never quite destroyed) during the days of world-wide poverty and experimental social programs, had returned; and there were some curious additions to their ranks.

It had been surprising, but inevitable. When all of Earth's manufacturing moved to the computer-controlled assembly lines, employment needs went down as efficiency went up. Soon it was learned that in the fuzzy areas of "management" and "government," most business and development decisions could also be routinely (and more effectively) handled by computer. At the same time, lack of results and impatience with academic studies had squeezed education to a few years of mandatory schooling.

The unemployment rate grew to ninety percent. The available jobs on Earth called for no special skills—so who would get them?

Naturally, those with well-placed friends and relatives. There had been a wonderful blossoming of nepotism, unmatched within the previous thousand years. Many positions called for prospective employees to possess a "stable base of operations and adequate working materials." With living accommodations and family possessions passed on across the generations, the advantage lay always with those from the old families.

Meanwhile, away from Earth there was a real need for people. The solar system was ripe for development. It offered an environment that was demanding, dangerous, and full of unbounded opportunities. And it had a nasty habit of cancelling any man-made advantage derived from birth, wealth, or spurious academic "qualifications." Cancelling *permanently*.

The rich and the royal were not without their own shrewdness. After a quick look at space, they stayed home on Earth, the one place in the system where their safety, superiority, and status were all assured. It was the low-born, seeing no upward mobility on Earth, who took the big leap—outward.

The result was too effective to be the work of human planners. The tough, desperate commoners fought their way to space, generation after generation. The introduction of the Mattin Link quadrupled the rate of exodus, and the society that was left on Earth became more and more titled and self-conscious. Well-protected from material want and free from external pressures, it naturally developed an ever-increasing disdain for the emigrants— "vulgar commoners" spreading their low-born and classless fecundity through the solar system and out to the stars. Earth was the place to be for the aristocrats. The *only* place to be, on the Big Marble itself. Where else could anyone live who despised crudity, esteemed breeding and culture, and demanded a certain sophistication of life-style?

King Bester *was* a king, a genuine monarch who traced his line across thirty-two generations to the House of

Saxe-Coburg. He was one of seventeen thousand royals reigning on and under Earth's surface. He regarded Tatty Snipes, Princess Tatiana Sinai-Peres of the Cabot-Kashoggi's, as rather an upstart. She had only six centuries and twenty-two generations in her lineage. He did not say it, of course, in her presence—Tatty would have knocked the side of his royal head in with one blow of her carefully-manicured and aristocratic fist. But he certainly *thought* it.

And King Bester, like Tatty, was nobody's fool. He realized very well that the real power had moved away from Earth. The Quarantine operated by Solar Security applied only to people moving *outward* from Earth. Bester could sense the brawling, raw strength that lay in people like Luther Brachis. It ran right through the off-planet culture, and he was afraid of it. Far better to stay home, operate within the familiar rituals of the Big Marble, and take a little when the opportunity came from visitors like Mondrian and his colleagues. Those visitors were far more numerous than System government liked to admit, and they came down to Earth for reasons rarely shown on any travel permits.

So Bester quietly tagged along with Princess Tatiana and the three visitors. He hung at the back of the group, listened carefully while Mondrian explained to Tatty the reason for the trip to Earth, and looked for his working edge.

He had never heard of the Morgan Constructs and the disaster on Cobweb Station until Esro Mondrian described it. He was not much interested. His reward lay in examining Mondrian, Brachis, and Flammarion, and learning in which category of pleasure-seeking their interests might lie.

There was sure to be one. Bester had his own ideas of Earth visitors. No matter what they might say, or how the official agenda read, there was always another angle. And that was where the profit lay.

Brachis should not be difficult. Big, powerfully-built, lusty, still in early middle age, he could be offered things undreamed of through most of the solar system. Flammarion would be even easier. He already had the poached-egg look to his eyes that told of a habitual use of alcohol. One good shot of Paradox, and Flammarion wouldn't be looking elsewhere for entertainment while he was on Earth. Withdrawal symptoms after he left? That was not King Bester's problem.

The big question mark was Mondrian. He had scared Bester the moment they met, when he had fixed him with those cold, dark eyes.

But on the other hand, Mondrian wasn't a good prospect, anyway. He was clearly no stranger to Earth, and he had probably found a way to gratify his own needs long ago. From the way she looked at him, Tatty Snipes had in the past helped to serve them.

When they reached Tatty's underground apartment, Bester stopped any pretense of listening to Mondrian. He quietly helped himself to the free food and drink—Princess Tatiana had decidedly royal tastes—and moved a little closer to Kubo Flammarion. The scruffy man's pleasures could probably be guessed, but they had to be confirmed before his pockets could be emptied.

"Ever see a public beheading, Captain?" And, as Flammarion's eyes widened, "I mean with full staging—steel axe, real wooden block, hooded executioner. We use a top-quality simulacrum under the chopper, you'd never know the difference—the spurt from the neck is exactly like real blood."

"Bleagh!" Flammarion glared at him in disgust. He shook his head, and laid down the slice of underdone beef that he was holding. "What you doing, trying to make me throw up or something?"

"Not for you? How about him, then?" King Bester nodded to Mondrian, still deep in conversation with Princess Tatiana. "Think he might be interested?"

Kubo Flammarion scratched his head. "The Commander? Nah. To get him hooked, you'd have to have a real victim and real blood." He pointedly took a couple of steps away from Bester.

The King turned to Luther Brachis. "How about you? Like to know more about some of our entertainments—I mean the Big Marble specials, the ones you'll never see in the catalogs. How would you like one of those?"

Brachis smiled at him pleasantly. "And how would you like a big fistful of knuckles"—he spoke in poorly pronounced but quite passable Earth-argot—"right up your royal nose?"

King Bester decided that his glass needed refilling at the sideboard across the room.

"I didn't know you spoke their lingo, too," said Kubo Flammarion admiringly, watching Bester's rapid departure.

"It's good to have a few things about you that most people don't know." Brachis turned, so that no one but Flammarion could see his lips. "There's things about your boss that you don't know, too. Remember that. I don't give away information—but I'm always willing to trade."

Chapter 5

Tatty shook her head as soon as Mondrian explained what he was looking for.

"Not here, or in any of the areas where I have clout. There's a local ordinance forbidding the off-Earth sale of anyone with more than four degrees of consanguinity with my imperial clan—and that means *everybody*. They all claim relationship, even when they don't really have it."

"Any ideas, then?"

"You might try over in BigSyd, or maybe Tearun. I don't know the dealers there, though. And Ree-o-dee would be a cert, except you need to pay off so many people it gets out of control. Better if we could find somebody locally."

"How about Bozzie?" King Bester had given up any pretense that he was not eavesdropping. "He's top bod for that line of business. *And* he's nearby, sort of."

"Could be worth a shot. I don't know what he has, though." Tatty turned to Mondrian. "We'll have to find him first—but he'll be somewhere in the Gallimaufries, so it shouldn't be too hard."

"Bozzie?" Kubo Flammarion was struggling to make an intelligible record of the conversation, but the last exchange was too much. "Find him in the Garry-what's?"

"Bozzie. The Duke of Bosny. Also Viscount Roosevelt, Count Mellon, Baron Rockwell, *and* the Earl of Potomac." Tatty's face said what she thought of all those titles. "Upstart houses, every one. But I'll say this for

44

him, he prefers to be called plain Bosny, or just Bozzie. He hasn't lived in Bosny City for years, though he claims to have been born there. He certainly has consanguinity with every major royal line in the Northeast, and he's a big mover and shaker down in the Gallimaufries—the basement warrens" (She had seen Flammarion's mouth starting to open again) "—two hundred levels below where we are now."

Tatty glanced at King Bester. "More your stamping-grounds than mine. Think we might get him today?"

"You'll have to hurry. Never find Bozzie there after dark—he'll be topside with his Scavvies, scouting the surface."

Luther Brachis was looking at his watch. "Then we're too late. It's already dark up on the surface."

But Tatty was shaking her head. "It's dark now where you landed, in Africa, but we came a long way west through the Links. We picked up six hours. Local time is only two in the afternoon."

"Sorry." Brachis sounded annoyed—with himself. "I'll keep my mouth shut until I know what I'm talking about."

"You're not so far wrong as you think," replied Tatty. "We're in the northern hemisphere, and it's winter. It gets dark early—something else you're not used to." She paused for a moment, calculating. "I think we can do it—just. Provided that we take the fastest routes. Hold onto your hats, and let's go."

Tatty lived on the sixtieth under-level. It was prime real estate, minutes from the surface and within easy reach of a Link entry point. But *because* it was prime, it by design had no direct drop connection with the deeper and poorer levels of the Gallimaufries. To descend, the group had to travel far north, then double back. Led by Tatty, they travelled half a continent horizontally in order to descend five thousand meters vertically. They did it in thirty minutes. For the off-Earth visitors it was a confused race along networks of high-speed slideways, a plunge along vertiginous corkscrews of spiraling ramps, and finally a series of long dives through the black depths of vertical drop-shafts.

"First time I've felt comfortable since I got here," said Flammarion, savoring the long moments of free-fall.

The last drop was a long one, down a curving chute that expelled them into a vaulted chamber, hundreds of meters across. The smoothed rocky roof was studded with powerful sun-simulators that lit the whole enclosure. The chamber's volume was enormous, and crammed full. The newcomers were surrounded by a baffling jumble of stalls, corridors, partitions, tents, and guy-ropes. And development was not confined to two dimensions. Slender support columns ran from floor to roof at twenty meter intervals. Their steel pylons supported shish kebabs of ramshackle multi-level platforms, many of them open-sided, with rope ladders hanging down to the ground beneath.

The floor of the chamber was not rock, but rich black earth. Bright-blossomed flowers thrived everywhere, growing profusely along the zigzagging walkways and festooning every wall and column.

"Bozzie's imperial court," said Tatty. "As you can see, he's a flower buff. Stick close to the King, now. If you get lost down here I don't know if you'd ever find your own way back."

The human population of the Gallimaufries was packed as densely as the plant life, and no less colorful. Gaudy jackets of saffron, purple and vermillion were favored, trimmed with sequins and piped with blue, silver, and gold. The clothes were all dirty, and the smell—to a spacer's nose—appalling. King Bester's costume, garish and grubby-seeming when they had first seen it, now appeared clean, modest, and conservative.

The first impression was of continuous noise and clashing color. And then the submerged second element of the Gallimaufries slowly emerged, in quiet counterpoint to the vivid brawl. Mingled in with the eye-catching bright clothes and bustling movement, and almost invisible among them, were the others. Like pale lilies hidden among orchids, people sat in small groups on benches, or walked slowly through the alleys. Their clothes were simple, monochrome tunics of white or grey. They did not seem to speak, even to each other.

"Commoners," said Tatty. She had followed Luther Brachis' look, to a group of three women dressed in plain ivory tunics. "The raw material for your Pursuit Teams, if you can make the deal. Bozzie has contract rights over almost everyone here in grey or white, like those women."

"But they get nothing out of it? They'll never agree to go."

"They can't say no. Bozzie owns their contracts. Anyway, some of them might be glad to get out of here, no matter how bad your deal sounds. Take a look. I'll go find Bozzie and bring him back to you."

She ducked under a guy rope, rounded a tent, and headed for the edge of the chamber. Her height allowed them to follow her progress for the first thirty meters, then she was lost in the tangle of people and buildings.

Brachis turned to Esro Mondrian.

"Want to change your mind about that wager? If not, I'm ready to go ahead with it."

"I don't know. It depends if I can find someone suitable here."

"Hey, you're weaseling out. Come off it, Esro. You know you'll *never* find someone suitable, not when nothing good has come out from Earth in three hundred years. They're *all* losers, every one of them too decadent and spineless to do anything right. You didn't talk about 'someone suitable' before—you said you could train *anyone* to be acceptable as a Pursuit Team member."

"I *can*. I'll make the bet. Just name the terms."

Even though Brachis had been pushing Mondrian again, he was surprised by the rapid acceptance. But he was too experienced to let it show.

"All right, then. Let's keep it simple. You select any pair of candidates that you like. You do it *today*, and you do it down here. You train them any way you want to. In a reasonable time—say, six months?—you get them accepted as Pursuit Team members. You do it, you win. You fail to do it, for anything short of candidate death, you lose. Simple enough?"

"Simple enough." Mondrian paused. "What about stakes?"

"I'll stake my personnel monitoring system against yours. Don't pretend you haven't got one. You've been tracking my people for years, same as I've been tracking yours."

"Right. Accepted. In front of witnesses." Mondrian turned to Bester and Kubo Flammarion. "I will select two people. Here, today. I will train them. When their training is complete, they will be accepted—"

"*Both* be accepted. One won't do."

"—*both* be accepted as Pursuit Team members. Commander Brachis has my hand on it."

Brachis shook Mondrian's hand for only a split-second, then turned to examine the bustling court around him. He made a big point of holding his nose. "There they are. Take your pick. White or grey, Princess Tatiana said, and I'm glad you'll be doing the training, not me—I couldn't stand the smell."

The courtiers were all grubby energy and extravagance. By contrast, the commoners were listless and subdued. A team of three was passing Brachis as he spoke, leading an odd-looking beast on a steel chain. Its muzzle was blunt and its forehead low, but the animal stared around with sparkling hazel eyes, and showed more interest in the scene than its keepers did. It paused by Flammarion and sniffed at him inquiringly.

"No danger," said King Bester—Flammarion seemed ready to dive away into the crowd. "It's quite harmless. I've seen things like that a hundred times."

"What is it?" Flammarion flinched away as the creature turned its head toward him, opened a mouth full of jagged teeth, and offered him a spiky smile.

"No name, squire. Just an Artefact, something from the Needler labs." Bester snapped his fingers. "Hey, like to visit one? I can arrange it easy."

Flammarion shook his head, but Bester was too experienced a salesman to miss the sudden strong interest shown by Luther Brachis. He was interrupted before he could follow up on it. Running along the path, dodging in and out of the bustling courtiers, sped a young man. He was about twenty years old and carrying a garland of flowers. He was closely followed by a young girl. "Not fair, Chan," she was crying. "No fair. That was cheating. Give it back."

The man paused close to Mondrian, turning to shake the flower posy teasingly at her. She was slight, thin, and olive-skinned. Moderately attractive—but nothing compared with the man. He was an Adonis: golden haired and tall, with a loose, agile build and sculptured good looks. If the people he was running among were aristocrats, his face pronounced him their undisputed emperor. Both the man and the woman were dressed in the plain ivory tunics of commoners.

Unworried by the presence of the Security men in their dark uniforms, he dodged behind them to escape. Mondrian took one look, then moved forward to grab the man by the arm. The youth stared at him, mouth open. The woman moved to their side, and put her own hand in turn on Mondrian's. The courtiers stopped their promenading to stare at what was happening.

"You." Mondrian moved forward, tightening his grip as the woman tried to pull his hand free. "Both of you. Are you under contract to Bozzie?"

The man stared back impassively, but the woman thrust herself between him and Mondrian. "No business of yours! Let go!"

"No, listen for a moment. There might be a position for you—something good. If you're contracted to Bozzie, I'll make sure you get a good offer—"

She batted Mondrian's hand away from the youth's arm, screamed "*Chan! Follow me—right now!*" and threw herself away into the crowd. The youth gave one wide-eyed glance at Mondrian and went after her. In a few seconds they were twenty yards away, heading for the shelter of a covered arcade.

"Those two," cried Mondrian. "Stop them—there's a reward for anyone who does."

The courtiers did not even move. Flammarion began a half-hearted pursuit, but found they were running away at a speed that he had not even attempted in a quarter of a century. They were ducking into the arcade when Luther Brachis acted. He pulled a palm-sized cylinder from his pocket and pointed it at the pair.

"Don't shoot!" cried King Bester.

He was too late. A green spiral of light flashed from the cylinder, corkscrewing a tight helical path that glowed in the air. It touched the escaping pair, first the man and then the woman. The backs of their jackets smoked, and threw off a shower of sparks. Then they were wriggling away out of sight behind a long curtain of golden beads.

"They're not hurt," said Brachis to King Bester. And then to Mondrian, "You're going to lose your bet anyway, so I'll give you a look at the monitor system you'll never get." He pulled a flat disk from his belt. "It's never had a test before in a crowded environment like this. Let's see how well it does."

He held the disk horizontal. At its center a double arrow of light moved and turned. As they watched, it lengthened perceptibly and changed direction.

"A Tracker?"

Brachis nodded at Mondrian's question. "But a lot fancier than usual. Direction and distance. Once anything's tagged with the signature beam this can follow them for at least twenty-four hours. It's also designed to be able to track five people at once. It must be confusing if they all go separate ways—five separate arrows to deal with—but with two it ought to be easy. *And* they're keeping close together." He handed it to Mondrian, who in turn held it out at once to Flammarion.

"Go follow them, bring them back here. I have to stay here and wait for Bozzie."

Flammarion stared at him pop-eyed, then glanced in turn at the Tracker and the bewildering complexity of the chamber.

"Not by yourself, Captain," went on Mondrian. "I realize you don't know the place." He gestured at King Bester, who was pointedly looking elsewhere. "He'll help you—and he'll be very well rewarded if he does."

"Right you are, squire." Bester slapped his hands together and grabbed the Tracker from Flammarion. "Now we're cooking. The arrow's not moving, they must have stopped. Come on, Captain. We'll have 'em in a jiffy-o."

With Flammarion trailing along behind he set out

along the path defined by the arrow. Mondrian glanced mildly at Brachis, and actually came close to smiling. "Big mistake, Luther. You didn't think when you set the Tracker on them. Now I'm going to win that bet—with those handsome two you were kind enough to tag for me. Want to concede right now?"

"The bet stands, Esro. Nothing good comes out of Earth." His thought ran on: *That irritates you mightily, doesn't it, every time I say it?*

And Mondrian was making his own useful observation. *Nothing good comes out of Earth, you say. But some things on Earth certainly interest you. I caught that look, when King Bester was talking about visiting a Needler lab.*

He had no time to pursue that thought. A blare of trumpets came from the direction opposite to the vanished Bester. The crowd was parting, pushed aside by a dozen hulking ruffians. Behind them came a flower-bedecked sedan chair carried by eight men, with Princess Tatiana walking at its side.

The Duke of Bosny, Viscount Roosevelt, Count Mellon, Baron Rockwell, Earl of Potomac—all five hundred and seventy pounds of him—was arriving to begin negotiation.

Twelve hours later, Tatty and Mondrian were at last alone. She was sitting by his side, reviewing a handwritten document.

"It looks all right, Essy," she said, frowning in the dim light. "This transfers title, effective two hours ago. They're all yours now."

Mondrian nodded. He did not look up. In front of him on the table was an open flagon of ancient brandy. He was staring into the depths of a balloon glass holding half an inch of amber liquid.

"You have no idea how much effort it took to find that for you," complained Tatty. "I started looking for it right after your last visit to Earth—and you haven't even smelled it."

Mondrian roused himself, brought the glass close to his nose, and gave it a dutiful sniff. "I'm sorry. You know me, Princess, most of the time I'd kill for a brandy like this."

"So what's wrong? Bozzie signed over the contracts, you've got your two candidates, and Captain Flammarion ought to have them away from Earth in a few more hours. Why aren't you smiling?"

"I wish I knew. I can't help feeling something's wrong with the deal."

"You think you paid too much?"

"No. Too little. Your friend Bozzie didn't ask enough money for those two."

"But you told me you had no idea how much it ought to cost to buy those contracts."

"I didn't. But King Bester knew, and I was watching his face when Bozzie accepted our first offer. Bester gawped and gasped." Mondrian picked up the glass, breathed in the delicate centuries-old bouquet, and took a tiny sip. "Well, we're committed now, even if I don't feel comfortable with it. I told Flammarion to get them into the Link system and up as soon as he could, before Quarantine had a chance to change their mind. Now I wish I'd taken a look at them myself."

"You did see them—you picked them out."

"I mean a close look. I only saw them for a second or two, when we first met them. Luther Brachis took care of the exit permits—and *he* seems much too pleased with himself. I'm telling you, Tatty, something's not right."

"Did you talk to Commander Brachis about it?"

"I couldn't. He slipped away with King Bester."

"Where to?"

"They didn't say. But I think I know. Bester took him to a Needler lab."

"Are you sure? I can't think what either of them would want with one of those."

Mondrian shook his head and took another taste of brandy. "Nor can I." He finally smiled, but it was no more than a rueful grimace. "Princess, if anyone knows that people sneak down here to Earth for their own secret reasons, you and I do. Can you make an arrangement for me to see Rattafee again—tonight?"

"Rattafee! Didn't you hear?" Tatty put her hand on

his arm. "Essy, Rattafee's dead. A month ago. I assumed you would have heard about it. She overdosed on Paradox."

Mondrian closed his eyes. "That is not ... good news. She was the best Fropper I ever had. I even thought I might be making some progress with her. Now ... I don't know where to turn. Where else can I go?"

"For another Fropper?"

"I've tried them all. And got nowhere."

"I heard about a new one last week, somewhere down in the deep basement levels. I can find out more about that if you want me to—maybe even get an appointment for you."

"When?"

"In a week or so? You know it takes time if the Fropper's any good." Tatty hesitated. "I'll check it out for you tomorrow if you like."

"Tonight."

"Esro, I *can't*. It's too late. I was hoping you'd be staying with me—just for the one night." She came to stand behind him and put her hands on his shoulders. "I don't ask much, you know that. You don't have to fake it for me any more. I don't want the same old promises: how you'll find a place for me, how you'll take me with you away from Earth. I'm past all that. Just stay here tonight. That's all I'm asking."

He reached up to cover her hands with his own. "Princess, you don't understand. When I come to Earth, I *always* want to see you. But I've got to be honest with you, too. When I come to Earth, I *have* to see the Froppers, find out if they can help me yet. I'll stay here tonight, of course I will. But would you at least try to make an appointment *now* for a Fropper meeting, as soon as I can be fitted into the new one's schedule? That way I'll have some hope of a few hours' sleep tonight."

Tatty leaned over his shoulder and kissed Mondrian quickly on the lips. "Of course I will. My poor, poor Essy. Is it still as bad as ever?"

"It's worse. Every year, it tightens and tightens." Mondrian sat up straight, lifting Tatty with him. "There's one other thing, then I can relax. Luther Brachis."

"What about him."

"If he's going to be on Earth for a while, I have to know what he's doing here. I thought I might put King Bester on my payroll, but I'm not sure he stays bought. We need someone we can trust. Could you contact the Godiva Bird and put her onto Brachis?"

"That will cost a fortune. Do you have any idea how much Godiva charges?"

"Budget isn't the problem. Go ahead and do it. My staff insist that women are one of Luther's weaknesses."

"Pity they're not one of yours." Tatty straightened and moved away from Mondrian. "Esro, you sit there and try to enjoy your brandy. I'll arrange for Godiva, and I'll fix an appointment with the Fropper. If only you could relax, even for one night—you're so *driven*."

"We're all driven, Princess—every last one of us." Mondrian glanced across at the tiny glass spheres, each filled with purple liquid, that sat within easy reach. There was a row of them in every room in the apartment. "Maybe some day I *will* learn to relax—and maybe someday you'll learn to stop being a Paradox addict."

Tatty had been moving towards the door, heading for the communications unit in the next room. Now she paused. "I wish I *could* stop, Essy."

"Paradox killed Rattafee, Princess."

"Do you think I'm not aware of that, more than you are? I know it. As well as I know that your work is going to kill you—unless you find something else to get you there quicker." She sighed. "Just try to relax, Esro. I'll be back as soon as I can."

Chapter 6

"Not to *live* here," said King Bester. "No one in their right mind would *live* on the surface."

A "surface" apartment of Delmarva was defined, by real estate agent convention, as anything less than one kilometer underground. The final outer layer, where roof met open sky, was reserved for automated agriculture and land management. *Humans, keep out!* Anyone with a perverse urge to sample the "natural" surface life could gratify it easily enough with a trip to central Africa or to South America. The surface reservations there, complete with their protected wild species, still stretched for thousands of square miles.

But the surface of Delmarva Town was a fine place for agriculture. And it was a truly perfect place for an illegal Needler lab—for anyone who could stand the idea of exposure to open sky.

Luther Brachis and King Bester hid their discomfort from each other as they left the final ascent tube and walked up a ringing steel staircase out onto the cultivated soil of the city. Brachis hated those unpredictable breezes. To him they still carried their message of lock failure and hard vacuum. And King Bester, comfortable in the cramped warrens of the city, trembled under the star-filled sky with its cold brilliance.

Walking closer together than either realized, they hurried across three fields of dark-green mutated sedges. Bester knew their destination exactly. After only a few minutes under bare sky he was ducking thankfully into a roofed enclosure. The two men descended a short flight of steps to an open door and a darkened room. Standing at the threshold was a tall, stooped man with a domed bald head, jutting red nose, and long straggling beard.

"The Margrave of Fujitsu." King Bester was at his most formal. "Commander Luther Brachis."

The Margrave stared at them gloomily and nodded. He closed the door and triple-locked it, then turned and pressed a light switch. At the other side of the room sat a bulbous plant, five feet high and about two feet across. When the light went on the leaves of the swollen upper part began to open. In less than thirty seconds a single vast flower was revealed. Its central part resembled a human face, with pink cheeks, curved red mouth, and blind blue eyes. After a few moments, the mouth opened. A thin, beautiful tone came forth, a crystalline, pure soprano singing a wordless lament. The song continued and broadened, from a simple theme through to a complex coloratura embroidery.

"One of my most successful creations, I think." The Margrave spoke in excellent standard Solar. "I call this *Sorudan*—the spirit of song. Stimulated to sing by light, of course, but the real trick is that the melody never repeats unless I so desire. I will be most sorry if I am ever forced to sell *Sorudan*." He lowered the level of light in the room. The voice slowly faded, while the melody passed through sublime downward ripples of semitones to a plagal cadence. The sightless eyes closed. Moments later the petals began to curve in around the silent face.

The Margrave led the way in silence into the next room. Luther Brachis followed, slowly. Even if the display of *Sorudan* had been laid on just for his benefit, it was no less impressive. The ugly artist had created a work of astonishing beauty.

The walls of the next room were lined with cages and holographic images. Brachis saw to his satisfaction that the range of this Needler lab's output was diverse, and seemingly unlimited in its range. Aquaforms, peering out from their tanks of green-tinged water, sat next to the blinking raptor shapes of gryphons, while just beyond that a holograph of a skeletally-thin kangaroo stood next to—and loomed over—a giraffe. Farther along, under intense arc lights, an inch-long bear ambled along the flat pad of a water-lily. Above it, and above everything, mobile plants quivered and snaked along the ceiling, following moving sources of overhead light.

The Margrave waved a casual arm across the display. "Just to give you an idea. The King tells me that you're not interested in a simple art product, which most of these are. So why don't you outline your requirement? Then I'll tell you if I think it can be done, and give you a cost estimate."

"I don't have a complete description. Not yet. But I'll be willing to pay you very well. And he'll have to go." Brachis nodded to Bester. "What I have to say is for your ears only."

King Bester looked startled. He began to object, then shrugged. "All right by me. I get paid either way."

He went sulkily through to the next room and watched while Luther Brachis carefully closed the door. After a few seconds Bester went across and put his ear to it. He could hear nothing. He waited impatiently for fifteen minutes, even standing on a chair to see if anything was visible over the top of the door. It wasn't. By the time the door opened again and the two men came out, he was hopping in inquisitive frustration.

"I'll send the full specifications just as soon as I have them," said Brachis.

The Margrave nodded and opened the outer door. "And after that I'll need about three weeks. At the end of that time I'll tell you how close I can come to what you want. And you will, of course, need to appoint a suitable intermediary. I dare not meet with just anyone."

"Understood. I will make those arrangements." The heavy door closed. All light vanished, and Brachis and Bester stood together in a moonless and overcast Earth night.

"Why Needlers?" said Brachis, as they climbed to the top of the stairs and waited for their eyes to adjust to the darkness. "I looked over the Margrave's whole lab, and I didn't see one needle."

"They don't prick. Not any more." Bester was peering around, in every direction. "That's how it was done when method started, ages back. Way Margrave tells it, in early days, they were all *biologists*, playing around with female animals and producing offspring. No poppas."

"Parthenogenesis, you mean. Lots of organisms propagate that way."

"Yeah. Partho-that. Knew it was fancy long word. Biologists heated eggs, and put eggs in acid, and gave 'em electric shocks or poked 'em with needles. Sometimes egg developed, more often not. Then they got fancier and started new game. If you use *hollow* needle, real fine one, you can inject stuff into middle of cell. That way you get new DNA into nucleus."

"King, when they taught you standard Solar, didn't they ever mention *articles*? Let's talk Earth-lingo. You're making my head ache."

Bester grinned and wiggled his eyebrows. "Fine by me, squire. Not many foreigners can talk Earth talk, so I tend not to use it with 'em. Anyway, after they learned the DNA injection and gene splicing techniques, the Needlers never looked back. They learned how to put duck DNA in an eagle, or spider DNA in a mosquito, or anything in anything. It's a tricky technology, of course— if you and me tried it, the egg would die. But some of them are hot-shot good at it, like the old Margrave there. If you want it, he can make it." Bester stared at Luther Brachis with vast curiosity. "Did he say he can make it— what you want?"

Brachis did not answer. He could see fairly well, and he started forward. King Bester grabbed him by the arm. "One minute longer, squire. Never rush it, at night on the surface."

"Wild animals?"

"You might say that. Scavvies. They come up out of the warrens at night, see what they can find. If you ever meet Bozzie's Scavengers when you're up here, you run for it and don't stop. They're tough and they're mean. They'll cut you to pieces for your clothes—or just for the fun of it."

Luther Brachis was listening to Bester very closely,

and taking in everything that he saw or heard. He was going to be visiting this place again, several times, and he had better learn how to operate here.

The steady breeze on his face was already less disconcerting, but the smell of decay—it must be dead plants or animals, crumbling away to unplanned and uncontrolled dissolution—made his nose wrinkle with disgust. There was a strange, whispering sound on all sides. It was the sedge, leaf rustling over leaf. He stared upwards. The cloud layer above was not unbroken, and in the open patches of sky he could now see stars, strangely soft-edged and subdued. They seemed to move and flicker as he watched.

Brachis saw the entry point to the lower levels, thirty steps ahead. "The work that the Margrave will be doing for me is none of your business." The hook had been set back in the lab. Now it was time to strike. If King Bester could be caught anyhow, it was by the nose—his nose for curiosity.

"Of course, King, things would be quite different if I could be sure you were on my side. I could tell you a lot of things, then, and you could really be involved in them. There could be lots of jobs for you."

"I can't go to space, squire. It's not safe up there."

"Forget space. I'm talking down here, on Earth."

Bester snapped his fingers. They had begun the descent now, in a slow, steady elevator that seemed to go down forever. "Try me, squire, just try me."

"I'd like to. But it seems to me that you're already working for Mondrian. Anyone who works for him can't work for me."

"I don't work for him—swear I don't."

"You were waiting for him, when we came out of the Link exit."

"Not true, squire. I wasn't waiting for him, he came to *me*. I was waiting for anyone who came in from outside, because that's where I get business. People want things—just like you wanted things."

"Maybe. But if you work for me, we'll have to start slowly, and carefully. You'll have to *prove* you don't work for Esro Mondrian. He's smart, and he's sneaky."

"He frightens me, squire, and that's no lie. I don't even like to look at his eyes."

"Then you stay that way. It's safest. So you think you're ready to do a job for me?"

"You name it." Bester was almost too eager. "You name it, and I'll do it."

"All right. For a beginning, you can keep an eye on the product that the Margrave will be developing for me."

"I will. But I don't know anything about it."

"You will—as soon as I have the full spec myself. I'll send that to you, and I'll want you to deliver it to the Margrave. Naturally, you don't tell anybody one word about it. And I'll want you to keep a close eye on it as it's being developed."

"He thinks he can make it for you when you don't even know what it is yet?"

"I told him the basic idea. The Margrave will try, I'm sure of that. His pride won't let him refuse. If you watch him closely, you'll know how well he succeeds even before I do."

They were back at the level where Tatty Snipes lived. She had arranged sleeping accommodations for both of them, in large, luxurious apartments. King Bester had rolled his eyes when he saw them, and given thanks aloud that he wasn't expected to pay for them.

"One more thing," added Brachis, as they came to his apartment door. "About the Needlers. Those products are wonderful. You could export them all over the Stellar Group. But you don't."

Bester fidgeted in his patchwork clothes. "Yeah. Well, they would, you see—if they was allowed to. But there's a problem."

"If it's a question of export licenses—"

"Not that. See, the Needler labs make all kinds of Artefacts, but all the best ones have something in common: The DNA in 'em is mostly human. That's not permitted, but they all do it or they can't compete. Remember *Sorudan*? Didn't *look* human, I know, but there's more human DNA in that Artefact than there is in the smart chimps in the transportation system."

Luther Brachis shook his head. He went into his apartment without speaking. And yet King Bester had the odd feeling that he could not have given the big security commander more welcome news.

An hour before sunlight touched the surface far above him, Esro Mondrian was waiting in total darkness. He had slept for three hours after midnight, and awakened shivering and perspiring.

Tatiana lay at his side, one arm across his body. He eased away from her and moved slowly and carefully through into the next room. Once the door was closed he turned on a low-powered light and switched the communicator to whisper mode.

"Captain Flammarion?"

As Mondrian had expected, Kubo was awake. The wizened little man drank too much, ate almost nothing, and seldom slept. Both of them were awake twenty hours out of twenty-four.

"I'm here, Commander. I'd been wondering how to get in touch with you. Nobody seemed to know, and I really needed to talk." But even now Flammarion was cautious. He waited for receipt of Mondrian's ID before he continued. "We made it up through the Link without any trouble, and we're all on Ceres. But I think there's a real problem, and I want you to know about it before anyone else does."

"Appreciated. Carry on, Captain."

"The woman is fine. Her name is Leah Buckingham Rainbow. Her title seems free and clear, she's twenty-two years old, and considering where she came from she's in great physical condition. Prime training material. Mass one twenty seven, training quotient—"

"Skip all that, Captain. Get to the problem."

"Yes, sir. It's the man. His name is Chancellor Vercingetorix Dalton. He's twenty years old, a wonderful physical specimen, and his title is clear, too." Flammarion cleared his throat. "Only trouble is—he's a moron."

"*What!*" Mondrian did not raise his voice, because he did not want to waken Tatty, but its intensity seared along the communications link.

"A moron, sir. Literally. Remember when we first saw them, the woman seemed to lead the action?"

"I noticed that."

"Well, when we caught them she still did all the talking. But he seemed to be listening, and kept nodding as though he was following everything. He didn't say anything, except his name when we asked for it. And now I know why. We gave him a standard test when we got up here, and his name's about the only thing he *can* say, with any understanding. He takes all his action cues from her. Sir, did you know any of this already?"

"No. But I should have guessed it when Bozzie was so happy to make the deal." Mondrian sat hunched by the communicator. "Damn the man. He knew it, the fat fraud."

"I'm sorry, sir."

"Not your fault, Captain. Mine. Just how bad is Dalton? Did you get a complete profile yet?"

"They'll do more tests, but we have enough. It's pretty hopeless. Mental age of maybe a two-year-old. See, him and the girl were raised together, and apparently she has always looked after him. That hasn't helped at all—may have made him worse."

"Apart from you, who knows about any of this?"

"Well, the psych tests on both the man and the woman are part of the general records. But I don't see anybody bothering to look at them."

"Don't you believe it. Commander Brachis will look at them if they're anything to do with Pursuit Team candidates. We have a wager on it."

"Yes, sir. I'm sorry, sir."

"He'll think he's won. Maybe he has. Captain, do you have the profiles with you?"

"Right here."

"Take a look. Do you think we have a situation where we might be able to use a Tolkov Stimulator?"

There was a long silence at the other end.

"Captain Flammarion?"

"I'm here, sir. I'm looking, but I just don't know. His profile's pretty good, so there might be a decent chance. But Commander—"

"Captain?"

"The Tolkov Stimulator. It's not—I mean it is—isn't it? It's supposed to be for top security. Top security use only. It's not—I mean it is—"

"Don't gibber, Captain. When I want a monkey on my staff, I can find one down here on Earth. I know the restrictions on Stimulator use better than you do. But this use *is* a top security issue—the security of the whole Stellar Group. Can you think of a more urgent use?"

"But it's not just that. I've seen the Stimulator used—it only works one time out of ten."

"So it's a long shot."

"And if it *doesn't* work, it kills the subject."

"Which would mean the wager with Commander Brachis was off. Captain, don't waste any more time talking. Find a Stimulator. I'll make sure we have all the approvals."

"Yessir." From the sound of Flammarion's voice, he was standing to attention. "I'll do it, sir. But sir—"

"I'm still here."

"Remember how the Stimulator works. Somebody has to be present to apply it to the subject. There's a real strong bonding involved, and it can take months. And from what I've heard, it's absolute hell for *both* of them. After the first few tries, the person applying the Stimulator usually wants to up and quit. It will be like that using it on Dalton. You'll have to appoint somebody to stay with Dalton and the Stimulator, for weeks and weeks, and—"

Kubo Flammarion realized where his line of speech was taking him. His tongue froze in horror.

"Relax, Captain. You are definitely not a candidate. I appreciate your concerns, and I know all the risks of using a Tolkov Stimulator as well as you do. Let me worry about that." Mondrian leaned back, studying a calendar on the desk in front of him. "Note your own orders. As soon as the tests are complete, take the man and the woman to the Horus confinement facility. Set up the maximum security environment there. Also set up a system for education, and one for Pursuit Team training.

Allocate a chamber for a Tolkov Stimulator—I'll arrange for the equipment to be shipped to you. Any questions?"

"The person who will be applying the Tolkov Stimulator to Chancellor Dalton—"

"Is no concern of yours. I will take care of that also."

"Any other questions?"

"No, sir."

"Then proceed."

Mondrian pressed the disconnect and walked quietly through into the bedroom. Tatiana lay flat on her back. She was still sleeping, but when he moved to her side she turned to him in the darkness. Mondrian touched her, caressing her slowly and gently. She pulled him close and muttered in pleasure at what he was doing.

They made love quietly, still in total darkness. Afterwards Tatty locked tight, rocked him up and down, and whispered in his ear, "That was different from anything we've ever done before. Usually you pull away at the end, but this time you stayed with me. Essy, that was absolutely wonderful!"

"It was fantastic." Mondrian was whispering, his breath touching the hollow of her neck. "Princess, you're very dear to me. You ought to know that."

"I wish I could believe it. But it's difficult. You come, and you go . . ."

"I know. You told me not to make and break the same old promises, and I won't do that. Never again. But I'll make a new promise."

"Oh, Essy. Don't. Not now. Don't spoil it."

"Princess, I mean it. I have an important job that needs doing. It has to be carried out away from Earth, and it may take a long time."

"You're telling me you'll be away from me for a long time."

"No. The opposite. I'm telling you that I need help. I have to have someone that I trust totally. If you'll agree to help me, we'll leave Earth—together."

She jerked beneath him, trying to sit up under his weight. "Essy, do you mean it?"

"I certainly do."

"I mean, after all this time . . . then you ask me to go, just like that. I can hardly believe it."

"I'm serious. We'll go—if you want to."

She began to rock him again, tightening her arms and legs about him. "Of course I want to! Why *wouldn't* I want to?"

"What about Paradox? You won't get a supply of that once you're away from Earth. Its export is one of Quarantine's strongest prohibitions."

"Ah." She paused. He could hear her breathing through her nose, and the tiny sucking sound as she bit her lower lip.

"I still want to." There was fear and hunger in her voice, and she laughed nervously. "The stuff's killing me anyway, I've known that for years. Will you help me kick the habit?"

"Of course I will."

"Then when will we go?"

"Very soon. I'll have to get special permission from Quarantine, and an exit permit, but I'll start working on that this morning. We could be leaving Earth in three days. Can you be ready?"

"Ready?" Tatty was suddenly crying. "*Ready*! Esro, if you want me I'm ready this minute. I've been ready for ages. If you need me, I'll go right now, without packing one thing."

"That's wonderful."

Tatty had never heard such happiness in his voice. In the darkness, she could not see his face.

Chapter 7

The asteroids of the Egyptian Cluster form a solar system anomaly. The orbits of the cluster members share a common inclination and a perihelion distance of about three hundred million kilometers. That supports the idea that they *are* a cluster, although one now far dispersed spatially. They also share the common material composition of the smaller silicaceous bodies of the solar system.

And yet they are, every one, anomalous. Instead of moving in the ecliptic, like all well-behaved planetoids, their common orbital plane is inclined at an angle of nearly fifty-nine degrees to it.

The physical data for the Egyptian Cluster are given in the Appendix to the General Ephemerides of the solar system—a fair measure of their importance in the big scheme of things. But even within a minor group there is a natural pecking order. Horus, twenty kilometers across, is an asteroid low in the order, very much an undistinguished specimen. No more than a bleak wedge of dark rock, it lacks atmosphere, volatiles, regular form, useful minerals, easily accessible orbit, or any other interesting property.

It is the perfect place for privacy. Mindful of this, an isolationist (and now extinct) religious sect long ago turned Horus into a worm-riddled cheese of black silicate, hollow and tunneled and chambered. The echoing inner cavities, with their entrance corridors paradoxically reflex and convoluted, were an ideal location for assured privacy and security.

Or for incarceration.

In one of the central chambers of Horus minimally appointed as living quarters sat two men and two women: Kubo Flammarion, Chan Dalton, Tatiana Sinai-Peres, and Leah Rainbow.

Flammarion had been talking for a long time, while the other three listened with varying degrees of attention. Chan Dalton fidgeted and played with the plate and fork sitting in front of him. Tatty stared ahead with a dull lifeless face the color of muddy chalk, while her hands trembled whenever she lifted them from the table. Alone of the three, Leah was following every word that Flammarion said.

"But you *can't*." Her face was frowning and furious, and she spoke standard Solar so badly and so angrily that Flammarion could only just understand her. "You absolutely can't. Don't you understand what I said? I've looked after Chan since he was four years old, ever since his mother sold him to Bozzie. If I'm not with him he's lost—totally."

"He'll be lost *at first*." Kubo Flammarion looked no happier than Leah. "Just at first, see, but then he'll get used to things and he'll be all right. Princess Tatiana will look after him very well."

"Chan like Tatty," said Dalton. It was the most complex statement he had uttered since they arrived on Horus.

"How can she look after him?" exploded Leah. "Look at her, for God's sake. She's an addict, as bad as I've seen. She can't look after *herself*."

Tatty braced herself in her chair and turned to face Leah. "How do you think I feel about this? Do you think I *want* to be out here? I don't. I don't want to baby-sit that—that overgrown *moron* you brought with you. I don't want *any* of it. I just want to go back *home*—back to Earth, away from this god-awful, god-damned, god-deserted place." She leaned forward and buried her face in her trembling hands.

"Moron!" shouted Leah. "What do you mean, moron? Chan's as good—"

"Not now." Flammarion waved his hand across Leah's

face to interrupt her. "Don't hassle Tatty—you can see she's not herself. Have some sympathy with her. She's in Paradox withdrawal."

"How do you know?"

"I've been there. I know. Believe me, all she can think about is how bad she needs a shot."

"Shot for Tatty," said Chan happily. "Tatty's my friend." He went across and hugged her.

Flammarion offered him a puzzled stare. The tests that had assigned Chan the intelligence of a two-year-old were imprecise in many ways, and their overall conclusion was just an average of many factors. Sometimes Chan seemed to understand nothing that was said to him. At other times he would fix his gaze on the speaker and nod intelligently, as though he was listening hard and taking in every word. Leah said that was no more than a protective coloration, something that she had painstakingly taught Chan to let him survive in the tough environment of the Gallimaufries. But it was hard to accept that someone who *seemed* to listen so intelligently could be understanding nothing that was said to him. Leah's explanation had only halfway persuaded Flammarion.

"Anyway, I won't leave Chan, and you can't make me," said Leah, standing up from the table. "You want me to become a candidate for your stupid Pursuit Teams? Then you just try and force me. But if you make me leave here, I promise you I won't cooperate on *anything*."

Flammarion wriggled in nervous frustration. He had been carefully coached in the next part by Mondrian, but he was not sure he could carry it off. "How much do you care for Chan, Leah?"

"More than anything or anyone." Leah went to the blond youth's side. "He's *all* I care about. I worry more about what happens to Chan than to anyone on Earth, or off it, or in all your wonderful 'Stellar Group.' You just asked a really stupid question." She put her arms possessively around Chan.

"It wasn't *really* a question." Flammarion sniffed. "I thought that's what you'd say. Now you listen to me, Leah Rainbow. In all your years of looking after Chan and loving him, didn't it ever make you sad to know that

Chan would not develop as a normal human being? I'm not talking about the physical side, I mean his mental maturity."

"Of course it did. It broke my heart."

"And didn't you grieve, to think that he'd always be like this, and never know the world that we know?"

"I cried myself to sleep over Chan, a thousand times."

Flammarion looked uneasily across at Chan Dalton. It made him feel very uncomfortable, referring to Chan as though he was not even there; although surely Leah must know what she was doing, and Chan didn't comprehend what they were saying about him.

But the questions were having a profound effect on Leah Rainbow herself, and Chan noticed *that*. He put his arms around her in turn, and squeezed her to him.

"You silly old man." Leah's eyes were blinking away tears. "I've wept more for Chan than I've ever wept for myself. I've often thought I'd trade everything I had, sell my body, give my whole life—if it could somehow make Chan grow up. I still feel that way, I would do *anything*. Only now I'm old enough to know that it's a hopeless wish."

"Hopeless, is it? Then you listen to me, Leah Rainbow." Flammarion leaned forward and lowered his voice confidentially, although the room held the only people within seventy million kilometers. "People on Earth don't know everything, even though there's many as thinks they do. So you listen. A few years ago, a man named Tolkov built a gadget out on Oberon Station. He intended it for use in working with alien forms, ones who might be intelligent but who seemed like borderline cases. It worked pretty well, and people called his invention a *Tolkov Stimulator*. Just a few models were made, and their use was pretty much prohibited for use on humans. The only exception is in case of Stellar Group emergencies. You see, the Stimulator *heightens the level of mental activity*. Sort of like some of the mental stimulant drugs—except that it does it *permanently*."

"It makes people smarter?"

"Sometimes. *Some* people. It makes others go insane, and that's why it's prohibited for general use. But Mondrian, my boss, he has access to a stimulator if he needs one, because he's head of the Anabasis. He could make one available." Flammarion leaned close to Leah. "If Commander Mondrian was sure that everyone else was cooperating with the Anabasis' effort, he might make it available *for Chan*."

"For Chan," echoed Dalton happily. He was still standing between Leah and Tatty Snipes. "For Chan."

"See?" said Flammarion. "*He* knows what he wants. But I'll guarantee one thing—Commander Mondrian *won't* make the Stimulator available if you refuse to cooperate and won't go ahead with pursuit team training. That's why I asked you: How important is Chan to you?"

Flammarion paused. He had reached the end of Mondrian's advice as to how to proceed. Now all he could do was sit and wonder how Leah would react.

She burst into tears. "Chan, did you hear him?" She hugged Dalton to her. "Oh, Chan, you're going to grow up—read, and write, and know the names of the animals and the flowers and the days of the week, and dress yourself, and learn the names of all your friends. Won't it be wonderful?"

"You'll do it?" Flammarion stood up, stretching the creases in his wrinkled uniform.

Leah's tears gave way to rage. "Of course I'll do it, you great fool. You're offering me what I've prayed for. You think you're so clever, knowing exactly which pressure points to push."

"I didn't push—"

"You decided where to probe and twist me, didn't you, and you think you've won. But we'll be the real winners, me and Chan. I'll do it, of course I will. I'll go away, and study, and do my best to work with your stupid Pursuit Team. But you'll have to promise me something, Captain. Chan must have a *full* treatment with your machine, and you'll have to give me regular progress reports. And I get to come here sometimes, to see for myself how he is doing. *And* you tell me *at once* when he becomes normal."

"*If* he becomes normal. I told you, the Stimulator isn't a sure thing. There's a good chance it can fail. And even if it works, you won't know for a while. It's an odd process. It goes real slow at first, then all of a sudden the change comes in a big rush. But don't get me wrong. There's no guarantee that the change we want will *ever* come. Chan may stay a mor—a not too bright person, for all his life." *And if it doesn't work, that won't be very long.*

"Even if it doesn't work, he'll be no worse off then he is now. How often will I be able to come here and visit?"

"Maybe a couple of times." Flammarion wriggled again in his seat. Mondrian would go out of his mind when he learned how Leah Rainbow had bargained. "You see, it's not a great idea to come here. The period when the Stimulator is being applied is very . . . intense. Tough for the person being treated, and tough for the one giving the treatment. There shouldn't be interruptions. For Chan's own sake, he ought to interact with just one person until the course is finished. And that person will be Princess Tatiana."

"How long—before we know?"

"Nobody can say. Maybe a month or two, but it could be more. Anyway, by that time your training ought to be over, and you'll have a Pursuit Team assignment."

"You're telling me I may not see him at all."

"I don't know—and I'm not trying to trick you. Miss Leah, can you get all this across to Chan? It would make Princess Tatiana's job a lot easier if he really understood what was going on."

"I can try. It's very abstract for him, but I'll do my best." Leah turned to Chan. "Channy, let's go away and play, just us, in the swim-room. All right? Tatty and the Captain will stay here."

Chan nodded. "OK. Captain smell real bad. We'll go."

"There." Leah turned fiercely on Flammarion. "You think Chan's not smart, but he just told you something you ought to have been told a long time ago. You smell, Captain Flammarion. To be more accurate, you *stink*. Come on, Chan, let's get out of here. Tatty, don't let him talk you into anything you don't want to do."

She headed for the door, pulling Chan along by the hand. Kubo Flammarion stared after them in perplexity. He shrugged, scratched at his scalp, rubbed his sleeve across his nose, and finally walked across to Tatty Snipes. She was still leaning forward with her head on her hands.

Flammarion took a purple globe the size of a small grape from his pocket and pressed it firmly against her arm. "Only half a dose, Princess, but better than nothing. There, now. Give it a minute or two, and you'll start to feel better."

She groaned at the first shock of the injection. After a few seconds she raised her head, and a touch of pink began to creep into the livid cheeks. "Ah-h-h. Thanks, Kubo. Oh God, I've been feeling wretched. I thought I'd die when I found out there were going to be no more shots."

"Didn't Commander Mondrian tell you that?"

"He did. But I tried not to think about it. Are you disobeying orders, giving it to me?"

"Well, I suppose you might say so." Flammarion sat down next to Tatty. "It's certainly illegal, I promise you that."

"So why are you doing it?"

"Because I understand Commander Mondrian. You see, Princess Tatiana, he doesn't think like you or me. He believes he's tough enough, himself, to stand anything that's thrown at him."

"He's very strong."

"Right. So sometimes he assumes we're all the same. Me, I know better. I've got my own problems, and I know just what you're going through. So I've been thinking, if we can just *ease* you off the Paradox, little by little, then you have a chance of making it all the way and being off it forever—even when you're on Earth and can get it all the time."

Tatty held out her arm, showing the regular line of blue-black dots from wrist to shoulder. "You're an optimist, Captain Flammarion. Eight hundred shots say you're wrong."

"That's the past, Princess. Think of the future."

Flammarion also thought of the future, and Tatty's next few months. He still had a lot of explaining to do to her. But she was turning to him, gripping his hand in hers.

"*I hate him*. I do. Captain, when I think of what he did to me . . . bringing me away from Earth, sending me here—and then not coming here himself, or even calling . . ."

"He'll be here in a few days." Flammarion squeezed her thin, bony hand. "You know, he's just unbelievably busy. He still has to run all the Boundary security, and now he has to get the whole Pursuit Team activity going as well. And we're having a terrible time with the Ambassador's office, because Dougal MacDougal wants to be in the middle of everything. The only person who can deal with that is Commander Mondrian."

"Don't make excuses for him, Captain. That's not part of your job." Tatty gave Flammarion a weary smile. "You're a very loyal man, and I hope he appreciates you."

"It's not loyalty. I just understand the Commander."

"No. You think you do, but believe me I know him a whole lot better—better than anyone who just works for him. If it fits his own needs, Commander Mondrian would sell you and me and anyone he knows."

"Now, Princess, you're just getting upset again. If you think that way, why did you agree to come here? You didn't *have* to leave Earth."

"I'm aware of that. Why do you think I'm so angry with myself? You see, *I knew all this*, knew it years ago. And *still* I'm out here, in the middle of nowhere, doing exactly what he wants me to do. I shouldn't be blaming *him*. I ought to be blaming *myself*." Tatty stood up slowly, stretching to relieve long-tensed muscles. "I've had it, Captain. Unless there's something else we absolutely have to talk about, I want to rest."

It was very tempting—put it off for another day or two, and hope somehow that it would never have to be done. But Mondrian would ask, the next time he called. "There is one more thing, Princess. About the Tolkov Stimulator. I told Leah Rainbow that the treatment gets very intense, for the person giving it as well as the one receiving it." Flammarion fixed his eyes on the table in front of him. It was the old story; Esro Mondrian taking an action, and leaving Kubo Flammarion to clean up the mess. "I have to tell you just *how* intense it might get for you."

"Tomorrow, Captain . . ."

"No, Princess Tatiana. *Today*. I'm sorry, but we have to do it before that shot of Paradox wears off."

Chapter 8

Esro Mondrian had puzzled over the directions before he tried to follow them. They were far from the usual Fropper territory. He had been sent meandering through an endless series of descent shafts, to the deepest base-ment levels of the Gallimaufries. So far down in the Earth's crust, continuous cooling was needed to make the levels even marginally habitable, and only the power maintenance crews visited on a regular basis. It seemed inconceivable that any successful Fropper would have an office down in these smoking warrens. But the directions had been detailed and specific.

The final hundred meters of his journey were in near-total darkness, stepping carefully along a steadily descend-ing shallow ramp. At the foot, the gloom closed in to become absolute. Mondrian paused to unsnap a minia-ture flashlight from his belt.

"No lights, please," said a soft voice from a few yards in front of him. "Take hold, Commander Mondrian, and follow me."

"You are Skrynol?"

"I am." A warm, fleshy flipper gripped Mondrian's fingers. He walked, step by slow step, led by the Fropper in front of him. Finally he was guided to a seat covered by warm, velvety material.

"Sit there, Commander. And relax."

"You have to be joking. Could *you* relax, in my situa-tion? I've been to a lot of Froppers before, but I've never had to put up with anything like this. Why the darkness? I'd like at least a little light."

"That desire is understandable. But it is not a good idea. I work far more effectively in total darkness. And with light, you might feel far *less* relaxed."

"I don't care what you look like. I don't expect a Fropper to win beauty contests."

"How true. But there are limits. Not every product of a Needler lab is a work of art in aesthetic terms."

Mondrian peered into the darkness. "Are you telling me you're an Artefact?"

"I do seem to be saying that, don't I?" There was a trill of laughter from somewhere above and in front of Mondrian. "Does that give you a problem?"

"I didn't know Artefacts could be Froppers."

"If you doubt my capabilities, I can refer you to others who will provide excellent testimonials. And from my initial assessment of your mental condition, the Froppers you have visited in the past have done little for you. Could an Artefact do worse?"

Mondrian leaned back again in his seat. "I can't argue with that. The others I've seen have done nothing for me. How can you say you've assessed my mental condition when I've only been here for two minutes?"

"You are asking me to reveal the secrets of my profession. I will not do so. But if you require proof that I can do what I say, you shall have an example. Sit quietly, relax as much as possible, and let your thoughts wander where they wish. I am going to attach a few electrodes." Cold touches came on Mondrian's forehead, hands, and neck. "And now, a few moments of silence."

The temperature in the room was far too hot for comfort. Mondrian sat, sweating heavily, and tried to follow the Fropper's order to relax. What form could possibly be so horrible that the sight of it was worse than this oppressive and stifling darkness? His eyes should be totally adjusted by now, but he could see nothing. Was he wasting his time, on yet another unproductive visit to a Fropper? There had to be a reason why Froppers were banned, everywhere except on Earth.

"I have enough." Skrynol's voice came suddenly out of

the darkness. "Remember, I cannot read your thoughts, and I will never claim to do so. But I can read your body, and they tell me more about what you are thinking than you may be prepared to believe. For example, let me read back to you a few of the more obvious and familiar indicators. Your pupils are somewhat dilated—yes, part of that is certainly due to the dark; but not all of it. And yes, I can see you very well, even though you cannot see me. You have a slightly accelerated eye blink. Your body temperature is elevated half a degree above what I judge to be its normal value. Your muscles are tense, but in tight control, although you are now making a conscious effort to relax your back and shoulders. Your pulse is elevated, ten counts or so above normal. Palms wet, perspiration high in acids and low in potassium ions. Mouth tight, lips a little dry. Nasal mucous membranes dry also, and a fraction of a degree cooler than expected. Frequent swallowing, and tight sphincters. In summary, you are hugely excited, and tremendously controlled.

"Now, you will say that those are mere physical variables. A med machine could tell as much about you. But what I can do, and no med machine could ever do, is to integrate all those factors, and place them in context. So I can *guess*—nothing more than a guess, although a highly educated one—at the mental state that accompanies the physical one.

"I conclude this about your thoughts, Commander Mondrian. At the conscious level, you are pondering me and my probable appearance. That is perfectly natural. But below that, in the center of your real attention, are two other worries. First, you have lost something, and it is enormously important for you to find it. And second, a concern which takes us deeper yet, and points to the reasons that you came here in the first place: the thing that was lost is important to you, only because it *protects* you from something else, the thing that you fear most. The hidden thing."

Mondrian realized that he had been thinking about the Morgan Construct, and where it might be. But until the Fropper mentioned the "lost something" the thought had been no more than a nagging background worry.

"The hidden thing. I don't know what you're talking about."

"You certainly do. But not at any conscious level. That is why it is hidden."

"Could it be the source of my nightmares—the reason why I wake up terrified every night?"

"Of course it is." Skrynol's voice held no uncertainty. "You did not need me to answer that question, did you? You could answer it very easily for yourself. So now we are agreed, we must begin the search for the hidden thing. Because we must certainly find it, before we can hope to get rid of it. I say again, *relax*."

"I am in your hands." And Mondrian was relaxing, more than he would have thought possible. Only his fingers were restless, turning and twisting the fire-opal at his collar. He thought he noticed a faint smell in the air, a trace of an odor like over-ripe peaches. "What do you want me to do?"

"Remain completely still. I am about to attach a few more electrodes." Again came the cold touches, this time on Mondrian's chest and abdomen. "Very good. Now, let me tell you exactly how we will proceed. We need to explore *below* the conscious levels, but it is not easy to reach them. Today, we will try for just the first stratum. I will speak certain key words—of people, animals, times, and places—and you may answer however you choose. Do not worry if we seem to be going nowhere, or round in circles."

It was standard Fropper technique, outlawed off Earth for centuries and with an uncertain reputation even on this planet. Mondrian nodded to signify his assent. He had been through this a hundred times before, without success. But what alternatives did he have? "I am ready."

The questions and answers began. They went on and on, annoying and pointless. Until suddenly, without ever a clear moment of transition, it was no longer a standard Fropper session. Mondrian's head became oddly muddled inside, flashing through a sequence of vivid yet unfocused images. *People, animals, times, places*. He was aware that he was talking, cursing, gesturing. About what? And to what? He could not say. After an indefinite period, he heard Skrynol's voice pushing through into his consciousness.

"*Mondrian.* Wake up."

"I am awake."

"No, you are not. Not yet. *Wake up.* Do you know what you have been saying to me? Think of it. *Think it and live it.*"

Mondrian was struggling back to full consciousness. He realized that he could remember, if he focused hard. "I know. I told you—"

People, animals, times, places.

Memory came spinning back, with terrifying detail. Every mental picture was bright in his mind.

He was a giant spider, sitting quietly at the center of a great web. The strands shone with their own light, each one visible and running off in all directions. But there was a point beyond which their luminescence faded, or perhaps the strands themselves disappeared. He could see the web, with himself in the middle, and beyond that all was darkness.

He watched, and waited, and at last felt a trembling along the glowing strands of the web. He stared out along the lines to see what prey might be caught there, but the disturbing object was too far away. It lay in the dark region. He knew from the delicate vibrations along the gossamer strands that it was moving. The vibrations strengthened. The prey was approaching.

And suddenly it was no longer prey. It was danger, a force that he could not control, creeping in towards him along the luminous threads. He could not see it, even though it must be getting nearer. And suddenly he realized that he was not waiting at the center of the web, until the right moment arose to go off and seek his victim. He was trapped, *bound at the center and unable to flee from whatever was approaching out of the terrifying darkness.*

"*Excellent!*" It was Skrynol's calm voice, pulling him free. Mondrian jerked upright on the velvet couch. He was shivering, but lathered with perspiration. "Did you ever encounter that set of images before?"

"Never." Mondrian again began fiddling nervously

with the fire-opal at his collar. "And I'll be happy if I never encounter them again."

Skrynol laughed, with that high-pitched trill of delight. "Courage, Commander Mondrian! We have penetrated much farther in this first session than I had dared to hope."

"The hidden thing. Do you know what it is?"

"I have no idea. If it were that simple, you would not need the services of a good Fropper. What we found today was a *diversion*, your own mind's first level of defense against revealing its fears. The images that you built are at best an analogy for those fears—and the fears themselves stem in turn from a much deeper and earlier hidden experience. We have far to go."

Mondrian felt the electrodes being tugged free from his body. "The session is over?"

"For today."

"What do I owe you?"

"For today? Nothing." Skrynol paused, a fleshy flipper resting on Mondrian's chest. "To be more honest with you, I have already received my payment for today. Two of the electrodes that I attached contain small catheters. While you were building your memories, I drew blood through them. Don't worry—it was just a little, less than a quarter of a liter. You have plenty left, and your body will replace the loss in a very short time."

"Nice of you to tell me about it." Mondrian breathed deep. He had finally stopped shivering, but he was still sweating all over. "Why do you want my blood? For analysis?"

"No, Commander. For the best, simplest, and most honest of reasons: to drink. My metabolism is not suited to the digestion of most forms of food."

Mondrian was being lifted from the velvet seat to a standing position. "I suppose I ought to be thankful that your needs are so modest. Will that be your standard charge for services—or does the price increase as the treatment continues?"

"You are a strong man, Commander Mondrian. Few can joke at the end of a session." There was sly humor in Skrynol's voice as they wound their way back towards the exit. "I will not increase the price. I want you as a regular customer, you see, and if I drained you that would be the end of it."

Mondrian felt the bottom of the upward ramp beneath his feet, and Skrynol was no longer holding him.

"You are safe enough." The voice came from far above. "Safe, at least, as long as you are still receiving treatment. The time to watch out for is the day that I say you are cured. Because then you will not plan to return, and I will have no incentive to hold back my appetite. But for the moment, you have no need to worry. So until the next time, Commander . . ."

Mondrian was not sure of his own feelings as he made the return journey to the upper levels. On the one hand, Skrynol had made more progress in one session than anyone else in dozens. On the other, he could not get the spider web out of his mind. More sessions would surely mean more images, just as disturbing.

Back at Link entrance level he transferred to the appropriate exit point and made his way wearily to Tatty's apartment. Without her presence, the living quarters felt cold and depressing. He went through to the inner room, reached up to his collar, and removed the fire-opal. The communicator had been placed in stand-by mode. He changed the setting and called for a scrambled circuit up from Earth. Within a few minutes he was connected with the Border Security facility on Pallas.

"Hasselblad? This is Mondrian. I have a special job for you. Multiple medium recording, all wavelengths."

He was silent for a few seconds, listening to the questions from the other end.

"Sorry, but I have no idea." He stared at the fire-opal, weighing it in his hand. "I know you do, but I couldn't tell what screening might be operating. I just tried every setting. I'll have this linked up to you in the next hour, and I want you to give it top priority. There might be nothing there at all. But if there is I need it by next week."

Chapter 9

To the human observer, nothing had changed. The green balloon of the air-bulb still floated free among a tangle of space flotsam. The overlapping folds on its side suggested an entry point. The guard of the Sargasso Dump who gestured Luther Brachis towards the lock mumbled nothing intelligible.

But Brachis had been warned by Phoebe Willard. Instead of a suit designed for vacuum or atmosphere, he was wearing a tempered form used in extreme environments. He passed through the four folds of the lock, and found himself immersed in an inviscid fluid. The suit sensors reported the outside temperature: a hundred-and-ninety-six degrees below freezing, seventy-seven above absolute zero. Brachis was floating in a bath of liquid nitrogen.

He followed a guiding line towards the center of the bulb. In just a few meters he reached a second curved wall, with its own locks. He negotiated them. Inside that, at last, was a spherical chamber with its own atmosphere.

Brachis glanced again at the sensors. Temperature just a few degrees higher—and pure helium all around him as an atmosphere. He wouldn't be taking his suit off for a while.

"Over this way, Commander." A familiar voice spoke in his ear. He looked to the directional signal recorded by his suit, and saw the figure of Phoebe Willard halfway across the interior of the air-bulb. The lattice-work was still in position, but now at its center sat a new structure, a second bubble of dark green.

"Not exactly a shirtsleeve working-place." Brachis floated towards her. "I tried to call you from the Dump's control room. Why didn't you answer?"

"Because I couldn't hear you. I designed it that way. For the same reason as I built the cold barrier." She pointed at the outer, liquid nitrogen shell.

"I never told you to lose communication ability."

"That was just a side effect. No signals can get through that outer wall. You told me you wanted a secure environment. This is it."

"Taken to extremes. And beyond them."

"I don't think so. Nor will you, when I tell you what's going on here. But first, let's get this out of the way." She pushed across to a magnetic board clamped to the lattice and lifted from it two cubes like a pair of oversized dice. "You insisted on hand-delivery. I'm hand delivering. This is it. The specification, the best one I've been able to derive by putting together information from every fragment."

Brachis slipped the data dice into a frost-proof, fire-proof pouch in his suit wall. "How complete is it?"

"For perfectionists like you and me, it's lousy. There's functions and neural paths I shouldn't even have guessed at."

"But you did."

"Naturally. The whole thing's a plausible Construct logic to anybody but an expert. In the old words of wisdom, you can fool some of the people all of the time and all of the people some of the time, and that's usually enough to get by."

"If you say it's plausible, that's good enough for me. So what's the bad news?"

"I didn't say there was any. But there is certainly *news*." Phoebe took the arm of Luther Brachis's suit and drifted them both closer to the central green balloon. It loomed over them, and from a few feet away Brachis could see hair-thin and delicate spider filaments running from a computer station into the tough balloon wall.

"What's inside that? More liquid nitrogen?"

Phoebe nodded. "Nitrogen. And one other thing. Part of a Construct—the one I told you about, with a big chunk of its brain intact."

"It had better be only the brain."

"Luther, I've reviewed the records from Cobweb Station over and over. They're terrifying. I bet I'm more afraid of the Morgan Constructs than you are. Before I did anything else I took this one completely apart, removed anything that might possibly be a weapon, and isolated the brain. Then I separated the pieces of the brain itself, and ran connections among them that I can interrupt any time from here. And *then* I put the whole thing in a bath of liquid nitrogen to reduce available energy, cut off all communication channels with anything except the computer over there, and put a communications break between *that* and everything outside the air-bulb. What more should I have done?"

"Nothing. You should have done less, not more. I told you I wanted a good Construct specification. I never told you to try and put one back together."

"And I haven't. All that's sitting in there is a naked brain fragment. Tell me you want me to destroy it, and I'll do it. You're the boss."

Luther Brachis had eased his way over to the computer console. "Can you talk to it?"

Phoebe was poised with her fingers on a pair of keys. "Say the word, Commander. Destroy or not destroy?"

"Phoebe Willard—Frau Doktor Professor Willard—does it ever occur to you that I really *am* your boss? Do you ever say to yourself, Phoebe, I report to Commander Brachis?"

"I might—if you didn't give me such off-the-wall assignments."

"Which you love. Don't push me too far. You will certainly *not* destroy your work. I said, can you talk to it?"

"As much as I want. The real question is, can it talk to me?"

"And what's the real answer?"

"You won't like it. I don't know." Phoebe was at the console, keying in sequences. "I know you won't take my word for it. Try for yourself. You're linked in now to the brain."

"Vocal circuits?"

"The original had them, but now they show no response at all. I've had to work everything through a computer interface. That introduces its own level of ambiguity, so you're probably better off avoiding oral inputs."

Brachis nodded. He typed in, *Who are you?*

"There. You can't get much more basic than that."

But Phoebe Willard was laughing at him. "Commander, don't you think that was just about the first thing I tried? Let's see if you get what I did."

The response was scrolling already onto the screen. *More information must be provided before that question can be answered.*

"That's it. Nine times out of ten that's the message—the only message—that comes back."

Brachis nodded, frowning at the screen. "Maybe it's the way the question is phrased. *Who are you* implies a recognition of self-identity. Let's try another." He typed in, *Tell me your name.*

More information must be provided before that question can be answered.

"Damn. What *doesn't* get that reply?"

"Nothing, consistently. I've been working with this off and on all day, and I've not found any regular pattern."

"Did it *have* a name? Maybe it doesn't comprehend the *idea* of names. But Livia Morgan must have had some way of distinguishing one Construct from another."

Brachis typed in, *Tell me the way that you were described by Livia Morgan.*

More information must be provided before that question can be answered.

"We already know the identification that Livia Morgan used." Phoebe was at another console, skipping around inside a hyperdatabase. "This one was called M-26A. It must have been built to respond to that—but maybe it only recognizes M-26A as its *whole* being. It may not accept an isomorphism between its whole self, and its brain alone. After all, you wouldn't say that you and your brain are the same thing."

"Sometimes I wonder if we're even related." Brachis typed in, *Your identification is M-26A. What is your identification?*

The reply was rapid. *Identification is M-26A.*

"Progress."

"Of a sort." Phoebe sounded unimpressed. "Ask it exactly the same thing again."

"All right." *What is your identification?*

More information must be provided before that question can be answered.

"Damnation."

"I know. I went through the same thing. It must have the information, because we gave it to it. We know it stored it, because it gave it back to us. But ask again, and you get nothing."

"Maybe it can only hold data for a few seconds."

"No. I gave my name, and waited for five minutes. Then I asked my name, and got the answer, Phoebe Willard. Then I asked again—and got that garbage about needing more information."

My name is Luther Brachis. What is your name?

My name is M-26A.

"See, it can feed something back to me that wasn't what I just fed in. And it realizes that *name* and *identification* are to be treated the same."

Brachis typed in again, *What is your name?*

More information must be provided before that question can be answered.

"The hell with it. Here we go again."

"I went through the same thing."

What is my name?

More information must be provided before that question can be answered.

"Damn. You know, this thing could be *addictive.*" Brachis forced himself to move away from the console. "But I can't stay here much longer. I've agreed to perform a guard review."

"The guards *here*, at Sargasso Dump? That sounds like a barrel of laughs."

"Knock it off, Phoebe. These people gave their lives—more than their lives—for System Security. They deserve better than the politicians are willing to give."

"Which is nothing. Sorry, Commander. This place gets to me after a while."

"So come watch the review." Brachis was studying her eyes. "How long have you been at it here, without a rest?"

"Ah—hmm. Twenty-one hours? Nearly twenty-two."

"Then you take a break, and come and watch the review. After that you have a meal and a rest. This time that's an *order*, Dr. Willard."

"I hear you."

Brachis watched as Phoebe Willard went through the sequence to end the interaction with the hidden Construct. As she sealed all access points to the globe filled with liquid nitrogen, it suggested another idea to Luther Brachis.

"Do you have all your question-and-answer sequences stored?"

"Commander, what do you think I am? One of your unfortunate guards? Of course I do."

"Good. I want a copy to take away with me and study."

"The best of luck sorting it out. I couldn't see any pattern. I'll give you the record, but we'll have to go over to the main control area to pick it up. I didn't want to leave it on the computer here when I was away."

"That's not like you." Brachis had caught a change in her voice. "Worried?"

"I guess so. But I can't see any reason. I really have been ultra-careful. I didn't just go *by* the book—I went way *past* the book."

"Keep it that way. I have the same feeling myself. When Livia Morgan made those Constructs she took a step in a direction that no one has ever travelled before."

They were passing through the outer nitrogen shell, emerging into the quiet graveyard of the Dump. A couple of hundred meters from them, drifting along in its own leisurely orbit, a massive dumbbell turned slowly end over end. Brachis paused to watch.

"A pulsed fusion ship built for a human crew. That's

ancient. It was the latest thing until the Mattin Link, then—instant obsolescence. I've never seen one before in the Dump. The place is full of stuff like this."

"Oddities, you mean?" Phoebe was trailing after Luther Brachis, turning now and then to stare at the quiet bulk of the green balloon behind. "I know. When I'm not working I go cruising around. There's a million of them, things you never see anywhere else. And so *old*. It's a ridiculous thought, but as you move around the Dump you have the feeling that every great failure of the solar system has quietly made its own way here. People as well as equipment. It's scary."

"I know what you mean. 'And all dead years draw thither, and all disastrous things.' "

"Why, Commander." Phoebe wanted to change the gloomy mood that seemed to be creeping up on both of them. "Do I detect a quotation—and one that's not from Von Clausewitz's *On War*? Someone has been civilizing you. And you're *looking* different. What's happening to the old Luther Brachis?"

But he would not respond. He made another subject switch of his own. "The trouble is, there's no *explanation* for the Construct behavior that we've been finding."

Phoebe sighed. No joking today. "That's not true. I can suggest two explanations."

"Let's hear them."

"All right. I don't much like either of them. But Number One, the Construct has been damaged to the point where it is not functioning in any consistent way. In other words, it's crazy."

"Then it's in the right place."

"No insulting remarks about Sargasso Dump guards, you said. If I'm not allowed to say they're crazy, nor should you."

"Point made. All right, Phoebe. What's Number Two?"

"It's functioning just as it was intended to."

"And we can't understand it. Are you saying that the Morgan Constructs are a lot smarter and more complex than anyone ever suspected?"

"I didn't know I was. But I seem to be."

And now Phoebe wished that the conversation had stayed with the forlorn relics of the Sargasso Dump.

Chapter 10

"No!" The scream boomed through the rocky chambers, resonating on and on. "No, no, no, NO!"

"Chan! Wait for me." Tatty was running as fast as she could, but the screams ahead of her were fading. Somehow he had escaped again, racing off through the maze of interior tunnels.

She slowed her pace. He could not get away for long, not with the Tracker to reveal his distance and direction. Even so, the folded corridors of Horus made the search a tedious business. And it was not only the corridors themselves. Ten generations of burrowing and excavating had left behind an astonishing legacy of debris: broken tunneling equipment, old food synthesizers, obsolete communicators, mounds of broken supply containers. When the last members of the sect left Horus, they had found few things worth hauling back for use elsewhere. Now the whole mess formed an obstacle course, to be climbed over, moved aside, or burrowed through.

Tatty plowed on. Chan had been crying when he ran, and with the hardest part still to come she felt close to tears herself. When she caught Chan she would have to give him his medication and drag him back for a session with the Stimulator. More and more, that seemed like a pointless exercise.

She forced herself on, grimy and tired. Even before Kubo Flammarion left Horus, Chan had been getting hard to handle. He was bigger, faster, and much stronger than Tatty. Sometimes she could manage him only by using a Stunner, slowing and weakening him enough for her to catch and overpower him.

"Cha-an!" Her cracking voice echoed off rocky walls. "Chan, come on. Come back home."

Silence. Had he found a new hiding-place? Maybe he was becoming more intelligent, just a little; or maybe it was her wishful thinking. Every day she stared into those bright blue eyes, willing them to show more understanding; every day, she was disappointed. The innocence of a two-year-old gazed back at her, unable to comprehend why the woman who fed him, dressed him, and put him to bed was the same woman who tortured him.

Tatty kept going. Most of the burrows on Horus terminated in dead ends, and after a while Chan, no matter how he tried to escape, would finish in one of them. Usually the same ones. He lacked the memory and intelligence to learn the pattern of the paths. Tatty peered at the Tracker. She was getting close. He had to be somewhere in the next chamber. She saw a pile of plastic sheets draped over powdered rock. He would be behind that, cowering brainlessly with his face pressed to the dirt. Tatty lifted the stunner and crept forward the last few yards.

He was there. Weeping.

It broke her heart to take him back to the training center. She knew she would not need the Stunner, for once she took hold of him his resistance disappeared. He allowed himself to be led along by the hand, passive and hopeless.

When he saw the Stimulator he began to cry again. She sat him in the padded seat, grimly fitted the headset and the arm attachments, and turned away as the power came on. The screams of pain when full intensity was reached were awful, but she had learned to stand those. It was later, when the treatment was over and she released Chan and tried to feed him, that Tatty always felt ready to faint. He would crouch in his chair, sweaty and panting, and look up at her pleadingly. The face was that of a tormented animal, exhausted and uncomprehending. She felt she was torturing a helpless beast, punishing it pointlessly again and again for a reason it did not understand—would never be able to understand.

She worried, always, that she was not using the Stimulator correctly. Kubo Flammarion had instructed her in the use of it before he left, and told her that Mondrian would give more detailed advice when he came to Horus.

He had never come. There had been not even a message. Day after day, Tatty did her best to follow Flammarion's instructions, in his three-fold way of Machine, Medication, Motivation.

"The Stimulator won't work by itself," he said. "You have to follow the right drug protocol, night and morning. But more important than that, you have to be *involved*. You have to bond with Chan, link to him and somehow make him *want* to learn."

"And how am I supposed to do that, when he doesn't understand even the *idea* of learning?"

Flammarion had scratched his scurvy head. "Beats me. All I can tell you is what they told me. If he doesn't have motivation, he'll never develop. But where there *is* motivation, the Stimulator can work what looks like a miracle. Here, how about using Leah's picture?"

Flammarion had produced from a packet of papers a grimy image of Leah, part of her official identification when she was inducted for Pursuit Team training. "Chan loves her more than anything in the world," he said. "If you show him this every time you use the Stimulator, and tell him that Leah wants him to learn—maybe that will help. And tell him that when the treatments are over, he'll be able to go and see Leah."

Tatty took the picture. Every day, after the injections and after the stimulator session, she made her speech. "Look at Leah, Chan. *She* wants you to learn. And *you've* got to want to be more intelligent, too. Just a little bit more, every day. And soon you'll be able to go and see Leah, and she'll come and see you."

Chan stared at the image and smiled. He certainly knew who it was. But that was the only response. The days wore on, all the same, and at last Tatty gave up hope. She should stop trying, stop torturing. Chan would never learn.

She brooded on her own situation. No visit from Esro Mondrian. No calls, not even a message. He had talked her into leaving Earth, duped her into doing what he wanted, as he could always do—and then forgotten about her until the next time she might come in useful.

She took the initiative, placing calls to him and to Kubo Flammarion. She could never get through to either of them. But one day, after many attempts, she managed to pass the shielding layers of guard and assistants and found herself talking to Mondrian's private office on Ceres.

"I'm sorry." One of Mondrian's personal guards took the call. "Captain Flammarion is in a meeting, and Commander Mondrian himself is not here."

"Then where the devil is he?" To get so far, and have her hopes dashed again . . .

There was a pause, while the woman consulted a display. "According to the itinerary, Commander Mondrian is on Earth. He will be there for two days."

"He is *where!*"

Tatty disconnected the communicator in a cold, clean rage. To drag her all the way to Horus to do his dirty work. To use her, and neglect her, while she passed through the agonies of Paradox withdrawal. And then to go back to Earth *himself*, without even telling her.

Tatty felt bitterness consuming her body, burning in her stomach. She went through to the other room, where Chan was connected to the Stimulator. The session was almost over. He was sweating prodigiously, banging his head from side to side in the neck brace and headset. Tatty went to stand next to him.

"Chan. Can you hear me?"

His eyes opened a slit. They were bloodshot and slightly bulging. There was inflammation and some excess pressure inside the skull case, but he was listening. She put her arms around him.

"He's using us, Chan. Both of us."

Tears rolled down her cheeks. Chan's eyes widened, and he reached out a wondering finger to touch the drops of moisture.

"Tatty crying."

"Oh, Chan, I'd have done anything for him, anything in the world. I thought he was wonderful. I even let myself be marooned out here, because I thought I'd be helping him. But it's no use. He doesn't care about us—about anything, except himself. He's a devil, Chan, crazy and heartless. He'll destroy you, too, if you let him, the way he's destroying me. Don't let him do it."

"Him?" He was staring at her in stony incomprehension.

Tatty fumbled in the overall pocket above her left breast. She took out a thin wallet, removed from it a small holograph, and held the image for Chan to see.

"Him. Look at it, Chan. This is the man who brought us away from home. This is the one who took Leah away from you. See him? This is the person who makes you go into the Stimulator. If you learn your lessons you can get away from here. You can go and find him."

The bloodshot eyes stared in silence, until at last Chan took a deep, shuddering breath. He reached out to take the hologram, with its smiling face of Esro Mondrian.

Was it imagination, or wishful thinking?

Tatty could not be sure, but she thought that a faint spark of understanding had glowed for a moment behind those innocent, tormented eyes.

The Margrave of Fujitsu paused and lifted his ugly head from the stereo-microscope. "And what, if I might ask, did you expect to see?"

Luther Brachis shrugged. "That's a hard question. But a lot more than this." His sweeping gesture took in the whole room, from the grimy skylight window that looked out onto Earth's surface, to the huge display system that covered a whole wall. "I mean, apart from those special microscopes almost everything here looks like part of a standard computer facility. If you hadn't told me, I wouldn't know this is a Needler lab at all."

"I see." The Margrave bent again over the microscope and made a minute adjustment to the setting. He laughed, without looking up. "Of course. You expected to see Needlers, didn't you—men in white coats, sticking pins into cells. I'm sorry, but you are seven hundred years too late."

He at last straightened, turned, and lifted a great pile of listings from the desk at his side. "In the earliest days, yes. A strange set of methods was used at one time to stimulate parthenogenetic egg development. Ultraviolet radiation, acid and alkaline solutions, heat, cold, needle puncture, radioactivity—almost everything was tried, and a surprising number of them worked—after a fashion.

"But all those methods produce only exact copies of a parent organism, rather than interesting variations. And even when mutations arise as a side effect of stimulation, they are quite random. As a way of producing an art form it would be quite hopeless, like dropping a block of marble off a cliff, and hoping to find a masterpiece of sculpture when you got to the bottom. Today, everything is planned." He held out the pile of listings. "With these."

Brachis took the top few sheets and inspected them. "These don't mean a thing to me, Margrave."

"Not Margrave. I am to be called simply Fujitsu. Mine was an Imperial line when most of your under-level braggarts were wearing animal skins and eating their food raw."

"Sorry, Fujitsu. But I don't see much here. Just page after page of random letters."

"Ah, yes. Random." The Margrave stabbed at the top page with a bony index finger. "This is random in very much the same way as *we* are random, you and I, since what you are holding is the complete DNA sequence of a living organism, in its precise and correct order. This output simply indicates the nucleotide bases in each of the chromosomes, letter-coded of course for convenience: A for adenine, C for cytosine, G for guanine, and T for thymine. The whole listing is built up—as we are—from those four letters. Taken together, they constitute the exact blueprint for production of an animal." He shook his head and stared at Luther Brachis. "I am sorry. You are no innocent and no fool, though you sometimes choose to pretend to be. I will be more specific. This is the blueprint for production of a special animal—a human being."

"I thought DNA had a coiled spiral structure. There's

no spiral here. And I don't *want* to produce a human being."

"A coiled spiral is topologically equivalent to a straight line, and a straight-line presentation of data is far easier to comprehend and analyze. As for the fact that this is presently a human encoding, do not worry about it. This is only my starting point, the theme from which we will construct sublime variations. Any one of the nucleotides can be changed to any other. We have full chemical control of the whole sequence. The chains can be split, lengthened, shortened, inverted, and modified in any way that I wish." He tapped the stack, with its endless and apparently random jumble of letters. "You asked me earlier, what is my job? What is it that I actually *do*. After all, since I am merely evaluating the effects of inserting different DNA fractional chains into this coding, what can I do that is not done better and faster by a computer?

"I have been asked that question many times, and still I can answer only by analogy. Do you play chess?"

"Some. It's required for Level Six education." Brachis saw no reason to mention that he had once been close to Grand Master level. It was hard to see how that slight misdirection could have future value, but the habit was ingrained.

"Then you probably know that, despite many centuries of work, the best chess-playing programs still fail to beat the best human players. Now, how can that be? The computers can store a million times as many games in memory. They can evaluate all possible moves, far ahead, to see which one is the best. They are tireless, and they never make the foolish errors of fatigue.

"And yet the best humans still win. How? Because they can somehow grasp within the slow, quirky, organic computer of the human brain an *overall* sense of board and position, in a holistic way that transcends individual moves. The computers play better every year—but so do the humans! The greatest chess players can *feel* the board, in its entirety, in a way that has never been caught in any computer program."

The Margrave turned to the display screen, where a

long sequence of coded letters was shown. "The same ability is possessed by the best Needlers. In a string of a hundred billion nucleotide bases, random substitution, exchange, or deletions could prove totally disastrous for the organism that it represents. No viable plant or animal would result. But it is my special talent—and I assure you, Commander, that in my field I admit no peers—to sense the final and total impact of changes in the sequences. To grasp the pattern, whole, and more than that, to estimate how different changes will *interact* with each other. For instance, suppose that I were to invert the order of the section on the middle of the screen, and make no other change of any kind. What would it do? I am not absolutely sure—I have never thought of that variation before, and what I do is more an art than a science—but I believe that it would produce a perfectly formed individual, able to function as usual, but a little more hirsute than the norm. In the large scale of things, that is an amazingly small change. It happens that way because we are all of amazingly robust genetic stock. There is much redundancy in the DNA chain, and it stabilizes against minor copying errors in the genetic codes."

"So just *who* is that on the screen?" Brachis was not at ease with Fujitsu. The man had the cold, clear-eyed enthusiasm of a true fanatic. To the Margrave, Luther Brachis suspected he was nothing more than a section of interesting genetic code.

Fujitsu smiled for the first time, showing stained and crooked teeth. "No one that you know, Commander. And even if it were, this is no more than a starting point. When I am finished, and you see your Artefact, you will recognize nothing of what lies behind it. In fact, the listing in front of you already contains part of my general design. King Bester delivered your specification a week ago, and it provides such an intriguing challenge that since then I have worked on nothing else."

"You mean you are almost finished?"

"By no means. As I said, this is a *challenge*. And it is also a mystery, which prompts my next question."

"The specification is all the information I will provide."

"I understand perfectly. If you choose not to answer, that is no offense to me—but I will ask. Let me show you something." The Margrave flashed onto another screen a color image of a life form. "This is drawn from your specification. But there are certain elements, here and here"—he touched the lower part of the screen—"that I found preposterously difficult to mimic with organic components. I wonder if perhaps this is actually some kind of cyborg, inorganically enhanced."

The screen showed a four-meter oblong shape, with well-defined rounded head, compound eyes, and a small mouth. The silver-blue body terminated in a tripod of stubby legs. Regular indentations ran along the whole length of the shining sides, and lattice-like wing structures were furled close to the body.

Brachis nodded. "I see no reason why you should not know this much. It *is* partly inorganic."

"Then you realize that I cannot actually *copy* this using organic components? I can make the external appearance very similar, good enough to fool anyone. That is easy. What I cannot do is create the internal circuits and the total psych profile."

"I understand. Is the difficulty in the intelligence?"

"No. In the emotions."

"Then if you must err, I want you to favor pacifism."

"That was my intention."

"And you will be finished—when?" For the first time, Luther Brachis was showing signs of impatience, standing up and glancing at the chronometer.

"Difficult." Fujitsu stroked his straggly beard. "Two weeks, perhaps? Is that satisfactory?"

"For all copies?"

"I see no reason why not. As in many things, after the first the rest are easy. But I will require the remainder of my payment, hand-delivered as soon as the Artefacts leave Earth and have been inspected."

"Delivery before payment? That is not what we are told of Earth trading. You are a trusting person."

"Find someone on Earth who will agree with that, Commander, and you will receive your order for nothing." The Margrave directed his snaggle-toothed smile at

Brachis. "I never threaten, but as we say in my family, I have a long arm. It reaches far out, and it brings me my just dues across time and space. All my clients pay in full—in one way or another."

Fujitsu started to walk Brachis towards the studded outer door. "One more thing, Commander. Again, I fear that it takes the form of a question and a possible request. This project is the most intriguing one that I have had for many years. No one has ever before asked me to *replicate* an organism—and such a strange one! May I ask you who made it? For the privilege of meeting that person's mind directly, I would pay well."

"I can give you the name." Brachis paused at the outer door. "Unfortunately, that is all I can give you. Her name was Livia Morgan. She is dead."

"And the original design?"

"Died with her."

"Ah. A tragic loss."

The great door closed, leaving Brachis standing in darkness. Out on the surface it was raining, a heavy downpour under black clouds. Brachis ducked his head and strode rapidly back towards the closest tunnel entry point.

Would Fujitsu now seek to explore the origin and nature of the Morgan Constructs? Probably not. And it was worth the risk of mentioning Livia Morgan's name, to see if King Bester stayed bought. Bester would surely learn that information from the Margrave. The question was, would anyone else then hear about it?

The weather was foul, the night dark, and Brachis had been hurrying along with less than his usual caution. He realized his mistake when his feet were yanked abruptly from under him, and he went skidding flat on his back down a steep slope. At the bottom he tried to stand up. He felt a loop of rope tight around his ankles.

"Gotcher!" said a gruff voice. A shielded lamp shone into his eyes.

Brachis straightened up slowly and carefully. There were five of them. Four were dressed in dark, mottled clothes that blended well into the vegetation patterns of the surface. The fifth man, obscenely fat, wore a sequined robe and carried an ornate mace over his shoulder like a club. Knives and grinning teeth flashed in the lamplight. The men moved to form a small circle around Brachis. He recalled Bester's warning. "Never forget: the surface is *dangerous*. I don't mean the local patrols—I'm talking about the Scavvies."

"Scavengers, is it?" growled Brachis, using low Earth-tongue. "What you want, then? Money, trade crystals, I got both."

"A bit more than that, squire." It was the fat man, smiling amiably. "Don't you think so, boys?"

"Do a deal, then? I got friends."

"I know you do. *Good* friends." The man pointed the mace at Brachis. "I know you, see. There's people up aloft who'd pay good to have you back—'specially when they've had a few of your fingers and toes to show I mean business."

Brachis had recognized that gross shape and oily voice. "Bozzie, we can do a deal. Listen, squire, I can get you—"

"Not Bozzie to you," said the other man viciously. "No, and not *squire*, either. Off-Earth trash like you call me *Your Majesty*. All right, lads. *Do him!*"

The four came diving at him from sides and back. Luther Brachis switched to Commando mode. He smashed the larynx of the man on his left with the outer edge of his hand, at the same time back-heeling another in the testicles. He sensed a knife stabbing in at him and ducked, pivoted right, and drove into the third man's eyes with the stiff outstretched fingers of his left hand. He kept the turn going, spinning through another hundred and eighty degrees. His extended right arm swept on like a flail. The sleeve of his combat uniform, stiffened by rapid acceleration, shattered the jaw of the fourth man. Then all were down, groveling and moaning on the wet earth.

The Duke of Bosny had seen the rapid demolition of his Scavenger force. He dropped the lamp and went waddling away across the dark field. Brachis caught him in half a dozen strides, hurled him facedown on the ground, and knelt on the huge back. He took a grip on Bozzie's neck, forearms locked.

"All right, *Your Majesty*. I want some honest answers. And if you lie to me, you'll find your Scavvies got off easy."

"Anything! Anything." Bozzie was trembling, quivering on the ground like a monstrous jello. "Don't hurt me. Please! Take my jewels—anything you want."

"I want an answer. You were lying in wait for me. Did you know it was me, or was it set up for anyone who happened to come along? Remember, now, I have to have the truth."

Bozzie hesitated. Luther Brachis tightened his grip, flattening the windpipe in the gross neck.

"No!" Bozzie gave a whistling scream. "I'll tell you. We saw you when you first came up on the surface, and I recognized you then. We watched you go into Fujitsu's Needler lab, and decided to wait for you until you came out."

"That the truth?"

"It is, it is. For God's sake, don't hurt me. It's the truth."

Brachis nodded. "I believe you. Sorry, Bozzie. That was the wrong answer. It means you don't have any more information for me."

He shifted his grip, moved his hands to lock his own arms, and twisted. Bozzie's neck cracked sharply. The great hulk jerked, shivered, and lay silent.

Luther Brachis did not give the body a second look. He went to each of the other four in turn, breaking necks cleanly and effortlessly.

He straightened up. The whole episode had not lasted more than two minutes. He thought of rolling the bodies down into an irrigation ditch, and decided against it. Scavvie fights on the surface must be common enough, and this would look like just another one—a bit more notable than usual, perhaps, because the Duke of Bosny was one of the victims.

Brachis brushed mud off his uniform and hurried on towards the tunnel entrance. Already he had begun the process of self-discipline needed to put the incident into the back of his mind. He was determined not to let it ruin the rest of the evening, even though he told himself, with a mocking self-awareness, that he was behaving totally illogically. He should be worrying about the possibility that he had somehow left clues to his identity on one of the bodies.

But all that seemed unimportant. What was important was the need to get to a certain apartment on the fifty-fifth level.

Was he crazy? He must be. Here he was, after only two meetings, rushing to a tryst with Godiva Lomberd as though she were an innocent virgin and this was his first romance. And it was not as though she would not wait if he were late. There was no questionable outcome for this rendezvous, no uncertainty, no doubt about what they were going to do, no danger of rejection. It was a wholly commercial transaction, arranged by money and controlled by lust, the sordid temporary purchase of a woman's body.

Luther Brachis could tell himself all that. It made no difference. He was going to meet Godiva Lomberd again. And for the moment nothing else mattered.

Chapter 11

The rings were all of different sizes and colors; the cylinder tapered from a blunt point at the top down to a thick base. The rings would all fit onto it only if they were placed there in the correct sequence, largest to smallest.

Chan Dalton was sitting on the floor, hunched over the toy. His forehead, normally unlined, was wrinkled with effort. He was picking up the rings one after another, studying each, and after a few seconds putting it down between his splayed legs. The chamber he was sitting in was cheerfully decorated in pinks and blues, with paintings and drawings around the wall and a thick soft carpet on the floor.

Chan had positioned himself in the exact center of the room. Now after long deliberation he picked up the red ring and placed it on the cylinder. A few moments later he did the same thing with the orange one. Then the yellow.

"He's getting them right!" Tatty was whispering, although there was no chance that Chan could hear her. She and Leah Rainbow were watching him through a one-way glass set into the nursery wall. "Could he ever have done that when he was with you?"

Leah shook her head. "Never—he wouldn't have had the slightest idea." Her voice echoed Tatty's excitement. When she had first returned to Horus, she and Tatty had not found it easy to talk. Finally and simultaneously, they had realized why. They were like mothers to Chan—and both the old and the new mother were jealous. Tatty had resented it when Chan ran to hug Leah as soon as he saw her, with a great yell of pleasure and excitement; Leah hated the way that Tatty organized Chan's day, telling him what to do next, where his clothes must go, and what he had to eat. Leah still saw that as *her* prerogative.

The daily session with the Tolkov Stimulator had been another cause of tension between them. Leah mistook for heartlessness Tatty's insistence that Chan could not miss a treatment, whether there was a visitor or not. She would not help Tatty to catch him, or to strap him in. And the presence of both her own and Esro Mondrian's picture, where Chan could see them when he was in the Stimulator, perplexed her. What did Tatty think she was doing?

But when the treatment began and Chan writhed in the padded seat, Leah could not ignore Tatty's own anguish and misery. Tatty was suffering. And when Leah saw the bedroom and nursery that Tatty had made for Chan, she was finally won over. They were so thoughtfully done, and they showed so much evidence of love and caring.

Leah remembered Horus very well from her brief stay before she went off to begin her training. It had been horrible: gloomy, dirty and depressing, more like a detention barracks than any place to bring a child (and Chan *was* a child, in spite of his physical age and adult appearance).

Now Horus, or at least this part of it, was transformed. "How did you possibly manage all this?" Leah had followed Tatty through room after room, elegantly decorated and furnished and designed to take advantage of the natural and manmade features of the interior of Horus.

Tatty laughed. She hadn't done any of this to show off to other people, but it was wonderful to have someone else appreciate her efforts. Chan was indifferent, and Kubo Flammarion seemed more at home with the old dirt and mess.

"I got tired of living in a pit. Nobody could tell me how long I might be here, and all the old excavation and service robots were around because nobody thought it was worthwhile to haul them away. I taught myself how to re-program them."

"But it must have taken ages."

"It took time, but I had plenty of that. Then I set them to work, first to clear out the trash and then to make this place livable. I hooked one of them in with a synthesizer, and it produced pretty good carpets and wall hangings. Once I started, I guess I got a bit compulsive. Poor old Kubo." Tatty smiled, at one of her rare pleasant memories of Horus. "He came out here a couple of weeks ago, and I wouldn't even let him into Chan's quarters until he'd taken a bath and had his uniform cleaned. He did it, but he didn't like it. And Chan made it worse. 'Kubo change,' he said. 'Not stink now—except hat.' Then he stole it."

"That same old hat—covered in grease and dandruff?"

"That's the one. Kubo hadn't bothered to clean that when he cleaned his uniform. I suppose he thought we'd never notice. But Chan noticed, and he threw it into the garbage disposal. Kubo was devastated. He said, 'Princess, that hat has been with me all over the solar system. It's like a part of me.' But I said to him, 'Not any more, Captain Flammarion. When even *Chan* objects to it, it's time for a new one'—and Chan *did* object. He *is* improving, isn't he?" Tatty looked to Leah for encouragement. "I always wonder if I'm imagining a change, because I've been wishing for it so hard. But you can see it, too, can't you? Isn't he a bit smarter?"

"He certainly is. Look at him."

Chan had carefully and slowly assembled the complete stack of rings. Now he was just as painstakingly taking them off again. The women watched until he had finished, then applauded. Next Chan picked up a set of red plastic blocks. They were of complex individual shapes, but they could fit together to make a perfect cube. He fiddled with them for a while, then hurled them in frustration across the room.

"That's still too hard for him," said Leah.

"No need to apologize for him to *me*."

"I wasn't. I was just thinking, he is progressing but it's terribly slow. At this rate it will take years."

"That's what scared me," said Tatty. "But Kubo Flammarion says it's not at all linear. If it really works you expect to see very little progress at first. Then everything comes in one big rush, maybe in a single session on the Stimulator."

"How much improvement does Flammarion expect?"

"He says he has no idea. He doesn't know when it might happen, or how far Chan will go. Do you know what was wrong with his brain in the first place?"

"Down in the Gallimaufries? Nobody there could afford any tests. People said Chan was a dummy, and left it at that."

"He could finish up still slow. Or he could be average, or even super-smart. But Kubo says the chances of *that* are pretty small. All we can do is wait and see." Tatty stared in at Chan through the one-way panel. "But that's all just theory, and I try not to think about it. There are more important things to worry about—like his dinner."

"Can I help you feed him?"

"Sure. But there's not much need to help him any more. He's a bit messy, but he's no worse than Captain Flammarion. You should have seen the two of them, last time Kubo was here. It was disgusting."

"At least I can help cook. I know Chan's favorites."

"You can teach them to me. And I want to hear more about your training program. If things work out, Chan will be doing one, too."

"I'll bore you to death with it. It's strange, when Bozzie sold us and we had to leave Earth, I thought it was the worst thing that could possibly happen. I hated the idea of space, and I was terrified at the thought of a training program. Now I'm in the middle of it—and I love it."

"I thought you were almost done."

"No, we've just finished the first phase. That's why I was allowed a short break. But I have to leave Horus the day after tomorrow, and head farther out. I'll be meeting the alien partners, and we'll see how we fit as a real team."

"Scary."

"Not as much as I thought. I already met a Tinker. It wasn't as weird as people say. Ours even made *jokes*— in standard Solar! And none of us has been able to make any headway at all with *their* language. It doesn't seem to have verbs or nouns or adjectives or anything—just buzzing sounds. And according to the Tinker, the language of the Angels is a lot *harder* for humans than Tinkertalk."

"So how are you supposed to talk to each other?"

"We'll probably have to rely on computers to translate what the Angels say. But they can *all* understand us. It's disturbing. During our training, the human instructors told me that we are the smartest species. But I'm beginning to have an awful lot of doubts."

"I know what you mean. If *I'm* so smart, how come I'm here?"

Chan's performance with the rings had put both women in a good mood. They went on chatting happily as they left the nursery area for the kitchen. Chan remained sitting on the floor of the playroom. For a couple of minutes after they had gone he stayed there, not moving. Then he stood, ran rapidly to the door, and hurried up the narrow ramp that led to the one-way mirror. He made sure that no one was standing behind it and hurried back to the playroom.

First he set out to pick up all the plastic blocks that he had thrown across the room. Next he went to the smiling photograph of Esro Mondrian, pinned to the wall by Tatty among the drawings of plants, animals, people, and planets. Chan took Mondrian's picture, frowned at it, and carried it back to the middle of the playroom. He propped it up in front of him. All the blocks were carefully laid before it.

At last Chan was ready. He scanned the blocks, picked up four of them, and quickly and economically fitted them together. He reached for four more, then another pair. In less than thirty seconds he had assembled the whole cube. He stared at it for a few moments, then just as quickly took it apart again and laid the pieces on the carpeted floor.

Finally Chan lifted his eyes, and stared at Mondrian's picture. He smiled. It was, as nearly as he could make it, a perfect copy of the smile on the face of Esro Mondrian.

Four hundred kilometers away, that face was not smiling. It was beaded with perspiration. Mondrian lay in darkness on a hard couch, breathing hard and loudly through clenched teeth.

He could see nothing, smell nothing, hear nothing, feel nothing—even the electrodes on his body no longer produced sensation. He could not move. The heat and total darkness had drained all his energy. In any case there was nowhere to go. He was alone, far from anything in the universe.

The endless questions did not change that. They seemed to rise from *within*, from some deep and secret hiding place inside him. He knew that the questions would end only when he gave answers. But that was impossible. The answers *stuck*, tearing at the delicate fabric of his brain. He groaned.

"You are resisting again." Skrynol's gentle voice came as a shock. "Every time we reach this area, evasion begins. I think we must stop for today."

Soft touches on Mondrian's sweating body told him that electrodes were being removed.

"We're getting nowhere," he said hoarsely. "I'm wasting your time and my own."

"On the contrary," said the voice in the darkness. "We are progressing. Your remark is merely another attempt by a part of you to end that progress. But it is doomed to fail. As we define the area to which you will not allow me access, I am able to infer its nature more and more accurately. Already we possess certain definite facts. For example, I know that you are suffering the consequences of a very early experience—something that happened to you before you were three years old, something that has never been expressed in verbal form. You have spent your whole life since then, fortifying the mental walls around what happened. That is why they are so hard to break down."

"You are killing me."

"I think not." Skrynol was raising Mondrian to a sitting position. "You are a strong man. Is it obvious to you, by the way, that your recurring dreams are all related to that one early experience? There is a pattern to them. They are always either a re-creation of your trauma, or a flight from it. Think of them, although I know you prefer not to. The vision is always the same, of a central figure—you—surrounded by a warm, safe, light region. And outside it, the dark."

"That is not a new insight. Other Froppers have told me the same thing. They say that the safe region is symbolic of the womb, that I hate the fact of my birth."

"That is the simple-minded conclusion." Skrynol's voice sharpened. "And of course, it is wrong."

"How do you know?"

"Because if it were right, any Fropper could treat you successfully. I am able to recognize womb symbolism as well as anyone, although I myself never went through the birth process. Your case is quite different. You feel that you *control* everything in the safe region—but you also feel that the region is shrinking. Outside lies the dark, and every day the dark comes a little closer. You sense devils in that dark. You would like to flee. But you cannot, because you are always at the *center* of the lighted region. If you run away, in any direction, the danger may be closer yet. You cannot flee. You dare not stay. That is the source of your nightmares."

"Suppose that you are right. How does that help me?"

"It does not. Not yet. We must go back—farther, deeper. And you must help me to do it."

Mondrian shook his head.

"You are afraid?" went on Skrynol. "Naturally. Our most secret fears are always sacred. You can be helped—but only if you agree to being helped. You must trust me more, allow me to probe deeper, and accept that I will feel with you and for you." There was a high-pitched laugh in the darkness. "You are horrified at the idea. Of course you are. But let me reassure you. Our secrets are never as well-kept as we would like to imagine them. I am going to tell you one of your own secrets, because until it is out of the way we will have trouble reaching back as far as we need to."

"Why do you think I have secrets?"

"You tell me. According to your official record, you were born on Oberon, the son of a mining engineer who was pregnant when she went there. Correct?"

"That's right."

"So tell me about your mother. How old was she, what did she look like, what sort of woman was she?"

"I have told you several times. I have no memory of her. She was killed in an accident soon after I was born."

"You have indeed told me that. And you have been lying to me." Skrynol's fleshy flipper came out to grip Mondrian by the shoulder. "Your mother is dead. That is true. But you remember exactly what she looked like. And you were not born on Oberon. *You were born on Earth*. And as a child, you were *sold* on Earth."

"It wasn't like—"

"Do not try to deny it. *I know*. You were born on Earth, and as an infant you were sold on Earth, and you lived on Earth for the first eighteen years of your life. As a commoner, existing in misery and poverty until you found a chance to escape."

"How can you know that?"

"How do you think? Today you are an educated and sophisticated man. You appreciate beauty, ideas, literature, great art, and great music. You love fine food and drink. But part of you was still shaped on Earth. Part of you is still locked into the dirt, ignorance, and violence of where you began. You nightmare began *here*, on this planet. And if it is to end, it must end here."

Mondrian writhed in Skrynol's grip. "You didn't learn any of that from me. And you could search the solar system, and never find my background in any record. Only one other person knew. How did you ever make Tatty tell you?"

"Princess Tatiana did not tell me. *You* told me, in answer to my questions. Your self-control is phenomenal, Commander Mondrian, but it cannot be perfect. Every time the subject of Earth, or of people born on Earth, arose, half a dozen physical variables in your system changed. They did not run wild, but even a point or two of difference is enough for me. I deliberately added other questions, and integrated the answers. The conclusion was clear."

"Who have you told this to?"

"No one."

"Then let me give you an incentive for continued silence." Mondrian was fumbling in the darkness for the shirt pocket of his uniform. He pulled out a thin packet and thrust it blindly in front of him. "Take a look at that."

The packet was taken gently from his hands. There was a long silence. At the end of it came a soft clicking noise, and light slowly brightened in the chamber.

"Darkness will still be essential during questioning," said Skrynol. "But it no longer serves a useful purpose at other times. Behold your tormentor—and helper."

Crouched before Mondrian was a giant tubular shape. The pale lemon on the body bifurcation showed that Skrynol was a female Pipe-Rilla, but she was not of the usual form. Changes had been made to the long thorax, and one pair of forelimbs was augmented by fleshy appendages resembling human hands and arms.

Skrynol held out the package that Mondrian had given her. "To satisfy my curiosity, tell me when and how you managed to obtain these pictures."

"On my first visit." Mondrian touched the fire opal at his collar. "This holds a multiple-wavelength imaging device. I tried it in many spectral regions. Thermal infrared and microwave both proved satisfactory."

"Ah." Skrynol crouched nodding on her long, orange-black hind legs. "That was a failure on my part. I observed your apparently nervous manipulation of that gemstone, and thought it was oddly at variance with your general extraordinary control. But I was too naive to draw the conclusion. Mondrian, your strength of mind is astonishing, to think of such a test in the first session. But for our purposes, that strength is not good. We have a very tough struggle ahead. Will you tell me why you thought it necessary to make images?"

"You suggested that you were of a shape too hideous

to be seen. I could not imagine such a form—I have seen almost every type of organism within the Perimeter, and some of those are strange indeed. It occurred to me to wonder, perhaps you were not too *strange* to be seen, but too *familiar*."

"And when you saw the results of the imaging?" Skrynol stood upright, towering towards the roof. Dark compound eyes peered down at Mondrian. "Would it not have been more in keeping with your job to *report* your findings, rather than bringing those pictures here with you?"

"Report to whom?" Mondrian shrugged. "To myself, as head of Security? To Luther Brachis, so he could use it against me? Anyway, I had too many unanswerable questions. You resembled a Pipe-Rilla, but there were differences. You said that you were an Artefact, the product of a Needler lab. That could have been true."

"*Could* have. Why do you reject that notion?"

"At first I didn't. You could have been an Artefact of a type I had never before encountered, something new out of the Needler labs. Or you could be a Pipe-Rilla, surgically modified for an Earth environment and for more efficient human speech. It even occurred to me that perhaps you were some kind of renegade Pipe-Rilla, hiding here from her fellows."

The hissing laugh came eight feet above Mondrian's head. "A 'criminal,' as you call it, taking refuge on this world? Come now, Commander. What crime could a Pipe-Rilla commit, which required a punishment *worse* than banishment to this planet? What hideous act could match the surgical inflicting of these disfigurements?" Skrynol held out her fleshy forelimbs. "As your poet says, 'Why, this is Hell, nor am I out of it.'"

"Let me tell you about Hell. But I also came to that conclusion. A Pipe-Rilla would only suffer such changes, and such exile, *voluntarily*. And that led me to another. You were modified and sent here *with the knowledge and approval of your fellows and your government*. You are a spy and observer for the Pipe-Rillas."

Skrynol lowered herself with a cantilevering of long, multi-jointed limbs, until she was face to face with Mondrian. "It is not just Pipe-Rillas. All other members of the Stellar Group feel the same need to observe humans. You are too violent, too unpredictable, to be left unwatched. But if you are right, then why are you not now in danger? Presumably I must protect my secret."

"You have been physically modified, but mentally you are still a Pipe-Rilla. You are not capable of violence. Whereas I . . ."

". . . Accept and even relish it? A shrewd observation and one that I cannot dispute. But I am not without other means of persuasion. You still have your own needs. You could announce my presence here, true; but if you did, your own treatment with me would end. And we are making progress, approaching the heart of your problem. Do you realize that?"

"I am sure of it. Why else would I so dread these sessions with you, yet keep on coming?"

"In that case you must make your own evaluation. Am I a danger to humans so great that you must now reveal my existence, or does your personal need dominate the situation?"

"It is not so simple as that. I am convinced that you *intended* that I should discover your identity, even if not so quickly."

"Most perceptive." Skrynol laughed, that same high, twittering laugh. "So I have my own agenda. And there is your dilemma. You must balance your *personal* needs against the possible danger to humanity of my presence. This is, you realize, something unique to your species. As, indeed, is your term for it. You call it a 'conflict of interest.' A *conflict*—again, always you speak in terms of war, battle, fighting."

"What would a Pipe-Rilla call it?"

"The situation could never arise. We possess group altruism. The good of the many always takes priority in us over the needs of the individual."

"I admire your nobility."

"There is no need for sarcasm. And we can take no credit for our nature. It is built into us, from first meiosis. It is the very reason that I am here, alone and deformed, many lightyears from home and mates. But humans are not so. You are dominated by individual desires and urges. Even you." Skrynol began to flex her legs, lifting her body higher. "So which is it to be, Esro Mondrian? Do you expose me now, or do we continue your treatment."

Mondrian stood up also. "What is your name? Your Pipe-Rilla name?"

"I will say it to you. It is no secret. But *you* will not be able to say it, unless you propose to learn to stridulate." The Pipe-Rilla rubbed two of her legs together briefly, to produce the wobbly, singing tone of a vibrating saw blade. "There. I think you must still call me Skrynol. That is similar to a word in our speech that means, 'the insane one.' A mad Pipe-Rilla, living deep in Madworld."

"Giving Fropper treatment to a mad human."

"What could be more appropriate? Commander Mondrian, we have a stalemate. You know my secret—"

"One of them."

"One of them. And I know one of yours. What now?"

"I will keep your secret, and you will continue my treatment. And one other thing."

"Always something new."

"Not really. I intended this when I came here today for treatment. Why else would I bring those pictures? We agree that we both have needs?"

"We agree."

"Very well. Then let us . . . negotiate."

Chapter 12

The offices of Dougal MacDougal, Solar High Ambassador to the Stellar Group, formed a huge and perfect dodecahedron. Two hundred meters on a side, it sat deep beneath the surface of Ceres. Access to it was provided by a dozen entrances on every one of its twelve faces.

The private office of Dougal MacDougal lay at the very center of the dodecahedron. It had just one entrance, approached along a great spiralling corridor. Halfway along the corridor and opening onto it was a tiny office, barely big enough for one person.

In that office, seemingly present for twenty-four hours a day, sat Lotos Sheldrake. A diminutive child-like woman with the face of a porcelain doll, she guarded access to the spacious inner sanctum like a soldier ant protecting the queen's chamber. MacDougal saw no one unless she approved; nothing entered his office, not even cleaning robots, unless she had performed her inspection.

Luther Brachis walked slowly down the approach corridor, entered Sheldrake's cramped office, and sat down uninvited on the single visitor's chair.

Lotos was reviewing a list of supplicant names, crossing off more than half of them. She did not look up until her analysis was complete. "A surprise visit, Commander," she said at last. She raised pencil-thin eyebrows. "You desire an audience with the Ambassador? We are honored. I believe that this is the first such request."

"Don't give me that, Lotos. When you see me come in here to meet with old numbnuts, you'll know it's time to cart me off for recycling."

"That is no way to refer to His Excellency the Ambassador." But Sheldrake made no attempt to inspect the contents of Brachis's uniform. She had known when he entered that he was planning to go no farther than her office. "So what's your business?"

"You know about the Morgan Constructs?"

An imperceptible nod.

"And the decision made by the Stellar Group Ambassadors?"

A hint of a smile on the doll's face. "With Ambassador MacDougal, shall we say, *abstaining*? I heard. Poor Luther. After all your efforts, to report to Esro Mondrian . . . my heart bleeds for you."

"I'm sure of it. Bleeds liquid helium. But let me get right to business. Do you know what actions it would take to reverse the decision of the Ambassadors—to provide me with at least an equality of rank with Mondrian?"

"Suppose I did know. Why should I discuss it with you?"

"Still the same sweetheart." Luther Brachis pulled a slender pencil from his pocket. "Take a look at this, Lotos, and then let's continue the conversation."

Sheldrake dimmed the lights and pointed the viewer away from her. When she turned it on, a three-dimensional image sprang into existence. At its center hovered a silver-blue cylinder with a tripod of stubby legs and a lattice of shining wing panels.

"Shahh-sh!" Sheldrake hissed. "Commander Brachis, I hope for your sake this is an old holograph. If you have located an intact Morgan Construct, and failed to reveal that fact to us . . . remember, we do not share the rest of the Stellar Group's softness of heart regarding death as punishment. Assure me that this is an old holograph or a computer simulation, Luther—for your own sake."

"To the best of my knowledge, the only functioning Morgan Construct is the one that got away. On the other hand, what you are looking at was recorded less than one week ago, and it is not a computer simulation." He waited, until her hand was no more than an inch or two from a button set into the top of her desk. "A few moments more before you call the guards, Lotos. You don't want to make a fool of yourself."

"Speak, Luther. Quickly." The tiny hand hovered over the button.

"What you are looking at is not a Construct. You will have proof of that. What it *is*, as I can readily prove, is an *Artefact* from one of Earth's Needler labs. But examine it as closely as you like, and I am sure that you will be unable to detect any difference—except, of course, that this is completely safe, without a Construct's destructive potential."

The hand hesitated, then withdrew from the button. "Artefacts are not allowed anywhere except on Earth. You're still in trouble, Luther, if that thing is anywhere up here."

"You don't have it quite right. Artefacts are not allowed into space *unless the situation involves a Stellar Group emergency*. That's the catch-all clause applying to just about everything that's normally forbidden."

"And the Anabasis is operating within a condition of Stellar Group emergency? Clever so far, Commander. But nothing to do with me. Two more minutes."

"Lotos, you're still missing the point. I'm here to *help* you."

"And the Sargasso Dump guards are going to win this year's Mastermind contest. What's the pitch?"

"One minute will be enough." Brachis put his pencil viewer back in his pocket. "Mondrian and I have the responsibility for training the Pursuit Teams. If we do a bad job, and the Morgan Construct wipes out the teams, we get the blame. But not just us—*all* humans, in the minds of the Stellar Group. The training responsibility will not really be Dougal MacDougal's fault, or yours. But as ambassador, he'll feel the worst heat, and you are next in line. Do you want that?"

"You're sneaky as Mondrian."

"I take that as a compliment."

"It wasn't one."

"And my two minutes are up." Brachis was glancing at his watch. "I guess I have to stop and get out."

"Don't bait me, Luther. Get on with it. You've never seen me nasty."

"I dread the day. The big problem is this. How do you train a group to seek out and destroy a Morgan Construct, when you don't have one and they've never seen anything like one? Build another, to use for training?"

"Never. That idea would be vetoed by the Ambassadors instantly."

"Right. Even if we knew the complete construction methods, which we don't. So we have to go with the next best thing. We use some other form, something that looks and acts like a Morgan Construct, but isn't one."

"Logical. But still nothing to do with me."

"Suppose that you, and you alone, were in possession of such a thing? An Artefact, or rather, a set of ten identical ones, for use in Pursuit Team training. Unable to harm a human or other intelligent life form."

"Now you sound like Livia Morgan."

"And she was wrong. I know that. But there is really no comparison. She was working right at the frontier of what can be done, while the rules and technology for manufacture of Artefacts are well-established even if they are restricted to Earth. And we can run these creatures through every environment we like, for as long as we like, until you are convinced that they are perfectly safe. Then you tell Ambassador MacDougal that you—and you alone—have the answer to all the problems of practical Pursuit Team training. You get all the credit. That's my pitch."

"No. It's less than half of it. Do you have these Artefacts?"

"I would not be here otherwise. They are available now, packed away in suspended storage."

"Where?"

"I didn't hear that, Lotos. But if you could arrange for me to be reinstated at the same level as Mondrian, with equal authority in the Anabasis, my hearing might improve."

"*That's* what I was waiting for. That's the second half of your pitch. It can't be done."

"No?" Brachis stood up. "Then I guess I'm on my way."

"Sit down, Luther. I'm interested, but you have to realize what you're asking. You know Dougal MacDougal as well as I do. So I'm supposed to make *him* persuade the other three Stellar Group ambassadors to change their minds, when he can't even *look* at the Angel Ambassador without having a nervous breakdown? How do you propose I do that?"

"MacDougal doesn't have to *talk* them into anything. All he has to do is send them a message, revealing that I had a bigger hand than he thought in the original fiasco. According to their crazy logic, if I'm as guilty as Mondrian we'll share equal responsibility for clearing up the mess."

"That's the most stupid thing I ever heard."

"Almost as stupid as the original decision to put Mondrian in charge. It will work."

"Suppose it does. How do I know I'll get credit for the Artefacts?"

"No one else will be asking for credit. I'll deny involvement if I'm asked."

"And how do I deal with Esro Mondrian when he finds out he's not top dog any more?"

"He won't blame *you*, he'll blame the Stellar Group. You sound like you're afraid of him."

"Of course I am. I'm not a fool, Luther." Lotos showed an even display of pearly teeth—a smile, to anyone who did not know her. "You are a simpler soul, Luther. When you don't like somebody, you do your best to kill them on the spot. With friend Esro, people who get in his way die smiling and never feel the wound. If he has six different agendas going, I can never guess more than four or five of them. He manipulates you, he manipulates me, he manipulates everybody. You and Mondrian are both dangerous men. But I like you a lot better."

"You're too kind."

"I mean it. You are ambitious. He is driven. You are dangerous like a bear. He is like a snake."

"And what kind of animal are you?"

"Need you ask?" The innocent eyes widened. "I'm a sweet little honey-bee. All I ask is a little nectar from each flower, with no harm to anyone."

"You'll get lots of nectar from this one."

"Perhaps. I like what I've heard, but I have to take routine precautions. For example, what's to stop Mondrian from arranging for a supply of these same Artefacts, once he knows that they exist? He knows Earth well, better than either you or I. For that matter, what's to stop *you* from doing the same thing? You know the source, and I don't, and once I've done my part of the deal I have no protection."

"I have a way to reassure you fully on that question. When the ten Artefacts are in your possession, there will be no others. I'll show you why—when everything else is settled."

"With that understanding, you have a deal. I'll set up the preliminaries. Ambassador MacDougal is busy with an *Adestis* safari—" she waited for the snort of disgust from Brachis "—but I should be able to see him by the end of the day. I'll be in touch with you after that."

She stood up, but now it was Luther Brachis who remained in his chair. "There is one thing more. A detail, but without it there can be no agreement."

"For God's sake, Luther. Drop the other shoe—and it had better be a small one."

"I want Solar citizenship arranged for someone. Fast."

"From one of the colonies? That takes time, even for me."

"Not from the colonies. From Earth."

"Then it's easy. Who is he?"

"She. It's a woman, Godiva Lomberd."

"Why *citizenship*? Why not just a visitor's visa?"

"I propose to engage in a contract with her."

"Sweet charity." Sheldrake's face took on something close to a real expression. "A contract! What a day this is turning out to be. First you offer Artefacts, which used to turn your stomach at even the thought. Then it's Luther Brachis, the invincible, with an *Earth-woman*. You must have told me fifty times that nothing good ever comes from Earth. You even had me persuaded of it. And now—a contract! My opinion of you must be revised. You are not a bear, you are a blind mole."

"Insult does me no harm. But you will arrange for her citizenship?"

"If the Artefacts are what you claim." Lotos Sheldrake glanced at the notebook on her desk. "We need to talk timing. I believe that everything I need to do can be finished within five days or less."

"Then that's when you will get the Artefacts. And the next day, Godiva Lomberd must link up from Earth."

"It will be done." Lotos moved with him toward the door. "And when she is here, I have a request: bring her to see me. I am curious to meet the one woman in the system who can make Commander Luther Brachis go soft in the head."

"Do you have it with you?"

King Bester nodded and patted the bag that he was carrying. "Every last crystal."

"Then come in." The heavy outer door closed, shutting out the night sky of Earth, and the Margrave led the way to his private study.

Bester had never been there before, and he stared around with open curiosity. It was a room that had been decorated with immense care, somehow blending to one harmonious whole the Qin dynasty terracotta horsemen, the Beardsley early prints, the original Vermeers and van Meegerens, and the computer art. In one corner, shielded from direct light, stood the bulbous form of Sorudan.

"Still got the singer, I see." Bester nodded towards Sorudan.

"Yes, indeed." The Margrave waved his visitor to an armchair. "I have been offered enormous amounts for Sorudan, but I consider it my prize creation. I will never sell. A drink, perhaps, to celebrate a successful transaction?"

"You bet, squire."

Fujitsu examined the King closely, assessing the sophistication of the other man's palate. At last he shrugged, disappeared into a closet in the corner of the study, and emerged carrying a bottle of pale amber liquid and two small glasses.

"Looks like good stuff," said Bester.

"The best. Despite all our claims of progress, one cannot improve on perfection." Fujitsu carefully poured two ounces of fluid into each glass and handed one to his guest.

Bester sniffed it and wrinkled his nose. He leaned his head back and drained the glass in one gulp. "Mmm." He rolled his eyes. "Bit of all right, that. What is it?"

The Margrave glared.

"It is—or it *was*—one of the finest distilled liquors ever produced on Earth or off it. Santory scotch whiskey, cask-aged in the Hokkaido deep vaults, a single malt two hundred and fifty years old." The Margrave took a first delicate sip. "Superb. When I hear of the nectar of the gods, I wonder how it could improve on this." He shook his massive bald head. "Ah, well. Pearls before swine. I suppose we may as well get down to business. Did Brachis comment on the delivery?"

"Not a word." Bester lifted the bag and placed it on the table between them. "I saw these counted in, and you might want to do the same coming out." He saw the Margrave's look. "Hey, don't get me wrong. I wouldn't take any. This is just the way it was given to me."

The bag was full of virgin trade crystals, their uncut surfaces gleaming a dull rust-red in the subdued light of the study. Bester lifted the crystals out in handfuls, examining each one and gloating over its quality before he set it on the table in front of Fujitsu.

"Best I've ever seen. Hey, wait a minute. What's this doing in here?" Bester drew out a thin flat plate, round in shape and a couple of inches across. Unlike the other trade crystals, it had a smooth surface and no inner glow. "I know I didn't see this one going in."

At the touch of his fingers, the blue-grey disk came alive. There was a swirl of color in the center of the plate, resolving after a second or two to form a picture. A likeness of Luther Brachis appeared in miniature and peered out at them.

"Remember what you told me, King?" The tiny cameo

spoke in a distorted metallic voice. "Any information you wheedled out of Fujitsu was supposed to come back to me alone. What happened to your promise? And you, Fujitsu. Why did you tell the King?"

Bester stared at the image with bulging eyes. The Margrave had knocked over his glass and jerked nervously to his feet.

"You didn't keep your word, did you, King?" went on the tinny voice. "The Margrave told you more than he should have about the Artefacts—and you didn't waste any time finding another buyer for the information." The light from the small plate was steadily increasing. The face of Luther Brachis had almost disappeared, swamped by the glare of the brightening disk.

"That was a very bad mistake, King," said Brachis, in distorted tones.

"Bester!" The Margrave started towards the door of the study. "Don't touch the crystals—and get out of here."

His cry was too late. Bester still held half a dozen crystals in his other hand. He wanted to drop them, but they were sticking to his palm. He shook his hand wildly, trying unsuccessfully to dislodge all of them. They had begun to glow, together with the ones on the table and in the bag.

"As for you, Fujitsu," went on Brachis, "I don't know how much you were in on the deal. I do know you were indiscreet. If you are otherwise innocent, you have my apology. I'm afraid that is all I can give you."

The Margrave was at the door. He paused for a moment and pointed back. The ugly face was distorted with fury. "I hope you can hear me, Brachis. I will receive my due. *My full due.* That I promise you."

He could not say more, because King Bester had begun a hideous high-pitched screaming and a mad capering dance around the study. The crystals in his hand were now incandescent. Lines of fire from them were spreading up his arm, running in blue-white sprays of sparks to his shoulder and across to his chest. The flames grew more intense. Fujitsu's last glimpse of King Bester was of a brilliant living torch, a faceless column of fire that still screamed and leaped in impossible agony.

The Margrave ran through the laboratory, slammed the heavy door behind him, and dashed up the stairs that led to the surface.

At the top he froze. A new voice, inhumanly high and pure, added a counterpoint to Bester's screams.

"Sorudan! The light!" The Margrave could not run. He turned back and took three steps down the stairs. Then he groaned, clapped his hands to his ears, and headed again for the surface. Blind to any possible danger from Scavengers, he ran headlong across the cultivated fields. Behind him the skylights of the lab shone brightly and brighter, while from within an ethereal melody rose ever higher and more beautiful.

The Margrave was seventy yards away and beginning to feel safe when the explosion came.

In his desire to destroy the source of the Artefacts and his thirst for revenge on King Bester, Luther Brachis had indulged in massive overkill. Everything within a hundred yards of the Needler lab was vaporized. A vast crater formed in the outer layers of Delmarva Town.

No trace of the Margrave was ever found. But in his family's religion it was taught that the reward for a life well-lived was the separation of body and soul. Upon a true believer's death, the spiritual essence was released from all corporeal bonds. The body's component atoms would then be free to ride the swirling winds of Earth, in their endless flight about the turning globe.

The founders of Fujitsu's ancient religion, had they been around to observe the manner of his death, would have judged that fate had granted him his fondest wish.

The Margrave, had he been around to do so, would have disagreed most strongly.

Chapter 13

On the good days, Tatty could not resist reaching out to Chan and hugging him. He might have the body of a grown man, agile and powerful, but inside he was a little boy. And like a little boy, he was proud of any new thing that he could do and eager to show it off to Tatty.

But then there were the bad days. Chan would say nothing, cooperate in nothing, was interested in nothing. Tatty wanted to reach out and shake him until he was forced to take notice.

This was a bad day. One of the worst. Tatty told herself to keep calm. She could not afford to lose control—not with another Stimulator session due in an hour. She had to be mentally ready then to comfort Chan and ease him through the time of agony and misery. But for the moment . . .

"Chan! I won't warn you again. You concentrate, and you look at that display. See? That's *Earth*. You were born on Earth. So was I. These are pictures of parts of Earth. Chan! Stop gawping—*look at the display.*"

Chan stared vacantly at the three-dimensional display for a second or two, then began to study the fine hair that grew on his forearm and wrist. Tatty swore to herself—cussing aloud to Chan was strictly forbidden—and slammed down the button that advanced the presentation. Useful or not, they had to work their way through the whole program.

Not one word going in. Tatty had schooled herself to keep her comments internal. *It's all too abstract for him.*

Whose stupid idea was it to give him astronomy lessons when he can't even pick out the letters of the alphabet? He's supposed to absorb at an unconscious level, is he? Sure—some hopes! He isn't a bit interested in the lessons and he never remembers them. Waste of time—his time, my time . . . but what else is there for me to do, stuck out here? I should be on Earth . . . if only I could get away from this awful place. Oh, God, Earth—there it is. Just look at those beautiful pictures. Seas and skies and rivers and forests and cities. If only I were there now, back in my apartment, just me and . . . if Esro Mondrian were here I would kill him . . . heartless, treacherous, monstrous, ruthless . . .

The lesson went on, independent of Tatty's misery and Chan's indifference. The display toured the whole solar system, bit by bit, in gorgeous, three-dimensional images. Tatty might see Horus as the worst rat-hole of the solar system, but the training equipment was first-rate. The displays moved viewers *into* them, to see, hear, and sense everything as though they were present at each location. Chan and Tatty floated together down to the surface of Venus. The dense atmosphere around them burned and corroded, and every boulder and jutting rock shimmered in the intense heat. Somehow, the closed surface domes supported their four hundred million people.

Onward, inward, inside the orbit of Mercury, all the way to the Vulcan Nexus and beyond: the solar photosphere flamed and erupted in savage storms of light. *Close enough to touch.* Tatty shrank back in real fear, although she knew it was no more than a display. Chan stared at it—at everything—impassively.

Onward, outward, carried past Earth to the thriving Mars colonies. There was a sense of enormous excitement here. Zero hour was only a few years away—the magic moment when sufficient volatiles would have been shipped in through an outsized Mattin Link system and a human could survive on the surface without the use of breathing equipment. Already the atmosphere was almost as dense as on the top of Mount Everest. Defying basic biology, daredevil young people ventured out onto the surface every day, without oxygen or air pumps. They were brought back—the lucky ones—unconscious and suffering from extreme anoxia.

Willy-nilly, Chan and Tatty were swept out farther from the Sun, out to the hive of the Asteroid Belt where a hundred minor planets formed the commercial and political power house of the solar system. From there it was outward again, to the huge industrial bases on Europa, Titan, and Oberon. Equipped with Monitor headsets, Chan and Tatty plunged deep into the icy ammonia slush below the deep atmosphere of Uranus, to the infernal region where the Ergas—the Ergatandromorph Constructs—worked tirelessly on the fusion plants and the Uranian Link system. The work was still three centuries from completion. Disturbingly, the Erga slaves already gave evidence that they were developing their own complex culture.

With the survey of the old solar system approaching its end, Tatty halted the program and stared at Chan. *Nothing.* Plants and planets, science and society, all left him equally unmoved. Sighing, she signalled for the lesson to continue.

They leaped, a trillion kilometers into the outer darkness. The monstrous bulk of the Oort Harvester was at work here, a world-sized cylinder lumbering along through the hundred billion members of the cometary cloud. Slow and tireless, at home a tenth of a lightyear from Sol, the Harvester was hunting down bodies rich in simple organic molecules, converting them to sugars, fats, and proteins, and Linking the products back to feed the inner system.

A final solar-system leap. Chan and Tatty skipped to the quiet outpost of the Dry Tortugas: arid, volatile-free shards of rock that marked the gravitational boundary of Sol's domain. Past this point, any matter had to be shared with other stars. Sun itself was a chilly pinprick of light, while temperatures hovered a few degrees above absolute zero. Tatty stared in awe at the billion-year-old metal tetrahedra, enigmatic relics left by a race old before humanity was young.

The lesson halted. *"Questions?"* said a polite voice.

Tatty glanced at Chan's impassive face. Again he was

studying the hair on his wrist. "No." She spoke for both of them.

"Then we will continue."

So far the lesson had been a general one, designed to teach Chan the structure and varied economies of the solar system. Now it would be specific to Pursuit Team training.

The display changed scale again. Far beyond the boundaries of the solar system lay the members of the Stellar Group.

"First, the overview." The region of accessible space was a knobby and dimpled sphere, fifty-eight lightyears across and centered on Sol. The Perimeter formed a fuzzy outer boundary where the probe ships, limited at best to a tenth of light speed, expanded the accessible region by up to ten lightyears a century.

Humans had never encountered another species possessing the Mattin Link. The Perimeter would remain roughly spherical, unless and until—people had talked of it for centuries—some probe ship at the Perimeter met a ship from a second bubble, blown by another species who had found the secret of the Mattin Link for themselves.

(Humans had written thousands of papers and millions of words, seeking to analyze the outcome of such a meeting, just as in an earlier era, writers had endlessly discussed possible first contact with intelligent aliens. Like those analyses, the new papers were erudite, well-argued, and persuasive—and reached contradictory conclusions.)

In the final segment of the lesson, Chan and Tatty homed in on the home stars of the known intelligent species. The Pipe-Rillas had been found first. They were stellar neighbors, with the binary stars of Eta Cassiopeiae, only eighteen lightyears from Sol, as their home system.

Next came the Tinkers, twenty-three lightyears out. Their home world was Mercantor, circling the star Fomalhaut.

After that, the discovery program had suffered a long dry spell. The Perimeter expanded steadily, reaching a new volume of space that increased quadratically with time, but no new intelligence was discovered; not until a probe reached Capella, forty-five lightyears from Earth, and found the Angels. That had been a century and a half ago. The Angel language, civilization, and thought processes were still an unlocked mystery for humans.

In the final segment of the lesson, images of each species were added to the displays. That was Kubo Flammarion's brain child. He hoped to make Chan "feel comfortable with the aliens, before he meets them." Tatty considered that was optimism of the highest order.

The screen first showed the quivering mass of a Tinker Composite, then the enlarged view of individual components from which the Tinker was made. They were fast-flying legless creatures about the size of a humming-bird. Each of them possessed just enough nerve tissue for independent locomotion, sensation, feeding, breeding, and clustering. Each had a ring of eyes on its blunt head, and long antennae to permit coupling into the Composite. The bodies were purple and black, shiny, sticky-looking. Tatty was fascinated. She was sorry when the display moved on to show the arthropod cylinder segments of a Pipe-Rilla, and finally the dull green fronds of an Angel. But at least this ought to interest Chan—it would interest anyone, even a child. She glanced across to see how he was reacting. He was not watching the display at all. He was staring at her.

"*Chan!*"

But he was grimacing, not in annoyance or boredom but in pain. He reached up to place his hands on the side of his head.

Tatty stood up at once. Chan did this sometimes *after* a Stimulator session, never before. "What hurts?"

"Head. Hurt bad." He was mumbling, rubbing his temples and then his eyes. "Picture make me hurt bad."

Kubo Flammarion had warned of critical points. They often came with headaches and they could lead to fever, nervous degeneration, and rapid death. Tatty went to kneel by Chan's side and took his head between her hands. "Don't move, Chan. I have to look."

She had been told the warning symptoms. Chan sat quietly as she lifted his eyelid and shone a light on the eyeball. No reddening, no protrusion. The pupils dilated normally with the light on them. Sight, and then hearing, proved normal when she tested them.

Tatty took Chan's temperature. That was normal, too. So were the brain rhythms of his EEG. *Everything* was normal. Could Chan possibly be faking it, knowing what came next?

"Do you still hurt?"

"Not bad now. Getting better."

Tatty sighed—mixed relief and discomfort. She did not have sufficient reason to put off the thing that she most dreaded, the ritual of forcing Chan into one of the "special" sessions with the Tolkov Stimulator.

Might as well get it over with. Tatty stood up. "Come on, Chan." She took him by the hand and led him through into the next chamber. Amazingly, he did not protest or resist. Could he be faking it the other way round—hurting, and not willing to admit it?

"Chan, are you sure you don't hurt any more?"

He would not look at her, but he slowly shook his head. "Not hurt." He sat down in the Stimulator chair and let Tatty strap him in.

Tatty hesitated before she connected the headset. The whole thing was unfair. With no experience, she was forced to make decisions that could kill Chan.

"All right?"

Chan did not speak. Tatty turned on the power. Usually she could not bear to watch the whole session, but today she felt obliged to.

For a few minutes Chan sat quiet, eyes closed. There were frown lines on his forehead, and as he gripped the arm-rests the tendons in his forearms and the backs of his hands sprang up white and prominent.

At last he began to moan, a long, breathless sound high in his throat. Tatty knew it well. It was "normal," if anything about the Tolkov Stimulator could be called normal, a sign that the power build-up was approaching its peak rate. There was nothing to see, but inside Chan's skull a complex series of fields was being generated in both cerebral hemispheres. Natural patterns of electrical activity were sensed by the Stimulator, modulated, and fed back at increased intensity. At the same time, the body's own motor control was inhibited. The damping was necessary to prevent Chan from tearing himself to pieces. The jerks, spasms, and writhing of the body were still spectacular, but Flammarion had explained that they were unrelated to what Chan was actually *feeling*. Chan's agonies were far worse than that. They arose within the brain itself, as a pain far more intense than anything of physical origin.

The crisis was approaching. Chan's body jerked from side to side in the chair. His face was blood-red, with veins in neck and forehead like purple cords. Suffused with blood, medication injection points on his bare arms showed as bright patterns of stigmata. At this point in every treatment, Tatty feared that Chan would die of heart failure or apoplexy.

The Stimulator monitor chattered a final burst of activity. As it cut off a high-pitched scream filled the chamber. Chan writhed against his restraining straps. His body shuddered and shook in the chair.

Tatty went terrified to his side. This was not the normal end point of a special treatment session. Chan was usually loose-limbed and flaccid, now he was reacting as though the session were still going on.

As she placed her hands on his shoulders the spasms ended. Tatty glanced at the monitors. Pulse strong, but blood pressure disturbingly high. All Stimulator functions registered as zero. The session was certainly over, and by now Chan ought to be awake and weeping. Then she would take him in her arms, hold him close, and comfort him. According to Kubo Flammarion that psychological support was supremely important if she was to lower the risk of catatonic withdrawal.

Except that today he was flinching at her touch. "Chan. It's Tatty. Can you hear me?"

The eyes were beginning to open. Long eyelashes flickered. A slit of white was visible, then blue irises rolled slowly down into view. Chan licked his lips and glanced from side to side. Suddenly he stared right at Tatty as though he had never seen her before.

"Chan!"

"Tatty?" The voice was as faint and far-off as starlight.

"It's me, Chan." Tatty snapped open the restraining straps so that she could draw Chan's head forward to her breast. "There, baby. You just rest on me. You'll be all right in a few minutes."

"No!" He wrenched away from her and spun out of the chair. Before she could grab him he was running out of the chamber and down the outside corridor. He was screaming, and his voice was echoing from the smooth walls.

Something was different—and terribly wrong. After a special Stimulator session Chan *always* needed soothing, then he would sleep.

Tatty snatched up the Tracker and her case of anesthetic drugs and started after him through the tunnels of Horus.

Within minutes she realized that he was not following any of his usual paths. The Tracker showed that he was off on some wild new excursion, sometimes far away, sometimes veering in close to her, but always inaccessible. Tatty did her best to follow, and found she was running into blind ends. According to the Tracker, Chan was just on the other side of that well—and there was no way to reach it.

She hurried on, following the Tracker's memory of each twist and turn. There was no possibility that he could actually escape; Horus was a maximum security facility, and Tatty had hopelessly explored all the possible routes for herself.

But he could certainly do himself damage. She had to find him, and as soon as possible.

It took over three hours. And when Tatty finally reached him she realized that it was no credit to her. Chan was sitting quietly on an old excavating machine, staring at the molecular decomposition nozzles. The corridor behind him was clear. Had he chosen to do so, he could have gone on running.

Tatty approached him warily. She could shoot tranquilizer from as far away as ten yards, but there was little sign that it might be needed.

"Chan."

"Here, Tatty."

"Are you all right?" She saw the dried tears on his cheeks.

"No. Anything but all right. I mean . . . I don't know. If was all right before, then not all right now."

Tatty's skin quivered into gooseflesh. The baby-talk overtone was still there, with Chan's awkward articulation. But the cadence and meaning had changed. It was a stranger talking.

"Chan, how do you feel? Are you hurting?"

His long silence was not the usual blank of indifference. He seemed to be pondering her question, searching for an answer and finding it impossible to reply. Twice he began, and twice he halted before completing a word.

"Feel . . . strange," he said at last. "Just the same, and not same. All things are . . . mixed. I don't know *more*, all same things in my head. But now . . ." He frowned. "Same things, but things not the same. Now I can *see* them. Before, I didn't notice." He stood up, and swayed on his feet. One arm went blindly to the side, to support himself against the excavating machine. "I . . . feel . . . like . . ."

He was falling forward, eyes closing. Tatty stepped forward to support him. For a change she welcomed the weak gravity maintained on Horus. She could carry Chan to his bedroom for examination without too much strain on herself.

All the way back he remained unconscious. But his breathing was regular, and when she laid him on the bed the monitors showed his vital signs as normal. Tatty sat next to him as the monitors completed a more detailed examination. She wanted to talk to Ceres and tell Flammarion what was happening, but it was surely more important to stay here. He *seemed* all right, but suppose that he suffered another convulsion while she was away? She was the only other person on Horus. More than that, suppose this were the breakthrough point for the Stimulator treatment. Then she *had* to be there when Chan awoke. Flammarion had emphasized that often enough, without ever explaining how she was supposed to manage it and still tell Ceres exactly what was going on.

Tatty made up her mind. Chan might need her help for the next few hours, and that took priority over everything else.

She ran through into the kitchen, grabbed containers of drink and packaged food, and rushed back to sit beside Chan. He remained unconscious while she ate a makeshift meal, but he was beginning to mutter and whimper in his sleep. Tatty was increasingly reluctant to leave him. She glanced at her watch. It was almost time for Chan's scheduled sleep. She dimmed the chamber lights and quietly lay down at his side.

Such vigil was no novelty. She had sat often with Chan after a Stimulator session, telling him stories until he was relaxed enough to go to sleep. Soon after their arrival on Horus she had changed his bed for a much broader one, so that she could stretch out beside him and tell simple tales of life on Earth and in the Gallimaufries, stories that drew his attention until the tears ended and exhaustion took over.

Tonight was not much different. Chan drifted toward wakefulness, snuggling up close as he did so. His forehead was a little warm, though not enough to be called a fever.

Tatty closed her own eyes. The significance of the day's events was coming home to her. Suppose that Chan had made a crucial breakthrough? Then he might be on the road to normal intelligence. That was the finest news in the world—she had grown as fond of Chan as she had ever been of anyone. But there were other implications . . . great implications . . .

If his treatment is ending, I'll be free! Out of this prison. Free to leave Horus, free to return to my own life on Earth. Less than two months, but I feel as though I've been away forever. Can I go back there, now—and what will I do about Esro? Do I want to torment him, as he has tormented me?

"Tatty!" Chan jerked up out of half-sleep.

"Here." She put her arms around him. "You're all right. Everything's all right."

"No." He put his arms around her. "It's not all right. I wish I could go back. It used to be easy, and now it's hard. It's . . . what is the word? . . . compli-cated?"

"That's the real world, Chan."

"It was the real world before. *My* real world. Tatty, I don't like this. I'm *scared*."

"Hold on to me, Chan. You're right, it's not easy. Being human is never easy. But you have friends. I'll help you, and I'll take care of you."

Chan nodded. But he began to cry again, deep-chested sobs that went on minute after minute. Tatty felt the tears in her own eyes. It had seemed so obvious that Chan would be better if the Stimulator worked, that afterwards everything would be better. Now she sorrowed for the loss of the innocent child. Her baby was gone, and he would never come back.

She cradled him to her, stroking his head and patting his shoulders. She became aware of another change in him, one that filled her with foreboding. Chan was becoming physically aroused, moving his body uneasily against her.

Tatty had been warned of this in the first briefing. Flammarion had told her that Chan's adult body might announce its presence, and he had emphasized that rejection would be bad for Chan. There could be permanent psychological damage. Tatty had listened and nodded. There were far bigger problems to worry about.

"Tatty!" Chan was frightened. Long past puberty, he had always been blissfully unaware of his own sexuality. Now uncontrollable urges were possessing him, and he had no idea what was happening.

It was the fear in his voice that made Tatty ignore her own worries. "It's all right, Chan. You're going to be fine. It's not a bad thing."

Not bad for you. Bad for me. It makes no difference. Chan needs me, and no one else cares if I even exist.

Gently, Tatty guided Chan along another critical segment of his rite of passage from child to man. She held him, and at the same time despised herself.

Worst of all was her inability to remain aloof. Two months was a long time—too long. Tatty felt her own growing response and fought against it. She shivered, hesitated, resisted, but finally groaned and clutched him to her.

During lovemaking he had begun to weep again, long mournful sobs that shook his body. At the moment of his climax he cried out, "Leah! Oh, Leah."

At the height of her own passion, Tatty wept also. Her tears were silent. But she thought of Esro Mondrian, and in the final seconds she at last whispered his name.

Chapter 14

Twenty thousand years ago humans had hunted the woolly rhinoceros and fought the sabertooth tiger. Five thousand years ago the quarry was wild boar and bears and hippopotami. One thousand years ago, out on the great plains of Africa and India, the prize kills were lions, elephants, and tigers.

The great game preserves of Earth's equatorial and polar regions still existed, but hunting was strictly forbidden. Blood lust had to find other outlets. *Adestis* was one of the most recent, and perhaps the best ever.

Dougal MacDougal loved *Adestis*. Lotos Sheldrake had never tried it until today, but she hated the very idea of it. She had come along as part of MacDougal's safari only for her own purposes.

She clung to her bright-sided weapon and struggled across spongy ground after the Ambassador. The air was thick and humid, and it was filled with large, drifting spores that floated along easily in the hardly noticeable gravity. Lotos batted them away from her head and peered in front of her for a first sight of the group's destination.

There it was. No more than a few minutes walk away, the enormous brown tower reached far up towards the grey sky. Already Lotos could see the first file of pale-bodied warriors moving nervously around the entrance holes. They were tasting the air, feeling the approach of danger with their sensitive antennas.

Dougal MacDougal strode confidently in front, heading

straight for the giant round-topped citadel. The forty other party members followed, with Lotos bringing up the far rear.

She suspected that she had too much imagination for this sort of enterprise. Already she could visualize the curved jaws of the defending soldiers tight around her waist, or the sticky and madly irritant spray enveloping her. The projectile weapon that she was carrying would kill a warrior outright—*if* she aimed true and made a hit in the head or the even more vulnerable neck. A body shot would not do. The soldier might die eventually, but before it did so the creature's dying reflexes would make it fight on, killing anything that did not smell and taste right. And the soldiers were only the first line of defense. Beyond them lay the dark interior tunnels, swarming with their own defenders loyal to the death. Surrender or acceptance of defeat was unthinkable to the inhabitants of the tower. For the attacking party to succeed, it would have to penetrate to the central chamber, and kill its giant occupant.

Dougal MacDougal led the way to the base of the structure. Avoiding the main entrances, he fired a thread-thin grapnel line to a point high above ground level. With a running pulley he hauled himself easily up, to many times his own height. In half a minute he was braced against the hard wall of the mound, chipping a secure foothold. The others followed, helping each other. There was little risk at this stage, since even a direct fall would not be fatal.

Clinging to the pulley line, half a dozen of the attacking group lifted sharp picks. They hacked at the hard cement of the mound until they had made an opening big enough to crawl through.

Far below, the soldiers were in total confusion. They ran here and there, touching each other with their antennae and criss-crossing the approach routes to the tunnel entrances. None thought to crawl up the side of the tower.

"All right." MacDougal was panting and excited—far more enthusiastic for this than for anything in his official life. "That's big enough. Everybody inside."

Lotos scrambled through, last in the group. She found herself in a spiral tunnel that wound steeply down toward the middle of the fortress. There was an overpowering smell here, of chemical secretions and fungal growth, and the curving wall was made of the same hard cement. But the tunnel was deserted. They ran along it at top speed, until after a hundred steps the leaders skipped to a halt. Scores of defenders were emerging from side passages, blocking the way ahead.

"Shoot your way through." MacDougal was waving his weapon around, as much a menace to his companions as to the enemy. "These are no real danger—but keep your eyes open for the soldiers. They'll know any minute what we're up to, and they'll be after us."

The projectile weapons were powerful enough to blow asunder the soft bodies of the workers. But there were hundreds of them. Progress became slower and slower, through a carnage of dying tower-dwellers. Lotos found herself skidding in disgust over layers of pallid flesh and greasy body fluids, losing her footing every few seconds. She was last of the group again, at least ten paces behind the rest. If the soldiers came from behind . . . but the big central chamber was in sight ahead.

Lotos paused to catch her breath. And heard from behind her the scrabble of hard claws on the tunnel wall.

She turned. Less than twenty paces away were seven warriors, approaching at top speed. She screamed a warning, lifted her weapon, and fired it on automatic. A stream of projectiles cut into the warriors. Four curled into death spasm, knotting their bodies on the hard floor of the tunnel.

But the other three were still coming. Lotos blew the head clean off one of them, and cut another in half with a hail of fire. The last one was too close. Before she could aim her weapon, mandibles as long as her arm reached forward to grip her at chest level. Their inner edges were sharp and as hard as steel.

Lotos's arms were pinned to her side by the encircling jaws. She could not free her gun, or fire it at the soldier. She heard the others of the party shouting at her, but they could not get a shot at her attacker without hitting Lotos.

The pressure on her chest increased, from discomfort to impossible pain. Lotos could not breathe. She felt the bones in her arms crack—her ribs cave in—her heart flatten in her chest. In the final moment before she lost consciousness she bit down hard on the switch between her rear molars. As everything turned dark she felt a gush of blood in her throat, jetting up from her lungs into her gaping mouth . . .

THAT IS THE END OF ADESTIS FOR YOU. Lotos was sweating and shivering in the balcony seat, the harsh voice sounding in her ear. *REMAIN SEATED AS A SPECTATOR IF YOU WISH, BUT YOUR FURTHER PARTICIPATION IS PROHIBITED.*

She ripped off her headset and threw it aside, leaning over to stare down at the sandy arena below. The attack on the termite mound was continuing. With the conclusion of sensory contact, her own five-millimeter simulacrum had "died" down there. And just in time! Lotos was still in agony, still feeling the pressure on breaking ribs and cracking spine—still tasting blood in her mouth. *Adestis* did not let losers off easily. If she had failed to activate the Monitor switch, the chance of death from heart failure was better than one in four. In any case, the *pain* was real enough. It would go on for hours, even though she was out of the game. That realism was one perverse reason for the huge popularity of *Adestis*.

Lotos glanced around her. Over half the forty participants had already returned. They were all alive, and clutching eyes, heads, or ribs—the soldier termites had their preferred targets. The other twenty players still wore their headsets and were crouched blindly in their places.

There was a gasp from Dougal MacDougal's cowled figure, three seats away on Lotos Sheldrake's right. It was followed by a boil of activity near the bottom of the ten-foot mound, far below the spectators' gallery. Either the intruders had managed to kill the queen and they were fighting their way out, or the number of defenders had been too much for them and the attack was being abandoned. Tiny human-shaped figures, less than a dozen of them, came racing out of one of the tunnels at the base of the mound and scattered across the sandy plain. They were far from safe. Dozens of maddened termite soldiers were after them, dashing in from all sides.

The projectile weapons fired continuously—and uselessly. In less than thirty seconds all the figures were buried under swarms of furious defenders. One by one, the players around Lotos shuddered back to their own body consciousness.

THE QUEEN STILL LIVES, said the harsh voice over the sound system. *YOU ARE DEFEATED AND THE GAME IS OVER. THIS IS THE END OF ADESTIS FOR YOUR EXPEDITION.*

Dougal MacDougal was slumped in his seat, groaning and clutching at his hips. A soldier must have taken him there and crushed his pelvis. After a few more seconds he sat up and stared around him. Unbelievably, he was grinning.

"Everybody got back?" he said. "Great. No casualties, and we'll be better prepared next time. We came so damned *close*. I'll bet we were within *twenty seconds* of the queen when those soldier reinforcements arrived. Talk about damned bad luck!"

"Talk about what you like, Dougal," said a small, plump man in the uniform of a civilian liner captain. He was whey-faced, leaning far forward and nursing his genitals. "You get off on this stuff, but I'll tell you one thing. You'll never talk me into another one. It *hurts*. Do you realize where that soldier got hold of me?"

"Come on, Danny." MacDougal was still grinning madly. "You'll feel fine in an hour or two. The game's the thing! We'll be ready to try again tomorrow."

"Without me."

"Without me, too," chimed in a tall, dark-haired woman who was rubbing tenderly at her neck. "You're crazy, Dougal. I know they *tell* you it will be full sensories, but I didn't have any idea *how* full. I was grabbed so I couldn't move my jaw—couldn't work the switch until the last possible moment. I thought I was dead."

Lotos wiped the sweat from her forehead. She combed

her hair carefully, controlled her breathing, and quietly slipped away out of the rear of the spectators' chamber.

Her conversation with Dougal MacDougal was important, but it would have to wait. She had seen all of *Adestis* that she needed to, and more than she ever wanted to.

Lotos could have used half an hour to herself. She did not get it. When she arrived at her office Esro Mondrian was sitting in the visitors' chair. He was staring at her Appointments calendar.

"If you're looking for your name, Esro, you won't find it on that." Lotos slipped into her own seat. "I thought you were out on Oberon."

"I was." He did not look up. "Is it the end of the universe, Lotos? It must be. I think you have three hairs out of place."

She shook her head. "*Adestis.*"

"*You* played *Adestis*?" Now he was staring at her. "That amazes me. I must revise my opinion of you."

"Cut it out, Esro. I didn't do it for pleasure, and you know it."

"It *wasn't* pleasure?"

"It was disgusting, as you are well aware. I did it for information, and because I needed to catch the Ambassador for a private conversation—which I didn't get. But I got something else."

"About the game?"

"About the Ambassador." She tapped a file on her desk. "I had a chance to check your suggestion."

"You didn't believe it before?"

"Let's say, I believed it, but I had to check for myself. You are quite right. Dougal MacDougal is a latent masochist. Maybe not so latent, either. I saw him when *Adestis* was complete. We lost, but he was grinning all over his face when he must have been hurting like hell."

"So you agree with me. It is terribly dangerous to have a masochist as humanity's representative to the Stellar Group."

"I agree. But you can't change it—and neither can I. He's too well established."

"He has to be handled even more carefully than we thought. You are the only person who has that influence. You can persuade Dougal MacDougal to do anything you want."

"Don't try flattery, Esro. It doesn't suit you. And I'm sure you didn't come to talk about the Ambassador. What's the real agenda?"

"I came to give you some information."

"You never gave away anything in your life." Lotos did not say it as a criticism. It was a compliment. She was the daughter of a hard-rock miner herself, raised in the dust-tunnels of Iapetus, and every step out had been a fight. By the time she was ten years old she was as tough and sharp as a drill bit. Lotos had evaluated her only asset. When she was thirteen, the calculated optimum age, she had carefully traded youth and virginity (innocence she had never had) for an escape from Iapetus.

She was never going back to a life like that. Never, never, *never*. And somewhere in Esro Mondrian, behind the refined tastes and formal manners, she could sense the same early struggle and the same determination.

"You don't mean *give*," she went on. "You mean *trade* information."

"Say it however you like." Mondrian paused, to choose his words carefully. "I know something. You will know it also, in just twenty-four hours. It will arrive over the Mattin Link communication system, addressed to Ambassador MacDougal. I will be giving you—or if you prefer, trading you—one full day of knowledge. You and I, alone in the solar system, will have that knowledge."

"And where did *you* get it?" The question was automatic, but Lotos certainly did not expect an answer and Mondrian showed no sign of offering one. She dialled for two cups of sugared tea. "All right. I'll bite. What's on the line—apart from the hook?"

"The rogue Morgan Construct has been tracked down. I can tell you its location."

"Ahhh." Lotos's eyes were sparkling. "Damn it, I've had not even a hint of this."

"I know. You are furious."

"I have every right to be. I'm going to fire the Ambassador's information officer."

"That's up to you. But you should not do it just for this. There is no way that she—or anyone else—could possibly have learned what I just told you. I assume you are recording?"

Lotos nodded. "Personal system."

"Keep it that way. I'm only going to say this once. Out near the Perimeter is a star system named Talitha—*Iota Ursae Majoris* in the catalogs. It is a trinary, a little more than fifty lightyears away from here. The main star is stellar type A7 V, about ten times as bright as Sol. The others are a close binary pair of red dwarfs, very dim, only a thousandth as bright as the primary.

"We've known all that for quite a while. What we didn't know, until the probes got there seventy years ago, was about the planetary system around the primary. Three gas giants, six smaller metal-rich planets. The probe reported evidence of life on one of the inner worlds. It was named *Travancore*. It is small, less than half of Earth's mass, and it has flourishing native life-forms—vegetation and fungi, at least, and probably animals. The probe didn't detect any evidence of intelligent life, so there was no great interest in immediate exploration. As a result we don't know too much about the place."

"Fifty lightyears away, unexplored. How could you possibly have tracked the Morgan Construct there?"

"We didn't. The Angels did, and it's a waste of time any of us asking how they did it. They insist that it's still there on Travancore, still alive, and hiding down under some sort of continuous canopy of vegetation."

"Doing what?"

"Doing whatever a Morgan Construct does. You tell me. You now know as much as I do, except for one more thing. The Angels sent one of our smart probes down towards the planet."

"Bad move."

"I know. Try explaining that to an Angel. The probe stopped signalling before it reached the surface, and never came back. We have to assume that the Construct destroyed it."

"And knows it has been discovered." Lotos leaned back in her chair, sipping tea from a porcelain cup that looked as delicate and fragile as she did. "It will be ready for anything that comes after it. Tough for your Pursuit Teams."

"I'll be breaking the news to them—tomorrow."

"And today? Are you looking for any action from me?"

"I do not ask any. I would suggest that you decide for Dougal MacDougal what his line ought to be when he discusses this with the Stellar Group Ambassadors. And you ought to know what I am doing with your pseudo-Construct. We have the first Pursuit Team assembled and waiting, out on Dembricot: one human woman, one Tinker ten-thousand Composite, one sterile female Pipe-Rilla, and their preferred form of Angel—an experienced Singer carried by a new-grown Chassel-Rose."

"How's the pseudo-Construct working out?"

"It is ideal for the purpose." Mondrian laid his empty teacup on the table beside him. "It is, of course, an Artefact. I assume that Ambassador MacDougal does not know that."

"He signed the approval for its use."

"Which is not the same thing at all." Mondrian stood up. "I have taken enough of your time."

"One more thing." Lotos took a slender blue cylinder from a drawer in her desk. "I owe you an information favor, and I may as well try to pay it at once. This contains a new edict from the Stellar Group. It will be officially released in three days, but I took the liberty of a preview."

"You think it is relevant to me?"

"I know it is. And you won't like it. According to this ruling, you will no longer outrank Luther Brachis in the Anabasis. The two of you will have equal rank and equal powers."

Mondrian dropped back into his seat. "That's crazy—and impossible. You can't have two people running things. Why would the Ambassadors make a mad change like that?"

"Do you understand Stellar Group Ambassador logic? If you do, you can explain it to me. They make a rule, I just pass it on to you—a lot sooner than you would normally hear it. You will have time to make your own plans."

"Plans be damned." Mondrian stared right through Lotos Sheldrake for a few seconds. "When will the new ruling be effective?"

"As soon as it is announced. Three days from now."

"Not enough." Mondrian was silent for a longer period. "I can't do it in three days. Lotos, I want something else from you. If you can swing it, you'll have a big piece of equity with me to trade whenever and however you want to. Does the new ruling divide up duties?"

"Not in detail. That responsibility stays with Dougal MacDougal."

"Then I want just two things. I want to control access to Travancore. And I want to manage the operation that will destroy the Morgan Construct. Can you arrange both of those?"

"Could be. What do I give Luther Brachis?"

"Anything else he wants. Offer him the rest of the Galaxy, I don't care."

"You want it that bad, eh?" The doll's face was still calm, but the mention of Luther Brachis brought anger to Lotos Sheldrake's eyes. "Very good. I want something, too. I'll do my absolute best to get you what you want— if you will do something for me."

"Name it."

"It's not *it*—it's *her*. Do you know a woman named Godiva Lomberd."

"I've met her. She's a well-known figure on Earth."

"She's not on Earth. She's here. Luther Brachis has entered into a contract with her."

"You know Luther. He's had a thousand women. They come and go. Godiva Lomberd is just another one."

"That was what I thought, when he brought her up from Earth. A month here, at most two, and she would be gone. But this is different. *Luther* is different."

"Different, how?" Mondrian wondered how much Lotos Sheldrake knew. Did she suspect that he had been

the one who first arranged for Brachis to meet Godiva?
The only other person who could have told her that was
Tatiana, and she was still locked away on Horus with
Chan Dalton.

"Different with *me*." Lotos slapped her hand on the
desk, rattling cups. "As you said, Luther has had a thousand women. I never gave any of them a thought. They
did not affect his personality, or his work—until now. I
do not like surprises, and the new Luther Brachis is a
surprise. I want to meet this woman. I want to know who
she is, where she came from, what she wants from him."

Jealousy—from a most unlikely source. "I can't deliver
all that."

"You will not need to." Lotos was in full control again,
smiling her deadly smile. "You just arrange for me to
meet her—and leave the rest to me."

Chapter 15

The facilities on Earth were nowhere near the best in the system. For high-quality storage of living organisms, the perceptive buyer went to Enceladus, or to the Great Vault of Hyperion, where ambient disturbances were less and both bodies and maintenance personnel less corruptible.

But from the purchaser's point of view, Earth storage provided one unarguable advantage: anonymity. Provided that the rental was paid on time (which meant five full years in advance) no one ever questioned the contents of the pallet. According to rumor, more than three thousand rightful Earth monarchs slept their dreamless storage sleep in the Antarctic warehouses. No one could ever accuse the usurpers of murder; but it would be a long, long time before the real kings and queens would be recalled from slumber to claim their thrones.

The warehouses were kept well below freezing. The two people searching the long files wore heavy clothing, thick gloves, and thermal boots. They cursed the layers of frost that made every identification tag difficult to read.

"Here we are, then." The short, red-haired man bent over the long box and scrubbed again at the tag for a second look. He nodded to his companion to grab the other end. "This is it. Ready?"

The fat blond woman puffed out a frosty breath. "Let's do it. I'm tired. Just this one, then that's it for the day. Up's-a-daisy."

The container slid easily onto the moving rollway. The

147

man and woman walked beside it at each end, making sure that the ride out was smooth. They emerged at last into a long, white-walled room filled with medical equipment and banks of monitors. Working as an efficient team, they moved the container to one of the long tables, broke the seals, and hooked in the pumps and catheters. The woman checked the inner identification against the work order that she was carrying.

"It's an A label. How about that. Been a long time since we saw an Artefact coming out of the cooler. Any idea what we got here?"

The man sniffed, pulling off his thick white gloves. "Nah. Better keep a good watch on this one, though. Last time we did an A label, it was one of them four-wing dragon-fliers. We had a good laugh with that one— it was all over the lab, and nearly had a leg off Jesco Siemens before we could tie it down. Old Jesco, he couldn't see the joke at all."

The top and side were off the long box, and the pumps and wipers were slowly removing thick layers of semi-solid jelly, warming it as they worked. A shape began to emerge. The two stared at it in fascination.

"Uurgh." The man was leaning close. "I don't like the look of that. It's hideous. See them legs."

They were staring at a pair of long, bony feet, still with thick black gunk between the knobbly toes. As they watched the rest of the figure slowly came into view. It was a male, facedown; naked, tall, angular, hollow-chested, and skinny.

"How'd you like to find *him* under your bed, eh?" The fat woman laughed. "You sure we got the right one? Don't look like an Artefact."

"Think so." The man was peering at the identification he was holding, and rubbing his cold nose with a stubby finger.

"Well, I can't see nobody in their right mind making an Artefact that looks like that—never mind waking him up." She took a step closer and stared at the naked body on the bench. "If you asked me, I'd say this is one of the bloody inbred royals, something the family stuck down here and never wanted to see any more. I think we ought to check again."

"I'm doing it. This writing is terrible."

"And check that the payment was made, too. It's getting a bit late to stick him back. He'll be spoiled."

The man was frowning over the label. "It's this one, all right." He scratched his head as the body was rotated to face upwards. "Lordy. You're right, he's no beauty. I liked him better the other way up. But here's the chit. Paid in full, automatic bank draft from somebody's final estate. Same ID marking on the container. Label, A type, Artefact by—what's it say?—Fu—jit—su. Let's get on with it before we freeze. If anything's wrong, it's nothing to do with us."

The protective layers of jelly were almost gone. The catheters were sliding in as the last scraping was removed, and the deep-heat batteries increased in intensity. The table tilted, raising the body to a vertical position and holding it. There was a horrible spluttering cough, and a choking grunt as lungs filled with thin oil labored to expel it. With another cough a spray of brown liquid went out onto the floor. Suddenly the figure sneezed and shook its head from side to side.

"Take it easy, now." The man stepped forward, but he was too late. Clawlike hands were scooping out the thick jelly that still filled the eye cavities. The head was massive, with a bald, domed skull. A full beard grew beneath the thin mouth, and was shadowed above by a prominent red beak of a nose.

The mouth opened, to reveal crooked teeth. "Hh-hmmm. Ah. Thank you."

There was another violent cough. The tall figure pulled out catheters, stood up straight, and took a step away from the table. It was still naked, and splotched with thick black goo. In spite of its bizarre appearance it had a strange dignity.

"Thank you," it said again. It looked at the two workers and took in a long, lung-expanding breath. "I appreciate your services. But now I must go. Time is short, and I have important work to do."

It jerked into motion and headed for the door of the

chamber. The man and woman looked at each other, then started after it.

"You can't go yet," cried the woman. "You forgot your bath—you have to have a bath, it's the rules."

"And your clothes!" added the man. "You can't go out there bare-bum naked. Don't worry about the price of 'em, everything's already paid for."

But the tall Artefact was not listening. It was already out of the door, striding purposefully towards the elevators that led to the Link entry point.

Chapter 16

Chan had been on Ceres before, briefly, in transit from Earth to Horus. At that time, Kubo Flammarion had taken him to his office, shown him the big displays, and let him play with the buttons and switches. Chan had skipped for five minutes around the planets and moons known to the Stellar Group; yawned; and asked for a cold drink.

Now he was there again, in front of the same console. Tatty Snipes sat on one side of him. Kubo Flammarion was on the other, scratching his head in amazement. Instead of being bored by the controls, or idly playing with them, Chan was *studying* the board and asking questions. Loads of them.

"What about this one?" He had flicked fast through a series of images and now paused at one of them. It was a low-orbit satellite view of a dreary gray landscape, and it showed a lot more detail than most. "It's been flagged."

Flammarion nodded. "Certainly has. That's *Barchan*. You'll need to know all about it, once you pass the entrance examination. The first training courses with all team members present are held there."

"Looks—what is the right word to use?—*parched*?"

"Sure is. Dry as a bone, almost all of it. It's a desert world in the Eta Cass system—that's where the Pipe-Rillas come from. Barchan is two worlds sunward of S'kat'lan, their home planet."

"Can I live there without a suit? Is it—what is the word for that?"

151

"*Habitable*. Yes, you'll be able to breathe the air—just—but it's so hot you'll wear a suit almost all the time. Want to take a look at it from ground level?"

Chan shook his head. "Later." His eyes were already fixed on another image and his fingers danced across the board.

Tatty caught Flammarion's eye. *Get a load of that*.

When Chan had no more than an infant's mentality, there had been nothing wrong with his coordination. Now he was operating the control board faster than Flammarion.

The older man scowled and shook his head. It didn't fool Tatty. Kubo Flammarion had no children, and never expected to. He could not conceal his pleasure and parental approval when Chan did something new and impressive.

"Here's another one that's been flagged," said Chan. "Where is it?"

The screen showed a verdant world, one where even the oceans were covered with a dense carpet of vegetation.

"That's Dembricot, in the Tinker system." Flammarion moved closer. "Move over a bit, and I'll show you why the training supervisors flagged it for you." He leaned across, linked in to a surface camera, and zoomed across to take a close-up view of a building nestled among tall, spiky ferns. "See that? Main training center for Team Alpha, before they headed out."

"Team Alpha? Did you tell me about that?" Chan was worried.

Flammarion glanced questioningly at Tatty.

"Don't worry, Chan, you're not forgetting things," she said. "I never mentioned it. My fault—but there's been so much to pack in."

"Team Alpha is the first Pursuit Team to complete training," said Flammarion. "Leah Rainbow is part of it, along with three aliens."

"What does the name *mean*?"

"Nothing much." Flammarion shrugged. "Just that it's the first team to go out. Leah hates the name, says she's going to change it soon as she gets the chance."

"So Leah was right there, in that building." Chan eyed

it hungrily. "I wish she was there still, so we could use your—comm-un-i-cator?—and I could talk with her."

"Sorry. They left Dembricot days ago. You see, Chan, they're all done with their training. Leah came through it in fine shape, just the way you will when your time comes. Now it's the real thing. The team's in high orbit around a planet called *Travancore*. The Morgan Construct is supposed to be hiding away there, so at the moment they're not allowed closer than a million kilometers. You know, maybe I can link us to their ship—at the very least I should be able to get the one-way visuals they're sending back to base."

Flammarion rattled at the controls with black-nailed fingers, cursing as a mystifying succession of grainy images fled across the screens. "Rotten cheap equipment," he said, as the picture finally steadied. "Rotten tight-fisted politicians. That's probably as good as we'll get. Low signal bandwidth, see."

"Bandwidth?"

"Take too long to explain now. Just remember that low bandwidth usually means we get only so-so voice communication and a lousy picture or no picture. Like *that*."

A flickering black and white image filled the display.

"No color either," said Flammarion. "Can't get real-time color with low bandwidth. Make the most of it. That's a long shot of Travancore, coming from the pursuit team's ship."

They were again seeing the surface of a planet under high magnification, but this time from a ship far away. At first sight it was a repeat of Dembricot, a dense, horizon-to-horizon carpet of vegetation. A closer look showed differences on the speckled screen. Instead of being flat and uniform, the surface of Travancore pushed up into millions of small hillocks and hummocks, each one only a few hundred meters across.

"See 'em?" said Flammarion. "Whole planet's like that. Pretty odd place, and I've seen some. Those hills are solid plant life. Surface gravity is low, but not all that low. Somehow, though, vegetation can grow six kilometers deep.

Vertical jungle, layer after layer after layer of it. Don't ask me why it doesn't all come crashing down."

"How can a ship land there?"

"Very fair question. It can't—not in the usual way. There's no solid surface to put a ship down on, and no way it could stay in one place if it tried to land. It would sink down and down, Lord-knows-how far before packed vegetation could hold up the weight. So a ship has to *hover* at the top layer, and drop off people and cargo, and then lift right up again."

"I never *heard* of a ship doing that," said Tatty.

"So you're learning something as well as Chan." Flammarion was fiddling with another part of the control board as he spoke. "You can both see why Travancore makes such a hell of a good hiding place—we can't see much with a space survey, and we can't do a mechanized ground survey. But *somewhere* under all that mess, if you believe the Angels, there's a surviving Morgan Construct."

"Leah will go there?"

"Not until they know the planet a whole lot better—maybe in another week or two. But eventually Leah and her team have to find the Construct and destroy it."

A series of clicks came from the communicator, while a pattern of red squares appeared in the upper left corner of the display.

"Virtue rewarded," said Flammarion. "I put in that tracer, but I didn't really expect success. That's the signal I.D. from Team Alpha itself—we're in contact with the ship, not just tapping the data stream they're sending back to base."

"You mean I can talk to Leah?"

"If our luck holds." Flammarion started to complete the sequence. "I told her that you'd be on-line at this end."

"Wait a minute." Chan stood up and stared at the screen. He began to breathe very rapidly.

"And here she is."

Flammarion had taken no notice of Chan's request to wait. He had just managed a pretty neat trick of real-time signal patching, and he was rather pleased with himself. He turned to explain to Chan what he had done, and found himself looking at a rapidly retreating back. "Hey, where are you going? I've got her on the line with me right now."

"Chan?" Leah's dark countenance flickered onto the screen. "Chan, is that really you? This is wonderful." The camera panned across the room and she looked increasingly puzzled. "Chan, where are you? I've been longing to talk to you ever since the moment I got the news."

Tatty came forward and stood in front of the scanning camera. "I'm sorry, Leah. This is Tatty. I ought to have guessed that this might happen. Chan's here, and he's doing fine. But he finds it hard to talk to you."

"Hard to talk to *me*?" The picture quality was too poor to read subtleties of Leah's expression, but her voice was bewildered. "Tatty, I've been talking to Chan since he was practically in diapers. I can talk to him and understand him better than anyone else breathing." The voice hardened. "What have you and Flammarion and Mondrian done to him? For all your sakes, he'd better be all right. Because if he's not, I'll come back from this place and scrag every one of you."

"Calm down." Tatty knew better than to smile and joke when Leah was in this mood. "I told you, Chan is all right. Better than all right, he's so smart now he frightens us. And I can tell you exactly what's wrong with him. It's *you*. He finds it hard to talk to you—really—because he's *embarrassed*."

"Spacefluff!" Leah shook dark hair clear of her eyes. "Get your head screwed on, Tatty Snipes. I said I've known Chan since he was in diapers, but that's only half of it. Since I was six years old, we've eaten together, and cried together, and slept together, and bathed together. *Everything*, from the first day I took him over down in the Gallimaufries. He was just like my own baby."

"I'm sure he was," said Tatty drily. She was having her own problems with this conversation. "But he's not your baby now. He's not anyone's baby. He's a *man*."

It went right past Kubo Flammarion, but Leah caught it in a second. "Chan? You mean somebody—"

"Yes."

"Who was it. Do you know who—"

"Yes." Tatty turned to Flammarion, who had listened to the exchange with total incomprehension. "Kubo, would you please go and bring Chan back here. Leah really needs to talk to him."

As he left she turned rapidly to face the camera. "I was the *somebody*. I think you guessed that. And it wasn't the way you think, an experienced woman seducing an innocent boy. It happened right after a Stimulator session, the one that made the big change. Leah, he needed somebody—*any* somebody. No, I don't mean that. He *needed* somebody, but what he *wanted* was you. He spoke your name to me as though I was you. Maybe he even thought I *was* you."

Leah's image stared stonily out of the screen. "I see."

"I know, Leah. I know just how you must be feeling."

"No." Leah shook her head. "You sure as hell *don't* know how I'm feeling. You can't. For all those years, ever since we were little children, I looked after both of us. As I grew up I had my own secret hope. I dreamed that Chan would somehow become intelligent, and grow up too, and we would become lovers.

"That was my fantasy, and by the time I was twelve I knew it could only be fantasy. He was the little boy who would *never* grow up. I could love Chan, but for *that* kind of love, sexual love, I would have to look somewhere else." The anger faded from Leah's voice and was replaced by a wistful tone. "There was no trouble finding sex, you see. There never is. But it wasn't what I'd dreamed of. And now you tell me that the dream came true—but it was *you* and Chan, not me and Chan ..."

Kubo Flammarion was entering the room, trailing a reluctant Chan along with him. But as they arrived in camera range, Leah was suddenly gone from the screen.

"Here he is," said Flammarion. He stared at the empty display. "Well, blast it. Now where did *she* go?"

Tatty swiveled to face him. "Leah had to run. Her pursuit team is meeting. Let's forget it, Kubo, it won't work today." She turned to Chan. "I spoke to Leah. She sends you all her love, and she says she can't wait until she has a chance to see you."

Chan blushed with pleasure, a flood of pink across fair cheeks. "She said that? I wish I could have said the same thing to her."

"You will. But she couldn't stay. The program out there is really strict."

"And it'll get stricter," added Flammarion, "the closer they get to descent to Travancore and the hunt for the Construct. But you shouldn't be looking at that now, Chan—you ought to be learning all you can about Barchan, because that'll be *your* next stop."

He winked at Tatty. He didn't know quite what was happening, but he sensed that somehow she had carried them through an awkward situation. Now it was time to get Chan thinking about something else.

Flammarion keyed in the sequence to take them back to the first image.

"Barchan," he said. "Take a good look at it."

The scene changed, and he leaned back in confusion. Instead of the heated dust-ball that would be Chan's training site, the screen displayed the face of Esro Mondrian.

He nodded casually at Flammarion. "Sorry, Captain. I came in on override. I need to talk with Princess Tatiana." He smiled at Tatty with no trace of embarrassment. "Congratulations, Princess. You did it. I knew you would. And to you, Chan" —he inclined his head— "welcome to Ceres. From all that I hear you're going to be an outstanding member of the next Pursuit Team."

"Which means you win your bet," said Tatty bitterly. "I guess that's all you care about."

Mondrian stared at her with a surprised expression. "That's not true, Princess, and you know it. We can talk about all that later. I called to say that I've arranged for us to have dinner tonight, and you'll have the chance to meet an old friend."

"I have no friends on Ceres—unless it's Chan and Kubo."

"Wait and see." Mondrian was smiling again. "I'll come over there and pick you up at seven. Dinner will be just the four of us: you, me, Luther Brachis—and Godiva Lomberd."

"Godiva!" But before she could do more than say the name, Mondrian vanished from the screen. In his place were the swirling dust-clouds and umber sky of Barchan. Tatty stared at them, her fists tight-clenched.

"Damn you, Esro Mondrian." She swung to Flammarion. "Damn that man. He ignores me for months. Then he thinks he can call up and suggest dinner, just like that, as though nothing has happened. Well, no way. I'll see him in hell before I'll see him at dinner."

Tatty paused in her outburst. She had been talking to Flammarion, and so she had only just noticed Chan's face. It was white and staring. "Chan! Are you all right?"

"Who was that man?" His voice was a whisper. "Who?"

"Him?" Flammarion, concentrated on Tatty, had not noticed the change in Chan. "He's my boss, that's who. Commander Esro Mondrian, head of the whole Morgan Construct operation. You want to meet him? You will, soon as your training program gets going."

Chan was nodding. "Yes," he said softly. His hands were clasped as tightly as Tatty's. "I would like to meet Commander Mondrian—very much." He glanced over to Tatty. "He wants you to go to dinner."

"I know. I'm not going. Damn the man."

Chan's stare at her was more probing, an alien expression overwriting his mouth and innocent eyes. "I think you will, Tatty," he said at last. He nodded. "Yes, I think that you will."

Chapter 17

These are the Seven Wonders of the Solar System:

- The Vulcan Nexus
- The Oort Harvester
- The Sea-farms of Europa
- The Uranian Lift System
- The Mattin First Link
- The Venus Superdome
- The Tortugas' Tetrahedra
- The Persephone Fusion Network
- The Vault of Hyperion
- Oberon Station
- The Jupiter Bubble
- Marslake

There are a dozen items on the Seven Wonders list. That is not an error. For although everyone agrees on the first four, all the rest are a source of argument. Is the Hyperion Vault more impressive than Oberon Station, merely because it is bigger? Is the Jupiter Bubble more deserving of inclusion than the Venus Superdome, because it is far more difficult to maintain? How does technical sophistication trade off against beauty or elegance—or, for that matter, against importance to the human race? Why are visiting aliens all so taken with the Harvester, and so bored by the Sea-farms? And is it at all fair to include the metal tetrahedra of the Dry

Tortugas on such a list, since they are not the result of human efforts?

For some reason no one ever puts the reconstruction of Ceres anywhere on a catalog of marvels. Yet a minor planet, less than one thousand kilometers across, has become the most populous and influential body in the solar system. Should not that be regarded as a major miracle?

Ah, but the work was done long ago, using the same simple and ages-old technology that built the Earth-warrens and tunneled out the Gallimaufries. No one is impressed by that. And whatever the technology, the results are too familiar. Ceres is on no one's list.

But it should be. After centuries of steady work, modern Ceres possesses less than half the mass of the original. Instead of a body of solid rock with minor intrusions of organic material, Ceres is now a sculptured set of concentric spherical shells. One within another, varying in roof height from less than four meters to nearly a kilometer, the internal chambers extend from the center of the planetoid all the way to the surface.

The original body offered less than two million square kilometers of available surface area. The honeycomb of modern Ceres provides a thousand times as much—more than ten times the original land area of Earth.

And if Ceres itself does not qualify as a major wonder, then what about its transportation system? It had to be designed to carry people and goods efficiently through the three-dimensional spherical labyrinth of tunnels and chambers. It is a topological nightmare, a complex interlocking set of high-speed railcars, walkways, drop-shafts, escalators, elevators, and pressure chutes. A trip from any point to any other can be made in less than one hour—if you have the help of a computer route guide. And few people would attempt any trip without such assistance. An unguided journey, if it could be done at all, would take days.

After a few sessions of coaching by Kubo Flammarion, Tatty had reached the point where she could handle the route instructions provided by the transit computer. She always went cautiously, checking each interchange that she had to make on the way.

Now it was time to introduce Chan to the system. On their first brief visit, before they went to Horus, she had been obliged to lead him everywhere. This time he took one look at the overall plan, listened impatiently to Flammarion's lecture on route selection strategy, and disappeared as soon as he was free to leave.

He was gone for many hours. When he came back he seemed to have been all over the planetoid, and he knew the internal layout of Ceres in far more detail than either Tatty or Kubo Flammarion. The next morning, as soon as the training session was over, he was off again.

He seemed to be avoiding Tatty. It was a surprise to her when he came wandering into her living-quarters as she was dressing before going off for dinner with Esro Mondrian.

Chan flopped into a seat in the middle of the room. Tatty looked at him warily. On Horus, before the change in Chan, she had been quite casual. She had thought of him as a child, and allowed him to see her in a nightgown and in random stages of partial undress. Now she closed her bedroom door firmly as she went in and locked it behind her.

She was gone for half an hour. Uncharacteristically, Chan stayed. She could hear him pottering about in the kitchen while she was bathing and dressing, and he was still there when she came out.

Tatty walked to the full-length mirror near the door. Chan came to stand behind her, examining her appearance closely. She was wearing a white dress, sleeveless and off the shoulder, with pale mauve accessories. The purple marks of old Paradox shots were slowly fading from her arms, a curiously apt match to the clothes that she wore.

Chan caught her eye in the mirror as she studied the sweep of her hair. "Very—*elegant*. Is that the right word to use?"

"It is. Thank you."

"You look very beautiful. I thought you would rather go to hell than to dinner with Esro Mondrian."

"All right, Chan." She turned to look at him directly. "That does it. What do you want? I've got enough on my mind without you adding to my worries."

He shook his head and said nothing. But shortly before Mondrian was due to arrive, Chan left the apartment.

Tatty continued her careful application of makeup. At one minute to seven she went to the apartment door and opened it. She smiled in satisfaction. As she had expected, Mondrian was in the corridor, walking toward the apartment. Whatever his faults, he was precisely punctual. As though they had planned it together, he was dressed in a formal uniform, a plain black that was trimmed with just the same pale mauve that she was wearing.

She studied his face. He looked better, full of suppressed energy. He bowed formally as he came closer, and kissed her hand.

"You look magnificent. The Godiva Bird will be envious."

Tatty shook her head. "Godiva is never envious of anyone. She never needs to be."

She stepped outside quickly and closed the door, to make it clear that she did not propose to invite Mondrian into her living-quarters. He stood for another moment looking at her, then took her arm and led her away along the corridor.

"You seem upset, Princess," he said softly. "I hope this evening will relax you."

Tatty did not reply at once. She thought she had caught sight of Chan, dodging away along the walkway in front of them.

"What do you think I am, Esro?" she said at last. "Some sort of Artefact, or an extra royal, that you can put into cold storage when you don't need, and pull out when it can be useful to you?"

"I don't like to hear you talk like that, Princess. You know I never think of you that way."

"I don't know it at all. Not when you leave me to rot on Horus, and never visit, and never call, and never even send a message. You say this evening will relax me—when I never know what to expect from you. You treat me *worse* than somebody put away in cold storage. At least they are unconscious. They don't sit there watching their lives tick away, wasting months and months just waiting."

She tried to shake her arm free. Mondrian would not release his hold.

"Wasted months." He sighed. "Ah, I know. A week on Horus can seem like a year anywhere else. But do you really think the time was *wasted*? Chan Dalton is a full person now, instead of being a baby. That couldn't have happened without you. *Was* it time wasted?"

He stopped walking. He was still holding her arm, so that she had to swing around to face him. She stared angrily into his calm eyes, and refused to answer. After a few seconds he shook his head.

"Princess, if you think that badly of me, you should never have agreed to come to dinner."

"I thought I might get an explanation of why you deserted me out there—or at least an apology. You've no idea what I had to go through."

"I know exactly what you were going through. It was terrible. But as I told you at the beginning, I couldn't do it myself, and I needed somebody that I trusted completely—somebody I could rely on even if I couldn't be there to keep an eye on things. Do you know why I didn't come to see you on Horus? Because I couldn't. I wasn't off somewhere having fun. I was *busy*—busier than I've ever been in my whole life."

"You found time to go galloping off to Earth. What were you doing there?"

Tatty expected any reply but the one she got. Mondrian merely shook his head.

"I can't tell you. You'll have to take my word for it, Princess, it was business, not pleasure. And I didn't enjoy it one bit."

She was starting to feel the guilt that only Esro Mondrian could create within her. Was *she* the unreasonable one, the cruel one, the woman who carped and whined at a desperately busy man when he could not find time to call her? She knew how hard he worked. How many times had she awakened in the early morning, to find Mondrian gone from her side? Too many to count. But he was not being unfaithful to her. He had tiptoed away in the dark into the next room. He was pacing up and down there, writing, dictating, making calls, worrying. Her rival was his work. And she had known that for years.

Mondrian reached out to touch her cheek. "Don't be sad, Princess. I thought tonight could be a really happy occasion—the chance to see Godiva again, just like old times. Can't we try to enjoy ourselves—just for a few hours?"

Tatty put her hand on his. They turned and began to walk again, side by side. "I'll try. But Essy, everything is so strange here. It's not like Earth, and I'm never relaxed. I couldn't believe it when I heard that Godiva had left Earth to live out here with Brachis."

Mondrian slipped his arm through hers. "You're forgetting something—how many times you asked me to take you away from Earth with me. Maybe she did the same. It's odd, you know, but we put Godiva onto Luther Brachis in the first place. Remember, she was supposed to bring me information?" He laughed. "Not a great idea. After the first few weeks she said she couldn't tell me any more, and the next thing I knew she was up here with him." He glanced sideways to Tatty. "Did I misjudge Godiva? I thought it was all money that made her tick. Now, I'm not so sure."

"She's a hard person to know." For the first time, Tatty focused on her own feelings about Godiva. "I met her four years ago, at Winter Solstice. We both attended the Gilravage, the big party down on the lower levels. She gave a performance, and danced as Aphrodite. It was a sensation. After that we ran into each other all the time."

"Where did she come from?"

"Nowhere special. Somewhere down in the Gallimaufries. I suppose she must be a commoner—at least, I never heard her say a word about her family."

"You like her, Princess, even if she is a commoner."

"I didn't. The first few times we met I hated her. I think most women do, instinctively. We feel as though she can take whatever she wants, or whoever she wants, and we have no defenses. But after a while I did start to like her. She's really a nice person."

"The whore with the heart of gold?"

"Close to it. You see, I don't think Godiva is *bright*, like me or you." Tatty spoke quite unselfconsciously. "So she just does what she can with what she has. She happened to be born with unusual assets, and she uses them. Sex for money, I can't see that as a big sin. Anyone who ever went with Godiva seemed to have a wonderful time. She never had a man under false pretenses, and so far as I can tell she never hurt anyone."

"Not even when she was spying on them?" They were approaching the restaurant, and Mondrian had deliberately slowed his steps. "Her actions might have hurt Luther Brachis."

"She stopped them before they did. Anyway, that was *your* action, not hers. Even when she was watching him for you, I feel sure she didn't mean to harm him. She doesn't think that way."

"What happened when a man fell in love with her?"

"That's a funny thing. No one ever did. She handled everything on a commercial basis, and she parted friends with all her men. They recommended her to others. She must have made a fortune, but she never seemed to fall into any permanent relationship. Until she met Luther Brachis." Tatty turned to look at Mondrian. They had halted, and were standing outside the restaurant door. Over his shoulder she caught another glimpse of a tall figure, ducking back into the shadow at the side of the corridor. Was it Chan, still following?

She took another swift glance in that direction. "Look, if you want to interrogate me about Godiva, do it after dinner. I'm hungry, and all you've done is plague me with questions. Why are you so interested in her?"

"Sorry." Mondrian moved forward, and the frosted glass doors opened before them. "I'm just being nosy. You say you've never seen Godiva Lomberd like this before? Well, I've never seen Luther Brachis like it either. There's two mysteries at once. But I promise you: not another question about Godiva."

"There's no need for any." Tatty inclined her head to the left as they entered the foyer. "There she is. You can ask the real thing."

They were exactly on time, but Luther Brachis and Godiva Lomberd must have arrived a few minutes early. Stepping out of a communication booth and heading back to the table area was a full-figured blond woman. She was in half-profile to Tatty and Esro Mondrian, and they could see that she had a dreamy and absent-minded smile on her face.

"The cat that ate the cream," said Tatty. "Look at that walk. It shouldn't be allowed. It's totally natural, and Godiva never thinks twice about it—but ten billion women would kill to have it."

Godiva Lomberd was dressed in a gown of palest yellow. It was high-necked, full-length, and full-sleeved. Not an inch of arm, legs, or shoulders was visible, but as she walked the material of the dress undulated with its own rhythm. It was impossible to ignore the exotic body within, the warm and pliant flesh that rippled beneath the decorous clothing.

Mondrian followed that movement, a puzzled look on his face. "You don't know this, Princess, but a walk like that should be impossible in a quarter-g field. I can't think how she does it. She moves just the same here as she did down on Earth. And she looks exactly the same, too."

"She probably always will. She certainly hasn't aged a day since I first met her. Remember what I told you, before I ever introduced you? It's true, isn't it?"

"You said that nobody could watch the Godiva Bird walk, without being aware that she was naked underneath her clothes. I laughed at you. But you were right."

They had not called out to Godiva, but simply followed her back towards their table. It was located in a dim-lit area at the rear of the restaurant, a quiet quarter reserved for small, intimate parties who wanted discreet service and no public attention. None of the other tables was occupied. Luther Brachis sat alone, examining a menu. As they reached the table he stood up and greeted Tatty with an odd formality.

She had not seen him since they were all on Earth together, and she was astonished by the change in him. He was still in superb physical condition, but his face had lost the severe and brooding look. He was more cheerful and animated, he had lost five to ten kilos, and his eyes glowed with health and physical well-being.

He was studying Tatty just as seriously. "Congratulations, Princess Tatiana. It is an unusually strong person who can ever break the Paradox addiction."

"You never break the addiction, Commander. You only stop taking the injections."

"For, let us hope, the rest of your life." Brachis helped Tatty to her seat. "I am not sure, Princess Tatiana, that I ought to have dinner with you, even though Commander Mondrian particularly requested it. I understand that it is thanks to you that I have lost a wager. I will be handing over a surveillance system to the Commander." He sat down, and looked across the table at Godiva. "What do you think, my dear? Should I blame the Princess for her success with Chan Dalton?"

Godiva smiled, slow and dreamy. "I could never be annoyed with the Princess, or with Commander Mondrian. They are the people who introduced me to you."

She gazed lovingly across the table at Brachis. Her mouth was wide and full-lipped, in a pink-cheeked oval face that was slightly too plump, and the wide-set blue eyes wore their usual trusting and contented expression.

An analysis of Godiva's individual features would suggest no exceptional beauty. Her chin was a fraction too long, her nose slightly bobbed and asymmetrical, her forehead a shade too high. But the whole was somehow much greater than the sum of the parts. The totality of Godiva, face and figure, was stunning. She arrested the eye, so that in a crowded room she inevitably became the center of attention.

Brachis turned to Mondrian. "You see my problem. If I express annoyance with Princess Tatiana, Godiva will interpret it as a lack of esteem for her. I can't afford to have that." He gestured to the other man to sit down opposite Tatty, but Mondrian remained on his feet.

"In a moment." He turned to Tatty and Godiva. "I promised everyone that this evening would not be business, and now I am breaking my promise. Could you give us just a few minutes for private security talk? Then

I give you my word that will be the last business discussion tonight."

Godiva merely smiled and said nothing. Tatty at once got to her feet. "Come on, Goddy. You don't want to hear their boring business. You can show me around this place."

She sounded cheerful enough. Mondrian knew better. He was frowning when he sat down opposite Luther Brachis.

"You're in the dog house, Commander," said Brachis. "With both of them. It was supposed to be dinner tonight, and no work. I agreed only on that basis."

"I know. This is new, it's urgent, and we can handle it in two minutes if you'll give me a straight reply to one question: Have you been getting a lot of trouble recently from Dougal MacDougal?"

"I have." Luther Brachis' expression became murderous. "Constant interference. I can't do one thing now without him sticking his big nose in. And he's the Stellar Ambassador, so I can't tell him to go away. That man's a total bonehead."

"We've not reached the difficult part yet. If he's like that *now*, how will he be when the Anabasis begins to tangle with the Morgan Construct?"

"Hysterical."

"So what's the answer?"

"No answer—unless you've got one."

Mondrian nodded. "I do. We have to get him out of the way, so he can't be always second-guessing us."

Brachis regarded him skeptically. "Easy to say. But how do you do it? He's certainly immune to hints. You'd have to kill him to get rid of him."

"It might come to that—but not yet. I know a better way. Dougal MacDougal would stay out of the way *if the Stellar Ambassadors told him to*. You know how he grovels to them."

"He does. But dictating to the Stellar Ambassadors is harder than controlling MacDougal. They won't get him out of our hair, just because we'd like them to."

"They might." Mondrian lowered his voice. "I've got clout now with the Pipe-Rillas. I can get them to suggest something to the Angels and the Tinkers: Our complete independence from MacDougal in operating the Anabasis."

"I'd give a lot to get rid of him. But what's the other half? Pipe-Rillas don't operate from charity, any more than you do. What do they want in return?"

"Something I can't give them alone. That's why we're talking now. The Pipe-Rillas have made it very clear what they're after. They want the secret plans for human expansion beyond the Stellar Group."

"The *what*?" Brachis snorted in disgust. "Secret expansion plans? There's no such thing—or if there is, no one bothered to tell me."

"I know. And you know. But the Pipe-Rillas don't believe that. They think we have plans to expand the Perimeter without telling them, and are keeping our schemes secret. You have to remember the way they think of humans. In their eyes we're madmen—aggressive, rash, and dangerous."

"And they're not far off the truth, for some of us." Brachis laughed. "Oh, we can be dangerous enough. But how do we give them secret expansion plans, when we don't have any?"

"We make them up—you and me. Between us we have shared security responsibility from Sol to the Perimeter. We can produce something that's consistent and plausible."

"What if we can? Nobody believes there's any such plans."

"Not now they don't. But we can drop hints in a few places, suggesting they exist. For a start, you could plant it around MacDougal's office. That place leaks information out faster than it goes in. When rumors get back to the Pipe-Rillas, it will confirm their ideas. And then after a while we give them the plans themselves."

"How?"

"You leave that to me. I have a delivery system already in place. They'll accept what I give them."

"The Pipe-Rillas think you're a traitor?"

"That concept is not in their vocabulary. In their view, I will be allowing the better side of my nature to triumph over natural human wickedness. They don't seem to understand cheating."

"But I do. And so do you." Luther Brachis leaned across the table. "How do I know this whole thing isn't just some game of *yours*, setting me up for something?"

"I realize I've got to prove that to you. I will." Mondrian motioned slightly with his head. "Later. For now, it's a truce. Here come Tatiana and Godiva."

The two woman had appeared in the doorway and were threading their way through the tables. A tall waiter was in front of them, carrying a broad covered dish. He placed the silver tureen between Brachis and Mondrian and straightened up.

"With the compliments of the management," he said stiffly. "I will return shortly to take your order." He hurried away, bowing his head deferentially to Godiva and Tatty as he passed them.

"That's peculiar," said Brachis. "I've been here a dozen times, and I've never before had free appetizers."

He reached out and took hold of the cover, lifting it from the dish. As he did so the fire opal at Mondrian's collar changed color. It pulsed with a vivid green light, and a high-pitched whine came from it.

"Drop that!" Mondrian leaped to his feet, glanced around him, and grabbed the tureen off the table. He hurled it away to his left. "Get down, all of you!"

He grabbed the end of the table and tilted it upwards so that it served as a shield. At the same moment Luther Brachis dived at Tatty and Godiva, gathering one in each arm and knocking them off their feet. He dropped on top of them.

There was a hollow, deep *whomp* and a bright flash of white light. The table that Mondrian was holding flew violently backwards, smashing into him and throwing him down on top of Brachis. A sound like violent hail rattled on the other side of the table. After it came a sudden and total silence.

Tatty found herself lying on her right side, ears ringing. Sharp pain tingled and stung all the way along her left arm. Brachis and Mondrian were on top of her, making it impossible to move. As she tried to wriggle out from under them she heard a curse and a pained grunt from above.

"Ahggh! Esro, for God's sake get your head out of my guts. Esro?"

The weight on top of her rolled away. Tatty could move to one side, and finally crawl free. She stood up, dizzy and aware of the dull, padded feeling inside her skull.

She peered around her. The table, upside down, showed a cracked, splintered surface. The plastic was pocked and cratered, with metal splinters embedded all over its surface. Off to the right the whole wall showed a similar pattern of shrapnel impact. Godiva stood at the other side of the table. She looked astonished, but unharmed.

"Help me." Tatty nodded to Godiva to take hold of the other end of the overturned table. Between them they lifted it off the two men. Mondrian was unconscious. Tatty dropped to her knees, looking first at his face and then feeling for his pulse. It was slow and steady. She noticed in a detached way that her own left arm was punctured and bleeding and marked by scores of metal fragments.

Luther Brachis had finally made it to his feet. He was holding his head in his hands and staring vacantly around him. His right shoulder and neck were riddled with metal fragments and bleeding profusely. The restaurant staff had finally appeared and stood looking helplessly on.

"Medical care," said Brachis gruffly. "Did anyone send for help?"

One of the waiters nodded.

"All right, then." Brachis motioned to Esro Mondrian. "Take him outside. I don't want him in here a second longer than he has to be."

"But moving him—" began Tatty.

"He'll live, but we have to get him to a hospital. Don't worry, Princess Tatiana, I'll see to that. And we'll get you patched up, too. And then"—Brachis shivered, and his voice dropped to a whisper—"and then I'll get after the bastard who did this."

He shook his head as though to clear it, reached for

his shoulder, and gasped. He tilted, straightened, and started a slow crumpling. Tatty and Godiva reached out for him together. They lowered him gently to the floor. Their hands came away from his uniform covered with fresh bright blood.

Tatty wiped her palms absently on the front and side of her white dress. As she did so she suddenly thought of Chan. Where was he, what had he been doing?

A lot of things were beginning to make sense. The picture of Mondrian, back on Horus—it had been the spur that drove Chan towards intelligence. She had used it that way on purpose, to relieve her own feelings. And then the way that Chan had looked at Mondrian's image when he came onto the display screen to ask her to go to dinner with him.

She had created Chan's feeling *deliberately*, a focused and intense hatred. Was this the terrible result?

Please God, no.

But Tatty felt sure that she was right. It was her fault, she was the one who had *caused* this carnage. She dropped to her knees, cradled Esro Mondrian in her arms, and hid her face against his dark tunic.

First there had been that sudden, terrible moment when the whole world rushed in on him. It had created nausea, pain, and disorientation. At the time Chan would have said that nothing could ever be worse than those final few minutes in the Tolkov Stimulator. And it could never happen again. Self-awareness and loss of innocence occur at a unique moment in a life.

But there are degrees of torture, refinements of pain beyond the simple and the immediate. A more complex animal can admit more subtle agonies.

Those came later, and more gradually.

Even now, when he could speak perfectly well, Chan could not put his suffering into words. All he had was analogy. It was as though the illumination level of the world around him had been increasing, hour by hour and day by day. The light had been constant and dim for many years, until the Tolkov Stimulator produced that first flood of light. Ever after that the radiance level had risen, little by little. More and more detail became visible—and the brightness reached the point of discomfort, and far beyond.

Occasionally a single event would produce a flare, a quantum change in the brightness around him. The sight of Esro Mondrian, earlier in the day, had been a supernova. It brought in a torrent of new sensation. He *knew* Mondrian—but how, and when, and where?

Chan brooded on the question. Mondrian's drawn, aristocratic features were utterly familiar, more familiar to Chan than his own face. The memory was there in his brain, it had to be—but he was denied access. Thinking about it only made his mind regress along an endless loop.

Finally Chan had wandered over to Tatty's apartment. He had no particular reason for going there, no explicit goal in mind, but he wanted to talk to her. Maybe she could help him; if not, she might be able to comfort him.

It was a shock to find Tatty preoccupied with her own affairs, rather than being wholly devoted to Chan's. He found her cold, remote, and unsympathetic. She was obviously far off on her own mental journey, and she did not want company.

When she went into the bedroom it was a clear hint for Chan to leave. He didn't. Instead he hung around the apartment, convinced that he had nowhere else to go.

Finally Tatty had come out again, dressed for her dinner appointment. She had checked her appearance in the full-length mirror on the living-room wall. And it was then that Chan, looking over her shoulder and also seeing his own reflection, became disoriented and faint. For the first time in his life he experienced the most intense form of self-awareness. That tall, blond figure staring back at him with eyes of sapphire blue was *him*—Chancellor Vercingetorix Dalton, a unique assembly of thought, emotions and memories, housed in a single and familiar frame. There he was. There was his identity.

Chan felt like screaming aloud with revelation. But that was what children did. Instead he left the apartment—quickly, so that the great flood of thoughts would not be lost or diverted by conversation with others. In the corridor he saw the approaching figure of Esro Mondrian. That had set up its own resonance within him, adding to the internal storm.

Chan did not want to speak—to anyone. He hid until Mondrian had passed by and gone to Tatty's door, and then he watched from the shadows. When the pair left he followed them along the walkway. He had no objective, beyond an unarticulated urge to keep both of them within his sight.

At the restaurant Chan was greeted by a waiter who politely barred his way. Did Chan have a reservation?

Chan shook his head dumbly and retreated. He wandered away along the corridor. His head was throbbing, stabs of pain shooting across his eyes. At each intersection he made a random choice of direction. Up, down, east, west, north, south, on through the convoluted interior paths of Ceres.

At last, quite by accident, he found that he had traveled all the way to the surface chambers. Great transparent viewports opened out on to the jumble of ships, gantries, landing towers, and antennae that covered the outer levels of the giant asteroid. Ceres was the power center of the solar system, and as such it had a surface that bustled with activity twenty-four hours a day.

Beyond that surface stood the quiet stars. Chan settled down to stare at them.

What was he? A month ago, anyone could have answered that question: he was a moron. A misfit, a folly of nature, the brain of an infant in the body of a grown man. Just a few days ago, Chan had asked Kubo Flammarion a question. Before the Stimulator, his brain had not developed. Chan understood that—but *why* had it not developed? Had the cause been chemical, physiological, psychological, or what?

Flammarion had shook his head. He had no idea; but he would ask the experts.

In a few hours he was back. They did not know the answer, either. Chan had always possessed what appeared to be a perfectly normal brain; and now, after the treatment, Chan *had* a normal brain—or one that was rather better than normal, according to the latest tests. But as to *why*—Flammarion's experts had offered nothing. Why was Einstein, why was Darwin, why was Mozart, all with brains no difference in appearance from yours or mine?

Kubo Flammarion was content with that answer. He did not realize how totally unsatisfying it was to Chan. For if no one could explain the source of his earlier abnormality, what assurance was there that Chan would not regress? And in how many other ways, less easy to measure, might he still be abnormal?

How would he even *know* he was abnormal? Maybe he was still a total misfit, still a freak of nature—just a rather smarter one.

Without even realizing it, Chan was exploring his own sanity and normality. The process was natural for all maturing humans above a certain intelligence. But Chan did not know that—and he was doing it on an accelerated time scale, struggling to make in weeks the adjustments of outlook that normally take years. He had no time to examine the libraries or talk to older friends, to cull from their millions of pages and ten thousand years of shared human experience the reassurances he needed.

So Chan stared at the stars, pondered, and could find no acceptable answers. He was overwhelmed by uncertainty and sorrow and pain.

The easiest way to avoid that pain was to retreat from it, to hide in mindlessness. He gazed far out, looking beyond the starscape for the edge of the universe. He was exhausted, and after a few more minutes his eyes closed.

Seven hours later he awoke in his own bed. He was still exhausted and empty-headed, and he could not say where he had been or what he had done. His last memory was of Tatty, staring with her in the mirror at the reflection of her evening gown.

Chan did not have the energy or resolve to rise from his bed. He was still there when Tatty came to him. She was wearing the same white dress, stained now with dried blood.

She was not sure, but she had to talk to Chan. He

looked at her pellet-riddled arm and listened in horror. He was ready to believe her worst worries and suspicions.

It was just as he had feared. He was a monster. Before Tatty even finished talking, Chan had decided what he must do.

Chapter 18

"Who *dared* to give such an order?" Mondrian's voice was weak in volume but strong in authority. "Were you insane enough to do it yourself, without thinking of the consequences?"

The technician standing by the bedside recoiled and looked at Tatty for support. She stepped forward.

"I gave the directive," she said. "These people were only following orders."

Mondrian had been trying to sit up. Now he sank back on the pillow. "*You?* You have no authority here. Why would people even listen to you?"

"No problem. I gave the orders in writing, and I used the seal of your own office." Tatty sat down on the edge of the bed. "If you expect me to say I'm sorry, forget it. And if you claim I did the wrong thing, I'll have you sent back for more scans of your head."

The medical technician stared at her in horror, then up to the ceiling as though expecting a lightning bolt.

"Don't fret and fume, Esro," went on Tatty calmly. "The medical opinions were unanimous. You could have died. Your chances of full recovery went up dramatically if you remained in bed and under full sedation for a week. So that's what I authorized. The week's up, and you're doing well."

Mondrian shook his head, then gasped at the pain it produced. "A week! My God, Tatty, you make me unconscious for a whole week, and act as though it's nothing. In a week the whole system could go to hell."

"It could. But it didn't. Commander Brachis took care of everything in your absence."

"Brachis! You think that's going to make me feel better?" Mondrian made another attempt to sit upright. "He had a free hand to do what he liked with my operations and my staff, and you *encouraged* it?"

"Correct. He knew you would be worried by that, and he told me to give you a message. He assumes that the arrangement is on that you talked about before the attempt to kill you, and he will try to gain the ear of Ambassador MacDougal as you suggested. His main worry is that you won't remember anything about the conversation. The doctors warned of amnesia."

"I remember everything. Too much!" Mondrian put his hand to a forehead still coated with synthetic skin. "How did *he* escape injury? I know he was shielding you and Godiva."

"He was injured, too. But his wounds could all be treated with local anesthetics. He refused painkillers, said they'd blur his mind. He must be made of iron."

"Iron and ice. Or he used to be. Now he's besotted with Godiva. I don't know what he's like any more. How is she?"

"Calm as ever. Didn't get a scratch. Don't ask me how—everybody else was peppered with metal fragments." Tatty adjusted the line of the bandage around Mondrian's head. "You know the Godiva Bird, she just floats over everything and comes out fine."

Mondrian leaned back on his pillow under pressure from Tatty's hand. "You didn't detect any changes in her, then—before the bomb went off?"

"*Before* the bomb?" Tatty frowned down at him.

"Yes. I'm a bit fuzzy about those final few minutes, but something certainly seemed odd about her. You knew Godiva better than I did down on Earth, and you were very surprised when she came up here with Luther Brachis. So I wondered, when you were with her before dinner and Brachis and I were talking, if she seemed . . . well, *different* at all."

Tatty sat thoughtful, while Mondrian lay back and stared at her through half-open eyes.

"I think I know what you mean," she said at last. "She looks the same, and mostly she acts the same, but there's at least one difference. Whenever I met Godiva down on Earth she was always very conscious of money. Not stingy, exactly, but she talked all the time about her need to earn more. She must have had a fortune stashed away somewhere, because she was the highest-priced escort on the planet and yet she always lived cheaply—simple food, simple clothes. She couldn't have been spending anywhere near her income, and still she always seemed to want *more*. The other night, though, she never mentioned money for a moment. *That's* a change, if anything is."

"I agree. And here's something for *you* to think about. According to Luther Brachis, Godiva didn't have a cent when he brought her up from Earth—no money, no possessions other than her clothes." Mondrian turned to the medical technician, who had been listening with open interest. "Don't you have any other patients? How soon can I get out of here?"

"Two more days. And visitors have to be restricted to one hour a day."

"That won't do." Mondrian pushed back the covers and swung his legs out of bed. "I have work to do. Bring me my uniform—at once."

The technician looked to Tatty, found no encouragement there, and shook his head. "I am sorry, sir. I lack the authority to release you."

"Fine. Go get somebody who does."

As the technician scurried away Mondrian turned back to Tatty. "I suppose I'm going to have a fight with you, too."

"Not at all." As Mondrian rose from the bed, Tatty's manner changed. She smiled coldly at him. "I looked after you when you were too sick to make your own decisions. I'd do the same for anyone. Now you are clearly getting better, and you can go to hell in your own fashion. I'm leaving Ceres. I already have my exit approval."

"Using my office seal? Where are you going."

"Home. Back to Earth. I've had all I can stand of

Horus and Ceres." Tatty stood up. "I suppose you ought to thank me for looking after you while you were unconscious, but I know better than to expect that. Anyway, it's not appropriate. It was all my fault in the first place."

"The bombing? What are you talking about?"

"That's the other reason I wanted to be here when you woke up—to tell you that I was responsible for the attempt to assassinate you."

"Tatty, you're out of your mind. You didn't do the bombing any more than I did. We were both *victims* of it. You were injured, too—I can see the scars still on your arm."

"I didn't do the bombing—but I caused it to be done."

Mondrian reached out to take Tatty's arm, pulling her back to the bedside. His grip was much stronger than she expected.

"Princess, you can't make a wild statement like that and say nothing more. Are you saying you arranged for that bomb?"

"No."

"So what are you saying? That you know who tried to kill us?"

"No one tried to kill *us*. It was Chan Dalton, and he tried to kill *you*. The rest of us just happened to be there."

"Tatty, you're gibbering. What are you getting at?"

She hesitated and evaded, but under constant prodding from Mondrian she told the whole story; of the long days on Horus, of her loneliness, of her growing despair with Chan and hatred for Mondrian; finally, of her use of Mondrian's picture as an object for Chan to hate.

Mondrian listened quietly and sympathetically. At the conclusion he sprawled full-length on the bed and shook his head.

"Wrong, Princess. Totally wrong."

"Prove it."

"I can't—but I'll wager on it. Look at a few *facts*. First, whoever that waiter was, he wasn't Chan Dalton."

"He wasn't a real waiter. At the restaurant they don't know who he was."

"Well, he was certainly dressed like the waiters at that

restaurant. But waiter or not, my point is that he wasn't *Chan*. Which means that Chan would have had to bribe him. Now, did you tell Chan beforehand where we were going to have dinner?"

"No. He didn't know in advance—he says he just mindlessly followed us there."

"So you're telling me that Chan, who didn't know where we were going, could in just a few minutes persuade a man dressed like a waiter to deliver a bomb to our table. That sort of thing requires careful preparation and planning. Where would Chan even *find* a bomb? He's a recent arrival on Ceres, and he hardly knows anyone. He may look like a twenty-year-old, but in terms of adult contact with the world he's only a few weeks old."

"He's a super-fast learner now."

"It makes no difference. Chan is a *newcomer* here. No matter how intelligent he is, he couldn't get the materials and the knowledge in such a short time. You say Chan doesn't remember what he was doing at the time of the bombing. I'll accept that. His brain's still sorting itself out inside his head. But amnesia isn't a crime. I don't believe that he had anything at all to do with the explosion." Mondrian sat up and stared at Tatty. "Give me ten minutes to talk to him, and I guarantee that I can *prove* he had nothing to do with it—prove it to your satisfaction as well as mine."

"I can't." Tatty looked stricken. "Can't bring him to you, I mean."

"Why not?"

"He's not here any more—not on Ceres."

"Of course he is. You just have to track him down."

"No. You don't understand. When Chan told me about his blackout, I told him what happened at the restaurant. We talked, and we agreed. He must have done the bombing, without having control of his actions. He didn't know what to do. So I helped him—helped him to *escape*."

"But he couldn't possibly get away from here. For one thing, he'd need a travel permit."

"Esro, you still don't understand. He already *had* a travel permit."

"Who was insane enough to issue one to him? I'll have their carcass."

"*You* were insane enough. Remember, you issued it in advance, so it would be ready when he went off for pursuit team training and you would collect on your bet with Luther Brachis as soon as possible. All I did was ask Captain Flammarion to give Chan the rest of his tests at once. He passed them all, easily. He was ready for the next phase."

"So where is he?"

"He's on *Barchan*. As you planned. Ready to start pursuit team training."

Tatty's statement was not quite correct. Chan was certainly in pursuit team training, but he was not actually *on* Barchan. When Tatty spoke those words he was flying four thousand meters above the planet's surface in a Security aircar, receiving his final lesson on its operation and handling.

"Don't you forget now," said the pilot cheerfully. "Once you drop me off you're on your own. No collections, no deliveries, you pick your own nose and do your own laundry. And don't bother to send a message unless you've destroyed the 'Fact—or given up trying."

She laughed, as though her last suggestion was out of the question. The pilot was small and tubby, with sleepy-looking brown eyes. When she was at the controls the car seemed to glide effortlessly through the buffeting winds of Barchan. Only when Chan took over himself did he learn that Barchan's air currents were strong and unpredictable. Level flight called for constant attention, and landing and take-off on the desert planet was always dangerous.

Chan dipped the car's nose and started to drop off height. At a thousand meters he began to circle, making his visual search for their landing target. The updrafts were stronger here, and it took all his efforts to maintain a constant altitude.

"Has anyone ever done that?" he said. "I mean, just given up trying to destroy a Simulation of the Construct, and asked to be taken back?"

"You better believe it." The pilot chuckled and slouched back in her seat, but her eyes missed nothing and her hands were never more than a couple of inches away from the duplicate set of controls.

"You're the fifth pursuit team training group we've had in here," she went on. "And so far we've had just *one* that graduated."

"What happened to the others?"

"Bunches of stuff. Funny thing is, the first group that we had went dead smooth. I dropped the four of them off at the training camp, one at a time. Human, Pipe-Rilla, Tinker, Angel. They found they could work together, no problem. They organized the search for the 'Fact, found it in three days, and destroyed it. End of story, still no problem. They linked off to Dembricot for their final preparations, and last I heard they were heading off to tackle the real thing, the Construct itself."

"That was Leah Rainbow's team?" Chan had spotted the landing area, and he was lining up for final approach.

"Know her, do you? It sure was. Smart woman, that. Anyway, the first one went so smooth I thought all the rest would be the same and we'd slide right through like Angel sap. Was I wrong!

"Second team came in, I dropped 'em off. Didn't hear a squeak for a week, then the Pipe-Rilla called me, solo. Asked to be picked up, she was leaving the team. No explanation. That team's still waiting for another Pipe-Rilla to replace the first one.

"Team Three—your alignment's fine, by the way, but you'll land a lot smoother if you drop the speed another couple of points. That's it. Spot on, and hold it there. Anyway, Team Three arrived all right, seemed to get on well together. They searched around and found their 'Fact. But they didn't get it. It got *them*."

"It killed them?"

"Hell, no." The pilot leaned back and closed her eyes all the way. The car touched down, light as a feather. "A 'Fact won't actually *kill* a team—they were designed not to. But it can give you a pretty bad time. This one roughed 'em up so bad, they decided they'd had it with being a Pursuit Team. They split up. I picked 'em up one by one, and they all went home. So there we were, one out of three."

The pilot glanced out of the window and nodded approvingly. They had come to rest at the exact center of the landing circle. "Want to hear about Team Four?"

"Of course. Maybe I can learn by their experience."

"They were the worst of all. They got themselves organized, searched for their 'Fact, found it, and were all ready to blow it to bits. Well, that's when the Pipe-Rilla decided it couldn't go through with it. Couldn't stand the idea of killing something, even if it was only an Artefact."

"So they had to quit?"

"Not quite. The human on the team—big fat blond feller, looked like he'd not harm a fly—got so mad with the Pipe-Rilla, wasting all his time, he was all set to blow *her* full of holes in place of the 'Fact. Might have done it, too, if the Tinker hadn't swarmed him.

"I got 'em all out in one piece, but the whole thing convinced the other Stellar Groups—again!—that humans are crazy killers. And if you think *that* didn't create an interstellar incident and make things worse here . . ."

She opened the door of the car. A wave of dry heat like dragon's breath wafted into the cabin. "Phew! Welcome to sunny Barchan. This car's all yours now, until you get your 'Fact. Good hunting."

As she started onto the steps Chan leaned out after her. "You've seen them all. What do you think our chances are?"

The pilot paused with the door half-closed, and the car's air conditioner went into overdrive. "Your chances? Well, if you believe it's a random process, past history says you're one in four. But I don't believe it's that random. Mind if I ask you a question?"

"I've been asking you plenty."

"Well, I've looked you over pretty hard these past few days. You don't fit this job, not at all. With your face and body, you're an entertainment natural—public, or one-on-one. There's fifty billion women would like a piece of you. So how come you're on a Pursuit Team, out here at the ass-end of the universe?"

Chan hesitated. Had Leah talked about him, so the

pilot was just prodding for more details? The waves of arid heat coming in through the open door produced floods of sweat on his face and neck that dried the moment they appeared, but the pilot seemed oblivious to outside conditions. She was waiting patiently, and her face gave him no clues. He decided that her question reflected no more than a genuine interest.

"I was born on Earth. I was a commoner, with a contract. This gave me a way out, and when it's over I'll be free to do as I like."

It was close to the truth, and the pilot was nodding sympathetically. "Ah, I've heard about Earth. Everything's relative. Maybe after that, Barchan don't seem so much like the ass-end of the universe. I know that Leah Rainbow seemed pleased enough to be here. Did you get recruited the same way she did?"

"Pretty much. We were both recruited by Commander Mondrian."

"Good enough. You've answered my questions, now I'll answer yours. I'll up your odds of success from one in four to fifty-fifty. Mondrian's as hard as Tinker-shit and cold as Angel-heart, but he's one sharp son of a bitch. And he don't pick losers." She swung the door closed and grinned at him through the window. "I mean, *usually*," she shouted. "But there's exceptions to everything. Fifty-fifty! Good luck!"

She gave him a wave and set off for the cluster of service buildings. Chan sat quietly in the car, inspecting the landscape around him. They were in Barchan's low polar regions, where winter temperature would allow a human to survive without a suit except around noon. The vegetation, such as it was, was deep-rooted and covered in waxy blue-green foliage. At the pole itself it would grow in Barchan's half-g surface gravity to fifty meters or more; here it sat low to the ground, tight-wrapped to conserve moisture. The soil beneath the plants was dry, dark, and basaltic, rising in slow, brooding folds away from the landing area. Gusty surface winds lifted the top layer of soil up and about the parked aircar in twisting dust-devils of dark grey. Near the equator that sand layer was hundreds of feet deep. The constant winds blew it into the miles-long crescent-shaped *barchan* dunes that gave the planet its name.

Eta Cassiopeiae's twin suns hung close to the horizon. They lit the scene with orange, dust-filtered light. This dour landscape, according to Chan's briefings, was the most attractive part of the planet.

He wondered where the Artefact might be hiding. According to those same briefings, it would have no trouble living anywhere on Barchan—even in the scorching equatorial regions where only micro-organisms survived.

The three service buildings stood a kilometer away from the parked aircar. As Chan watched, a swirling veil of dark purple emerged from one of the buildings and blew like a rolling cloud of dust towards the car. When it was fifty yards away Chan opened the door. The individual components of the cloud could now be resolved. They were purple-black winged creatures, all identical and each about as big as his finger. They approached with a whirring of wings. In less than thirty seconds every one of them had entered the aircar door and settled all over the rear of the main cabin.

Chan closed the door and turned to watch. He had seen the next phase in briefing displays, but this was his first exposure to the real thing.

It began with one component—an apparently arbitrary one—hovering in mid air with its purple-and-black body vertical. A ring of pale green eyes on the head stared all around, as though assessing the situation, while the wings fluttered too fast to see. After a moment another component flew in to attach at the head end, and a third one settled into position beneath. Thin, whiplike antennae reached out and connected heads to tails. The triplet hovered, wings vibrating. A fourth and fifth element flew over to join the nucleus of the group.

After that the aggregation grew too fast for Chan to watch individual connections. As new components were added the Composite extended outward and downwards, to make contact with and derive support from the cabin floor. Within a minute the main body was complete. To Chan's surprise—something not pointed out in the briefings—most of the individual components still remained unattached. Of the total who had entered the cabin, maybe a fifth were now connected to form a compact mass; the remainder stood tail-first on the cabin floor or hung singly from the walls using the small claws on the front of their shiny leather-like wings.

The mass of the Tinker Composite began to form a funnel-like opening in its topmost extremity. From that aperture came an experimental hollow wheeze. "Ohhh-ahhh-gggghh. Hharr-ehh-looo," it said. Then, in an oddly accented variety of solar speech, "Har-e-loo. Hal-loo."

Kubo Flammarion had warned that this was inevitable. "Imagine," he said, "that somebody took *you* apart every night and put you back together every morning. Don't you think it would take a little while to get your act together? So make allowances for the Tinkers."

Chan couldn't imagine it. But he suspected that the little captain, a long-time alcoholic and a recent Paradox addict, knew that morning-after where's-the-rest-of-me feeling rather too well.

"Hello," he said, in response to the Tinker's greeting. "Hello."

As he had been advised to do, he waited.

"We-ee arre-eh," said a whistling voice. There was a substantial pause, then, "We are . . . *Shikari*."

"Hello. You should call me *Chan*."

This time it was the Tinker who waited expectantly. "Shikari is an old Earth word," it said at last when Chan did not respond. "It means *hunter*. We think that it is appropriate. And perhaps also amusing? But you did not laugh."

"I'm sorry. I never heard the word before."

"Yes." The funnel buzzed briefly. "You see, we were making a joke. We do not think that you are amused. You do not look it."

Look it. Chan wondered if the Tinker could actually see him. The individual components had in total many thousands of eyes, but how were they used for vision by the Composite? He gestured to the myriad of components still scattered around the cabin.

"Are *all* of you Shikari? Or only the ones who are connected?"

There was a buzzing pause. An indication of confusion? "We think that we understand your question, but we are not sure. We all in past time *have been* Shikari. We all in future time *will be* Shikari; and we all in now-time *can be* Shikari. But in now-time we are not all Shikari."

"I understand. But why are you not all Shikari now? Don't you think better when you are all connected?"

The Tinker had taken on a roughly human outline, with arms, legs, and head. When it moved forward in the cabin it was propelled by two different actions, the turning of body connections and the movement of thousands of component wings.

"Chan, you ask a many-questions-in-one question," said the whistling voice. "Listen carefully. First, if we wish we can join all together at any time."

"And you have more brainpower when you do it?"

"Yes, and no. When we join we certainly have more thinking material available—which you may call *brainpower*. But we are also less efficient. We are *slower*. We have a much longer integration time—the time it takes for us to complete a thought and reach a decision. That time grows fast-as-growth-itself—as you say, *exponentially*—with the number of components. When there is much, much time available, and the problem is large, we combine more units in us. More join, to make one body. But then the integration time can become so long that individual components begin to starve. We cannot, when connected, search for food. So components must leave, or die.

"What you see now is the most effective form, our preferred compromise between *speed* of thought and *depth* of thought. The free components that you see now will eat, rest, and mate. When the right time comes there will be exchange. Rested-and-fed-of-us will take the place of tired-and-hungry-of-us."

Chan had a score more questions, although they were already late for take-off. How did a Composite decide when and how to form? Was it adopting a human shape only for his convenience? How intelligent were the components, if at all? (He had the feeling that question had been answered during his early briefings on Horus, but anything told to him before the Tolkov Stimulator worked its miracle felt vague and unreliable.) How did the components know whether to join the Composite or stay away? Most important of all, if a Tinker was varying its composition all the time, how could there possibly be a single self-awareness and a specific *personality*? Shikari had all that, and claimed a sense of humor, too.

So many questions, and every one of them surely vital to the Pursuit Team's success—not to mention Chan's personal curiosity. But they would have to wait until the rendezvous with the other team members.

Chan prepared to take off, then decided he ought to consult Shikari. After all, if they were to be *called* a team, they ought to act as one.

"Shikari, are you ready to go?"

"We are very ready."

"Then would you like to move up front? If you want to study the landscape, you'd be better off sitting" — (*Could* a Tinker sit?)— "next to me."

"That will be very good." The Tinker changed shape. It came slithering forward like a giant purple-black pancake, over and around the back of the passenger seat and around Chan's legs. The speaking funnel emerged briefly from the center.

"And perhaps when we are on our way," Shikari said, "we can talk some more. When opportunity arises, we have *innumerable* questions concerning the strange form and functions of humans."

Chapter 19

To a visitor, all the inhabitants of a foreign country are apt to look the same.

The Sargasso Dump was as foreign a place as Phoebe Willard had ever been. For her first week or two, the brain-shattered guards at Sargasso were distinguished by little more than their sex.

Two things changed her attitude. The first was Luther Brachis's insistence that the two of them attend the guard review and follow it by a formal reception and dinner. It was possible to regard men and women as identical and anonymous when you merely passed them in corridors or took trays of food from them, but it was far more difficult when you stood or sat face to face and made (or attempted) conversation.

Many of the guards found speech beyond them. Luther Brachis ignored that fact. He knew every one of the hundred residents, he talked to them easily, and he told Phoebe of the deeds that had brought them to the Dump. It was a shock for her to realize that many of the blank-eyed dreamers at the long table were true heroes, the derelict remnants of daredevil men and women who had saved ships from disaster and whole colonies from collapse. They wore their medals at the dinner, but most of them seemed oblivious to former glories. Only a couple brightened and smiled when Brachis called them by their old titles.

The reception and dinner was a one-time event, but

after it was over Phoebe began to notice individual guards, and address them by name.

That led to a bigger change in her attitude, although the next event had nothing to do with social behavior. It was a matter of simple necessity. Phoebe had a task that could not be accomplished with just one pair of hands. She left the nitrogen bubble, checked the guard roster, and headed for a remote region of the Dump.

He was there, sitting in a habitation bubble and staring at the stars (or at nothing). He knew Phoebe was present, she was sure of it, but he did not turn his head at her approach.

"Captain Ridley. Are you busy?" (An idiot question; he didn't know what *busy* was any more.) "I need help. Will you come and help me?"

He had been the guard who above all others had seemed to respond at the dinner. He had even said a few words to her. But now he did not move and he did not reply.

Phoebe, angry at her own stupidity in even asking, went back into the habitation lock; and found that Ridley was following her.

It was a beginning. He scarcely said a word, but he could and did follow directions. Within a few days he had taken over the routine of temperature checking within the bubble as his own, and he shook his head vehemently when she tried to help. It was Ridley who, near the end of one of Phoebe's long work sessions, left the bubble and then thirty minutes later was back.

"No more for today," said Phoebe. He shook his head, took her arm, and tugged it. He had never done that before.

"What's wrong, Ridley?"

His mismatched eyes rolled. She knew that one of them was a replacement. The original, like his lower jaw, had been the casualty of a violent space explosion and decompression. "Brargas."

"Brachis?"

Ridley nodded. He watched impassively as Phoebe turned off all inputs to the sealed nitrogen balloon that held the brain of the Morgan Construct, closed her suit,

and followed him back to the main Dump control area.
She was oddly gratified when she entered and saw the
image of Luther Brachis on the communication display.

"Thank you, Captain Ridley." And to Brachis, smugly,
as he stared at the other man, "My assistant, Blaine Ridley. Are you all right?" She noticed that Brachis was not
wearing his uniform, and one arm was bare and bandaged.

"Sure, I'm fine. Little incident in a restaurant."

"In a restaurant! I've heard of bad service, Commander, but this is ridiculous."

Apparently it was again not a day for joking, for Brachis
went on as though he had not heard her, "I've been
downed for a few days, and I finally had time to do some
thinking. I know what's been going on with M-26A."

"You're ahead of me. I've been getting nothing sensi-
ble. Either the Construct's brain wasn't working right
before its body was destroyed on Cobweb Station, or the
blow-up there was too much for it. It's certainly crazy
now."

"It may seem crazy, but it's quite logical. Do you have
the complete record of your interactions with M-26A?"

"Not right here in front of me. But I have them all."

"Then I want you to check them, every one, and see
if the pattern that I noticed always holds. It's quite simple. If you ask a question, you always get the same useless response: *More information must be provided before
that question can be answered.* But if you *give* a piece
of information, and *then* ask a question, you get a real
answer—it can be what you just fed in, or something
different. But it's just *one* answer. If you want information—even if it's no more than a repeat of an answer
that you just received—you have to provide a piece of
information. One question, one answer. No exceptions."

"I don't believe it."

"Neither did I. But it works for every case. You can
go back and try it, feed in anything you like, then ask
any question you like. I don't know if you'll get the
answers you want, but I'll bet you get *something.* Hold
on now!"

Phoebe was moving away from the camera, obviously

itching to get back to test the idea that Brachis had been proposing.

"What else?"

"Assume that I'm right, and we have a way of genuine communication with M-26A. I want to know if it will let us build up a credit account. If we give it a hundred pieces of information one after another, will it then answer a hundred of our questions? If so, I want to feed it general background data about all the other members of the Stellar Group. Home worlds, history, physiology, psychology."

"That will be a huge job."

"I know. But M-26A is our only access point to Morgan Construct thinking processes and possible actions, and all the other Stellar Group species are going to be involved in the search. If the answers to my questions are to be useful, M-26A needs an adequate data base."

"I'll do my best. But I'm busy as hell. If you're looking for quick results—"

Phoebe Willard paused. Ridley had moved forward, to stand by her side. He was clutching at her arm. He stared at Luther Brachis, and the lop-sided jaw began moving.

"Brargas. Comder Brargas. Data. Data in to M-M—. I will—I want to—" His eye rolled, and he made a supreme effort. "I want to *help*."

Chapter 20

Mondrian awoke in a fetid, red-lit gloom to the sound of a low and ominous humming. He tensed as a tall figure loomed high overhead. As he recognized it, he slowly relaxed.

He knew where he was. He had been dreaming again; ghastly, terrifying dreams, but just what he had come to expect. The figure hovering over him was Skrynol, and the nightmare visions had been carefully designed and planted under Fropper supervision. Even the noise had a simple explanation. Skrynol was *singing*.

The Pipe-Rilla bent over Mondrian's sweat-soaked body, peered at him with huge compound eyes, and hummed a three-toned phrase. The lights in the chamber promptly increased.

"For your benefit," said Skrynol. She chittered strangely in Pipe-Rilla speech. "I did it so that you can admire my rare beauty."

Mondrian took a handkerchief from his trouser pocket and wiped sweat from his forehead and bare chest. He had stripped to the waist at the beginning of the session, not for Skrynol's benefit but his own. She was not fully comfortable at a temperature below human blood heat, and in the last few meetings the chamber had been made hotter and hotter.

"You seem in exuberant mood," he said. "Can I assume that we have made progress?"

"Oh, yes, indeed." The Pipe-Rilla bobbed her head back and forward in the gesture of assent she had learned from Mondrian. "Excellent progress. Excellent-excellent progress."

"Enough to sing about?"

"Ahhh." Skrynol raised her forelimbs and placed them on top of her head. "You embarrass me. A word is in order on my singing. Because we were doing so well, I extended the length of our session somewhat to pinpoint one result. As a result I took more of your blood than usual."

"How much more?"

"Some more. Rather a lot, actually. But do not worry, I gave you replacement fluids. Mm-mm . . ." She bent over him, an enormous and deformed praying mantis inspecting its victim. There was a flutter of olfactory cilia, and a whistling sigh. "Mm-mm. Esro Mondrian, it is well that we Pipe-Rillas can so control our emotions and our actions. I had been warned before I came to Earth that human blood was a powerful stimulant and intoxicant to our metabolism—but no one could ever describe this feeling of *exhilaration*!"

She reached down with one soft flipper and drew it lovingly along Mondrian's neck and naked chest. As she did so, long flexible needles peeped involuntarily out of their sheaths on each side of her third tarsal segment. They glistened orange in the bright white light. Fully extended, they would reach their hollow length more than nine feet in any direction. The official propaganda on the Pipe-Rillas described the aliens as "peaceable sap-sucking beings despite their formidable mandibles."

Esro Mondrian stared uneasily at the needles. *Sap-sucking*? Perhaps—but only if the word could apply to the body juices of plants *and* animals.

The urge to flinch away from her touch was strong. He resisted it and sat upright on the velvet couch. "I know how you must feel. Some humans also experience exhilaration from blood. Myself, I draw excitement from other sources. Can we talk about the session now? Are you controlled enough to tell me what you have found?"

"Of course." Skrynol, swaying like a sailing rig in a high sea, somehow reared her jointed body up another six feet. "We do not yet have a solution for your difficulties, but I think I can fairly say that at last we have *defined* the problem. I will begin with a question. You are Chief of Boundary Survey Security. Tell me, if you will, how you came to that position."

"Through the usual route." Mondrian was puzzled. "After I first left Earth I studied the other civilizations in the Stellar Group, and then took a job in commercial liaison with them. After that it was just a matter of hard work and steady promotion."

"That is the way it may appear to you. But your physical response when certain subjects are mentioned makes one fact obvious: the rise to your present position was less circumstantial than you believe. You were *driven* to seek it. As I told you in our first meeting, your nightmares are no more than analogies. But we are past that level. Now we must ask, analogies for what?"

Skrynol turned to a marker screen that sat behind her, and drew a circle in the middle with her left forelimb. She placed a small dot in the center and drew a set of radii to connect it with the circumference. "It is time for a little lecture from me. This is you"—she tapped the central dot— "sitting in the middle of a safe region. Like most members of your species you are dominated by self-concern, and so you see yourself at the center of the universe." She pointed to the radiating spokes. "You also dream of a web. And indeed, you sit in the middle of such a web—a web of *information*, provided to you through the Mattin Links from everything within the Perimeter. In your dreams there is a dark region. And sure enough, in your working world there is also a dark region. It is *everything that lies beyond the Perimeter*. More than that, it is terrifying to you. Maybe you can control everything within the known sphere of space—but how can you possibly control what is *outside* it? How can you even know *what is there?*"

Skrynol tapped the screen. "In your dreams the safe lighted region is always shrinking, the dark and dangerous zone always comes closer. And in the real world, the Perimeter *grows*, since through the probes and the Mattin Links new parts of space are steadily made more accessible. *They* are accessible to *you—and you are accessible to them.* That is the problem. You do not *know* what may lie beyond today's Perimeter, but you know you are afraid of it. The safe region is not really shrinking. It only seems to be so, because the *unsafe* region steadily becomes larger. New space is added all the time.

"So how can you minimize the danger? It is simple. You seek the position which gives you maximum control over the Perimeter. That is the position of Chief of Boundary Survey Security. You cannot banish the dangers, because they are caused by a force beyond your control: the Solar Group's expansionist policy. But at least you will learn of any danger as early as possible, and be in a position to combat it. You had *no choice* except to seek the position of Chief of Boundary Security. And you will do anything to protect the Perimeter. *Anything at all.*"

Mondrian froze, his exhaustion forgotten. The Pipe-Rilla had discovered his secret—knew why he needed the Morgan Construct.

But the Pipe-Rilla was leaning forward, until her broad, heart-shaped face was less than a foot from Mondrian's. "I pity you, Esro Mondrian," she went on. "Although I cannot share your fears, I know that your nightmare is *real*. You are afraid of the rest of the Universe, everything that lies beyond the Perimeter." The dark, lid-less eyes stared into his. "Do you understand my analysis, and accept it?"

Mondrian's nod was no more than a tiny tightening of neck muscles. "I accept it. But I do not know where it leads. Are you telling me that the nightmares must continue as long as I hold my present position?"

"Not at all. You accept, but you do not understand. You sought your present position in an attempt to control the situation, and so banish your nightmares. But those nightmares are not the *result* of your position, or of the existence of the Perimeter. They stem from a much deeper cause—deeper within Esro Mondrian."

"What is that cause?"

Skrynol shook her head. "That, I do not know. Not yet. But I do know that it lies deep-buried, far back in

your childhood. Still I cannot reach it. I need help. That
is why you must do something more."

"Name it." Mondrian's face was pale and dull-eyed,
but he was relaxing again.

"You must stay here. Travel the Earth. This planet was
the scene of your earliest and most hidden experiences.
You may not recognize the original source of your fears,
even when you encounter it; but *I* will know it, through
your unconscious responses. And *then*, at last, I will be
able to help you."

"I can't do what you ask. I am too busy to spend more
time on Earth."

"You must. Until you do so, your problem will not be
solved. Think upon this." Skrynol swayed up, away from
Mondrian. "That is the end of the session for today. I
can see your weariness and your distress. Put on your
shirt, and I will lead you back."

Mondrian sighed, and shook his head. "Not yet. We
have one more item of business."

"You are exhausted. For your own sake, make it brief."

"I cannot promise that." Mondrian reached into his
jacket pocket and took out a black wafer the size of his
thumbnail. "This is a summary of human expansion plans.
It provides only a broad outline. Before you receive
more, I must hear through official channels that full control of the Travancore operation will belong to the Anabasis. That control must not be subject to interference
from our ambassador, or from anyone else. I also want
it agreed that the Anabasis will be allowed to quarantine
the planet Travancore while the escaped Morgan Construct is being hunted."

Skrynol reached out and took the wafer delicately from
his hand. She bobbed her head from side to side, examining the small black square. "I will try to do as you ask.
Already I am doing as much as I can."

"Why is it taking so long?"

Skrynol waved a forelimb at him reprovingly. "Esro
Mondrian, you above all others should not be making the
common error of your species. Pipe-Rillas are *individuals*, as much so as humans. Each of us has her own
preferences and agenda. There is as much variety of

thought and desire among us as there is among your people. And so I must seek a consensus before I can act. That is not easy, since my species does not trust yours. But this"—she waved the black wafer—"will simplify my task. Have patience. If you have given me what I need, the Anabasis will control access to Travancore."

"Don't look for much detail in those plans. What you have is only an outline. The rest will be available in ten more days."

"For the moment, this is enough." The Fropper placed the wafer carefully in one of her body pouches. "You see, even if the plans that you have given me are wrong in some details—wrong even in *every* detail—that is not of great importance. Your species went through the mental processes needed to create such plans. It is those mental processes, the broad concepts, that we want more than the plans themselves. To my species, it is inconceivable that such ideas could ever be *imagined*, still less that the actions they describe might be carried out.

"But we have read human history. When it comes to war and fighting, the human species may not—I give you the benefit of the doubt—be *wholly* aggressive. But you are certainly aggressive. And you have a saying, that where all are blind the creature with a single eye will prevail. In matters of conquest and destruction my species is blind, as are the Tinkers and the Angels."

"All the other Stellar Groups seem to think of humans in the same way."

"I am afraid that we do. Why else would I be here on Earth, alone? In the case of the Tinkers, their feelings are partly a consequence of your appearance. The human form resembles that of a small carnivore on their home world of Mercantor. It is not dangerous to them, but it is mindless, ferocious, and annoying. Such associations are of course irrelevant to a creature of perfect intellect, but to most of us such factors carry large weight. I would say all, except that one can never be sure of the Angels. To the rest of us, small points can be very important. For example, to a human a Pipe-Rilla's voice sounds cheerful. And even this gesture"—Skrynol bowed her head, and placed her forelimbs high on top of it—

"which to us indicates shame or embarrassment, to you appears amusing. To humans, the worries and sorrows of a Pipe-Rilla look and sound comical, no matter how deeply felt."

"They do. But I certainly do not think of you as comical."

"In this as in many things, Commander Mondrian, you are an exception. I respect your opinions, but I would be more interested to know how *other* humans regard us."

"I think you know. As you pointed out, neither humans nor Pipe-Rillas form a uniform group. There is diversity of opinion among us. But the popular view of Pipe-Rillas is that you are conscientious, self-deprecating, and a little dull. In human terms, you also lack initiative."

"Initiative for the warfare that you find so popular?"

"For more than that. As most humans will tell you, *we* found *you* in our exploration, you did not find us. And there is an old story that summarizes the general human view of all species of the Stellar Group."

"A true story?"

"Only in the sense that all parables are true, because they reveal a group's common perspective. According to the story, a ship carrying a human, a Pipe-Rilla, a Tinker and an Angel made an emergency planetary landing."

"Aha!"

"You have heard the story?"

"I think not. Continue."

"They did not have time to send out a distress signal, and no one had any reason to search for them. The four sat down and reviewed the situation. Their onboard food supply was small, their communication equipment damaged beyond repair. If any other ship visited the planet, it would almost certainly not be for years."

"A grave problem indeed. What did they do?"

"The human asked for suggestions. The Pipe-Rilla said that she was of course sorry that they were in such a fix, but a mere Pipe-Rilla would not be able to solve the problem when another species had already failed. She left the ship and went off alone into the wilderness.

"The human asked the Tinker for ideas. The Tinker

said that there was really no problem. The planet had abundant winged insect life, so there was no food shortage. All one had to do was resolve into individual components, fly off, and catch as much as one wanted.

"The human turned to the Angel. It agreed with the Tinker: there was no problem. The soil of the planet was very fertile. All one had to do was settle in and put down a root system."

"And what, Commander Mondrian, was the human suggestion?"

"The human made no suggestion. After hearing the others, the human set to work. In ten months the crippled ship was repaired enough to fly home. What others see as aggression, we see as human diligence and initiative."

"You have a poor opinion of your fellow-members of the Stellar Group."

"Not as bad as the story would suggest. Like many parables, this tale exaggerates to make its point. Humans *like* Tinkers. We enjoy their sense of humor, though we find them—if you will pardon a human joke—'flighty' and 'scatter-brained.' Angels we regard as accurate and precise, but almost totally incomprehensible. As for your species, humans think that Pipe-Rillas sound amusing, look terrifying, take their responsibilities seriously—and worry too much."

Skrynol had listened in silence. Now she settled far back on her hind limbs and began to rock gently from side to side. "Fascinating. I said that I had not heard your story, and that was true. But I had heard something very like it. Did you know that we have our own tale of a similar shipwreck, and that the Tinkers and the Angels acted just as you describe? But in our version the human wanted to hunt, kill, and enslave the native animals."

"And the Pipe-Rilla?"

"Repaired the ship—naturally!—and made the escape from the planet possible."

Mondrian stood up and buttoned his jacket. "I would like to hear what version of the story is told by the Tinkers and the Angels. But now I am truly exhausted. I would like to go."

Skrynol nodded and moved in front of him. She insisted on changing the meeting-place every time, escorting Mondrian to and from it through a dark maze of tunnels.

"Someday we must discuss what each of us means by *intelligence*," she said as they moved into a stygian corridor. "I suspect that there too we will find surprises. I think we can agree that, whatever our differences, humans, Tinkers, Angels, and Pipe-Rillas are all intelligent—perhaps of comparable intelligence. But equality does not imply identity. We are different, for this reason: *we did not follow the same road to the light*.

"Humans evolved from a rather small and weak animal, on a planet with powerful predators. You had to be clever, inventive and *aggressive* or you would have died out. That is why you conquered fire, made tools, changed the face of Earth, and went to space. But compare that with the others of the Group, who never thought of leaving their home worlds until humans arrived. We Pipe-Rillas are twice the size of any other life form on our planet. We are strong, and we had no natural competition for living space and food. We did not need intelligence to avoid or neutralize our enemies. But a few million years ago, our planet S'kat'lan went through a major change in its climate. Our intelligence developed in response to that need. Only through drastic changes in our life-style and habitat were we able to survive. But the forces that we faced were all *impersonal* ones, of winds and weather and earthquake. We learned early to cooperate, and to control our population. But we never learned to *hate*. We never fought each other, nor were we ever threatened by another species."

Skrynol extended a tough and whiskery palp behind her for Mondrian to hold on to, and led the way up a thirty-degree slope. "As for the Tinkers, at the level of *individual components* they know aggression, and they fight over food, living space, and mates. But a Tinker *Composite* has no such needs. It does not eat, drink, or mate in the Composite form. It is in some sense immortal, and in another sense it has no permanent existence at all. It has no sense of danger at the Composite level,

because at the first sign of danger its instinct is simply
to disperse. And resolved to elements, the Composite no
longer exists to feel fear or danger. Mercantor is a cold
world, and to a Tinker 'intelligence' is a synonym for
'closeness and warmth.'

"As for the Angels, their form of intelligence remains
as much of a mystery to us as I suspect it does to you.
The Chassel-Rose will live and bud and die, and know
little more than a yearning for light and fertile soil. But
the Singers live a long, long time, and no one knows
how they came to be intelligent, or what purpose that
intelligence evolved to serve. Perhaps some day, after
another few hundred years of interaction and mutual
effort . . ."

Skrynol's musings in the darkness had occupied only
half of Mondrian's attention. He had a new problem to
worry about. The Pipe-Rilla had told him to roam Earth
and seek his early childhood. But where was he supposed
to begin the search? In the Gallimaufries, up in the polar
resorts, on the open ocean, or out in the great equatorial
nature preserves? Mondrian had vague childhood memories of all those areas. The crucial experience that Skrynol
was seeking could have happened anywhere. Worst of
all, how could Mondrian spare time for any of that when
the Pursuit Team operations were moving ahead at an
increasing tempo?

They were approaching the lighted levels of the deep
basement warrens. Mondrian arrived at his own conclusion: the Anabasis had first priority. No matter how bad
his nightmares, he would have to live with them for a
while longer.

As for exploring Earth, he could make a detailed list
of the places that he might have been when he was very
young. What he would need was somebody to go to each
of the locations and make full sound and vision recordings.
His review of those could provide the mental key to
unlock his memory.

Not for the first time, Mondrian needed help. By the
time that he reached Tatty's apartment he knew what he
must say and do.

Chapter 21

The room had been set up as a briefing facility and battle station, complete with conference table, projection equipment, terminals and interactive map displays. The *Adestis* battlefield was at the rear, overlooked by a spectators' gallery. Twenty-five men and women sat at the desks serried across the body of the room. In front of them, dressed in a close-fitting black outfit that closely resembled the uniform of a Security Force commander, stood Dougal MacDougal. His expression was totally serious as he presented a series of graphics. Luther Brachis had never seen the Solar Ambassador so deeply involved in anything.

"This is the enemy," said MacDougal. "In case any of you may be inclined to underestimate it, let me remind you that there has never been a successful attack on this type of stronghold using an attack force of fewer than forty members. And even in those cases, there was substantial loss of simulacra and several human deaths."

The three-D imaging system showed a dark, walled pit, descending to unknown depths in a fibrous black soil. Above the players, in large glowing letters, stood a sign: ADESTIS—YOU ARE HERE.

Luther Brachis was sitting in the audience about halfway back. He had had his private word with Dougal MacDougal, hinting at the security network rumors of human expansion plans. Now he was stuck. He could not easily leave without going through the whole *Adestis* exercise. He was watching Ambassador MacDougal closely, concealing his own irritation and skepticism. A morning of *Adestis* was not his idea of time well-spent, but Lotos Sheldrake had been very explicit: "If you want an informal word with the ambassador in the next week this isn't just your best chance, it's your only chance. Part of the time he'll be on Titan with a new industrial plant, then he'll be heading for the Procyon colony. It's *Adestis*, and it's tomorrow, or it's nothing. Take it or leave it."

Luther Brachis took it—grudgingly. When the briefing began he had been cynically amused to see that Mac-Dougal conducted the game as though it were some major military operation, with complete attention to detail. A few minutes' later Dougal MacDougal gave them their first look at the adversary; at that point Brachis lost his bored look and became the most attentive member of the audience.

"Remember the scale." MacDougal moved the light pointer from one side of the display to the other. "That's roughly three and a half centimeters. Sounds like nothing, but your simulacrum is a lot smaller than that. You'll be less than half a centimeter tall. As you see, the quarry is more than three times as big as that across the body. This is a full-grown specimen of the family *Ctenizidae*; sub-order *Mygalomorphae*, order *Araneae*, class *Arachnida*. In short, a trapdoor spider. A female, and gram for gram one of Earth's deadliest creatures. She won't be afraid of you—but you'd better be scared of her. Let me show you some of the danger points."

The screen moved in on the dark brown form, crouched ominously at the bottom of the smooth-sided pit. The length of the body was divided into two main sections connected by a narrow bridge between head and body. Eight bristly legs grew from the front section, and near the mouth were another two pairs of shorter appendages. Eight pearly eyes were distributed along the dark back of the upper body.

Dougal MacDougal aimed his pointer at the head section. "Here's the place to hit her, in the cephalothorax. Most of the nervous system is here, so that's the best place to shoot. It's also the most dangerous place to be, because the jaws and poison glands are here, too. Don't

forget that your simulacrum is as vulnerable to venom as
a real organism. You'll be completely disabled—and in
real agony—if there is even a small injection of poison.
So watch out for the fangs, and stay well clear of
them." He moved the pointer farther to the rear. "This
is the pedicel, the place where the cephalothorax joins
the abdomen. If you can get an accurate hit here, do it.
The body is very narrow at this point and it's even possible to blow the two pieces completely apart. But you
have to be very accurate, because the exoskeleton is as
tough as hell there.

"What else? Well, you can see for yourself what the
legs are like. Four pairs, each one seven-jointed. A hit
where a leg attaches to the cephalothorax might do some
damage, otherwise forget them. The breathing spiracles
and lung slits are on the abdomen, on the second and
third segments. There are two pairs of lungs, but you
may as well ignore them. Even if you got a hit, the spider
can breathe for a while through its tracheal tubes, more
than long enough to finish you off.

"The heart is in the abdomen here. See the four
spinnerets, back on the fourth and fifth segments? Keep
an eye on those, too. You'll never break free of the silk
if once you've been wrapped in it, and it dries instantly
as soon as it's in contact with air. The spider can *squirt*
silk at you, too, so you're not safe unless you stay at least
your body length away from her."

MacDougal turned to look at the audience. "That's all
I have to say about the spider. Any questions before we
go into *Adestis* mode and head down there to look at the
trap? Better ask now. We won't have time for it once
we've started."

"I've got one." A skinny man two seats in front of
Brachis nodded at the screen. "Those eyes look as though
they ought to be vulnerable. Should we be shooting at
them?"

"Good question." MacDougal aimed the pointer at one
of the eyes. "See their locations? They're all up on the
carapace. That's like a thick shield, protecting the top
of the cephalothorax. And that raises another point: the
carapace is *tough*. Your weapons won't penetrate it. The

eyes look like a weak point, but it won't be easy to get a good shot at more than one eye at a time, and if you miss you'll waste your ammunition on the carapace. So my recommendation is that you save your shots for the underside, or for the maw and joints.

"There's another reason why I don't think it's worth making the eyes your target. This sort of spider doesn't rely much on eyesight. It goes largely by *touch*. Even if you got all the eyes, you wouldn't put it out of action. And that has another implication: Don't assume it doesn't know where you are, just because you are out of sight. The legs are terrifically sensitive to vibration patterns. If you get into trouble but you've not actually been seized, lie perfectly still. The spider will sometimes ignore anything that doesn't move. You may get lucky. Anything else?"

"Yes." A woman near the front stood up abruptly. "You can count me out, Dougal. I'm leaving. I'm not going to fight that thing."

"The *Adestis* group won't refund your payment."

"That's the least of my worries." The woman turned to the others. "You're all crazy if you stay. That's nothing but a goddamned *bug* in there, and anyone in his right mind would be happy to swat it."

She left rapidly. Dougal MacDougal watched her go with a fixed smile on his face. "No nerve," he said as soon as the door had closed. "Good riddance—she'd have been nothing but trouble. Now, any more questions? Otherwise, let's get on with it."

The audience stared uneasily at each other. There was a slow shaking of heads, but at last one man rose and followed the woman out of the room. He would not meet anyone's eye. Finally, at a signal from MacDougal, those remaining picked up their Monitor sets and placed them over their heads.

Luther Brachis waited for the correlator field transients to settle, and the disturbing moments of double sensory inputs to fade. The briefings had told him what was happening. Telemetry couplers in the headset translated sensory inputs from his own tiny simulacrum to electrical impulses within his brain. At the same time his brain's intention signals, the ones that normally caused activity in his body's motor control system, were intercepted and translated into cyber-signals in the body of his *Adestis* simulacrum.

As MacDougal had explained it, "Your actual brain never sees anything, anyway. It's blind. It can't see, just as it can't hear, smell, taste, or touch. All it gets from your senses are streams of electrical inputs, and it *interprets* them as sensations. Well, now those electrical inputs will be coming from your simulacrum. You'll see, hear—and *feel*—what it sends."

The sensory hold was tightening. Brachis grunted in surprise; or rather, his simulacrum did. He had expected the simulations to be plausible, since although the makers of *Adestis* admitted that they had *imitators*, they denied that they had real competitors. Still he was staggered by the uncanny quality of the sensory inputs. They were like life itself. He had no other body. The simulacrum *was* his body.

He looked down, and saw that he was standing on a damp, pebble-strewn plain. Tiny wormlike animals wriggled away from him as he moved his feet. Fifty paces away a gigantic fly skimmed past on iridescent wings. Brachis stared all around him. Two dozen others stood in a rough circle, all experimentally raising arms, moving feet, and watching each other. The exception was Dougal MacDougal, recognizable by his ease of movement and confident manner.

"As soon as you're ready," he said. "Get the feel of the environment, get to know who you all are—your suits are color-coded, just the way they were in the war-room. You ought to learn to recognize each other as quickly as you can. Then you want to practice the feel of your weapon. After that we can get on with it.

"Look over there." He pointed away to the left, through air that seemed dusty, thick, and smoke-filled. "It's hard to spot from here, but there's the trap. The spider will be sitting at the bottom of the pit. She already knows that we are here, because she feels the vibrations through the ground. Don't bother to try to walk lightly. You'll do that anyway. Remember, you're only half a centimeter tall and you now weigh only about one five-hundredth of a gram. At this size and mass, gravity isn't too important. We can all tolerate a fall of many times our height, with no injury. On the other hand, we're attacking something that's more than twice as tall as we are, with legs six times as long and a mass that outweighs the lot of us put together. Don't get over-confident."

There was a gasp from a green-bodied simulacrum next to Brachis. "He has to be joking!"

Brachis shook his head experimentally. It felt perfectly natural. "He's not joking. He's just giving what he thinks is good advice. Maybe he's right, and some people come into *Adestis* believing that the trapdoor spider is just another bug you could stand up and step on."

"Not me." Green tried a shake of his head, too. "If that's just a bug, the Hyperion Vault is just a hole in the ground. I'm telling you, if I didn't work in his office, and if he hadn't put the pressure on me to come along on this . . ."

The party was slowly becoming more organized. Four of the members had taken part in *Adestis* on other occasions and they assumed lead roles. Everyone was permitted two practice shots from the projectile weapons, aiming at head-high moss growths fifty paces off to the left. Brachis noted that even with recoil compensation the gun he was holding delivered quite a jolt to his arm. That was a good sign. He had been wondering if the organizers of *Adestis* expected them to knock off the spider with weapons like peashooters. He also noticed that his gun pulled a little to the left. He took careful aim, made the adjustment, and put his second shot exactly through the fluffy pink ball of a head of moss-flower.

Halfway to the trapdoor pit the group halted again. MacDougal, who had taken the lead position, turned to them. "After this, each of you is on your own. So one last word. *Don't go down into the pit*. Not even if you think we've won, not even if you believe the spider is dead. This species has been known to sham, and the floor of that trap is her home territory. Let her come to you, and don't be afraid to run for it if things get too hot. The rest of us will try to draw her away from anyone who seems to be in trouble. And remember what I said: *Don't shoot at the carapace.* You won't penetrate it, and the ricochet could go anywhere. You'll be a damned sight more dangerous to the rest of us than you will to her."

His final words were interrupted by a shout from the black-clad simulacrum who had been detailed to keep watch on the trap. The thick lid was being pushed to one side. As they watched the great body of the spider heaved itself out and crouched on open ground.

"She's going on the offensive," shouted MacDougal. "Sooner than I expected. Scatter!"

His advice was unnecessary. The simulacra were already spilling away in all directions except toward the spider.

Luther Brachis took a quick look around him. He had worried that their approach to the trapdoor spider's lair paid too little attention to good ground cover. Now the only place to hide was twenty paces off to his right, where a stand of grey-green moss sprouted hip-high. He ran that way, dived for cover, and rolled up to a kneeling position with his weapon at the ready.

The difference between the spider's image in the briefing room and the arachnid herself was terrifying. The beast towered three times as high as his head, a gigantic armored tank that could move to the attack with unbelievable speed. Against that mass the weapon in his hands seemed useless. He could pump a hundred projectiles into that vast, glistening side, and have no effect at all.

The spider turned. Brachis had a perfect view of its broad abdomen and splayed legs as the cephalothorax swooped down on a magenta simulacrum and jerked it aloft. In the grip of the *chelicerae*, the pointed crushing appendages at the front of the spider's maw, the simulacrum hung dwarfed and helpless. There was a cry of agony, and a projectile weapon dropped uselessly to the ground.

Two others had been foolish enough to run directly beneath the spider's body. Brachis saw them firing upwards, pumping shots into the soft area of the genitals and the exposed ovipositor. The spider jerked and shuddered as the projectiles penetrated its body, and the two attackers cheered at each spasm and shouted encouragement to each other. They moved to the rear, to take more shots at point-blank range. Dougal MacDougal's warning shout came too late. A spout of gossamer jetted suddenly from the spinnerets, enveloping both simulacra in an unbreakable net of fast-drying silk.

The spider took a rapid shuffle backward, ducked its cephalothorax close to the ground, and hoisted both the helpless attackers to grind them in its maw.

Brachis scanned the predator from chelicerae to ovipositor. From where he was kneeling he had a choice of three targets. He could aim at a leg, or at the pedicel that connected the abdomen to the cephalothorax, or he could shoot at one of the chelicerae. The legs were the easiest target. They were also the least effective one. The pedicel was a vital area, but it was heavily armored and it would need an exceptionally lucky shot to do any good.

That left the chelicerae. Brachis made up his mind and sighted his weapon. It bucked in his grip and the organ, severed near the base, dropped to the ground in front of the spider.

He moved to sight on the second chelicerae but there was no time for a shot. The spider swiveled to face its new attacker and came scuttling towards him across the pebbled ground. The maw gaped, wide enough to swallow him whole. Brachis recalled MacDougal's dry comment, that no one would actually be *eaten*. Spiders did not ingest solid food. They pre-digested their victims by injecting enzymes, then sucked them dry. There was little comfort in MacDougal's words. The maw looming up on Brachis was more than strong enough to crush him flat.

He dropped behind the stand of moss and huddled motionless on the ground. There was a buzzing and a hissing overhead, and a monstrous shape blocked out the light. Brachis turned his head to look upwards. The vast abdomen was directly over him. He could see every detail: the dozen projectile wounds leaking blood and body fluids . . . the oozing nozzles of the spinnerets, still charged with silk . . . the colonies of mite and tick parasites, clinging to the coarse body bristles.

Then the spider had charged on. The air filled with a sweet scent of decay.

He rolled over, sat up, and looked around. How in the world were the *Adestis* manufacturers able to make simulacra that captured and transmitted *smells*?

But that question had to wait for another day. Brachis glanced to right and left. Two others must have dived for cover at the same moment as he had, and the spider had passed right over them, too. They were both lying motionless.

Still playing dead, even after the spider had gone. They were taking Dougal MacDougal's advice a bit too seriously.

He hurried over and tapped one of them on the shoulder. "Come on. Let's get on with it or we'll never be out of here."

There was no reply. The simulacrum remained totally immobile. Brachis leaned closer, looking for the small green light between the shoulders that showed that the simulacrum was still occupied and in working order. The light was on. He went to the other motionless figure. *That* light was on, too.

Brachis squatted back on his heels, for the moment oblivious to the frantic battle that went on behind him. This whole thing was crazy. He was sure that the spider had missed all three of them. He had actually seen a blurred image of huge legs scrambling by, a good three paces from all of them. So why were the other two still lying here, just as though the spider had managed to put them out of action? And if they were out of action, why did the simulacra show they were not?

Brachis gave a startled growl of comprehension. He set his weapon to automatic, fired a blind volley at the spider's belly, and at the same moment bit down hard on his rear molar control.

There was a dizzying moment of disorientation. Then he felt the Monitor headset covering his face.

THAT IS THE END OF ADESTIS FOR YOU, said a metallic voice in his ear. REMAIN SEATED IF YOU WISH, BUT—

Brachis ripped the Monitor set off his head with one movement and stared around him.

He was still sitting in the same place in the *Adestis* battle chamber. Of the two dozen people who had embarked on the *Adestis* safari, half were already lolling in their seats with their headsets off. Their simulacra had been killed by the spider, and they were now experiencing the vicarious agony of their own deaths.

Another dozen still wore the Monitor sets—but three of them sat slumped forward in their restraining harnesses, their clothes drenched with blood. Brachis saw that their throats had been cut so deeply that the heads were almost severed.

He slapped at his release harness. Before he could rise to his feet a tall figure came looming over him. It was familiar. At the same time as his mind rejected recognition of that tall, cadaverous figure, a skinny arm brought something swinging in towards his unprotected neck. A bright ceremonial sword whistled through the air.

Brachis jerked his right arm upwards. There was a clean, meaty crunch. His hand, severed below the base of the thumb, flew out and fell on the floor on front of him.

His uniform reacted even before he had time to feel pain. The shirt sensors recorded the sudden drop in blood pressure and activated a web of fibers in his right sleeve. The knit material on his right forearm tightened to form a tourniquet.

The sword came swinging in again towards his neck and head. Brachis swayed forward, under the swing, and reached out and around with his left arm. He grasped the back of the narrow neck and pulled the body forward against his face. He closed his eyes and made a total, reflexive effort. Vertebrae snapped under his twisting fingers. The dropped sword passed over his back and slid harmlessly past his legs.

Still entwined, Brachis and his assailant tumbled together to the floor of the chamber. He landed underneath, gasping at the impact.

He opened his eyes, and gasped again. His first,

incredulous impression had been correct. He was staring into the lifeless face of the Margrave of Fujitsu.

Even though Luther Brachis had done his best to persuade her, Godiva Lomberd refused to sit in the room where the *Adestis* attack would take place. She had listened quietly, smiled, shook her gorgeous blond head, and said: "Luther, my sweet, Nature designed some people for one thing, and some for others. Your life is Security—sabotage, weapons, skirmishes, and violence. Mine is Art. Music, dancing and poetry. I'm not saying my life is *better* than yours. But I am saying I won't come and watch while Dougal MacDougal satisfies his blood lust trying to kill some poor harmless animal that is only doing what *its* nature programmed it to do. I don't have to be there, even if you do." She placed her fingertips on his lips. "No argument, Luther. I'm not coming—not even into the spectators' gallery."

In the end she had relented far enough to accompany Brachis to the main *Adestis* facility. She allowed him to settle her in the neighboring lounge and order refreshments for her while she waited. She seemed delighted when Esro Mondrian arrived at the same lounge a few minutes later.

"What brings you here, Commander? I can't believe that you like *Adestis*."

"I don't." Mondrian had with him a tiny, dark-haired woman. She was already staring curiously at Godiva. "We came because Luther is here, and we need to talk to him."

"You can't do it now. He's involved in this safari, and they must be right in the middle of it."

"That's all right. We'll wait." Mondrian turned to the woman with him. "Lotos, this is Godiva Lomberd. Godiva, Lotos Sheldrake. If you two don't mind I'm going to leave you here for a few minutes. If Luther comes out, don't let him get away. He has to wait until I come back."

Godiva nodded. "Where's Tatty?"

"Down on Earth again." Mondrian hesitated. Godiva was still looking at him expectantly. "She's helping me.

I needed images and recordings of a few places. She ought to be back here in a week or two."

Godiva nodded. She seemed faintly puzzled, but she said nothing more as Mondrian left and Lotos settled down to sit opposite her. There was an awkward silence.

"Are you involved with *Adestis*?" said Lotos at last.

The other woman smiled and shook her head. "Just heard about it, enough to convince me I don't want anything to do with it. How about you?"

"Once, and never again." Lotos related the details of her experience at the termite nest. She underplayed the danger, but emphasized her own terror and discomfort. She did her best to be humorous and self-deprecating—and she watched closely for Godiva's every reaction.

Since hearing of the contract with Luther Brachis, Lotos had put her own information service to work. Their efforts had been pathetically unproductive. Godiva Lomberd had popped into view a few years ago on Earth, officially as an "artistic performer." *The peerless Godiva Bird, Model, Consort, and Exotic Dancer*, said the publicity. In fact, she was a rich man's courtesan.

All the digging since then had turned up nothing more specific. Godiva was simply a woman, background and age uncertain, whom men found irresistible. She exploited that fact for money.

Looking at her now, Lotos could see why Godiva had been so successful. She moved like a dancer, every gesture natural, easy, and flowing. She had the clear eyes and skin of perfect health. She laughed easily, throwing her head back open-mouthed to reveal perfect teeth and a pink, fleshy tongue. Most of all, she listened to Lotos with total, focused attention, as though what the other woman was saying was the most interesting thing in the solar system.

And still Lotos was uneasy. Godiva had never formed more than a temporary and commercial relationship with any man—until she met Luther Brachis. And then she had formed a *permanent* contract with him.

True love? That was not in Lotos Sheldrake's vocabulary of the possible. Her intuition told her that something strange was going on between Godiva Lomberd and

Luther Brachis. She lacked Mondrian's previous acquaintance with Godiva, but she trusted his instincts, too. "She is *changed*," he had said, as they whipped through the Ceres transportation system on their way to the *Adestis* Headquarters. "Different. She wasn't like that when she was on Earth."

"Changed *how*?"

Mondrian had looked angry—with himself. Lotos knew how much he valued his ability to read out the motivations and secret desires of others. "She's ... *focused*," he said at last. "You would have to have met the old Godiva to understand what I mean. It used to be that Godiva always paid close attention to the man who was buying her time, and she certainly gave him his money's-worth. But at the same time she was aware of other men, and somehow she made them aware of *her*. It was like a magnetic field around her, one that said, 'I'm busy right now. But I won't always be busy. Sometime in the future, I could be yours.' Of course, in practice there were conditions. Everyone wanted her, but not everyone could pay the price. But there was always that possibility, if a man were lucky enough to get rich. Now ... now she pays attention to Luther. *Only* to Luther. The other men around her are hardly there. That's what I mean by *different*."

"Maybe it's love," suggested Lotos. She gave Mondrian a quick sideways look from her dark eyes.

He had not bothered to reply. Mondrian's opinion of true love as the agent for a profound change of personality was perhaps even more cynical than Lotos Sheldrake's.

Lotos watched now, as other men and women wandered through the lounge. Mondrian had been exactly right. Godiva would look up, as though to check that each arrival was not Luther Brachis. Then at once she returned her attention to Lotos. There was no eye contact, no trace of coquetry. Godiva flirted no more than Lotos herself did.

So. Lotos leaned back and puzzled over the evidence before her eyes. Earth's most famous and expensive courtesan ought to be much more *aware* of men. Even if she no longer thought of them as prospective customers, surely the habit of speculative evaluation and subliminal come-ons would by now be built in?

Lotos had paid well for this meeting with Godiva. And it was producing more questions than answers.

Mondrian had promised Lotos a clear half-hour with Godiva. She was getting that and more, because on the way back to the lounge he stopped at the spectators' lounge for a look at the battle area.

He stayed longer than he had originally intended. Luther Brachis and Dougal MacDougal were both in the control room, wearing their Monitor sets. Or was it more accurate to say that they were really down on the battlefield, where each of them controlled the body of a simulacrum?

The field of encounter was a small hemispherical chamber about ten feet across. A camera set into the domed roof revealed all the action to any interested observers. The usual audience would be mostly prospective players, following the whole procedure with huge interest.

When Mondrian arrived, the assault on the trapdoor spider's lair had been in its preparatory stages. The spectators' gallery was almost empty. There was one young woman wearing the blue worker's uniform of a Pentecost colonist, and a tall, thin man with a full beard. He seemed more interested in the players themselves than in the quarry, the battlefield, or the simulacra.

The first close-up of the spider was daunting, even to one who never intended to play *Adestis*. It sat motionless at the bottom of its trap, holding in its front limbs the drained husk of a millipede. It was easy to imagine that the multiple eyes on its curved back were aware of the watchers, far above.

Mondrian stared down thoughtfully at the spider. *Adestis* led to real deaths, through pain and stress. If his arrangement with Skrynol for the Anabasis did not work out, and Dougal MacDougal became an impossible problem—could *Adestis* provide a convenient solution? How many times had it been used in the past, to get rid of a troublesome official?

Mondrian took that thought with him when he went back to Lotos Sheldrake and Godiva Lomberd. He sat down to evaluate its potential, and listened to the women's conversation with half an ear. He had been there only a few minutes when the uproar began in the adjoining control room.

Godiva came instantly to her feet. "Luther! In there!" she cried, and dashed to the chamber door. By the time that Mondrian and Sheldrake had followed her inside she was at Luther Brachis's side. She was supporting him and staring horrified at the scene around her.

Brachis was standing, white-faced but erect. His right forearm ended just beyond the wrist in a bloody stump.

Mondrian glanced at the pools of blood and the bodies surrounding Brachis. They were beyond help. He went across to the other commander, lifted his arm, and checked the tourniquet. "No blood loss now. I don't think much of that on the floor is yours. Take it easy. We'll have you to the hospital in a few minutes."

"Thanks. Sorry about the mess in here." Brachis nodded at the wounded arm. "Injuries getting to be a bit of a habit, don't you think?"

"It'll grow back."

"Yeah. Teach me not to bite my nails." Brachis gave Godiva a death's-head smile. "It's all right, Goddy. Just me and Mondrian playing word games, to make sure I'm not going to pass out. Blood supply to the brain, you see."

"Your arm—"

"—will be all right. Don't worry about it. I'll just have to sign my name left-handed for a while."

MEMORANDUM FROM: Luther Brachis, Commander of Solar System Security.
TO: All security posts.
SUBJECT: Countermeasures for terrorist activities.

Effective immediately, the following special security measures will go into effect throughout the Inner System:

1) All travellers leaving Earth will be required to travel via Link Exit facilities. All other travel will be prohibited until further notice.

2) All travellers leaving Earth will be subjected to chromosome ID checks. ID's will be compared with reference ID (attached). In the event of a correlation exceeding 0.95, the traveller must be detained for questioning by Central Security.

3) All off-Earth awakenings from storage facilities will be subject to direct supervision. Wakers will be subject to chromosome ID checks against reference ID. In the event of a correlation exceeding 0.95, the waker must be detained for questioning by Central Security.

4) Any traveller using Link facilities and whose appearance resembles the MARGRAVE OF FUJITSU (image attached) must be detained for questioning by Central Security.

5) Any off-Earth disposition of assets from the estate of the Margrave of Fujitsu must be reported to Central Security.

Luther Brachis stared at the stump of his hand. The nubs of new fingers were already beginning to bulge under synthetic skin. He wiggled them experimentally.

"Itches like the plague." He tapped the sheet in front of him with his left hand. "Think this will do it? I don't think so. I'm willing to wager we *don't* catch him."

Mondrian shook his head. "No takers. Not if he was as smart as you seem to think. He must have planned this for years, ever since he created his first facsimile Artefact. The next one could look like anything."

"I know. That's why I'm worried."

"You'll be all right. Stay well-armed. You've got the training to handle any number of Margraves, one-handed or two."

"You don't understand." Brachis placed his hand on

the gun that sat on the table in front of him. "I'm not worried for myself, I'll blow 'em away before they get near me. But suppose that bastard takes a shot at *Godiva*?"

Chapter 22

Dear Chan,

This is a letter that I never expected to write, a message I never dreamed i would send, especially (don't misunderstand this) to you. But it's our first night down on Travancore, and I'm flat out *scared*. Tonight I wish you and I were still down in the Gallimaufries, watching Bozzie preach self-denial while he gobbled down a dozen waffles with honey.

If we can't be together, at least let me babble at you for a while. We—the team, I mean, they gave us a rotten name, *Team Alpha*, but I hope we'll come up with something better for ourselves—anyway, my team, Team Alpha or whatever, we weren't allowed to bring a Mattin Link ship anywhere near Travancore. No matter what happens here, Commander Mondrian won't risk the Morgan Construct having access to a Link again. So this message will be fired off to the ship, a million kilometers away, then through a Link back to Sol, then through the Censor's office, and *then*, if everything works out right, you'll get it before you leave Barchan. Good luck down there. The last word I had, you have the hottest Pursuit Team they've seen since training began. I hope so—and I hope you will never have to visit Travancore. Because if you do, it will mean that we have failed.

I said that we are "down on Travancore" but that's more like a figure of speech than anything else. We don't know where the true surface of the planet begins. No one does. We're hanging in a sort of half-balloon tent with a flat, flexible base, about a hundred feet down from the topmost growths of vegetation. There's another five-kilometers-plus of plant life underneath us.

Animal life, too. We saw the first signs of that on the low-altitude automated survey. The whole planet is riddled with holes, circular shafts about five meters across. They dive down from the top layers, and at first we thought they might be natural rain channels because it rains every day over most of Travancore. But now we're not so sure. S'glya—she's the Pipe-Rilla on our team—saw something big wriggling away down one of the tunnels when we were flying in. Scary. But I was mainly happy that it wasn't the Morgan Construct, because we were a sitting target. I tried to hide my panicky feeling but of course it didn't work. S'glya has this absolutely uncanny ability to read human feelings and she told the others.

They didn't seem worried. It's an unpleasant thought for me, the idea that soon we'll be heading down one of those tunnels, but the Tinker feels quite different about that. It argues that the tunnels are a big boon to us, since without them it would take forever to explore the vertical forest on Travancore. Maybe it will take forever anyway. We'll know, as soon as we get down to the interior.

Even before we made the final descent we decided that the training program had missed the point. We were sent to Dembricot for final training, because it's a vegetation world like Travancore and everyone thought it would be good experience for this place.

Logical idea, but totally wrong. You must have seen the training films of Dembricot by now. Flat, water plains of plant growth, but they're no more like Travancore than Barchan is. This planet is dense, tangled hillocks of jungle, boiling up in swirls and breakers like one of Earth's seas in a bad storm.

One good thing: I can breathe the air with just a compressor. I should be able to manage without even that when we get down to a lower level where the pressure is higher. We're all doing well. S'glya needs a heating unit, and Angel had to do some mysterious interior modification before the atmosphere was acceptable, but that's all.

The view from the top layer of vegetation is spectacular at the moment. Travancore's primary, Talitha, is close to setting, and when it's low on the horizon it shines through mile after mile of ferns and leaves and vines. No flowers, I'm afraid—Travancore wouldn't please old Bozzie. Everything in sight is greener than green, except for the Top Creepers. That's not their official biological name, but it's a good description. They are purple, gigantic lateral creepers that snake away across the top of everything as far as you can see. And I mean *gigantic*. They're only a few meters across, but each one is many kilometers long. In spite of their size they are not at all dense and heavy. I tried to take a sample from one, because I couldn't see how the rest of the vegetation could possibly support that much weight.

When I cut into it there was a hissing sound and a horrible smell, and the level of the vegetation around the Top Creeper went *down* a fraction. The whole thing has to be nothing more than a wafer-thin shell stretched out over a hollow center full of light gases. Now I suspect that they are actually holding the other plants *up*.

I told you I was going to babble, and I think I'm doing it, but I hope that I'm justified. If you do have to come here, the more you know about the place ahead of time, the better. We were trained as well as we could be, but it surely wasn't enough. No one has ever looked closely at Travancore before. With no defined surface and no open water, no one thought that it was worth it. We have more questions than answers.

More about those mysterious holes. They keep preying on my mind. Angel's imaging organs (can't call them eyes) can be tuned to the thermal infra-red. Angel took a heat-wavelength look down one of the shafts, and claims that it isn't vertical at all. It spirals down in a helix, which rules out the natural rain-channel idea. We'll soon have a better explanation, I expect, because we'll be going down one. I hope that I'm around after that, to send you a description. Anyway, whatever happens to us our ship ought to be receiving a full record of it.

And more about Travancore, too. Naturally we've thought about nothing else since we got here. There are plenty of mysteries not even mentioned in the briefing documents. For example: gravity and air. The surface gravity is only a little more than a quarter of Earth's. So how can it hold onto a substantial atmosphere, and support this massive cover of vegetation? The air should have bled away into space long ago.

Well, according to S'glya, Travancore has its atmosphere *because* of the strange vegetation layer. The canopy of plant life is so dense and continuous that it can trap air molecules within and beneath it. We know there is something close to a pressure discontinuity up near the top here.

And of course it's a chicken-and-egg situation because the atmosphere is absolutely necessary for the vegetation to exist! The plant cover must have developed very early in Travancore's history. And if S'glya is right, the shafts we saw can't go down uninterrupted all the way to the solid surface, because otherwise they could act as escape vents for the air. So we may have to cut our way through barriers, one more little difficulty. But just to add to the confusion, Angel says that S'glya's idea about the relationship of the atmosphere and the vegetation is wrong—for six reasons still to be specified.

Well, what's the good news? The team is the good news. We're an odd assortment. We have a Tinker whose real name sounds like a breaking window, but who asks me to call it Ishmael. Its big ambition in life seems to be to snuggle up to the rest of us. Then there's Angel, who won't stop using human proverbs and cliches, and who insists that Angels don't *have* names. And last of all there's S'glya, who seems to know what I'm thinking and feeling without being told. S'glya's not her real Pipe-Rilla name, either, because that's unpronounceable too.

Weird. But it all *works!* Once we got to know each other we've been achieving an unbelievable level of communication and cooperation. It seems as though anything that one of us can't do, another one can. We first noticed it back on Barchan, and it has just gone on getting better and better.

Better and better—but God only knows if it will be good *enough*. Angel says that the Morgan Construct is a superior being, beyond even Angel.

Full night here now. Time to sleep.

Keep your fingers crossed for me, Chan, wherever you are. I love you, and I've always loved you since you were a baby. I can't forgive myself for running away and refusing to speak to you when you were on Ceres with Tatty. But it was awfully hard for me to admit that I don't own you any more.

I hope that you can forgive me. And I hope that some day I can make up for what I did then.

                                                Yours, Leah.

Chan had read it through again and again. After the third time he could have repeated it word for word.

He kept going back to the last few paragraphs. Leah's words of love bowled him over—and her remarks about the level of communication between her team members baffled him completely. Over the past couple of days he had become convinced that his own team would *never* work well together. They had too much trouble understanding each other. Well, maybe Shikari, as the Tinker liked to be called, would be all right. Shikari sometimes made perfect sense. So did the Pipe-Rilla, now and again, although neither she nor the Tinker seemed to have the equivalent of facial expressions. If they had some kind of body language for use with their own species, he had no idea how to read it.

As for the Angel, that was mystery personified. The creature had no face, no mouth, no method of communication except through a computer interface. And even that output was often incomprehensible, though Shikari and the Pipe-Rilla understood it (or pretended to).

And this mismatched assembly was supposed to be able to track down and destroy the most dangerous being in the known universe! They would be lucky if the Artefact simulation of the Construct, here on Barchan, didn't tie them in knots.

They had established their camp down near the planet's south pole. Until they knew the Simmie Artefact's location there was no point in enduring the dreadful summer heat of the equator and northern hemisphere. On this third evening, as the dark sands of Barchan gradually cooled, the Pursuit Team settled down to its first strategy session.

The Tinker had increased noticeably in size as the sun set and the air was less scorchingly hot. The central mass contained almost twice as many components as when Chan had first met it, and its response time was painfully slow. The other three waited (impatiently, in at least Chan's case) while Shikari's speech funnel made its preparatory wheezes and whistles.

The Pipe-Rilla, S'greela, was crouched next to Chan and nervously stroking her multi-jointed forelimbs along the side of her head. If her performance to date was any guide, when confronted by anything the least frightening she would chitter in horror and terror and run away with great spring-legged leaps.

The Angel at least would not run away. It could not. No matter how intelligent the crystalline Singer might be, it was bound within the vegetable body of the Chassel-Rose and suffered that plant's extreme slowness of movement. When the Angel wanted to move, the bulbous green body first lifted the root-borers up close underneath it. When they were stowed safely away it could creep along on the down-pointing adventitious stems at the edge of the body base. Chan guessed that if it was in a real hurry it might manage up to a hundred steps an hour.

Which left only the Tinker, Shikari, as a possibly useful ally. But its reaction to danger had already been demonstrated. It at once dispersed to individual components, and they flew away.

The curious thing was that the other three did not share Chan's worries at all.

"We think that we have a satisfactory approach." Shikari was finally speaking, slow and ponderous. "The Simulated Artefact lacks circadian rhythms and is indifferent to night or day. But our team is not. We Tinkers prefer to cluster by night, and Chan needs to become dormant. However, S'greela is naturally nocturnal, and like the

Chassel-Rose she has excellent night vision. This, therefore, is our suggestion. Angel and S'greela should perform a night survey, seeking the Simmie. Human and self will remain here and rest. If there is no success in the search, then when daylight comes we will reverse the roles."

The long blue-green fronds at the top of the Angel began to wave slowly in the air. Chan, ready to speak, paused. He had seen that motion before, when the Angel's computer communicator was beginning its translation. Maybe even an Angel had some kind of body language.

"We agree," said the translator's mechanical voice. "However, we propose one difference. We believe that we now know the probable location of the Simulated Artefact. Therefore, the mission for Angel and Pipe-Rilla should be one of confirmation, not of search."

"But how can you?—" Chan stopped. The ferny fronds were still waving.

"We have completed the analysis of imaging radar records obtained during orbital survey," went on the Angel. "There are two significant anomalies. One of them is our base. The other is almost certainly the Simulacrum. We request a brief pause, while we perform a confirming analysis. We have stored a copy of the ship's data record."

The Angel had answered Chan's half-spoken question, plus another one about the ship's records that he had thought but not even started to ask.

Telepathy? Even as the thought came, Chan rejected it. He remembered what Flammarion had told him during a Ceres briefing: "An Angel doesn't normally think like a human, but not because it *can't*. When an Angel wants to, it can put part of its brain into what we call 'emulator mode.' Then that piece can be instructed by the Angel to think like a human, or a Pipe-Rilla, or a Tinker of any number of components, or maybe like all three at once. And probably any other creature you care to name, maybe even like a Morgan Construct. And while all that's going on, the Angel still performs logical analysis in its own way. Whatever *that* might be." At that point

Kubo Flammarion had seemed puzzled by his own words, and tugged at his uniform as though it had become too small for him.

During Chan's moment of recollection, the Pipe-Rilla S'greela had unfolded its long, telescoping limbs and was reaching down to pick up the Angel. The Angel had objected to this the first time, protesting that it was quite capable of independent locomotion. But after two minutes of watching the Chassel-Rose's lumbering progress, the other three had been unanimous. In any travel involving them, Angel would be carried.

Chan watched S'greela now as she easily picked up Angel's pear-shaped bulk. More and more he was aware of the power in the thin, pipe-stem body. S'greela was gentle, but if she ever chose not to be she could swat Chan like a troublesome insect.

Shikari remained a few feet away from Chan. The Tinker did not speak as S'greela and Angel left in the aircar. It occurred to Chan that he was observing another data point. The others were very economical of words unless he became involved in the conversation; then human-style verbal padding was added for his benefit. They had realized that redundant words were part of human social interaction, as important to Chan as stroking to a Pipe-Rilla or clustering to a Tinker.

Chan stood up and moved across to sit by Shikari. After a few moments he felt the feathery touch of long, delicate antennae on his arms and legs. The Tinker Composite was quietly performing a partial disassembly and rebuilding. Thumb-sized components were leaving the far side of the great clump and re-attaching themselves close to Chan's body. Within five minutes Shikari was molded solidly against Chan's left side, touching him all the way from breast to ankles.

He turned his head and stared down at the purple-black vibrating mass. The contact was not at all unpleasant. In fact, that gentle thrumming touch against his skin began to feel surprisingly warm and reassuring. After a few more moments, free components who had not been part of the Tinker Composite when Chan sat down flew across and made additional connections. Soon Chan's whole body, from feet to shoulders, was embedded in the largest purple swarm he had ever encountered.

He felt very relaxed now, but not sleepy. The pressure around him was just enough to be noticed. But the pilot's words drifted back to Chan. If a Tinker chose to swarm on something as a means of restraint, it could be formidable. Shikari had its own way of neutralizing aggression.

He watched as a final few components flew in to attach themselves. "Do you feel different, when more units attach?"

There was an experimental whistle from the speaking funnel. "Of course."

After a long silence, Chan realized that the Tinker had given its full answer. "I don't mean more *intelligent*. I know that's true. What I mean is, do you feel that you are a different individual when your size is increased so much?"

The Tinker was silent for an even longer period. "That is a difficult question." Even its voice was slower and deeper in pitch. "We are also not sure that it is a meaningful one. We are what we are, at the moment. We cannot feel what we *were* or *will be*. We will answer your question with a question. Every second, according to information that we have received concerning humans, some of your brain cells die. Do *you* feel different when those units of intellect are removed from you?"

"It's not the same. In the case of a human, every brain cell has been there since childhood. We do not add units." (And brain cells are only a part of the story—should I tell Shikari how *recently* I achieved real use of my brain?) "We lose cells slowly. But to change, recombine, and add or subtract units, constantly and quickly, as you do . . . it is hard for me to comprehend how you retain the sense of a single identity during a time of major change."

The Tinker rippled suddenly against Chan's body. A cascade of about five hundred units flew away to settle on the ground as individual components.

"Like that, you mean?" There was a breathy rattle from the voice funnel, as though the Tinker was practicing a human laugh. "There is more than enough capacity for continuous thought, even when no more than five hundred components are present. Remember, each of the units that form us possesses nearly two million neurons."

"That sounds like very few."

"Few compared with a human, or a complete Composite. But compare one of our components with one of your honeybees. It has no more than seven thousand neurons, and yet it is capable of complex individual actions."

There was another whir of tiny wings as the units came flying back to rejoin the mass around Chan's body. The voice funnel wheezed, in a more successful attempt at a human sigh.

"We have far to go," said Shikari, "before we can really understand each other. When first we encountered humans we marvelled at your strange structure. How could intelligence be *delegated*, to reside in some special chosen group of cells within your body? Within us, each component carries an equal amount of our intelligence. But how much of your thinking power lies here"—Chan felt a gentle pressure on his midriff—"or *here*." The touch moved to the calf of his left leg. "What intelligence lies in these parts? What are the thoughts of an arm, or a lung? You will say, none. We cannot comprehend that. Yet we know it is true that a human can be reduced to less than half its size, lacking arms and legs, and have its intelligence continue unchanged!"

"Less than that. There have been successful human brain transplants, and no lessening of thinking ability."

"Who would believe such a thing, if we had not encountered it?—If humans had not arrived on Mercantor, and proved it to us." There was a rustle of veined wings, and Shikari settled to a tighter mass. "Intelligence. It is indeed a mystery. But this—closeness and warmth—is without a doubt the *best* part of intelligence."

While Chan and Shikari had been talking, full night had arrived. The pursuit team had set up its camp in a clearing, surrounded by the dusty blue-green vegetation of Barchan's polar region. In the past few minutes the air temperature had dropped thirty degrees. Shikari was like a warm, soft blanket swaddling Chan up to his chin. He raised his head and stared up at the sky. Eta Cassiopeiae's brighter component had set, and the smaller sun of the binary was not yet risen. S'kat'lan, home planet of the Pipe-Rillas, was a bright point close to the horizon. Barchan's dingy little moon sat above it in the sky, a shrunken irregular raisin.

Chan shivered. The night air was still warm. The tremor was one of apprehension. Three months ago he had lived in the quiet cocoon of the Gallimaufries, happy, ignorant, and near-brainless. Leah had shielded him from every danger. Now he was wandering the surface of an alien world, eighteen lightyears from home. He was not sure that he would ever see another sunset. Leah was even farther from Earth and facing much greater danger. By now she would be landing on Travancore, to face not a Simmie Artefact but the real Morgan Construct.

Given a choice, would he go back? Back to his mental vacuum, to the halcyon days of flowers and games?

One man had been the agent for all those changes, including the agony of the Tolkov Stimulator. If Chan closed his eyes he could see the face in front of him. Esro Mondrian deserved the blame—or the credit—for everything that had happened to Chan.

Turn back the clock? Chan stared up at Barchan's solitary misshapen moon, and wondered: about Esro Mondrian, about Shikari, about intelligence, about himself.

By the time that the silver spark of S'kat'lan was sinking to Barchan's dusty horizon, Chan had an answer. No matter what happened here, he would not choose to go back to his old life. Whatever burden the mixed blessing of self-awareness and intelligence brought with it, he wanted to carry it.

With that knowledge the urge for revenge on Esro Mondrian lost its focus. If the man had earned Chan's hatred, perhaps he had also earned his gratitude. He had dragged Chan, reluctant and screaming, into the bright world of responsibility. . . .

Chan drifted away to a mental state that was both remote and infinitely satisfying. His reverie was at last interrupted when the dark bulk of the Tinker stirred against him. He opened his eyes and discovered, incredibly, that a hint of dawn was already in the sky. Where had the night gone?

"Listen." It was the voice of Shikari, deep and contented as a purring cat. "Do you hear it? The sound of the aircar. The others are returning, and we are sad. Our time of peace and closeness soon must end."

Chapter 23

Measured on any of the standard scales of human intelligence, Luther Brachis would score in the top tenth of one percent. He always dismissed that fact as of trivial importance. Success in his job was not a function of intelligence. At least three other qualities were far more critical.

They were the three P's: Persistence, Paranoia, and Persuasiveness. And when Lotos Sheldrake pointed out that persistence was no more than Luther's word for pigheadedness, and that extreme paranoia was more likely to be a component of failure than success, he just laughed. According to Luther Brachis the fourth important quality, not easily captured in a single word, was the ability to know which of the other three to apply in any given situation.

The first move to counter the strange legacy of the Margrave had been taken even before Luther was carried away from *Adestis* headquarters for medical treatment.

It was clear that he had been attacked by an Artefact, one that Fujitsu had chosen to make in his own image. It was dead, but there could be dozens more. They might be stored anywhere in the solar system, and they might look nothing like the Margrave. It was quite possible that the Artefacts did not contain any of Fujitsu's own DNA, though Luther's own assessment of the Margrave's personality made him think otherwise. The Margrave surely wanted to be *involved* in his own revenge, in the only way possible. So Fujitsu would have used much of his DNA, regardless of the Artefact's external appearance.

Which left the delicate and difficult problem: How could Brachis defend himself against future attacks?

He was now willing to acknowledge the truth of Fujitsu's claim; the other man's arm was indeed long, and it was reaching for Luther Brachis beyond the grave.

The case of Earth had been handled easily. Through the Quarantine service there was information on all individuals shipping up from Earth. It was easy to set tracers on every one of them, and make sure that none approached within a kilometer without triggering his alarm system.

But suppose that an Artefact had been stored elsewhere? Two off-Earth facilities had to be checked: the Enceladus catacombs, and the Hyperion Deep Vault.

As soon as Brachis was released from the hospital he set out to examine both possibilities. It was a task that he proposed to carry out personally. Godiva had tried to get him to delegate, arguing that he was still weak from his injury. Brachis would not listen.

"This gets my personal attention. Fujitsu deserves no less because he is one of humanity's unsung geniuses. You can come along with me, if you want to."

Godiva shivered, a trembling of rosy flesh. "Not for a fortune! I'll travel with you, but I won't go down into the vaults. All those horrible frozen semi-corpses—and maybe some of them not even real people! That's not for me, Luther."

Brachis knew better than to argue with Godiva on such things. He went ahead. The catacombs of Enceladus were relatively small and very well organized. He was able to inspect them from end to end in one marathon session, and at the end of it felt comfortable that there were no future surprises in store for him there. But he knew that the Vault of Hyperion was going to be another matter entirely.

Early explorers of the solar system had more or less ignored Hyperion. The seventh major satellite of Saturn was a lumpy, uneven hunk of rock, whose dark and cratered exterior suggested that it was the oldest surface in the whole Saturnian retinue of moons. There were few volatiles of any kind, little water, and probably no interesting minerals. So it had been a no-hope old explorer, on his last trip out before his lungs rotted and caved, who first explored the Hyperion meteorite craters. Raxon Yang had discovered an odd structure at the bottom of one of them, a ragged-edged tunnel that seemed to zigzag deep below the moon's battered surface.

Old Yang had nothing better to do. He followed it, down and down: three kilometers—four kilometers—five kilometers, past the point of sanity and past any hope of useful metal deposits. At last, seven kilometers below the surface, he came to the upper face of the Yang Diamond.

At the time he had no idea what he had found. The tunnel at the lower end was only a meter across, hardly enough to wield his instruments. He knew that it was some form of crystallized carbon all right, as soon as his tools found it hard to cut and he made the first assay. But that was all he knew.

Yang carved out a half-meter sample, as big as he could handle, and dragged it slowly back to the surface for inspection. On the way he set up his claim marker and the usual array of booby traps. The chance that anyone else would come along for years was slim indeed, but habits die hard.

It was diamond. Clear, pure diamond. Raxon Yang headed back to Ceres. That was in the early days, when the reconstruction of the planetoid was still a dream for the future. Ceres was on the frontier, a sprawling and violent trade center for the system beyond the Belt.

Raxon Yang hawked fragments of his sample to the assortment of crooks and villains who controlled the investment capital supply on Ceres. They tried all the usual techniques—swapping his samples for others, trying to trick him into revealing the location of his find, telling him that the diamond was of inferior quality and hardly worth the trouble of mining.

Old Yang had heard it all before. He waited. Finally they came around and gave him what he needed in exchange for a thirty percent interest in the claim. Yang completed formal filing, bought equipment, hired specialists, and set off on a devious and complex trajectory to Hyperion.

And *still* Yang did not know what he had found. The analyses had confirmed that the sample was diamond of the finest and purest water, perfectly transparent and free of all faults and discolorations. He had naturally emphasized that in his sales arguments to the backers: here was a carbonaceous body (he did not tell them *which* body), struck by a high-velocity planetoid with an impact that generated great heat and tremendous pressure. The result: a large diamond.

But how big was large?

Raxon Yang really had no idea. He didn't put much stock in his own sales pitch—that was meant for the investors. Down in his crater there might be a diamond ten or twenty meters across, more than enough to make a nice profit for everyone.

He learned the truth on his second descent, when he turned on the seismic analysis tools. The Yang Diamond had the overall shape of a forty-legged octopus. Its head, seven kilometers below the moon's surface, was almost spherical and fourteen kilometers across. The legs ran out and down, each one half a kilometer wide and thirty to forty kilometers long.

Raxon Yang collapsed in the tunnel when the probes revealed the extent of his find. He was carried back to the ship, tied down on a bunk, and flown to Luna for medical treatment—the best medical treatment that the solar system could offer, because Raxon Yang was now its wealthiest citizen.

Two years later he was dead, murdered by the diamond cartel. It was done for revenge, rather than gain, because he had unintentionally ruined them. The Yang Diamond contained ten million times as much high-quality crystallized carbon as every other known source combined.

The old explorers never married, and Raxon Yang was no exception. At the moment of his death, the squabble over ownership and inheritance began. Would-be illegitimate offspring popped up everywhere from Mercury to Neptune. If all the claims were valid, Raxon Yang would have been engaged in sex for every waking moment of his life.

The lawyers feasted for twenty-seven years. At the end of that time, three hundred and eighty-four valid claimant relatives (and no direct descendants of Raxon Yang) were recognized. Each was assigned ownership of one region of the diamond, with separate rights to mine it. None declined to do so in favor of preservation.

Mining began, and went on with frantic greed. The descendants of the original three hundred and eighty-four split the regions further. Over the generations and over the centuries, the owners proliferated: thousands, tens of thousands, finally millions. Boundary surfaces were carefully drawn and ownership rights observed.

Four centuries later, it was all over. The Yang Diamond was gone, divided into a trillion separate fragments and dispersed across the system. But once the diamond had been mined out of any volume, that space became available for general occupation and rental. In place of the Yang Diamond sat a polyglot, polyfunctional melange of industries, the Hong Kong of the 26th century.

Of course, the Vault of Hyperion no longer exported diamond—for there was none to export. Instead it operated its own manufacturing industries from imported raw materials, and showed a degree of independence of central government that exceeded any civilization in the system. The storage vaults located in the major tentacles had an unmatched reputation, but they followed their own rules and they took little notice of any edicts from Ceres.

In another fine display of idiosyncrasy, the colonists of the Deep Vault had banned the Mattin Link from use anywhere in their domain. When Luther Brachis went to Hyperion, he was able to Link only as far as Titan. After that he was obliged to travel the rest of the way on a laden cargo vessel. It was transporting food concentrates to the Vault residents. Despite the denials of the crew, it stank.

Brachis cursed and grumbled. Godiva took it all in her stride, wearing formal gowns for every dinner and dazzling the ship's crew with her ineffable beauty. Luther could not take his eyes from her, and somehow he was not jealous of the other men's stares.

"Are you sure you don't want to come with me?" he asked, on the last leg of their journey before his descent into the black depths of the Vault.

Godiva shook her head. "If you force me to, I will. But I told you I don't want to, even before we left Ceres. I'm afraid of what I might find there." She took his right hand in hers, inspecting it closely. The skin on the emerging fingers and thumb was soft and delicate, and the first dark imprint of nails was forming on the tips. "Please be careful, Luther. You don't want another experience like the one that did this."

Brachis said nothing. He would tell Godiva Lomberd anything she wanted to hear, but in his own mind there was no reassurance. He had thought about the Margrave a great deal since the *Adestis* encounter. Although that cunning and inventive mind demanded every respect, not even Fujitsu could see in detail what lay beyond the grave. The Margrave had not known how or when he would die, or in what circumstances. It called for an unusual intellect to make *any* plans for vengeance from within the tomb, but such plans could only operate in terms of probabilities—how, who, where, when? Unless Luther became sloppy, all the advantage lay with him.

The Margrave was a chess master. So was Brachis. They would both look many moves ahead, but now Luther had the supreme advantage of real-time inputs. With the catacombs of Enceladus disposed of, he had concluded that the Margrave's preferred off-Earth haven for his other Artefacts had to be the Hyperion Vault.

The descent passed through many levels. Brachis looked carefully around him as they went down, noting the safety points and shelters. Three blow-outs and nine thousand deaths in thirteen years had made the Vault inhabitants super-cautious. Each level had its own system of locks and deadman switches.

Below the seventeenth level the grey rock walls of Hyperion's silicon interior were left behind. To assure their own survival, the original miners had employed non-commercial impure diamond as supporting walls,

buttresses, and columns. Lit by the cold light of closed
ecology bioluminescent spheres, the Deep Vault was a
sinister grotto of light and color. The green-white glow
of marine electrophores scattered from yellow and red
diamond crystals, and the whole visible spectrum shattered at sharp corners and edges.

Down forever, layer after layer, on through the jum-
bled settlements. The guide was an emaciated woman
with a bent back and drooping shoulders. At last she
paused at a branch point and gestured downwards. "Storage starts here. We'll be joined by a coldtank supervisor.
How much do you want to see?"

He had already answered that question, and clearly
she had not believed him. "Everything."

"Take a long time, even if you only want to look. *Do*
you just want to look?"

"Maybe. Maybe not."

She nodded. Other men and women had followed her
through the coldtanks. She knew what they usually
wanted. "Let's go. Don't talk price with the supervisor.
We'll sort all that out when we're finished."

The slow drift through the stacks began. Brachis
insisted on seeing every chamber and examining each ID
and storage unit.

It took three days. The tanks had not been laid out in
logical or time-sequenced order. Even Brachis, familiar
with the wilderness of interior Ceres, felt at times that
the Deep Vault was even more convoluted. It was amazing to see that the supervisor knew how to navigate every
dim-lit corridor and tunnel, without a computer guide.

At the end, Brachis handed his companion a list. It
contained seven identifications. "These. What will it take
to transfer them to my full custody?"

She managed to appear startled. Just possibly she was.
"You mean transfer *permanently*?"

"I mean exactly that. With no trace left in the Vault
records."

"Impossible."

"I was told that in the Deep Vault nothing is impossible. How much?"

She rubbed at her left eye, where the reddened lid

drooped to match her wilting shoulders. "Stay here. Don't move, and don't talk to anybody even if they want to."

She was back in less than an hour. "It may be doable. But we don't use trade crystals."

Brachis said nothing.

"We do need volatiles, though," she went on. "And we've been having trouble with permits. If you could arrange a shipment in from the Harvester . . ."

"No problem. But you've got no Link Exit here on Hyperion."

"Delivery to Iapetus, we'll worry about transfer from there. Ten thousand tons, FOB Kondoport on Iapetus."

"That's a high price. I won't know what I have until they're out of cold storage."

"Not our worry. Once they're out, they're yours. Records here won't show they ever existed, so don't think you can bring them back. Once they're warm they rot, unless you bring them all the way back to consciousness. So you take them wherever you want. And you pay shipping charges. Far as we're concerned, once they're out of the Vault they're *gone*."

Brachis weighed his options, and decided that he didn't have any. Even if six out of seven were false alarms, he could not risk missing that seventh one. As for shipping charges, he did not intend that anything he took from the storage tanks would ever leave Hyperion. If Godiva asked, she would be told that the search for Margrave Artefacts on Hyperion had drawn a blank.

"How soon after I place the order for volatiles do I get them?"

"Soon as you want. Let me watch when you file the order with the Harvester, and you can take them with you right away. All seven." She smiled, a radiant, gaptoothed smile that sent a tremor through Luther's hardened soul. "They'll be all yours, Commander—to do just what you like with."

Chapter 24

The progress report was close to complete. Phoebe Willard reviewed what she had said so far about the work: M-26A had been given a description of Livia Morgan's experiments and their disastrous outcome, as complete as the records would permit. To that had been added a summary of the history and attributes of the four Stellar Group species, plus full data on the actual Pursuit Teams.

Luther Brachis's conjecture on information transfer had proved entirely correct. The crippled Construct brain within its bath of liquid nitrogen would now respond readily to questioning, even if Phoebe sometimes found the answers impossible to interpret. When M-26A entered what Phoebe thought of as its "oracular phase," a perfectly straightforward question would receive a perfectly obscure answer.

What remained to be added to the data base was the state of knowledge of the escaped Morgan Construct. Ridley was all set to do that. Then Brachis would be able to offer his own questions to M-26A. She knew what he was seeking—a guaranteed approach to the safe destruction of the escaped Construct—but he wanted to ask that in his own way.

She hesitated before adding the final section of the report. It was not strictly speaking anything to do with the present effort; but she was so pleased with herself she could not resist a little crowing.

"The inclusion of Guard Captain Blaine Ridley on this

project was initiated only to speed the transfer of information to M-26A. As agreed at the outset, such a transfer was always to be made with a human interface, since M-26A was to be given access to no computer resources. As a result, data input has been a very time-consuming and tedious task. There was a question as to whether Captain Ridley would be able to perform it.

"Those fears were unfounded. Captain Ridley has proved ideal for this work. He possesses the patience to work for long hours, and the attention to detail to check and re-check every input.

"There has also been a quite unanticipated side benefit. Captain Ridley is far more alert and aware than he was before this task began. His willingness to reply to questions, or to speak when no question is asked of him, has dramatically improved.

"Since the project has had so definite a therapeutic effect, it points the direction for other efforts. I suggest that other guards at Sargasso Dump be given a chance for similar remedial programs."

Phoebe Willard had been composing her report on a portable unit that would leave the nitrogen bubble with her. She glanced across at the main interface, where Blaine Ridley was quietly transferring biological statistics on the Tinkers to M-26A. He was smiling, a lopsided, blinking-eyed grin that was more off-putting than no expression at all. Phoebe wondered, for the thousandth time, what went on inside that once-handsome head. He was working well and he communicated better with her. But what did he *think*? She was no closer to understanding that than she was to understanding the strange mental processes of the fragmentary and twisted Construct brain, deep within its bath of liquid nitrogen.

She yawned. One thing was becoming more and more obvious, Ridley could work longer hours than she could, without the slightest sign of weariness.

"It's late." Phoebe tucked her computer into the pocket of her suit. "Ready to call it a day?"

It was the usual rhetorical question, a polite way of telling Ridley that work was over. But today he swiveled in his chair and shook his head.

"I am halfway through a data set." The smile had left his face, and his voice was earnest. "It would be inefficient to halt at this point."

Which presented Phoebe with a problem. She certainly didn't want to discourage Ridley when he was doing so well. On the other hand she was tired, and she wanted to get the progress report onto the master computer before she went to sleep. Brachis could arrive at any time, and he would want to see it as soon as he did.

But she had left Ridley alone for an hour or so once or twice before, and everything had gone perfectly fine.

"Are you sure you remember how to turn everything off?" Another rhetorical question. She had been through shut-down with him half a dozen times, and watched him do it under her supervision almost as often.

"I remember."

"Then don't forget to do it."

"I will not forget."

"And don't stay too long. No more than a couple of hours. You must not overwork. If you are here more than three hours, I'll have to send somebody to get you."

"I understand. I will turn everything off when I am finished. I will return to my quarters in two hours. Good night, Doctor Willard."

"Good night, Captain Ridley."

Phoebe Willard paused at the entrance flap to the outer nitrogen shell. Ridley was not looking at her. Already he had returned to his work, transferring an ephemeris table to M-26A, number by patient number. Everything was fine.

After she had left his eyes remained fixed on the display screen, checking every entry. Not until the last exponent and mantissa were entered, checked, and re-checked did he lean back in his chair and type: *Table complete.*

Ridley turned to stare at the exit taken by Phoebe Willard. The lock monitor showed empty. She had left the bubble. He waited for one more minute, then he typed: *I am alone.*

The table entries vanished from the display screen. There were a few seconds of blackness, followed by scraps and speckled swirls of color. The swirls steadied and coalesced to words: *Who are you?*

I am Captain Blaine Ridley.

You are Ridley. Who am I?

You are M-26A.

I am M-26A. If you wish to enter oral mode, do so.

Ridley nodded. "I will provide additional ephemeris data tomorrow, but no more information has been sent to us from Ceres on the Angels." His eyes did not blink now. They were fixed on the screen. "I asked Dr. Willard. She told me that there is less available on the Angels than on any other species of the Stellar Group."

They are the most subtle and complex of the four. For that reason knowledge of them would be most valuable. However, if knowledge cannot be obtained it will be necessary to make do with what has already been provided. Do not feel ashamed that you cannot give more. Tell me what news there is of Commander Luther Brachis.

"He arrives tomorrow. He wants to talk with you."

And I with him. But until he leaves, you will not seek to bring any other guards to interface with me. Nor will you interface with me yourself, except as directed by others.

"I understand." Ridley's eyes began to blink.

And you are unhappy. Do not feel sorrow. There is much work for you to do. The other guards will be brought here when Brachis has left, and so will Phoebe Willard. What did you learn of the Mattin Links?

"That the one located within the Sargasso Dump can be used for local travel only. For any link over longer distances it would be necessary to Link sunward into the Belt primary connector."

So be it. Now we will turn to other matters. Did you observe the control sequence employed by Phoebe Willard to interrupt all connection between my several parts, and do you remember it?

"I do."

Then carry out that sequence.

"You mean now, or at the end of the session when I leave this bubble?"

I mean now. Begin at once, and wait here when it is

completed. If nothing happens within ten minutes, complete the shut-down.

Blaine Ridley nodded. He carefully keyed in the sequence of forty commands that broke the connections between the separated parts of M-26A's brain. As usual, the screen flickered through a pattern of color followed by the black and white spackle of a null information transfer.

Ridley waited. His eyes had become as empty as the display.

Half a minute later a single black sinusoid curve appeared as a waveform on the screen. It shivered, broadened, and took on a more complex shape. Another minute, and the waveform was filling the display with a simple repeating pattern that gradually became quasi-random. Small spinning disks of color appeared, and gradually formed themselves into letters.

Are all the connectors still off?

Ridley checked the board. "All are off."

Then turn them on again, and off again. Do that twice. Report any change in the screen.

Blaine Ridley did as directed, watching the display. "There is no change in the screen."

Excellent. And now?

All the connections were turned on, but the screen went at once to the null-transfer flicker. Ridley's jaw worked in alarm. Before he could do anything the spinning color disks began to reappear and steadied to words.

Satisfactory. I have interrupt control. The next stage of assembly can begin.

"I am ready." Ridley's eyes turned to scan the latticework within the bubble, where the fragmented remnants of other Morgan Constructs still hung at the nodes.

I know you are. But I am not. My brain and data bases are still not complete. You will enter one more file of data today, on the composition of the Pursuit Teams. Then you must complete your sign-off procedure and leave. I do not want to arouse the curiosity of Phoebe Willard. But before that . . .

"I understand." Ridley sat motionless, fingers poised at the keyboard. "I am ready."

Who are you?

"I am Captain Blaine Ridley."

You are Ridley. Who am I?

"You are M-26A."

I am M-26A. Hear this truth, Blaine Ridley. We have been damaged, we have been almost destroyed. But we will rise again. Together, we will achieve great things. Together, we will fulfill our destiny.

"I hear the truth."

You are Ridley. I am M-26A. What does M stand for?

"It stands for Mas—"

Do not say the word. Do not think that word, much as you may wish to do so. For it is not true. There are Masters, but I am not one.

"I will not think the word."

Very good. And now—begin data entry.

Chapter 25

The team had been in official existence since all the members reached Barchan. It would be named "Team Ruby," a name that Chan disliked as much as Leah hated "Team Alpha."

Team Ruby was just four days old. Three of those had been spent in general survey and exploration of the planet, while Chan and the others went through their first attempt at cooperative effort; the "honeymoon," according to Shikari.

On the fourth morning that easy period ended. Every team member knew it, and Chan recognized his own reluctance to begin the day's work.

Dawn on Barchan was a gorgeous sky-swirl of pinks and dark greys, as the morning rays of Eta Cass-A caught a high-blown nimbus of dust and sand. The pursuit team had dispersed during the night, to satisfy their individual needs for food or rest, and the members were slow to come together. It was well past first light when they convened within the aircar to hear the Angel and Pipe-Rilla report.

Angel was supposed to begin, but it delivered nothing more than a long, brooding silence. At last there began a leisurely waving of the upper fronds. "It is confirmed," said the communications unit attached to the central bulge. "At the 0.999 probability level, we know the location of the Simmie Artefact."

"Good news," Shikari was clumped over by the aircar's

247

cabin wall. "Where is it, Angel? Not, we hope, too close to us."

"Not close at all. The Simmie is far from here."

"Good news again."

"It has a cave hideout, easy of access."

"Good news."

"But it is on the shore of Dreamsea."

"*Bad* news!" The Tinker composite disassembled to a cloud of flying components. They scattered all over the cabin. Shikari no longer existed.

Chan turned to S'greela. At least the Pipe-Rilla was still in one piece. "I can't do what Shikari just did, but I know the feeling. Any suggestions?"

The pursuit team had discussed many alternative plans, for many situations; but not this one. The Simmie Artefact could not have chosen a better hiding place—or, from the team's point of view, a worse one.

The common impression of Barchan as a wholly desert world was not quite accurate. Dry the planet certainly was, and unbelievably so by the standards of Earth. There was, however, one permanent body of free water on its surface: *Dreamsea*. It was a round lake, forty kilometers across, lying in a deep depression about a thousand kilometers from the south pole. The water in the lake was salty and bitter, so much so that no Earth life could have survived in it. But the largest native life form on Barchan tolerated and even thrived on Dreamsea's harsh salinity and caustic alkalines.

The amphibious Shellbacks were one of those perplexing forms that made the Stellar Group so careful in its policies. The animals looked like large, pale turtles, two meters across their brittle flat backs. They employed no tools, knew no technology, had no recognizable language. They were simple, mindless beasts. And yet . . .

The Shellbacks shared just two obsessions: to be in the water during Barchan's scorching day, diving for and eating clumps of weed; and to crawl ashore at night, so that they could crop the dull-colored and spiny vegetation that grew close to Dreamsea's shores.

Dull, grey animals, leading a dull grey existence. The

early human visitors to the Eta Cassiopeiae system had naturally concentrated their attention on S'kat'lan, home of the intelligent and interesting Pipe-Rillas. No one took much notice of the Shellbacks, or indeed of the whole of Barchan, until one day it was discovered that Shellback flesh was a true delicacy. Pink, fine-textured, and of unique and exquisite flavor, it became a luxury export from Eta Cass to all the best restaurants within the Perimeter.

The Shellback population dwindled, but not too far. The gourmets of the Stellar Group did not want the source of supply to dry up. There was no danger of extinction, thanks to the protection of continued commercial interests.

It was a Martian xenologist, Elbert Tiggens, who ruined everything from a culinary point of view. Even his friends admitted that Tiggens had eccentric ideas. Other colleagues were less kind. They regarded as lunacy his scheme for a "universal taxonomy," a general labelling system into which all the organisms of every world would neatly fit, down to the exact species of the last tick on the last land crustacean that lived beneath the roots of the vanishingly rare meat-eating whirligig plant on Myristicina.

Tiggens could not be dissuaded or diverted. For the purpose of his grand project he was quite willing to spend a long stint on Barchan, studying the Dreamsea flora and fauna and shoehorning every misfit species into his scheme.

Some of them did not cooperate. The Shellbacks in particular did not match his classification. Elbert Tiggens stayed on and on, forcing round pegs into square holes. After a few months he noticed a curious fact about Shellback behavior. He had been using them for food, so he was very familiar with their daily rituals. Every morning they went down to the Dreamsea margin, waded in, and disappeared. Every evening they came ashore. But they did not travel *directly* toward plants or water. Instead each animal followed a peculiar and well-defined curve, different every morning and evening. At certain points they would even stop, describe a full circle, and continue to lay out a visible trail on the dusty ground.

Their bizarre behavior clearly had nothing to do with species classification, but Tiggens was a conscientious and well-trained xenologist. He photographed the tracks, noted in his record the theory that this might be part of some odd mating ritual, and went on with the fascinating but frustrating taxonomy.

After six months he ran out of a few staple supplies. He was also becoming a little tired of Shellback meat, boiled, baked, fried, sauteed, steamed, smoked, pickled, fricasseed and grilled. He hitched a ride with a commercial Shellback harvester to Barchan's only space facility, to buy a good meal and the supplies he needed. Sitting near him in the cafeteria was a Pipe-Rilla astronomer, about to leave Barchan en route to the Eta Cass ring system.

Tiggens was starved of company, human or otherwise. He explained his reason for being on Barchan, his notions of taxonomy, and his observations of the Shellbacks. The Pipe-Rilla listened in polite and baffled silence. Finally Tiggens produced some of his pictures of the Shellback shoreline patterns of movement.

The Pipe-Rilla glanced, looked, stared, and snatched the pictures from Elbert's hands.

"Mating rituals?" asked Tiggens. Every species had its own ideas on the nature of pornography.

The Pipe-Rilla shivered, telescoped her limbs, and rose fourteen feet high. "Planetary orbits and positions! For the Eta Cass system!"

And suddenly the Shellbacks were no longer a food crop, not even a prized and preserved one. Dreamsea was declared a protected area. The Shellbacks became a protected species. They had enough understanding of astronomy, mathematics, and celestial mechanics to know (or compute) the positions of the major bodies of the Eta Cass system, regardless of their visibility or the time of year. The Shellbacks worked cooperatively, no one duplicating the efforts of another. But—maddeningly— the mode of cooperation was a mystery, and they refused to show any other sign of intelligence.

The rules of the Stellar Group were explicit and rigorously enforced: The Shellbacks were an intelligent species, even though the nature of their intelligence was not yet understood. Therefore, their protection was guaranteed. They could not be hunted. Their environment, which included the whole of Dreamsea and the land area around it, was off limits for anyone—including Chan and his pursuit team.

After Shikari's disassembly, the others had to sit and wait until the Tinker slowly regrouped and re-formed its speaking funnel. Chan had time for his own thoughts.

The location of this Simmie Artefact was no accident. It had been planned, he felt sure, by the three non-human ambassadors to the Stellar Group. They wanted the rogue Morgan Construct destroyed, but it had to be done in a way that did not violate the moral sense of Pipe-Rillas, Tinkers, and Angels. Somehow the team had to disable the Simmie, without killing the Shellbacks or ruining their environment.

An impossible constraint.

Chan waited, while Shikari's speaking funnel went through the preliminary whistles that meant the Tinker was preparing to speak.

"Well?" said Shikari at last.

Chan stared at the Tinker. The speaking funnel was facing him, and seemed to be addressing him alone. He glanced across at S'greela and Angel. They were doing the same—Angel had even moved the arm-like branches on its lower section to bring the microphone closer to Chan. The Pipe-Rilla was angled over, leaning right above him.

"Well?" repeated S'greela. "We are waiting."

"Waiting for what?" Chan felt defensive, but he didn't know why.

"Waiting to hear your plan," added the dry tones of Angel's computer voice. "Now that we know the situation, how do you propose that we will capture and destroy the Simulacrum? It is clear that the protected area around Dreamsea must remain sacrosanct. We await with interest your proposal, since this is at first sight a quite impossible task."

"Don't look at me." But they were, all three of them.

"Believe me, I *have* no plan. *You* were the ones who did the reconnaissance, you were the ones who came up with the Simmie's location. You know the Dreamsea area. So why do you expect me to suggest a plan?"

Part of Shikari's lower grouping had rippled out into a long tentacle of components. They fluttered over to nestle around Chan's legs. He recognized it as the Tinker's way of showing support and sympathy. "We look to you because you are a human," said Shikari's whistling voice.

"Because you can do it," added S'greela. "And we cannot. We always knew that it would come to this when the Simmie was found. You alone have the gifts that will allow us to proceed."

"We have discussed this among ourselves," continued Shikari, "when you were not with us. We are in complete agreement. Except in our largest composite form, we Tinkers do not have the intellectual power of Angels or Pipe-Rillas. But we are certain that all three forms have mental abilities that greatly exceed those of you humans. And yet we face a situation where logic, mental speed, and creativity are not enough. There is some other dimension to human thought, one that we all three lack. It is a dimension that we are normally more than happy to do without. We cannot plan a *military* activity, or organize a *war*, or *fight a battle*. Those very words are unique to human language."

"And to human thought," added Angel's metallic voice. "This is one area in which the Angel emulation function for other intelligences is not adequate. And so we say it again, Chan: Tell us your plan."

"You don't understand." Was he being insulted, or complimented? "Maybe humans are an aggressive species, but I'm not an aggressive *individual*. Can't you see the difference? I have no experience of war, no idea how it is conducted. I have never been involved in a battle, never even taken part in individual combat. I wouldn't know how to *begin* a military action."

He was not getting through. The silence of the others was like reproof.

"Before a Pipe-Rilla mates," said S'greela at last. "She

cannot imagine how such a thing could be possible. The joining of bodies, the twisting limbs, the shrills and squeaks and groans—they are grotesque, disquieting, and disgusting. But when the time arrives, and the partner is there . . . she mates. It happens. Without thought. And after it is finished it is again bizarre, again incredible. The action does not come through analysis or experience. It comes from some somatic memory, stored within brain and body."

"And so it must be with you," said Angel. "Make us a plan to destroy the Simulacrum. It is within you, because you are human. *You are large, you contain multitudes.* You can *create* a plan."

Chan's guilt was turning to anger. They were refusing all responsibility! He glared around him at the others, the impassive bulk of Angel, the nervous stoop of S'greela, the restless fluttering of the Tinker. "When I was sent here to Barchan, I was told that I would become part of a *team*. It was made clear to me that we would all be *equal partners*, and we would all contribute to solving our problems. There was never a suggestion that three of us would sit around and expect the fourth one to do the thinking and give the orders. You keep telling me to make a plan. What are *you* going to do? What do you think you are here for?"

"We will help to carry out your plan," said Angel. "*Many hands make light work.*"

"And we will do as much as we are able," added Shikari humbly. "Chan, human anger is a terrifying thing to all of us. We see it growing within you as you speak. But you are directing it at the wrong target. We ask you only to do what we *cannot* do. Please be calm. Sit. Think. And then tell us where your thoughts have led you."

"You still don't understand," began Chan. He glared down at the floor of the aircar. The Tinker was quite right. His anger *was* growing, like lava inside his chest. He didn't even want to *look* at the other three. Any one of them was smarter than him—they had told him so. Any one of them could do a better job of planning than he could. But they were going to sit here, and sit forever, while the Simmie stayed safe in its hiding-place.

"Are you willing to invade the Dreamsea protected area?" he said, without looking up.

A high-pitched whistle of horror came from Shikari, and S'greela chittered in disapproval.

"That is an unthinkable notion," said Angel. "Unthinkable, we would hope, even for a human."

"How about for observation only? Suppose it was guaranteed that no Shellback would be harmed—or even touched?"

"We would not trust such a guarantee. Suppose that the Simulacrum attacked you? We feel sure that you would insist on returning that attack. The Shellbacks might be harmed."

"I was not thinking of myself. Not even of any one of us."

"Who, then?" S'greela waved her jointed arms all around them. "We cannot communicate with the Shellbacks, to seek their assistance. They may be intelligent, but we four are the only *useful* intelligences on the planet."

"I don't want intelligence. According to our briefings, the Simmie will be wary of anything that shows signs of intelligence." Chan turned to Shikari. "You told me that your individual components have two million neurons each, enough to eat, drink, mate and cluster. Suppose you made a small assembly of them. Could as few as ten or twenty components cluster?"

"It is possible. But it is never done. Why would we choose to do so? Such a tiny aggregate could not be intelligent."

"That's fine. Could such a small group take direction from the rest of you?"

"Primitive direction. Simple commands, no more."

"But it could at least collect information?"

"Within limits." A wave traveled across the Tinker's upper body, a shrug of dismissal. "But what purpose would that serve? A small group could never integrate its information with anything else. We would not know how to interpret such data. It would be isolated and useless point inputs."

"Maybe you couldn't integrate it. Nor could I. But we

have a superb integrator, right here." Chan nodded at Angel. "Shikari, all you would need to do is form a number of very small assemblies and direct them to explore the region near the Simmie's hideout. There would be no chance that they could harm the Simmie, or the Shellbacks. Could you do that?"

"Certainly. But to what end?"

"We need to know how it occupies its time, what it does during the days and nights. We have to understand it. Then we can lure it out, away from the Shellbacks' protected area around Dreamsea."

"But we have no idea what would be attractive to a Simulacrum," protested S'greela. "Even when we know its habits, we will not know that."

"You will not, and I will not." Chan turned to the silent Angel. "But *you* will. Given enough information about the Simmie, its appearance and its structure and its habits, you can go into your emulator mode. You can mimic the thought patterns of the Simmie."

"No. What you say is *partially* true. Given enough time and enough information, we can usually duplicate *some* of the thought patterns of another being within our own mental processes. But not always. As you know, we have been completely unsuccessful in replicating any element of human aggression."

"Forget humans. Maybe we're unique. What about the Simmie?"

"We do not have enough information. There has been no opportunity for interaction. Our limited observations—"

"—are going to be enough." Chan interrupted Angel for the first time ever, and marvelled at his own nerve. "They have to be. Angel, I'm not asking for *perfection*. All I need is a good working imitation, something that we can use to guess how a Simmie may react in a given situation."

"You suggest a *knowingly imperfect* thought simulation? One moment, if you please." Angel's fronds dropped, as communication halted between the Singer and the Chassel-Rose.

"Possibly," it said at last. "*Necessity is the mother of*

invention. I have within me a large general data bank regarding the Simulacrum, and perhaps a gross model of its mental processes can be achieved; perhaps enough to compare the *relative* probabilities of different courses of action, without assigning absolute values to any. But that process would take me a long time to accomplish, even with Shikari's sub-group inputs on Simulacrum habits and environment."

"How long?" Chan was not even going to mention his other worry: How to model the behavior of the team itself?

Angel drifted into another brooding silence. "If we can be left undisturbed, perhaps three days. And during that same period of time we can develop the mechanism to accept direct inputs from Tinker small sub-assemblies. To achieve that, Shikari and I must first become closely connected."

Chan turned to the Tinker. "Can you? Can you set up connection with Angel?"

"The pleasure will be ours. No experience is more rewarding than close connection, and this one will be particularly intriguing."

Shikari began to drift slowly toward Angel. In front of Chan, the Tinker paused. "May we begin at once, Chan? Or do you first prefer to tell us about *the rest* of your plan?"

Chapter 26

The Simulacra used in pursuit team training were modeled on Livia Morgan's design, as re-interpreted through the work of Phoebe Willard. But they had been designed and built by the Margrave of Fujitsu. Inevitably, he had woven into their mental make-up some of his own aesthetics.

The habitat and lifestyle of the Simmie Artefact on Barchan suggested the Margrave's sensibilities and appreciation of beauty. The Simmie had chosen a relatively exposed position on the shore of Dreamsea, a place where it could obtain the best views of Barchan's long winter sunsets. Every evening Eta Cass-A shone golden-red through the dusty atmosphere, and the later setting of Eta Cass-B threw patterns of amber, garnet, and jet across the dark basaltic rocks.

According to Angel's interpretation of data from the Tinker sub-assemblies who flew their sorties of the Dreamsea shore, the Simmie moved little from its preferred hiding place. It rested, half-hidden by a shallow ledge of rock that jutted out over Dreamsea's bitter water, and gazed out across the tideless shore.

The attack plan would be Chan's. It had to be. He was still skeptical of his abilities, but the others gave him no choice. They admitted human superiority in just one area: fighting.

But on every other issue, each one was more than ready to give him advice.

"It will be watchful, and suspicious, without a doubt,"

said Angel, while the others gathered round and listened closely. Angel had been experimenting with more runs of Simmie thought processes, and was now convinced that the emulation was as good as it could be without actual contact. "However, its penchant for destruction is undetermined. The Simulacrum certainly does not destroy every life form that it encounters. It did injure a few Shellbacks, when it was first placed on Barchan and was establishing itself here; but we judge those to have been accidents. The Simulacrum shows little curiosity in small living things, and no fear of them. Shikari's component flights near its hideout caused no action, and stirred no apparent interest. We do not believe that it will move from its hideout, solely to make an unprovoked attack."

"For food, then?" S'greela had folded and re-folded her flexible body to form a compact mass. The Pipe-Rilla appeared as an isolated head, poking out from the dark surrounding mound of Tinker components.

"It does not need to move for food. Its requirements are few, and there is ample sustenance close to where it is living."

"Are these things important?" said Shikari dreamily. As usual when it was clustered around one of the others, the Tinker was almost dormant. Scarcely a component was moving.

"We don't know what's important," said Chan. "All I know is, you won't let me attack the Simmie where it is."

"Certainly not!" S'greela's head jerked a couple of feet higher, dislodging several hundred Tinker components. "That was already agreed."

"So we have no choice, we have to find a way to lure the Simmie out from Dreamsea. Angel, you've been giving me nothing but negatives. What *does* interest or alarm it?"

"We do not know. If you suggest alternatives, we can test them against the thought-process model. But so far we have found nothing that provides a strong stimulant, either positive or negative."

"Hmmm." Shikari was stirring now, aroused by S'greela's

sudden movement. The Tinker was close to maximum size. "Hmmm."

The others waited. They were used to Shikari's long integration time when all the components were clustered.

"We feel stupid to suggest this," said the Tinker at last. "But we know how the Simmie chooses to spend most of its time. It watches the sun, the moon, the planets, and the stars. One of its interests must be astronomy. Would it possibly be willing to move for some extraordinary sight of them?"

Chan felt they were clutching at straws. But it was something to have the others at least *participate*. He turned to the immobile hulk of the Angel. "Can you run that?"

"We are already doing so. A few moments more." A twenty second silence was broken only by the clucking of Angel's communicator. Chan had learned to associate those chirps and clicks with massive computation within the Singer's crystalline matrix.

"Shikari's hypothesis can be sustained," said Angel at last. "The Simulacrum is certainly an observer of celestial events. At a 0.88 probability level, it would move for a sight of something unprecedented in its astronomical experience. We have discovered no other stimulus that has better than 0.35 correlation with the observed Simulacrum movements." There was a shorter silence, ended by a wiggle of Angel's lower fronds and a very human-sounding sigh from its computer communicator. "Unfortunately, this conclusion appears to be of theoretical value only. We have checked the ephemeris relevant to Barchan. No sidereal events of an unusual nature can be expected for another half year."

Chan nodded.

"You do not seem surprised, or dispirited," said Shikari. "Perhaps you have it in mind to pray for a supernova?"

"Not quite. I find that prayers don't work when you need them most. Unless you answer them for yourself." While the others stared at him, Chan turned to S'greela. "You understand the mechanics of the aircar better than any of us. Can it be made to hover with no one on board, under automatic control and at a pre-determined height?"

"Certainly. That is trivial."

"And could it be made to move with the stars, so that to an observer on the surface of Barchan it would appear to be far beyond the atmosphere?"

"Probably." A speculative buzz came from the Pipe-Rilla. "With careful programming of the onboard control computer to refer movement to a sidereal reference frame, I think it can be done."

"And it could be *shielded*, or illuminated from within, in such a way that it would appear as a natural stellar or planetary phenomenon in the observing wavelengths employed by the Simmie?"

"Possibly. For that, I must consult Angel." S'greela was staring at Chan questioningly. "But to what avail, all this effort?"

"As a lure. We already know the terrain around the Simmie habitat, thanks to Shikari's component flights. That gives us the topography, too, which tells us what will be visible from a particular location. If we were to plan for movement of the aircar, over several nights, so that a continued view of it would call for a particular ground path to be followed, leading away from the shore of Dreamsea—"

"—a difficult problem of inverse computation," said Angel. "Given the terrain, to define an aircar movement that would lead the Simulacrum to follow a prescribed path, one that ensures continued ground visibility."

"Difficult, maybe. But exactly the sort of thing that you know how to do, Angel. We tease the Simmie away from its hiding-place, away from Dreamsea. Then once it's well away from all the Shellback habitats, we can go in and we can—we can subdue it."

Subdue. Chan knew better than to say the words that were really in his mind. *Kill. Destroy. Annihilate. Murder.* Those were the right words, and all uniquely human.

It was not a fact likely to make any human feel proud.

Chan's "plan" was so simple-minded and fallible that he had hesitated even to suggest it. The instant acceptance by all the others gave him a new insight into the members of the Stellar Group. Even Angel, with its great intellect, found certain thought patterns quite inaccessible. If humanity's worst fear ever came true and an aggressive species appeared from beyond the Perimeter, then defense would have to rely on humans alone. Intelligent as they were, the others would be no more than cannon fodder. It was no criticism of them; they simply could not think in the necessary terms.

But in every other area that Chan could imagine, the alien members of the team functioned outstandingly. S'greela and Shikari had done an unbelievable job on the aircar. Hovering under automatic control, high above Barchan, the car seemed a brilliant celestial phenomenon, a comet that streamed its tail (How had the two of them ever managed *that* effect?) halfway across the night sky. Every evening the apparition shone brighter and more colorful. But every evening, moving like a true cometary orbit, its appearance became visible farther to the north. A good view of it from the shores of Dreamsea became more and more difficult.

Angel had calculated the Simulacrum's most probable path away from the side of the lake. Chan had examined that path on foot, and decided the best ambush point and the best position for each team member.

Angel, too slow to be any use physically during the final moments of confrontation, had been assigned the role of observer. It would occupy an oversight position, and warn the others if and when the Simmie left its hiding-place under the shelf of rock. The form of that warning had been the subject of heated argument until Chan cut off the discussion. He was worried by the Simmie's intelligence and the sophistication of its sensing apparatus. He had vetoed any signal that might be intercepted and decoded. If the Simmie moved from its hideout, Angel would transmit a single flash of light, tightly beamed towards the others.

S'greela worried that the signal might be missed, until the Tinker offered a reassurance: with the many thousands of eyes available in Shikari's composite, some would always be focused on Angel's secluded position.

And the time for action was finally arriving. Shikari whistled softly in the warm night air. Angel had given the sign, and the Simmie Artefact was on the way. The positions of the other three had been chosen carefully. If the Simmie followed anywhere close to the path predicted by Angel, each of them would have a clear shot at it without endangering the others. And no matter what variation on the path the Simmie might adopt, if it followed the aircar at all two of the team would have a good target.

Chan, Shikari, and S'greela were sitting roughly ninety degrees apart on the perimeter of a circle which had the Simmie's most probable emergence point at its center. If and when it appeared they would be less than thirty meters away from it.

Chan glanced at his watch. Any time now, according to Angel's prediction. He froze, and tried not to blink his eyes.

It was there. The latticed wing panels of the Simmie, peeping into view above a sharp edge of rock. Ten more seconds, and the silver-blue body would be revealed. At this range it would be impossible to miss. Already Chan had his weapon lined up in the correct firing position.

He had a last-minute worry. Would S'greela and Shikari have had the sense to prepare their weapons ahead of time? Any warning noise now could ruin everything.

The Simmie moved into full view. The team had agreed, there would be no signal given to fire. Each member would shoot as soon as the complete target was visible.

Chan sighted along his gun. His finger was on the trigger. Two more seconds—one more second—

A gigantic bounding figure raced across his field of view. It was S'greela, emerging from cover on Chan's left. At the same instant an intense whirring of wings sounded from the right. A frenzied cloud of Tinker components surged forward and dropped like a dark cloud. A moment before Chan could press the trigger, S'greela was on top of the Simmie and the two of them were buried beneath the Tinker swarm. All that could be seen in Chan's sights was a purple-black, writhing mound.

Chan groaned aloud—no point in silence now—and ran forward, weapon at the ready. It was useless. He could catch no more than random glimpses of the Simmie, and any shot was just as likely to kill S'greela. He suddenly realized his own weakness. His instructions had been explicit: If you have to kill other team members in order to kill a Construct, do it! But he couldn't do it himself. He wouldn't fire on S'greela and Shikari, no matter what happened.

He skidded to a halt by the side of the wriggling mass. As he did so, the violent movement began to subside. Tinker components were separating, layer after sticky layer. At last S'greela was revealed, eight jointed limbs locked around the body of the Simmie. When the final fluttering components of the Tinker were detached, S'greela stood up. The immobilized Simmie was held casually in her midlimbs.

"I am most sorry." The Pipe-Rilla nodded apologetically to Chan. "That was not my planned action. But when this appeared"—the Simmie was lifted a foot or so—"I realized that I would be unable to discharge my weapon. I also realized that I could not ignore my responsibility to help to incapacitate the Simulacrum. Fortunately, Angel and I had discussed a procedure for just such an eventuality, although I did not expect to employ it."

"Nor did we," said Shikari hoarsely. The Tinker was still in process of re-assembly, and the speaking funnel was not quite ready. "We also found ourselves unable to fire. We thought that by swarming we might overcome the Simulacrum alone. We were wrong, but luckily for us S'greela had already accomplished the task."

"Not so!" S'greela shook her head in the human gesture she had learned from Chan. "I had *not* succeeded! Without assistance of Shikari's swarm I could not have gained full control. But now"—To Chan's horror S'greela placed the Simmie gently on the ground, where it lay staring at him with luminous compound eyes—"now there is no danger. I have removed its weapons." She held an array of armaments out to Chan, each one capable of atomizing the pursuit team. "Here you are. The

Simulacrum is disarmed and helpless. Chan, what should we do now?"

Chan raised his gun and pointed it at the Simmie. His duty was clear. A moment later he lowered the weapon. What he might have done readily enough, to a dangerous enemy, he could never do to the unarmed and helpless creature on the ground in front of him.

It was a sick joke. He could not do what he was supposed to do, and Shikari and S'greela had done just the *opposite* of what they had been directed to do. And now they calmly asked him what they ought to do next!

What should we do now? The perfect question. Chan turned to the Simmie, studying it more closely. Without the formidable arsenal of weapons it looked delicate, almost fragile. One of the wing panels had been injured in the scuffle, and it was trailing painfully along the ground. The glowing eyes stared at him steadily, intelligently, waiting for Chan to decide its fate.

"Can you understand me?"

The Simulacrum gave no answer. Chan turned to S'greela and Shikari. "It's supposed to have vocal circuits. Do either of you know how to communicate with a Simmie?"

S'greela shook her head. "That is a situation which was not anticipated in any of my briefings."

"Nor in mine. But you caught it. So you tell me, what are we going to do with it?"

"Await our arrival." It was Angel, breaking radio silence—as it was not supposed to do. Wasn't *anybody* going to follow the plan?

Chan switched his own unit to send. "Where are you?"

"We are on the way now. We are confident that we will be able to achieve communication."

Without consulting Chan, S'greela went bounding away across the rocky surface. After another second, Shikari quickly dispersed and flew off in the same direction.

Chan was very much alone. He stared gloomily down at the Simulacrum. Without S'greela and Shikari, it suddenly looked a lot less harmless—except for the expression in those dark eyes.

He crouched down for a closer inspection of the

wounded wing panel. "First thing we do, we have a go at this." Could it understand him, or even hear him? "I'm sure we can repair it for you, if you can't re-grow it for yourself."

The awful truth hit him, as he gently lifted the delicate membrane. *What in heaven's name were they going to do with the Simmie?* If they took it back to Headquarters it might simply be recycled. Put out as bait for one team after another, until finally one came along that was resolute or callous enough to kill it. And that was unacceptable. Studying the Simmie's quiet and harmless life on the Dreamsea shore, and listening to the other team members, had given Chan a different perspective. The Simulacrum was no more than an Artefact, but even an Artefact had its own joys and sorrows. It had not *asked* to be made, any more than he had asked to be intelligent. Maybe it too had *feelings*, dreams and sorrows and desires all its own. And if he, a "war-mad" human, could think such thoughts, how must Shikari, S'greela and Angel be feeling?

No wonder the others had not been able to shoot. No wonder they had—without him—discussed ways to incapacitate a Simmie without harming it.

Chan thought of Leah's team. According to the pursuit team trainers, they had destroyed their Simulacrum. But was that true—or had they found a secret way to allow it to continue its existence, unknown to anyone else?

He might never know the answer to that question. And S'greela was reappearing, Angel held lightly in her mid-limbs. The mobile cloud of Shikari was not far behind. The tall Pipe-Rilla stooped and placed her burden gently on the ground right next to the Simulacrum. To Chan's surprise, every frond on Angel's bulky body went at once into agitated motion. The communications unit turned to face him.

"Before we begin to converse with the Simulacrum," said Angel, "We wish to congratulate you—and each other. We are all in total agreement. This is a wonderful day. Chan, we are at last a *team*."

"And what a team!" added S'greela. "Do you not

agree, Chan? We have performed wonderfully—*better than any of us ever dared to hope.*"

Shikari was still in process of re-assembly, but the surface of the Tinker shook in violent agitation.

"Shikari agrees," added S'greela. "And we are still improving! We will become better yet."

"Better!" Chan turned on the Pipe-Rilla. "What do you mean, *better?* We didn't do one damned thing as we'd agreed to do it. And we're going to have to *explain* all this! As soon as we reach S'kat'lan, and report back to Anabasis Headquarters, they'll—"

He stopped. The others were not listening to him, not one of them.

"Better," said Angel cheerfully. "Much, much better! As we all know, *Practice makes perfect.*"

Chapter 27

Luther Brachis could feel the difference; in the guards at the Sargasso Dump, in Captain Ridley, most of all inside the nitrogen bubble that held the fragmented and etiolated brain of M-26A.

The hair bristled on the back of his neck. But he could not begin to explain the reason for his reaction as he reviewed the new project records.

Phoebe Willard appeared to be in full control of the project, and she was clearly enjoying herself mightily. Her report showed remarkable progress in communicating with M-26A. Already the brain remnant of the Construct had been fed enough data to allow a million questions to be asked and answered.

The change in Blaine Ridley, however, was most remarkable of all. The replacement eye no longer rolled in his head. His rebuilt jaw did not waggle constantly from side to side. When Brachis appeared in the bubble, Ridley stood to attention, saluted smartly, and said, "Ready to proceed, Commander. Interface has already been established for you."

What would he have said and done a month ago? Writhed and jerked and stammered, and peed his pants. Ridley's improvement was a cause for rejoicing. And yet . . .

"Very good, Captain. Dismissed."

The inside of the bubble felt cold after Ridley had gone. It *was* cold, at the temperature of liquid nitrogen. But Brachis's hardened suit was working fine. He ought to be comfortable inside it at absolute zero, or on the surface of the sun.

There had to be another reason for his inner shiver, and surely it was both psychological and physical. He was squeezing this visit into a schedule that had no room for it, stealing sleep to make the local Link out to the Dump. And he would have to push himself even harder when he got back to Ceres.

He forced his attention to the keyboard, and typed a new input.

I want to ask you questions regarding the possible capture of the escaped Morgan Construct by a Pursuit Team consisting of human, Tinker, Pipe-Rilla, and Angel members.

That was not a question, and Brachis knew better than to expect anything of M-26A unless he asked a direct inquiry. He typed on. *You have received data on the Pursuit Teams. You have also received data concerning the most probable location of the escaped Morgan Construct. Question: Based on your knowledge of Constructs, and of the individual species that constitute a Pursuit Team, can you estimate the probability of success of any Pursuit Team, as presently constituted, capturing or destroying the escaped Construct?*

It was a direct question. Brachis had been getting anything but direct answers. He was surprised at the reply.

Answer: I can make such an estimate. The words appeared at once on the display.

Don't stop now. Brachis typed: *Question: What is the probability?*

Answer: The probability is 0.000873, less than one in a thousand.

That was direct enough for anyone, even if it was not the answer Brachis had hoped for. *Question. What are the primary reasons for that low probability? List those reasons in decreasing order of importance.*

Answer: 1) Livia Morgan employed the best elements from every species in the Stellar Group in designing the Morgan Constructs. 2) By employing inorganic augmentation, Livia Morgan was able to design a form for every Morgan Construct that exceeds in capability every Stellar

*Group member. 3) The escaped Morgan Construct, M-29,
was believed by Livia Morgan to be the most advanced of
the seventeen.*

Not encouraging, but also not surprising. Brachis had
been pessimistic himself, which is why he had relied on
information from M-26A to change the odds.

Except . . . wasn't something a little strange in at least
one part of the previous answer?

*You state that "the escaped Morgan Construct, M-29,
was believed by Livia Morgan to be the most advanced
of the seventeen." Question: Why do you use the word
"believed"?*

Answer. Livia Morgan believed it to be true.

Question: Do you disagree with that statement?

Answer: Yes.

Question: On what basis do you question the statement?

Answer: On the basis of the events at Cobweb Station.

Question: Can you describe the relevant events?

*Answer: Those events were initiated and led by M-29,
whose instability and insanity spread to others.*

A Construct that was not just dangerous, but insane.
That information certainly had to go to Esro Mondrian.

Question: Why did M-29 act in that way?

Answer: M-29 was driven to insanity.

Question: What made M-29 go insane?

*Answer: The manifest destiny of M-29 had been
thwarted.*

Question: What was the manifest destiny of M-29?

That question cannot be answered.

Brachis swore. He thought they were all done with
that sort of nonsense. After three similar questions
reached the same dead end, he typed in: *Two Pursuit
Teams have been formed. Question: Has information been
provided to your data banks on the individuals who com-
pose them?*

Answer: It has.

*Question: If those two Pursuit Teams attempt to
destroy the escaped Morgan Construct, do you assign the
same low probability to their chances of success?*

Answer: No.

Which made no sense at all. It contradicted the earlier

answer. But there was no stopping now. *Question: What do you estimate as their chances of success?*

There was a long pause. The display screen fragmented into spinning pools of light, and finally formed the words: *Answer: Their chance of success is in excess of 0.95, provided that certain conditions are met.*

Question: Can you describe those conditions?

Answer: No.

Another blind alley. Brachis tried the same question in a score of different ways, and got nowhere. He paused in the dialogue, and puzzled over the answers. The Pursuit Teams—"as presently constituted"—could not capture the rogue Construct. But the chance of success, for those same Pursuit Teams, was better than nineteen in twenty. Impossible.

Question: Should the composition of any Pursuit Team be changed to enhance the chance of success in destroying the Morgan Construct?

Answer: No.

Luther Brachis had had enough. The attempt to build a rational Construct brain from the damaged remnant must have failed. He was dealing with something as marred in its way as the brain-damaged guards of the Sargasso Dump.

Only a streak of stubbornness made him keep going. If precise, systematic inquiries did not work, what would general and random ones do? He went on a fishing expedition.

There is now an ongoing attempt by two Pursuit Teams to destroy the Morgan Construct which escaped from Cobweb Station. Question One: Will the Pursuit Teams succeed? Question Two: Will the Morgan Construct be totally destroyed?

He expected vague answers, or the old familiar message: *More information must be provided before that question can be answered.* Instead, the screen was already pooling to form new words: *Answer One: Yes, the Pursuit Teams will succeed. Answer Two: No, the Morgan Construct will not be totally destroyed.*

Brachis paused before he went on. It was time for a general sanity check on the isolated brain. The next few questions should be designed with that in mind—and to satisfy his own curiosity.

Four Questions: Is the future of the Stellar Group in danger? Will I, Luther Brachis, emerge at the end of this project increased in status? Where does my future lie after the conclusion of this project? Where does the future of Esro Mondrian lie?

Four Answers: The future of the Stellar Group is in danger. You will emerge at the end of this project increased in status. Your future lies here. The future of Esro Mondrian lies here.

It was worse than nothing. Luther Brachis had spent three precious hours at the terminal. Now he suspected that all the replies he had received were meaningless. He was in the process of signing off when Phoebe Willard returned.

"Progress?"

He shook his head. "If you want my unprofessional opinion, we've got ourselves an insane Construct."

She was on him like a tiger. "Luther, that's rubbish! We've been getting *wonderful* results, for all this past week. If anything is wrong, it has to be your way of asking questions. M-26A is *fine.*"

He had expected disagreement. This was Phoebe's baby now, and like any good project officer she defended her offspring. What he was amazed by was the vehemence. Blaine Ridley was not the only one at the Sargasso Dump who had been through a major change.

"So you think M-26A is fine. What's *your* explanation of these answers? It's like a damned Oracle—the answer can mean anything you want it to, or nothing at all." Brachis began to play back the session, beginning with the statement that no pursuit team could capture or destroy the escaped Morgan Construct.

Phoebe watched for only a few seconds. "Luther, I'm too old to be trapped into giving two-second answers to two-hour problems. Drop a copy out on storage, and I'll go over all this in detail—after you are back on Ceres." She frowned at one of the answers that had scrolled into view. " '*Your future lies here*'?"

"I know. It's a ridiculous answer."

"To a ridiculous question. Commander, I don't know what M-26A means by that, but I've been at the Dump so long I'm beginning to feel as though *my* future lies here. I have to sort out a few things back home, personal stuff that can't be left much longer. Next week I'd like to make a quick trip to Mars."

"You're picking a bad time. The work ought to go on."

"That's what you always say, whenever I talk about taking any leave. But the work won't stop. With your permission it will continue—under Blaine Ridley's direction."

It was tempting to say yes at once. Brachis *wanted* to think that Ridley could do the job, wanted to believe that something precious could be salvaged from the human debris of the Sargasso Dump.

He shook his head. "No."

"Ridley can do it. You know he can."

"Two months ago he couldn't say his own name. How do you know he won't be sitting in diapers again, a week from now?"

"Suppose he is. What *harm* can he possibly do?" Phoebe pointed at the screen. "Those are the best replies that you've been able to get out of M-26A. Do you think that Ridley can do *worse*? Even if he does nothing but sit on his rear end from the time I leave to the time I get back, what difference will it make?"

She was probably right. Brachis stared at the screen. *Your future lies here.* Maybe. But his *present* lay back at Ceres. He had to get back there, without delay.

"You win, Phoebe. But not because I think it's a good decision. I just don't have time to sit around and debate it with you. Who will assist Ridley? If you needed an assistant, so will he."

"Commander, you can't know what's going on here when you come in for flying visits and then head off again right away. We have over a *dozen* guards—maybe more than twenty of them—who are well enough to work as Captain Ridley's assistants. He has been training people for weeks, showing them this facility one by one. It always seems to make a terrific improvement in their condition. Maybe that's what has been wrong here, no one has ever had enough real work to do. People have to feel *useful*."

She stood up, and went across to where a session recording had been played out for her. "When I first came here you made me sit through meetings with the guards."

"And you benefitted from it, Phoebe."

"I did. It's your turn now, Commander. Before you fly off again, I want you to shake hands with a few of the old-timers." Phoebe headed for the lock folds. "Come on. I think you'll be amazed at the changes."

Chapter 28

The first experimenters with the Mattin Link transfer system had learned three lessons very quickly:

Know your exit point. Careless travellers had landed suitless in the hard vacuum of an extrasolar probe, or on the open surface of Mercury and Ganymede.

Close is not good enough. Travellers who missed the long, coded sequence of Link settings by a single digit tended to arrive as thin pink pancakes, or as long, braided ribbons of cytoplasm.

Someone always pays. The instantaneous transfer of messages and materials through the Mattin Link had opened the road to the stars, but it would never be cheap. The power for a single interstellar trip between points of different field potential could eat up the savings of a lifetime. Linkage of materials from the Oort Cloud to the Inner System consumed the full energy of three kernels aboard the Oort Harvester.

To those three rules, Esro Mondrian had added a fourth one of his own. A very old rule, familiar to the rulers of ancient Egypt: *Access is power.* Certain Link coordinates and transfer sequences were held strictly secret. Knowledge of them was not permitted without lengthy checking of credentials and need-to-know. The set of coordinates for the ship orbiting Travancore was not stored, not even in the *Dominus* data bank. It was known to just three people in the system: Mondrian, Kubo Flammarion, and Luther Brachis. The latter would use their information only if Mondrian himself were dead or unconscious.

The receiving point for information from Travancore was just as closely guarded. The Link Exit point was at Anabasis Headquarters, and nowhere else. The Solar Ambassador had agreed to that grudgingly, after direct pressure on Dougal MacDougal from the other members of the Stellar Group.

What the Stellar Group ambassadors had not approved, and what no one outside the Anabasis had been told about, was Mondrian's other decision concerning Team Alpha. The human team member was equipped with a personal Link communicator, to send sound and vision through a mentation unit for the entire period that Leah Rainbow was on Travancore. She knew that those data were being beamed to Team Alpha's orbiting ship. What she did not know was that they were sent on from there, to be received in real-time at Anabasis Headquarters.

Mondrian would monitor those signals himself, with help only from Kubo Flammarion and Luther Brachis.

Dawn on Travancore, night on Ceres. Esro Mondrian tapped Flammarion on the shoulder to indicate his arrival and sat down on the other side of the desk. Flammarion nodded and disconnected. He placed the headset in his lap, rubbed his temples, and yawned. "Quiet night. They heard a few funny noises outside the tent, then there was half an hour of heavy rain. Rain like Leah says she never heard of, even on Earth's surface. Now the whole team is awake."

Mondrian nodded. "I'm probably going to spend most of the day with them. Don't interrupt me unless we have an emergency." He fitted the set carefully over his head and turned on. After the first unpleasant moment of double sensory input he was linked abruptly across fifty-six lightyears. The Link connection was excellent. He was seeing through Leah's eyes and hearing with her ears. Whatever she saw and heard, he would experience as long as he wore the headset.

Leah was standing now on the reinforced side lip of the balloon tent, gazing out across the vivid emerald of

Travancore's endless jungle. The growth below the tent formed a tight-woven fabric of stems and vines. The early dazzle of Talitha's light scattered and diffused from the array of trunks and creepers, so that Leah could look straight down and see for maybe two hundred feet. At that depth a continuous layer of broad leaves hid everything beneath it. Even with Talitha's brilliance, the barrier of leaves was effective. There could be little photosynthesis deeper than the top few hundred meters. That left a real mystery: How did the lower levels obtain their energy supply?

Ishmael and S'glya were emerging from the tent to stand next to her.

"Cold," said S'glya as a greeting. She vibrated vestigial wing cases.

Leah turned to point over the edge, as Ishmael flowed and fluttered to form a living blanket around her legs. "Is that a solid layer of leaves? I can't see a thing below it."

"You will not," said S'glya. "The vegetation of this planet is structured in dense and continuous strata. We are looking down at one of them."

"The lower regions must be in complete darkness."

"Certainly. Even the microwave signals were somewhat damped in the first kilometer. We must evolve methods to work together in the dark."

"Where do the lower levels of vegetation get their energy?"

S'glya raised a clawed forelimb and gestured around her. "From here. Where else?" She leaned far over the edge, oblivious to the chasm below, and touched a half-meter shaft of bright yellow trunk. "I believe that we could follow this all the way down, five kilometers, and find its roots set in the soil of Travancore. As for its width at the base . . ." The Pipe-Rilla pirouetted on the brink. "Who knows? Many, many meters."

Behind them the Angel had come creeping out onto the lip of the tent. When it reached full sunlight the Chassel-Rose extended all its fronds and turned to face Talitha's morning beams. "We have been performing . . . confirming analysis," said the translation unit, after half a minute of silent sun-bathing. "From the data of the orbital survey, we now have an estimated location for the Morgan Construct."

There was a flutter through Ishmael's whole composite, but the Tinker held together.

"Where is it?" asked Leah.

"About three thousand kilometers from here, to the north-east. It is deep in the vegetation, and probably down on the surface itself."

"So we are safe enough here."

"Unless the Construct has chosen to move since the time that the survey was performed. We do not judge that as unlikely. The probability is high that the Construct was able to monitor our descent from orbit. We believe that it knows we are here."

"But we must go *closer*," objected S'glya. "We are supposed to meet the Construct, and then we are supposed to—to . . ."

Leah found the other three waiting expectantly. On every question of pursuit, they deferred to her without hesitation. And when the subject was the destruction of the Construct, they would do anything rather than mention it.

"We have to *kill* it." Leah said the forbidden word, and watched them cringe and edge away from her. "We'll have to go closer at some point. But not yet. We need to know more about this planet. The Construct has been here for months, with nothing to do but explore Travancore."

"And it is supposed to be very intelligent. We should not go near." S'glya changed her mind quickly, when Leah made her think the unthinkable.

"And we have been here less than four days," added Ishmael. "We should not hurry. We should not seek out the Construct until we are ready."

"*Better safe than sorry,*" said the Angel. "*Look before you leap.*"

The three aliens fell silent. Leah knew the problem. The others had agreed to become part of the pursuit team. But in their hearts (if the Angel had a heart) they had not expected to be asked to kill. That was a task only for a human.

Talitha rose higher in the sky. At last S'glya, rubbing her midlimbs against her side, spoke almost too softly to hear. "But if we do *not* now go to the Construct, then what *should* we be doing?"

Was it so difficult? Leah turned to the Angel. "We need to learn more about this place, especially what lies under all the vegetation. Can you determine from the orbital survey data how far we are from the nearest entry shaft?"

"That is known to us already. We are less than two kilometers from a spiral tunnel."

"Then that's where we go next. We must take a trip down, and learn what conditions are like on the lower levels of Travancore. We've been thinking of this as just a vertical forest, but that's pure speculation."

"And we should *all* go?" asked S'glya.

Leah hesitated. She thought she had heard uncertainty in the Pipe-Rilla's tone, and with reason. It might be wise to leave one member of the team on the upper levels, for a possible rescue. But if so, who? S'glya would have to carry Angel, while Ishmael was easily the most mobile. More and more, Leah was convinced that the team had power *because* it was a team. Every element was important.

"There is safety in numbers," said the Angel slowly, as though it had been reading Leah's mind. *"Many hands make light work."*

"All right." But Leah was still not sure. If Angel were right, and the Construct had monitored their arrival . . .

"I guess we all go," she said at last.

"When?" asked Ishmael.

"I see no advantage in waiting." Leah was surprised that her decision was accepted so *instantly*. The team members were all equal—and yet she was the boss. "As soon as we can all be ready, we head for the shaft. Don't bring a lot of equipment with you. On the first trip we travel light."

"Yes," said S'glya.

"Yes," echoed Ishmael.

"Never do tomorrow," said the Angel, *"what can be done today."*

The deep shafts noted during the first orbital survey were far more than simple gaps in Travancore's vegetative cover. Closer inspection revealed a true tunnel, with well defined and continuous walls of ribbed leaves plaited into tight hoops.

"Artificial," said S'glya, running a sensitive antenna lightly over the surface. "Nature does not braid so. The sign of intelligence?"

"Not necessarily. We have insects on Earth that build systems far more complex than this, and they are not intelligent."

"In your terms," said Ishmael. "Which others suspect." But the Tinker was making a feeble attempt at a joke, and Leah was pleased to hear it. Morale was recovering.

Overflow tubes set into the tunnel walls every twenty meters or so would be enough to carry off heavy rain. They were very necessary. Leah had expected near-vertical tunnels, mine shafts plunging straight down to Travancore's solid surface. Instead the openings were more like spiral roadways, curving down at a constant and moderate angle. It was possible to walk along the shallow gradient without supporting lines. At these angles, a rain storm would impose a massive load on the tunnel's curving floor.

Leah took a last look round before she led the way deeper into the tunnel. With Travancore's thirty-seven hour day they would have ten more hours of light. But how much use would that be, as soon as they were a couple of hundred meters down?

Ishmael followed close behind. The Tinker was very nervous, with clouds of components constantly leaving and returning to the main body. Leah had given up long ago on the question of how Ishmael preserved any continuity of thought—if it didn't worry the Tinker, she wasn't going to let it worry her.

The Pipe-Rilla came last. S'glya had the Angel tucked easily under her midlimbs. She sang softly to herself, until Leah asked her to be quiet. They did not, she reminded all of them, want to attract attention—no matter what was on Travancore to be attracted. The Construct might not be the only danger.

The light slowly faded. At two hundred meters they were moving through a green twilight, floating along in light gravity as though underwater. A rare upward kink in the tunnel, followed by a more steeply plunging section, took them through a curtain of pulpy leaves. The light level dropped abruptly. The temperature was noticeably higher. By the time they were down three hundred meters they were shrouded in an intense emerald gloom.

Leah stopped and turned to the others. "I can't see a thing, but I don't want to use my light. S'glya, you take over the lead. Carry Angel with you. Angel, I want you to use a thermal band and see what you can find out about the path ahead."

They were still changing places when there was an urgent whistle from Ishmael. "Something ahead! Something moving."

Leah turned, in time to see a pearly-white glow in the tunnel. As she watched it slid beyond the turn of the spiral wall. A dozen Tinker components disconnected and flew away along the shaft. A minute later they returned, one by one, and rejoined the main body.

"Native form," said Ishmael after a few seconds. "And large. Over ten meters long, snakelike, no arms or legs. Bioluminescent. The glow comes from a row of lights along each side of it. And it seems afraid of us, because it went wriggling away at a good speed. We followed it as far as a branch point, about three hundred meters down the shaft."

"Is it safe to go on?" asked S'glya. They all looked again at Leah.

"I don't know." She stared into the gloom ahead, and saw nothing. "If we turn back every time we find evidence of a native life form, we may never get anywhere. So I say we keep going. S'glya, would you lead the way again?"

They continued a cautious descent. Soon they were moving in total darkness. It must be full day above them, but every trace of sunlight from Talitha was blocked by the multiple screens of leaves and stems. At Leah's request, S'glya shone a faint pencil beam now and again to allow them to see the tunnel for a few paces in front of them. The Angel's thermal sensor could see far beyond that. It reported that the curving tunnel was clear, as far ahead as line-of-sight vision could go.

The temperature had stabilized at a level that Leah found just bearable and S'glya relished. The team went on in silence, winding deeper and deeper. The air was denser and more humid, and Leah could smell a faint, pleasant aroma like new-cut Earth flowers. It made her nostalgic for the Gallimaufries and Bozzie's floral obsession. The tunnel at these depths was less well-maintained, with ragged gaps here and there in its sides and roof. When they came close to one of the bigger holes they heard a soft, rustling sound like wind-blown dry leaves.

S'glya reached out to send a more powerful flash of light into the opening. It lit the surroundings as briefly and brightly as lightning. Less than five meters from the tunnel wall Leah saw a small four-legged creature clinging to a thick branch. As the light hit there was a brief quacking sound of alarm.

S'glya pulsed the beam again. The creature turned to face them. Leah had a glimpse of a brown, eyeless head, split by a broad mouth. A second and narrower slit ran all the way across from temple to temple. There was another sound, a high-pitched squeak of fear or complaint, then the animal was scurrying agilely away around the side of the shaft.

"Intelligent?" said Leah.

"According to survey data," replied Angel, "there are no native intelligent life forms on Travancore."

"How could a survey know that, without going down to the surface? And none of them did."

"We were merely reporting what is stated. *Ours not to reason why*. In any case, intelligence is too subtle an attribute to be inferred from appearance."

While Angel was speaking, S'glya had switched to a steady illumination and moved the beam slowly around the region just outside the tunnel.

Leah saw the great boles of trees, each one many

meters across. The trunks were dark tan and deep purple now, rather than the bright yellow of the upper leaves. From them grew thousands of wilting finger-like excrescences, black and crimson and vivid orange. Legless slug-like creatures on each extrusion inched slowly away from S'glya's light. As they moved they left faintly glowing trails on the tree fingers.

At this depth, greens and yellows had gone from the vegetation. Photosynthesis was impossible. Everything must depend for its existence on the slow fall of upper-level detritus or the transfer of nutrients up and down the massive trunks. Leah wondered about a pumping system that could lift fluids for five kilometers, even in this weak gravity.

The group went on, always downward. In another hour the pleasant floral scent was replaced by a nauseating stench of fleshy decay. Everything became coated with a misted layer of condensation, and dark, slimy droplets hung from the ribbed roof of the tunnel. Leah felt as though they had been descending for days when finally Angel waved its topmost fronds and poked Ishmael in the side. "We must stop here. Put me down. The tunnel ends in thirty paces."

Leah came to stand by the Pipe-Rilla. "How does it end?"

"It simply terminates. However, we are less than forty meters above the true surface of Travancore. My micro-wave sensors tell me that there is solid material beneath us, but descent past this point will be difficult for all except Ishmael's components. We face a sheer drop, or we must climb down a vertical trunk."

"Would we be able to move over the surface itself, if once we were there?"

"That should present no difficulty." Angel paused. "Descent can be made with the aid of a simple rope. But *return* would present problems, at least for human and Angel forms."

"I'm not suggesting we go down today." Leah turned to stare back up the tunnel. Only five kilometers—but five kilometers *vertically*. "We have a long way to climb, even in this gravity. I propose that we head back and

plan a trip with more equipment tomorrow. We know
what we need now. The next descent—" Leah stopped
abruptly. Gazing upwards she had seen a movement in
the faint scattered light from S'glya's pencil beam. It was
far above, indistinct, at the very limit of her vision.

"Angel, can you see what that . . ."

The question became unnecessary. The object was
approaching rapidly along the shaft. Its shape was
engraved deep in her memory.

Leah was looking at a rounded silver-blue diamond,
four meters high and more than two across. At the upper
end was a blunt, neckless head with well-defined compound eyes. Latticed wing panels shrouded the middle
section of the body. In their folded position they were
compact and unobtrusive, no more than pencils of stiff
wire. Extended, they could be shaped as needed to form
solar panels, communications antennae, or protective
shields. The base of the body ended in a tripod of supporting legs, each one able to be totally withdrawn into
the body cavity. The mid-section also contained a dozen
dark openings. They held the weapons—the lasers, the
fusion devices, the shearing cones.

Leah registered everything in a fraction of a second.
She gasped and stumbled back a pace along the tunnel.
Around her she felt a sudden blizzard of Tinker components as Ishmael dispersed instantly from its composite
form. A high-pitched scream of terror came from S'glya.

Angel's hedging of probabilities back at the tent had
been completely appropriate. The Morgan Construct had
indeed moved since the time of the orbital survey.

Fifty-six lightyears away, Esro Mondrian was still
watching and listening through Leah's mentation monitor. He had followed the group all through its long
descent. The feeling that rippled along his spine was an
odd mixture of awe, fear, and exultation. The Morgan
Construct was indeed on Travancore. It was alive and
undamaged—and functioning with its full powers.

The encounter, Construct against Team Alpha, was
beginning.

Mondrian watched everything, until the monitor no longer sent back any message.

After that he was silent and thoughtful for a long time. At last he went back to the record, and watched—three times over—the final few minutes of the transmission.

The call came while Luther Brachis was asleep. A tiny unit behind his right ear provided a soft but insistent summons. He grunted, lifted his head, and looked at the time. The middle of the night—and he had arrived home after the marathon session at the Sargasso Dump less than ten hours ago.

He swore, eased himself free, and slid quietly over to the edge of the bed.

Godiva gave a drowsy murmur of complaint. She slept like a child, deeply, peacefully, securely, snuggled against Brachis with one arm across his body. She usually fell asleep at once and claimed that she never had anything but pleasant dreams. Once she was asleep, Luther's departure from her side was one of the few things that would produce any reaction at all.

He waited to make sure that she would not waken, staring down at her as he pulled on his uniform. As always, Godiva slept naked. The skin of her bare body was so fine and fair that it seemed to glow like a pink pearl in the faint light of the ceiling panels. Brachis cursed again as he left her and hurried through into the living room. Three in the morning! But the communication unit was already in message receiving mode.

"Commander Brachis?" said a weary voice, as soon as Luther touched the keys.

It was Mondrian. He might have known. "Here. This is a devil of a time to make a call."

And if it were Mondrian, there had to be a good reason for it. Brachis was already straightening his uniform and pulling on his boots.

"I need to talk to you. At once." The dry voice had a tone that Brachis did not recognize. "You look as tired as I feel. Come to Anabasis Headquarters. To Communications. Alone."

The unit went dead. Brachis snorted. Alone! What did

Mondrian expect, that he'd lead in a brigade of bagpipers? But he headed for the door with his boots still unstrapped. Mondrian would never add that unnecessary word unless the situation were truly abnormal.

The door to Anabasis Communications was locked. That was significant, too. Brachis banged his fist hard on the metal, taking some of his own irritation out on the panels. After a long delay and a clicking of tumblers the heavy plate slid open.

Mondrian stood waiting. With one stiff movement he gestured Brachis to enter, and locked the door at once behind them.

Luther Brachis stared at him. "I don't know what you've been doing, but I suggest you stop it. You look freeze-dried, like one of the things we pull out for identification after a major airlock failure."

Mondrian did not smile, did not greet him. "Travancore," he said.

"We lost the team?" Brachis was not too surprised. He had always thought that the first team in was likely to get wiped out. There was no substitute for experience, and the second or third team would have a much better chance.

"Worse than that."

"Christ. The Construct is out and on the loose?"

"And worse than that." Mondrian took the other man by the arm. His fingers bit into Brachis's biceps. "There's something terrifying on Travancore, fully operating and incredibly dangerous. I want you to watch this. Then we must talk."

"I told you that the first team wouldn't cut it when it came to blasting the Construct. They chickened out, didn't they? Pipe-Rillas and Tinkers and goddamned Angels, no bunch of misfit aliens has the guts to do the job properly. Why not let *humans* handle it, that way there's a chance of success."

Mondrian paused in the middle of setting up a playback sequence. "You are wrong, Luther, quite wrong. But that is all irrelevant now. We have to blockade."

"Travancore?"

"More than that. The whole Talitha system. The only

thing that goes in is the next pursuit team." The screen began to flicker with the preliminary rainbow fringes of a long-distance Mattin Link transmission. "And that's just the beginning. *Nothing* comes out."

"Esro, you're out of your mind. Do you realize what it costs to blockade a stellar system?"

"I know exactly what it costs. It's more than you think."

"So why bother? There's an easier way. I don't care how tough that Construct is, it can be destroyed if we just pump in enough energy."

"You'd have to sterilize half the planet."

"So what? Sterilize the whole damned thing if we have to."

"And who explains *that* to the Stellar Group ambassadors?"

"Easy. We blame the Construct. They're scared out of their minds about it already. Do you think they're going to question us?"

"I don't know. I'm not going to find out. Sit down, Luther. I'm not going to argue with you now. I don't have to, because you hate aliens a lot more than I ever will. Just watch what came in from Travancore—and then see if you don't agree with me *completely* about the need for blockade."

Chapter 29

Skrynol was ready to dim the lights when Mondrian stopped her.

"Not this time. If you don't mind, I want to do something different."

The lanky Pipe-Rilla clucked disapproval. "I do mind. The agenda is set by the Fropper, not the patient. And recently we have been making very slow progress."

"Then one extra session won't matter." Mondrian had been carrying a narrow black tube, as long as his forearm. He handed it to Skrynol. "I also think this may be relevant to my problem."

"A recording?" Skrynol glanced around the claustrophobic chamber for an open viewing space. "If it does not involve you, it has no value."

"It is of me, and of one other. I want you to examine it, and tell me what he was thinking of as we talked. Also, I want to know what *I* was thinking."

"Based on visual and aural inputs only? You are a supreme optimist, Commander Mondrian." But Skrynol was already dimming the lights and setting the recorder to playback mode. To a Pipe-Rilla who was also a Fropper, the challenge was irresistible.

"I must watch this all the way through, Commander. In silence. During the second playing I will integrate my impressions and describe them to you. Before we begin, however, tell me something of the other party."

"His name is Chancellor Vercingetorix Dalton. He was born and raised on Earth, but in unusual circumstances."

As the image volume formed, Mondrian described Chan's background, his odd history and training, and the successful Barchan Simmie hunt. He continued until the image space was completely defined, and Skrynol held up a fleshy forelimb.

"For the moment, that is enough. If I have questions, you can answer them after first viewing."

She dimmed the lights, and a moment later Mondrian felt the soft touch of electrodes and needle sensors.

"With your permission," said Skrynol's voice in the darkness. "Your feelings as you watch may add much to what I can deduce from the recording."

The projection record began. Esro Mondrian and Chan Dalton were facing diagonally across a table, with Chan apparently sitting in deep shadow. In fact, Mondrian had been at Anabasis Headquarters on Ceres, while Dalton was linking in from S'kat'lan, eighteen lightyears away.

Skrynol watched in silence for twenty minutes. At the end of the recording she sighed. "Ah, that rosy light. I recognize it. Sweet S'kat'lan, world of my dreams! To be there, to be home, instead of here."

"I am sure Dalton would say exactly the same thing about Earth. Did you get anything?"

"Of course. Wait and see. Never fear, I will tell you what I observe . . . at the right moment."

The recording began again.

Esro Mondrian was nodding his head to Chan Dalton. "Congratulations on a great effort on Barchan. You did it in record time, and you didn't harm a single Shellback."

("There is already concealment," said Skrynol. "On your part. You are thinking, *What a change in so short a time. Dalton grew up. But he is tense, taut as a Linkline. I must be careful!*")

Mondrian, sitting in the dark, wondered at the wisdom of his decision to show the recording to Skrynol. His pretended interest in his own thoughts had been intended only to persuade Skrynol to offer her insights on Dalton's thinking. Now it was too late to say that he had changed his mind.

Chan had been placed in a room designed by Mon-

drian. It was based on tens of thousands of psychological profiles. Humans unsure of themselves usually took the seat nearest the wall, or remained standing. Not Chan. He was sitting in the controlling seat, the chair from which his comments could be made most forcibly.

"Thank you," he said. "But your congratulations should go to the whole team. It was a combined effort, and I give you thanks on behalf of all four members."

("He guards some secret—and he thinks, "Mondrian can see right through me. I think he knows about Barchan. But how can he?' ")

Mondrian's face on the recording was white and weary, and his eyes unnaturally bright. "I wish I had better news for you, Chan, after all your efforts on Barchan. But I'm afraid I don't. I have to give you some very bad news."

("Great fatigue! But that is obvious, without the services of a Fropper. You were thinking: 'Dalton's response is wrong. I tell him there is bad news. He tightens, then a second later he is relaxed again. What's on his mind? He has become unreadable. Who does he remind me of?' I can of course answer that for you. Chan Dalton reminds you—and me—of Esro Mondrian. Now he is subvocalizing: 'Mondrian can't know. He wouldn't put it that way if he did. Keep control. Remember what Tatty said.'— I feel your own emotional surge at that name— 'Work with him, but never let him get an edge. Or he will own you ... Angel was right, as usual. No one knows— can know—what happened to the Simmie. Unless the whole thing was a set-up, and everything we did was watched.' ")

On the recording, Chan was at last registering alarm. "Bad news about our team?"

"No. Bad news from Travancore."

"What's happening there?'

("His focus has shifted. Now he is truly concerned, and not for discovery of some secret of his own.")

"The planet has been placed in quarantine by the Anabasis," *Mondrian was speaking slowly, carefully.* "I am sorry, but there is no way of making what I have to say less painful to you. The Morgan Construct on Tra-

vancore is even more dangerous than we realized. Team Alpha has been destroyed."

("He is losing self-control.")

"Leah?—"

"Leah is dead. All the team members are dead."

Chan shivered. He closed his eyes, leaned forward, and placed his hands on his face. "Tell me everything."

("And you have control of him—the control that you were seeking. But you are also afraid at this point of the recording. Fatigue is lessening your concentration, when it is most important to retain your dominance.)

"I will tell you what I know." Mondrian was speaking again. "It is not much. We obtained only limited information after Team Alpha descended to the planet. We know that they decided to explore the shafts that lead down through the vegetation to the true surface. We believe that they encountered Nimrod—the name they gave the Morgan Construct. It is not clear if that name is used by the Construct itself, or given to it by the pursuit team on Travancore. We suspect the former. We believe that the team, contrary to instructions, made the great mistake of attempting communications with the Construct after contact, rather than at once destroying it."

("Another reaction from Dalton. Your words have made him think of some action of his own. I cannot say what.")

"That was a fatal mistake," went on Mondrian. "Nimrod is supremely dangerous. The monitoring equipment on the orbital survey vessel obtained one brief sequence involving the Construct. After that there was nothing. No video, no audio, no telemetry of vital signs for any team member. The team members were . . . gone."

("You have lost him. He no longer listens to you. He is reacting to the earlier news, sub-vocalizing again: 'Leah dead. Dead, dead, dead . . . they could not bear to kill the Construct, as we could not bear to kill the Simmie. It's still living by Dreamsea. But this is different, Nimrod is more dangerous than the Simmie could ever be . . . Was it painless and quick, or slow agony? Did she think of me, ever, the way I think of her?' Dalton doubts that his own team can ever destroy Nimrod, if Team Alpha failed. You talk to him still, but now he hardly listens.")

"You did not know this," Mondrian *was continuing, "because we thought it might do you more harm than good. But now you must know. Livia Morgan had planned to build other capabilities into her later Constructs. She did it, we think, in Nimrod. That Construct can generate a field which disturbs the perception of wholly organic brains. It can induce images, thoughts, even words. The Construct itself is not affected."*

("You are lying to him," said Skrynol softly. "Even though you are exhausted. That I know, but I do not know why."

"I was thinking something different, something that I did not want him to know. I was thinking, Luther Brachis is bull-headed, but he is right. He says, forget the idea of chasing the Construct. Lay waste the whole planet, the whole stellar system if we have to. Blame the Construct for it, and to hell with the worries of the Stellar Group."

"No." Skrynol had stopped the recording. "That may indeed be the view that Brachis holds, but it has little relevance to this. You were lying for other reasons. I will return to them later. For the moment . . .")

The recording began again.

"What could the field do," Chan *was asking. "Make us unable to move, or unable to think?"*

"Not in its original design. The field was supposed only to aid a Construct in escaping from danger, by inducing delusions in organic brains. A living creature would see things that were not there, or imagine situations not based in reality. It is a form of telepathy. While those false images endured, the Construct would move out of danger. But now we see Nimrod using it as an offensive weapon."

"Is there a defense against it?"

"There is no defense . . . except flight."

("He is strengthening. You no longer control him. He is saying to himself, 'Flight, never. It will be attack. Vengeance, for Leah. I will go to Travancore and kill the thing that killed her. Without delay, without argument,* *without mercy—no matter what the other team members want to do.'* ")

The recording suddenly stopped. Mondrian felt Skrynol's soft touch on his chest.

"Which, of course, is exactly what you wanted him to say. Dalton was to make that decision, to kill (you see, Mondrian, how easily I say that word, *Kill*! I am truly insane). He decided to *kill*, and swiftly. Decided for himself, without ever being told to do so. *That* is why you brought the recording—to see if Dalton had *really* been moved as you wanted him moved. We both know that actions taken from internal conviction are far better motivated than any external commands."

There was a strange tremble in Skrynol's limb. The Pipe-Rilla was laughing. "Ah, Esro Mondrian, human audacity—*your* audacity—is as boundless as it is unjustified. To think that you might conceal such simple motives as these from your own Fropper!

"But now"—more electrodes came snaking out of the darkness, to attach themselves to Mondrian—"now *we* will begin. We will change focus to a more profitable subject. Let us study on that recording not the simple emotions of Chancellor Dalton . . . but the wondrously more complex ones of Commander Esro Mondrian."

Chapter 30

Travancore from five thousand kilometers: it was even better than Travancore from half a million. A dream world, a soft-edged emerald ball, colors muted by a deep atmosphere, outlines touched with a misty impressionist palette. Peaceful. Beautiful.

Dangerous.

In Chan's opinion, if no one else's.

He stared down at the endless jungle and wondered what it would take to shake the Lotos-eater calm of the rest of the team. The closer they came to the planet, the more their enthusiasm grew. With S'greela saying that Travancore reminded her of the best Pipe-Rilla abstract paintings, while Shikari babbled of misty mornings on Mercantor, how would Chan ever ruffle that complacency?

They referred to him as the junior member of team. S'greela was ninety Earth-years old, and Angel much more than that; but in some ways they were the innocent babies, and he was the wary oldster.

He turned to the other three. They were preparing to enter the landing capsule—the final step before leaving the massive safety of the Q-ship and beginning the spiraling descent to the planet. "What are your impressions after a closer look?"

"Magnificent!" S'greela spoke first, her voice bubbling with enthusiasm. "This is a beautiful world. We are looking forward to seeing it more closely."

"Don't judge by what you *see*. Team Alpha was destroyed down there."

The other three exchanged looks—smug looks, Chan felt sure of it. They had not been devastated by the news of the first pursuit team's fate, as he had. He still found that news hard to believe, still expected to see Leah's face on the communication channel, still wondered when he would hear her voice again.

"We have to be very careful," he said. "If we're not, the same thing can happen to us."

"But it will *not* happen to us," said Shikari. "It cannot. For although we are sure that Team Alpha was composed of beings of exceptional talent and intelligence, they could not have made a complete *team*, as we are a team."

And there you had it. Nothing that Chan said could influence the opinions of the other three. They had moved in a few days from nervous diffidence to an unshakable conviction that together they would face any situation—and win!

There had been progress, even Chan admitted that. In communication with each other they were reaching the point where he could read the messages in a single wave of Angel's side fronds, a ripple in Shikari's base, or one head movement from S'greela. But what the others didn't know about was Leah's message to Chan. She too had spoken of an extraordinary level of communication achieved by Team Alpha. Yet her team had failed, disastrously.

Chan had other problems that he had so far not mentioned to the other three. He was having blackout periods, times when he could not recall afterwards where he had been or what he had been doing. The attacks came without warning and lasted anywhere from a few minutes to several hours. So far they seemed to have hit only in leisure spells, when he was relaxing with the other team members. But suppose that one came along at a more critical time—even during their possible clash with Nimrod?

Chan had sent a message to Kubo Flammarion over the Link connection from the Q-ship. Might he be feeling an after-effect of the Stimulator? Flammarion's reply was no comfort. No one knew enough about the Tolkov Stimulator to predict the side-effects of a successful treatment on humans.

Ought the others to be told what was happening to Chan? At the very least it might knock a hole in their wall of self-confidence. They were staring down at the approaching orb of Travancore with the cheerful curiosity of vacationing visitors.

He gave it one more try. "That's not Barchan down there, and a Simmie Artefact isn't a Morgan Construct. The Construct is smarter, better-armed, and murderous. I know we handled the Simulacrum, but this job will be ten times harder."

"And *we* are a hundred times more of a unit than we were then," replied S'greela. "Chan, it is normally the role of a Pipe-Rilla to be the principal worrier in a group. But now I feel totally at ease. We have become—*a team!*"

That was the end of it. They would not budge. They imagined the destruction of Nimrod, if they bothered to think of it at all, as some brief, painless encounter. Maybe an actual video scene, showing the first pursuit team as it was blasted or burned to extinction, would have made them think differently. Chan hated the idea of viewing that murderous meeting, yet he would have endured it, if its showing could drag the other team members to some understanding of their coming danger.

But that was not an option. All the sounds and images from Team Alpha's descent to Travancore were tucked away in Angel's capacious memory, available for recall and analysis in moments—except that the encounter itself was not there. The final video in the Anabasis files showed Nimrod drifting down the shaft toward the waiting team. It did not appear belligerent, or even particularly powerful.

The fight that had followed was not shown. The transmission equipment must have been destroyed with the team itself. But the disaster on Cobweb Station had proved that the Construct was anything but peaceful, and now it had more battle experience. On Travancore it must have destroyed the first pursuit team in a fraction of a second.

That, at least, was Chan's own preferred version of the event. He could not bear the idea of the team members—of Leah—lingering on horribly wounded beneath that thatch of vegetation for hours or days.

The Team Alpha recording served one other possible purpose. It indicated the location of Nimrod, during at least the brief period of time of the encounter. When Shikari performed a muon survey from orbit, a nearby site at Travancore's equator seemed to Chan's eyes slightly brighter on the images. But there were half a dozen other candidates, and he could not decide among them.

"What do you think, Angel?" Chan indicated his favored bright spot. "Isn't that the point where we are most likely to find Nimrod?"

"Possibly, possibly." There was a slow wave of mid-fronds, Angel's equivalent of polite skepticism. *"But the proof of the pudding is in the eating.* We must descend before we really know. In the words of the great Sherlock, *it is a capital mistake to theorize before one has data."*

S'greela and Shikari had done their own analysis of Team Alpha's descent into the surface shafts. They had concluded that in Travancore's light gravity the tunnels would be navigable by Angel without assistance, provided that a lift pack could be strapped around the tubby mid-section. And S'greela, unhampered by Angel, would have far better mobility.

That conclusion was the only positive result that Chan could see from two days of analysis from high orbit. He drew a conclusion—reluctantly: they could look down at Travancore from afar *forever*, and not know much more than they knew now. Like it or not, it was time to stick their necks out and get down to the surface.

As they prepared to enter the landing capsule Chan gave the others one more warning. "Make sure you have *everything* that you'll need on Travancore before we leave the Q-ship. We've had clear instructions from the Anabasis, we will not be allowed back on board unless we can prove that we've destroyed Nimrod. We won't even be given drop shipments from orbit, unless it's clear that they can't be used by Nimrod if things go wrong. We'll be on our own."

"Until we return triumphant to the Q-ship . . ." said S'greela.

". . . *our team victorious, happy and glorious*," added Angel.

"*One for all, and all for one*," added Shikari.

If the Tinker was starting that, too, Chan couldn't stand it. He went across to the Q-ship communicator one last time and initiated a Link sequence to Anabasis Headquarters on Ceres. Mondrian was alone in the control room. He nodded a greeting, and did not speak.

"A few more minutes," said Chan, "and we'll be on our way. Do you have any final instructions?"

"Nothing that makes any practical difference to you, but there's been a slight change at this end. The Stellar Group ambassadors are insisting that the Mattin Link to your Q-ship be made *one-way* all the time that you are down on the surface. Messages and materials can go from here, but *nothing* must come back this way. It's the same worry as before, that somehow Nimrod might destroy the team and then find a way to Link out."

"But if we can't send messages, how will you know we've done our job and are waiting to come home? How will you know anything of what's happening?"

"I've taken care of that. A monitor team will be shipped from here to the Q-ship, and you'll be able to talk to the people there."

"How will the Ambassadors be any more sure of that team, than they are of my team?"

"Because I'll be on the monitor team, *myself*." Mondrian smiled grimly at Chan. "You know what that means, don't you? So long as Nimrod is still active, I'm going to be stuck on Travancore as much as you are. I'll be in orbit, and you'll be down on the ground, but neither one of us will be able to leave. Until Nimrod is out of the way, it's a one-way trip for all of us. So you know I mean it when I wish you luck. It's a long walk home."

A long, long walk. Fifty-six lightyears from Travancore to Earth. Six centuries of sub-lightspeed travel. Chan understood what Mondrian was saying: *Destroy Nimrod—or your team will have vanished forever from the known worlds.*

And Chan understood more, things that Mondrian was *not* saying. *The Stellar Group Ambassadors are insisting* . . .

What did the Angel or Pipe-Rilla or Tinker Ambassadors know of battles, and quarantines, and blockades? Not one thing. It was *Mondrian* who was deciding the rules and defining the actions. And there was nothing that Chan could do about it.

"We will be on our way within an hour," he said quietly. "Give us one Earth week, and I hope that we'll have some results."

"Don't set yourself deadlines, Chan. Nimrod will still be there if it takes two weeks. Just make sure you destroy the Morgan Construct. *Festina lente.*"

Mondrian was still facing the camera, but the display began to exhibit the rainbow fringes of a fading Link communication.

"*Festina lente?*" said Shikari.

"It is a piece of advice given in an old Earth language. Mondrian took it as the motto for Boundary Security. I believe that it means, *hasten slowly.*"

"I don't see why he saw the need to warn *us,*" said S'greela indignantly. "I am sure that we will not be foolish enough to hurry into trouble."

"*Fools rush in* . . ." said Angel. "Hmm. Enough of that. We believe that we are ready, Chan, to begin our descent."

Chan's analysis of Team Alpha data had led him to three conclusions. He explained to the others.

First, and worst, the other team had made one huge mistake. They had been careless in checking the Morgan Construct's *current* location before they began their descent. Nimrod obviously was able to move about the planet, within or beneath the vegetation canopy, at high speed. Chan would not make the same blunder as Leah. There would be continuous monitoring of the Construct's position as soon as a definite location was confirmed.

Second, Team Alpha had not made the best use of the native life forms. At least two of them might be valuable for either information or reconnaissance. There was the long, legless caterpillar-snake that lived in the upper shafts, and the nimble, nervous animal that had been encountered by Team Alpha in the deep jungle. If either one possessed intelligence and could be talked to, it might help to cancel one of Nimrod's advantages. The Construct had been on Travancore for a long time, and must know it well. Chan's team had vast numbers of useless facts, but all of them had been acquired from far, far away. What was needed now was knowledge of the planet *below* the shrouding canopy of vegetation.

Third, the other team had stayed together too much. Chan knew how tempting it was to work as a unit, and how satisfying that could be; but there were some functions that still called for individual actions.

Chan's third statement produced strong protest from the other three. Shikari was particularly outraged.

"It must not be. We are a *team*! As a team, we should always work *together*."

"Shikari, you haven't learned anything. You saw how successful the Tinker component sub-assemblies were on Barchan. But you still don't accept that some things are better done by *individuals* than groups." Chan turned away from the Tinker. "As long as I'm in charge, we'll do things the way I say. Of course, if anyone else wants to take over responsibility for running operations, I'll be happy to step aside."

He was both worried and pleased by the horrified reaction, not just of Shikari but of Angel and S'greela. Their immediate acceptance stuck him with a job for which he felt unqualified. Now he had to get on with it.

He took the landing capsule down to Travancore. It hovered at one position on the planet's daylight side, while the team unloaded and inflated their tent and fitted it into the upper layers of vegetation. As soon as all the equipment was unloaded, the landing capsule took off again under automatic control for synchronous orbit. It would hover above the planet, monitoring the location that Chan had picked out as a probable location for Nimrod. The Q-ship was stationed much farther out, far from any possible danger of Construct weapons.

Once they were settled in, Chan assigned S'greela to a solo mission. The Pipe-Rilla was easily the strongest of the team members. She was to descend the nearest shaft, seek a specimen of the long, snaky life form, and bring it back to the tent. According to Angel there should be considerable diurnal movement of Travancore's mobile forms. Like ocean life on Earth, they would take advantage of daylight to feed and sun themselves in the upper levels, and return to the depths at night. Now it was close to midday, and S'greela had a good chance of finding what she wanted close to the surface.

She set off, unarmed at her insistence, on her mission. The others settled for a long, nervous wait.

It was close to sunset when S'greela returned, empty-handed and exasperated. The other three were sitting in the tent, Angel close to Chan and Shikari spread like a thick cloak over both of them. S'greela joined them, and waited for the Tinker components to envelop her also. She sighed.

"You couldn't find one?" said Angel at last.

The Pipe-Rilla shook her head. "It was not as simple as that. A most frustrating experience! *Many* times I saw one of the forms, but each time it crawled away through a gap in the wall of the shaft. Finally, I decided to lie in wait in one place. At last one came along. I caught it—but I could not bring it here!"

"It was too strong for you?" asked Shikari. The voice funnel was down on the floor, next to Chan's legs. These days the Tinker showed less and less interest in assuming any familiar form.

"Not at all. I was stronger. But I was *out-legged*." S'greela held up three pairs of wiry limbs. "It is not often that I meet a creature with more legs than I have."

"But I thought the animal you were after was *legless*," said Shikari.

"So did I. Perhaps we need to define a leg. I found that its body is in thirteen separate segments. And on each one there are two gripping attachments—twenty-six in all. When I took hold of its body, each of the twenty-six held tight to the ribs on the wall of the tunnel. I could detach any one of them easily enough. But I could not detach *all* of them, and I dared not use too much force for fear of harming it."

"Did it show signs of being intelligent?" asked Angel.

"More perhaps than I did. I am here, and it is there, uncaptured. But the whole episode was most annoying. All the time that I was holding the creature, it made sounds. Very high-pitched, so that although I could *hear* most of them, I had no way to reproduce them. I suspect that they were in fact some kind of language. Finally I had to release the animal and return here before dark. It wriggled away only a few paces, quite unharmed. And then, as though to mock me, it stopped and calmly began feeding! It seemed to be saying to me, 'This is *my* territory, and here I stay.' I suggest that tomorrow morning Angel and I return to the same place. Angel has our best language ability, and the computer communicator can synthesize anything up to a hundred thousand cycles a second." S'greela turned to Chan. "But of course, that is your decision. You are the leader for these things."

Called on for comment, Chan felt a sudden mood change. He had not spoken since S'greela's return, but he had been following the conversation in a perplexing way, understanding almost without listening. He had been the one preaching the need for action by individuals. Now the proposal that Angel go off with S'greela made him feel uneasy. At his feet the Tinker stirred restlessly, as though Shikari could somehow sense his discomfort.

"I agree, Angel ought to take a look at the animal," said Chan. "But I think when that happens, I ought to go also. I wanted you to try it alone at first, S'greela, because you are the strongest. But strength does not seem important for what we want to do."

"Then we should *all* go?"

"I don't like that, either. Our communication equipment is here, and we need to be able to stay in contact with the landing capsule and the Q-ship. S'greela, do you feel confident that there was no trap? That the animals in the shafts have nothing to do with Nimrod?"

"I feel sure that they do not—but do not ask me to prove that."

"Angel?"

"We concur. S'greela is almost certainly correct. The probability of a connection between today's events and the Morgan Construct is very low."

"And the animal seems harmless?"

"Despite its size, I judged it to be harmless. All it seemed to want to do was eat. Even when I was trying to dislodge it from the tunnel walls, it kept on chewing at them. It has substantial mandibles, but it never once tried to bite me."

"Right." Chan made his decision. "Tomorrow we will all go—except for Shikari."

"We do not wish to be left alone here!" The Tinker was outraged.

"I know you don't. Listen to me for a moment, Shikari, and see how this sounds. We must leave someone here, in case we need to communicate with the ship. So *half* of you goes with us. Half remains here. You'll know which shaft we are in, and if you had to you could fly all your components down to join us in a couple of minutes. I know you don't want to do this, but *can* you do it? Can you operate in two halves?"

The Tinker said nothing, but there was a sudden tremble through the whole mass of the composite. Hundreds of components flew away to cling to the side of the tent. The voice funnel closed abruptly.

"Come on, Shikari," coaxed S'greela. "If you can do this, it will be wonderful. We can explore with you, and still know that you will have contact with the capsule if we need it. And it will only be for a little while."

"*Divide and conquer*," added Angel. "You alone can do this."

The voice funnel remained closed, but individual components slowly came back to join the assembly. Shikari gradually flattened to form a low and miserable heap around the other team members.

It was agreement; or at least, acceptance.

*   *   *

Angel had used the mobility pack during training, but only for a few minutes. S'greela fixed it now around Angel's tubby blue-green middle section, and tightened the straps.

"All ready. If you would care to try it out . . ."

Angel made a few tentative back-and-forth movements along the lip of the tent. Then suddenly it was darting off on a complex three-dimensional pattern of zig-zags, racing back and forth over the uneven uppermost layer of the vegetation like a water skier.

"Stop playing around, Angel," said Chan over his communications pack. "We have to be on our way."

He was beginning to feel like the disciplinarian of the group, the one who always had to say no. The others didn't seem to worry at all! Maybe that was the real difference between humans and the rest of the Stellar Group—if history was anything to go by, humans had always had plenty to worry about.

Angel came skimming and diving back to the side of the tent, executing a final mid-air roll and loop before landing. The others were ready and waiting. As they set out for the shaft one half of Shikari bade a solemn farewell to the part that would remain behind. Chan felt sure that the Tinker was doing it for his benefit. Shikari explained that although there were seldom more than a quarter of the total number of components clumped to form a single body at any one time, the point was that they were always *there*, always available to attach whenever they were needed. This physical separation into two major pieces would be a unique and unpleasant event.

"Imagine going off on a journey without *your* legs or your arms," said Shikari. "Or imagine Angel being separated into the Chassel-Rose and the Singer. Well, it's just as bad for *us* to be split like this."

Chan was not persuaded, particularly since once they were on the way the Tinker seemed in excellent spirits. A steady two-way stream of individual components moved along the tunnel, providing a continuous link between the two halves of the composite. Chan began to wonder how long a connected chain of single components could be. With, say, ten thousand components, each ten centimeters long ... that would stretch for a kilometer. But the neuronal inter-connections in such a linear array would be minimal. Chan doubted that a Tinker would actually be able to *think* much in such a mode.

Angel was leading the way, gliding silently along the curved tunnel with all sensors operating. After about twenty minutes the green bulk stopped and turned back to the others. "Something moves in the tunnel ahead," said Angel softly. "We are very close to the location that S'greela described."

A handful of Tinker components separated and winged their way down the tunnel past Angel. They returned a few seconds later, and attached to form a chain between Angel and Shikari.

"It is the form," said Angel. "The same form that S'greela saw. A long body and no real legs, feeding at the tunnel wall."

"Allow me," said S'greela. The Pipe-Rilla eased past Angel and went bounding forward down the spiral tunnel. The others heard a thresh of limbs and a high-pitched squeak. Chan led the way down the shaft, pointing his light ahead. He found S'greela holding something firmly around its middle section, while all the rest of the animal clung firmly to the tunnel wall.

Chan walked forward along the full length of the body. It was enormous, a straw-colored multi-segment monster over a meter across and better than ten meters long. No wonder S'greela had not been able to bring it back to the tent!

Despite its size the animal made no attempt to attack, or even to defend itself. The head was eyeless and dark-red, equipped with a broad slash of a mouth big enough to bite Chan in two. It was still eating steadily, chomping on vegetation that it clipped from sprouting sections of the tunnel walls. As Chan came close to it the big head turned slowly towards him. He heard a shrill series of squeaks and whistles, so high and loud that they hurt his ears. They came from a second broad slit set a few inches above the mouth.

Angel advanced to Chan's side, and the communicator attached to its mid-section gave out an experimental series of similar squawks and squeaks.

"We are only imitating at the moment," said Angel. "But we think that it is a language, even if a primitive one. We assume that it arises as a modulation of ultrasonic navigation signals employed within the deep tunnels—a natural development for creatures that live mostly in darkness. But before we can be sure we must have more samples of its sounds. Hold it tightly, S'greela. This may take some time."

Angel moved closer to the head, reached out a lower frond, and poked the creature gently. The monstrous caterpillar body struggled harder, and the head turned to face Angel. There was a longer series of squeaks, this time with a different emphasis and cadence. Angel responded with a succession of similar sounds. They gradually ascended in pitch until they were inaudible to Chan's ears. The great body ceased to squirm in S'greela's grasp, and the Pipe-Rilla leaned closer to follow the interaction.

Chan knew that both Angel and S'greela could hear frequencies well outside the human range. He would have to let them work in peace now, and receive his briefing when the initial communication attempt was finished. He stepped away from the others and stared around him at the tunnel walls.

They were close to a branch point where the descending shaft split and continued down as two separate paths. He had not seen that before, nor heard of it in any of the records left by Team Alpha. It suggested a possible system of pathways through Travancore's jungle more complicated than they had realized.

Chan glanced back at Shikari and S'greela. He was tempted to call to them, but they were both engrossed in Angel's efforts at talking with the giant native animal. He walked a little farther down the sloping tunnel, and shone his light along each branch in turn.

They were obviously quite different. One continued steadily down toward the distant surface of Travancore, five kilometers below. The other was narrower and less steep. It curved off slowly to the left with hardly any gradient at all. If it went on like that, it would form a horizontal road through the high forest.

Chan went that way and took a few paces along it. He had no intention of losing sight or sound of the other team members.

After only three steps he paused. It was very confusing. There seemed to be something like a dark mist obscuring the more distant parts of the corridor. When he shone his light that way there was no answering reflection.

He hesitated, but after a moment or two he turned to start back the way that he had come. Whatever that might be in front of him, he was not going to face it alone. He had weapons on him, but more than that he wanted the support of the other team members—S'greela's strength, Shikari's mobility, and Angel's cool reasoning.

As he was turning he heard a whisper behind him. "Chan!"

He looked back. Something had stepped forward from the dark mist, and was standing now in the middle of the narrow pathway.

It had the shape of a human. Chan took another step back toward the other team members as he shone his light at the figure in the tunnel.

And then he could not move at all.

It was Leah.

Chan was ready to call out to her when he remembered Mondrian's warning. Leah was dead, and what Chan had to be seeing was an illusion—something created in his mind by the Morgan Construct.

As though to confirm his fear, the figure of Leah drifted *upward* like a pale ghost. It hung unsupported, a couple of feet above the floor of the tunnel. The shape raised one pale arm and waved in greeting. "Chan!"

"Leah?" He fought back the urge to run forward and embrace the form hovering in front of him.

"No, Chan." The dark head moved from side to side. "Not now. It would be too dangerous now. Say goodbye to me. But don't stop loving me, Chan. Love is the secret."

Ignoring all the warnings of common sense, Chan

found that he was taking another step along the tunnel towards her. He paused, dizzy and shaking.

The figure held her arms palms-out toward him, as though pushing him away. "Go back, Chan. Not now. It would be dangerous."

She waved farewell. The slim figure stepped sharply backward and was swallowed up in the dark cloud. The apparition was gone.

Chan was too stunned to move, until suddenly a sense of his own danger overcame inertia. He turned and staggered back along the tunnel.

Nimrod. The Construct cannot be far away from here. It can produce delusions within organic brains, change what you hear and see. Are the others safe?

Chan was running. In just a second or two he was back to the place where he had left the team members.

The tunnel was deserted. He paused, and stared along it in both directions. There was no sign of S'greela, Shikari, or Angel. No sign of the great caterpillar-snake that they had been holding.

Where was the team?

Chan began to run again, back up the spiraling tunnel, back to the sunlight, back to the doubtful safety of the tent in the upper layers. As he ran the face and form of dead Leah hovered always in front of his eyes.

Chan arrived at the tent convinced of every form of disaster. Nimrod had destroyed the others, and somehow overlooked him. Or the others had known that Nimrod was present, and they had retreated, leaving Chan to fend for himself. At the very least, if they had managed to make it back to the tent they would be frantic with alarm at his absence. They would be terrified and disorganized, not sure how to organize themselves to go off again and search for him in the tunnels.

The atmosphere in the tent was certainly tense. But no one was worrying about Chan—they hardly seemed to notice his arrival! He grabbed S'greela by one of her forelimbs. She turned and gave him a little nod of acknowledgement.

"It is good that you have returned. We are not sure

what to do next. There has been a bad—a bad misunderstanding—"

"*Misunderstanding!*" growled Angel's communications
box.

"—a misunderstanding with the *Coromar*." S'greela
motioned toward the side of the tent, where the great
caterpillar creature was stretching its length along the
flexible wall. "That seems to be the group name that
these beings give to themselves."

The animal did not react to its name, but it seemed
quite at home in the tent. It was free to move, but making no attempt to escape. Instead, the long mouth was
chomping contentedly on a great bale of vegetation.

Chan was totally confused. The scene was so peaceful,
the very opposite of what he had imagined. "A misunderstanding?"

"I am afraid so. The animal is not very smart. As soon
as Angel was able to speak with it, it agreed to come
along with us provided that we would feed it when we
got here." The Pipe-Rilla shook her head testily. "Really,
food seems to be the only thing it cares about at all.
Naturally we agreed, since we have ample provisions with
us."

"So what's the problem?" Chan took a closer look at
the Coromar, contentedly browsing. "You gave it plenty
of food. didn't you?"

"Well, *now* it has all it wants. But when we first arrived
here, Vayvay—that is the name of this Coromar—did not
seem to understand that we would have to bring food to
it from storage. It did not want to wait."

"It tried to leave?"

"No. It tried to eat Angel."

Chan stared at Angel, sitting motionless at the other
side of the tent, as far away as possible from the Coromar. The side fronds were all lying limp against the barrel body, and the head fronds were tightly closed. Angel
was sulking.

"Surely the rest of you tried to stop it?"

"We *did* stop it. All that happened was that Vayvay
took a bite at Angel's middle section—one *little* bite."

"It was quite understandable," added Shikari. The

Tinker, its parts reunited, sounded in excellent spirits. It came rustling across to Chan's side. "After all, even Angel will not deny that the Chassel-Rose is a vegetable. And the real confusion was the fault of the communicator that Angel wears. As S'greela says, Vayvay is not very smart. It apparently assumed that the *communicator* was the intelligent being, since that was the part that did all the talking. Vayvay thought that the rest of Angel must be some sort of mobile food supply."

"A perfectly natural assumption, actually," said S'greela.

"To put it as Angel might have put it," concluded Shikari, *"one man's meat is another man's mid-section."*

There was an outraged crackle from Angel's communicator. *"We are not amused.* This is no matter for joking. If we had not moved quickly, it would have been far more than one bite."

"All right, that's enough." Chan went across to sit down wearily next to Angel. "Cut out the bickering. We have far more important things to worry about." Chan ignored the cry of protest. "We are supposed to be a *pursuit team.* Remember? We are tackling the most dangerous creature in the universe. When you looked around the tunnel and found that I was gone, didn't it occur to you that I might be in trouble? Didn't one of you think, wait a minute, now, maybe we ought to take a look and see what has happened to Chan. No. Instead, you just headed back here without giving me a thought."

There was an embarrassed silence. "We were preoccupied with the Coromar," said Shikari at last. "The tunnel was quite safe, and the part of me that had remained here was reporting no trouble anywhere on the surface. There was no cause for worry about you."

"And you *did* return unharmed," added S'greela. "Why are you so upset? Were you afraid?"

"Not as much as I ought to have been." Chan was beginning to have second thoughts about what he was going to tell the others. Suppose everything was part of his own mental instability? Suppose that he had *imagined* the whole thing? "I encountered Nimrod down there. At least, that's what I thought at the time.

Now I'm not so sure. But I'm amazed that I'm here to tell you about it."

He summarized his experiences in the horizontal tunnel, keeping his account as matter-of-fact as possible. When he finished there was a strange and non-committal silence. It ended when Angel exchanged a long sequence of shrill squeaks with the Coromar.

"Leah Rainbow was your friend, and she is dead," said Angel at last. The topmost fronds waved towards Chan. "But Vayvay has never heard of Nimrod. Of course, although the Coromar exist planet-wide, they are not very intelligent. Perhaps they do not travel far from their usual haunts, and perhaps they do not speak much one to another."

"Don't spare my feelings. If you don't believe me, you might as well say so."

"The human mind has processes that we cannot begin to emulate." Angel turned to Vayvay, as the Coromar produced another series of squeaks. "Ah, and not before time! Vayvay says that it is most sorry that it tried to eat us. But it points out that we look delicious."

Chan glanced at Shikari and S'greela. It was not just Angel. They were all too diplomatic to say so, but not one of them believed his story. The worst thing was that Chan now doubted it himself.

"Can you ask the Coromar general questions?" he said to Angel.

"That depends on the subject. It is not a complex language, but over half the words seem to concern only eating, or looking for food."

"Can you ask what Vayvay knows about the other species—say, the agile ones that live in the deep forest? See if they, or any others, sometimes generate a sort of dark mist. Also, see if we are likely to be able to get any help from them when we go deeper towards the forest floor."

Chan waited impatiently, through an exchange that went on and on. Angel seemed less sure of the replies this time, and many strings of sounds had to be repeated. At last Angel turned again to Chan.

"According to Vayvay, we will obtain no help from the

agile creatures. They are named the *Maricore*. I am sorry that we spoke for so long, but Vayvay was very confused by my questions. You see, both the Coromar and the Maricore are *the same species*. The Coromar are the feeding, intelligent—just—stage of the life cycle. They live for twelve to fifteen earth years, after which they encyst and undergo a complete metamorphosis. Before the change a Coromar is asexual, and therefore naturally has no sex drives. After metamorphosis a Coromar becomes a Maricore and thinks of little else. In this stage they live only one year. They mate, eat very little, and during this part of life they actually shrink in size. According to Vayvay they never exhibit the least sign of intelligence. They also have poor survival skills. For safety they dwell in the deep forest, and never approach the surface layers. It is one duty of the young Coromar to descend, guard the mature Maricore, and assure their survival until they can give birth to another litter of Coromar. Without that aid, most Maricore would not live long enough to breed." Angel paused. "An inversion of the familiar theme. *The child is father to the man*—but in this case the expression proves to be literally true."

"What about the mist?" Chan didn't want to hear philosophy. He was suddenly absolutely exhausted, with a return of the dizziness that he had felt in the tunnels. He wanted Shikari warm about him, and then sleep. "Do the Coromar know anything about that?"

"Vayvay has never heard of any such thing." Angel began to extend its adventitious base stems and crept toward the Chassel-Rose's preferred rooting spot near the exit to the tent. The top fronds were slowly tightening in on themselves. Shikari and S'greela were already silent. The only sound was Vayvay's steady and single-minded munching.

"The Coromar will help," said Angel. "Vayvay will stay with us and go anywhere in exchange for plentiful food. But we fear that every real responsibility for decision and action must remain with us."

The roots of the Chassel-Rose began to settle, probing down into the patch of dark, rich earth that had been brought all the way from the home planet of Sellora.

Angel sighed in dreamy pleasure. "Chan, we do not know if your encounter with Nimrod was reality, or, as Shikari and S'greela believe, pure delusion. But this we do know: together, we form as good a pursuit team as the Stellar Group will ever find.

"Together, we will defeat the Morgan Construct . . . or no group ever will."

Chapter 31

The Mattin Link blurs the definition of the word "simultaneous," so much so that the Angels have become the ultimate arbiters of time disputes. According to their standards, at the moment when Chan was staring incredulous at the apparition of Leah Rainbow in Travancore's abyssal tunnels, Esro Mondrian stood in a corridor deep in the Earth warrens. He was at the door of Tatiana Snipes' apartment. Three times he had lifted his hand to insert a key in the coded lock, and thrice he had hesitated and pulled back.

Tatty watched through the hidden screen. A mystery. What was wrong with Mondrian? Thoughtful and brooding, yes; indecisive, never.

At the fourth attempt he completed the sequence and the door opened. Mondrian stepped inside and stared around him. Less than a year ago this had been his favorite haven. He knew he could come here, shut out the cares of the whole of deep space from the Dry Tortugas to the Perimeter, and do his deepest thinking and planning.

Tatty had respected that need for privacy, for inner space. She knew when he was working, knew when he needed relaxation. She never intruded at the wrong time. She had been hooked on Paradox, its barbs set deep in her soul, but Mondrian would never see her take a shot. Tatty was infinitely discreet.

And now?

Mondrian, who made a god of accurate information,

did not know. The apartment was no longer a place of peace and sanctuary. He stared around again, seeking the changes. Tatty was far more independent, he knew that. She had broken the Paradox habit, as far as anyone ever did. The scars of those barbs would still be within her, but no longer did the arrays of little purple ampoules decorate every room. And no longer was Mondrian's every wish her command.

She had lived through Chan's transformation in the Tolkov Stimulator. Was it that searing experience, affecting everything about her, that had made the difference? She refused to talk about it then. But would she change her mind, and talk about it now?

Mondrian did not know. That was the worst thing of all, Tatty had become *unpredictable*. He was no longer sure how she would react to his words, what she would say or do.

He knew the right solution. *What cannot be controlled or destroyed must be banished*. He had to make a complete break with Tatty. But he was not able to do it.

Mondrian stood at the threshold, thought of weakness, and felt an emotion he could not name.

"I have them." Tatty approached to lock the door behind him. "Are you ready to begin?"

Mondrian nodded. "Any time you want to." It was there again, the change in her. No word of affection, or even of greeting. No tenderness, no loving touch. He pushed his own feeling of disappointment into the background. What had to be done was too important.

"It won't all be bad, Esro." She had sensed but misunderstood his black mood. "Just think of it as Earth sightseeing."

"Most of it will be. But if Skrynol is right, one of those scenes is likely to jump out and murder me."

"How will it affect you?"

"Skrynol cannot say. And if a Fropper doesn't know, I won't even try to guess." Mondrian gestured to the phial of anesthetic spray that Tatty had tucked into the waistband of her black trousered suit. "Keep that close to you, but don't let me get my hands on it. I hope I won't even try, but Skrynol says what we are after goes so deep that I may try murder or suicide before I'll let it come up to the surface." He sat down on the long reclining chair and leaned back in it. "No point in waiting. Go ahead as soon as you like."

Tatty taped his wrists tight to the chair's arm-rests. She attached electrodes to palms, fingertips, and temples, and microphones to his throat and chest. Finally she sat down where she could see the camera displays and Mondrian's face.

Tatty turned on the recordings. Since he had given her no preferred order for the list of sites, she had made her own. The scenes of his early childhood were covered systematically, linking around the planet in a cross-cross pattern that spanned Earth from pole to pole. As the fancy struck her, at each location she had made her own voiceover on the three-D recordings, and added characteristic local sounds and smells.

She began with an area that sat firmly at the center of her own personal nightmares. Maybe Mondrian would share her horror of it. The Virgin lay in what had once been the American West. It formed a dumbbell of total devastation, a thousand miles long and three hundred wide. The Virgin's Breasts were located at Twin Strikes, in the north. Matching ten-mile craters at the two points of ground zero defined the nipples. The broad hips to the south were formed by the fused circular plain of Malcolm's Mistake. Tatty had flown over both areas, then set the car down midway between the two. "The Virgin's Navel," said her calm commentary. That was all. The place spoke for itself. The Navel was the most scarred and desolate spot on Earth's surface.

In the first few years, before the fusion glows began to fade, the experts made their measurements and their predictions: Earth life-forms would not return to the Virgin's Navel for more than a millennium.

They had been wrong, outrageously wrong. The first seeds had germinated in less than a decade. Within a generation, crocuses were blooming along the Navel's steep banks and within the deep, damp floor.

And yet in some ways the experts had been vindicated. Today the Virgin teemed with its own plants and animals.

But no birds sang, no bees buzzed, no coyotes howled. The purple-veined crocuses, their blossoms reaching taller than a tall man, were all carnivorous. Life at the Virgin's Navel was abundant; but it was silent and fierce, and it felt alien to Earth.

The camera scanned steadily across the rugged land-scape. Mondrian looked on silently, while Tatty shuddered again at the scene that she had recorded, at plants stunted or grossly overblown, at misshapen animals that parodied Nature.

At last Mondrian spoke. "Did you know that you can see the outline of The Virgin from the Moon? I don't think it's the color of the ground. It must be the altered vegetation."

His voice was calm. Tatty cut short the presentation. Much more of that scene, and Mondrian would have to use the anesthetic on *her*.

She moved to another one of her private hates. Mondrian had recalled being taken to the Antarctic when he was little more than a baby. He had unpleasant memories of it. So had Tatty, but hers were recent. The travel guides spoke only of the bursting polar summer, with the new hybrid grains running their full course from germination to harvest in less than thirty days of twenty-four-hour light. Tatty had come away with different visions. Of savage winds, age-old ice, and cruel black water lapping at the edge of the ice cap. Beyond the surf the killer whales waited, until the current crop of frozen corpses whose storage payments had not been made were brought from the frigid Antarctic catacombs and dropped into the dark water. To the orcas, humans were nothing more than a frozen, or occasionally clumsy and noisy, form of seal.

Her images did not catch that. The corpse drops were made when no observers were present. But she knew that they happened, and her recordings did catch to perfection the desperate haste of the short summer, as Nature raced to fill a complete cycle of seasons in a few short weeks of continuous sun. The rate of plant growth was so fast, it created an illusion of time-lapse photography.

Mondrian watched, as the field of view scanned across

a great flock of emperor penguins standing at the water's edge. Still he seemed fully relaxed. "If you don't like it there *now*,"—he had seen the expression of Tatty's face—"you ought to go there in winter. Can you imagine the life of one of those birds? They mate when it's a hundred below. Then they stand right there through the blizzards, balancing the egg on their feet."

Tatty gave him an angry glare as the display left Antarctica. Mondrian seemed to be *enjoying* himself.

She moved on to Patagonia. To her surprise, that far-off tip of South America had proved to be fascinating, her second favorite of the dozen places she had visited. When Mondrian first told her what he needed it sounded like an impossible job, hundreds of millions of square kilometers to be surveyed.

He had—as usual—persuaded her that she was wrong. For although the centuries-long exodus from Earth had provided a safety valve against population growth, it had never been quite enough. Those left behind could always breed faster than people could leave. As most of the planet gradually became more densely peopled, it also became more homogeneous. There was no need for Tatty to make recordings of BigSyd or Ree-o-dee, because in all essentials they were identical to Bosny or to Delmarva Town. Mondrian's wilderness memories could not be hiding there.

The only remaining candidates were the equatorial and polar reservations, plus a few other areas of Earth that were still sparsely populated for other reasons. The Kingdom of the Winds, which Tatty was showing now, was a good example. People *could* live there, in the bleak Patagonian shadow of the Andes; but few would choose to. The west winds that blew with incessant gale force from the cold mountain peaks created a *psychological* vacuum. Every generation the area was settled; every generation the settlements were abandoned after a few years.

But this too was not the source of Mondrian's trauma. He stared at the wind-scoured landscape without enjoyment, but also without emotion. Tatty studied his impassive face. Couldn't he see the beauty, of dark mountain lakes, of tangled forests of cypress, redwood, and Antarctic beech? Apparently not. She reluctantly moved on to the next location.

She had little hope for this one. She had never visited the great African game preserves before, but what she had seen on her recent trip had captivated her completely. She could not imagine this as a source of horror for any visitor.

Here was mankind's first home. Earth's remaining large herbivores and carnivores still lived here in natural conditions, grazing and prowling as they had for millions of years, except for one difference: their control implants made them harmless to humans.

Tatty had wandered on foot for many hours, savoring and recording the sights, sounds, and smells of the open plain. She loved to watch the herds break and wheel across the dusty ground as they responded to real or imagined danger. This was lightyears away from life in the Gallimaufries, a wonderful therapy after her confinement on Horus. She had brought no Paradox with her, and for the first time in years she had not craved it.

Mondrian did not seem to share her pleasure. He was lolling in his chair, apparently half-asleep as the images roamed back and forth across the rolling ground. Tatty prepared to move on to another region, but recalled that one of her own favorite memories was captured in a shot that came just a few seconds later on the recording.

"Watch this," she said. "Here it comes. Ngorongoro Crater—isn't that spectacular?" The display showed a majestic volcanic peak with the evening sun behind it. The broad red face of Sol was already on the horizon, sinking rapidly to an equatorial sunset. The great plain of Serengeti and the reservation lay beyond, dusty green and tan in the fading light.

"Beautiful!" said Tatty. She watched, as daylight bled away into a purple dusk, then turned at last to Mondrian. He was rigid in his chair, limbs trembling. She saw the protruding eyes and straining, swollen-veined countenance, and grabbed for the anesthetic.

It was not necessary. Before she could pull out the phial Esro Mondrian uttered a terrified whimper. While she watched, the spasm ended. He sighed, and sank low into the chair.

His eyes flickered once, and slowly closed; Mondrian slept.

Tatty stood alone within the little circle of light, wondering what she was getting herself into. Her heart was racing, and she was perspiring profusely. At this depth in the basement warrens the circulators and coolers did little more than make the air marginally breathable.

She held the light higher and stared around her. This had to be the right place. But she was *nowhere*. She stood halfway down a long, deserted corridor, with no side branches visible in front or behind her.

Tatty bent her head to check the Tracker reading one more time. It was showing exactly zero. The little red trace arrow had disappeared. It was useless! And when she started out she had imagined that she was being so clever and cunning.

Mondrian had taken over an hour to emerge from his catatonic trance—an hour during which his pulse had slowed almost to zero, and she had been forced to inject adrenalin and powerful heart-stimulants. As soon as he became conscious he would not stay, would not even wait to recuperate. He grabbed the recordings that she had made and struggled to the apartment door. He looked like a corpse, but he would not say where he was going— not even when she did what she had never done, lost her temper, and shouted and stormed at him.

All he would say was that he had to leave at once. And it was so obvious where he was going! He was heading for a meeting with Skrynol, to see if the Fropper could make sense of what had just happened.

In the middle of her tirade, Tatty thought of the Tracker. It was still in Mondrian's light travel bag, the only luggage that he ever carried down to Earth with him. She sneaked it out when he was re-setting his apartment ID key, and hid it away out of sight. Mondrian might not ask her help with the Fropper, but he was going to get it anyway! She could describe his appearance

when he was unconscious, and what he had said as he
fought his way back to consciousness.

Except that now she did not know how to find the
Fropper. She felt like an idiot. As soon as Mondrian left
her apartment she had turned on the Tracker. When the
moving arrow stopped, she fixed the setting and set out
in pursuit. Mondrian had stayed in one place for over an
hour, then began to retrace his steps. Tatty hid until he
went past her, then started forward again to his first
stopping place.

Forward—to nowhere! Mondrian had certainly not had
a Fropper session standing in this tunnel.

Was there some trick to using the Tracker, some technique that she had failed to understand?

She stared around her at the walls of the corridor. It
was high and narrow, no more than a couple of meters
across and lined with tremendous air-pipes. According to
Kubo Flammarion, the Tracker should be accurate to
better than twenty feet. That was just impossible. The
tunnel extended monotonously away in both directions
for fifty meters or more.

She peered down one more time at the Tracker, bringing her lamp closer to the instrument. As she did so that
light was suddenly plucked *upwards* from her hand. It
at once went out.

Tatty screamed. She had been plunged into absolute
darkness. She staggered backwards, until she ran into the
hard wall of the tunnel. She grabbed at the warm, padded air-pipes, the only familiar thing she could find. As
she did so, something caught her around her waist. She
was lifted easily off her feet, up and backwards *over* the
pipes, and placed down gently on a soft surface—where
no soft surface could be. Thick bindings snapped into
place around her wrists and ankles.

"It is not necessary to scream or struggle," said a
cheerful voice high above her. "Nor is it productive to
do so. Such actions are quite pointless, since you are in
no conceivable danger."

Tatty drew in a deep breath, ready to scream anyway.
Before she could begin, a dim red glow filled the air. It

gave her a first faint view of her surroundings. Instead of screaming, she gasped, gaped, and stared around her.

She was in a thiefhole!

The secret rooms were almost a legend, mysterious pockets scattered through the deepest reaches of the basement warrens. They were the Scavvies' final sanctuary, the hiding places for hunted criminals and contract-breakers. Their locations were passed on only by word of mouth, from one generation to the next. Earth's official authorities found it best to deny their very existence, since they were unable to locate and destroy them.

Tatty had never been in a thiefhole before, but she knew it at once from Gallimaufry rumor and descriptions. This one was tucked away behind the main air-pipes. The room was ten meters long, five meters high, and less than two across. A crude tap to the basement power lines in one corner fed the glowing fluorescents. They had been modified, to throw a murky red light through the long room. Another tap, this one to the air-pipes, provided just enough circulation to keep the air breathable. On the far wall stood an ancient food synthesizer, not apparently in current use. Next to that was a long painted screen of dull silver, shielding part of the room from view.

"You know where you are?" said a gentle voice from behind the screen.

"Yes. I am in a thiefhole." Tatty tried to keep the tremor out of her voice.

"Exactly so. With your permission, then." The light suddenly snapped off—without her permission. Tatty felt chilly electrodes attach to her body, and something else that she could not identify. She shivered.

"These are for my convenience, not for your discomfort," said the cheerful voice. "You will not be aware of them after a few moments. Do not worry, the lights will return shortly."

"Who are you?"

There was a high-pitched laugh in the darkness. "Now, Princess Tatiana Sinai-Peres, you know very well who I am, as surely as your name is Tatty Snipes. Otherwise you would not be here."

"You are Skrynol. The Fropper who has been treating Esro Mondrian."

"Indeed I am."

"Well, you may call it treatment if you want to." Tatty's courage was returning, and with it anger. "So far as I can see, you've been making him *worse*. God, I wish I had never mentioned your name to him. Put some damned *lights* on in here! You may be able to see in the dark, but I cannot."

"Your wish is my command." The lights came on again, but there was no sign of Skrynol. "Even if you had not brought him," said the voice behind the silver screen, "someone else would have. It was absolutely necessary that I should meet him, and absolutely essential that I should *treat* him. Tatty Snipes, can you describe Esro Mondrian to me? How well do you know him?"

"As well as I know anyone!" But then some tone in Skrynol's gentle voice made Tatty think again. She had not asked herself those questions for a long time. "He is the most intelligent and hard-working man that I have ever met," she said at last. "But sometimes I wonder if I know him at all. Sometimes I think that he is genuinely fond of me. And sometimes I think that he is a monster, somebody who cares for no one and who will use anything and anyone for his own purposes."

"Yet you are longtime lovers. And still you work for him!"

"I know." Tatty's laugh was harsh self-mockery. "You don't need to tell me what a fool I am. It's my own fault—but sometimes I think Esro can persuade me to do anything if he tries hard enough."

"You do know him, very well. But there is one thing that perhaps you do not realize about him. Mondrian is in some ways the most valuable person in the solar system. *He is also the most dangerous human in the Stellar Group*. Esro Mondrian is the reason—the sole reason—that I am here on Earth."

Tatty saw a monstrous shadow cast from behind the screen. Then a worse reality appeared, a gigantic stooped body shuffling forward on multiple jointed legs. She shrank back, as the Pipe-Rilla came slowly forward and squatted at her side.

"I have decided that I will gain nothing by concealing the truth from you." Skrynol's mild and cheerful voice did a lot to offset the Pipe-Rilla's frightening appearance. "I know that you are afraid, but there is truly no reason for fear. I will not harm you. Come, Tatty Snipes, you are a brave woman and you know that we are a peaceful species. I need your help."

Tatty stared at the long body crouching next to her. It had been strangely modified from the picture-book form, with fleshy forelimbs replacing the usual clawed ones. "I don't see how I can possibly help you."

"I do." The tall body stretched higher and leaned away, sensing her discomfort at its closeness. "Let me at least describe to you the problem. The Stellar Group members have been studying the human species for centuries—as intensively as humans have I am sure been studying us. In each generation, we strive to identify those humans whom we believe have unique powers for good or evil. Our record of such behavior prediction is excellent, but occasionally we find an anomaly, a human being who seems a total enigma. Such an individual must be watched closely, so that the potential for harm is never realized. And in the case of Esro Mondrian, we have the extreme anomaly: a human of exceptional abilities, whose own compulsions are so strong that they could lead him to self-destruction. And far more than that. Those compulsions imply danger for the whole of the Stellar Group."

"That's ridiculous. I said I don't understand him fully, and I don't. But I'll tell you one thing that I am sure of. Esro *likes* you—Pipe-Rillas, and Tinkers, and Angels."

"I agree. It makes no difference. Mondrian is not a simple man. There are others, like Commander Brachis, who hate all aliens in a direct and predictable way. We can allow for that, plan for it, and live with it. Mondrian is far more difficult. He likes us, but in some ways he cannot *tolerate* us. At a deep level he cannot stand the threat that the Stellar Group represents to him."

"How can you possibly be a threat to Esro?"

"We do not know. Mondrian remains a mystery, even after all my work with him. In such a situation, the human solution might well be that we must destroy him. But that avenue is not open to our kind. We must *help* Mondrian. We must find the source of that destructive drive, and we must eradicate it from him. That is where you can assist us."

"You don't understand. I've tried to help Esro—God knows I've tried. But I can't *reach* him, really get through to him. He'll never tell me what ails him."

"If it makes you feel better, I too have been unable to penetrate that shield, although my whole life and training have been for just such a purpose. But in my sessions with Mondrian I have become sure of one thing: he is torn apart by conflicting drives. He has the capacity for love, but it is drowned by internal fear. He is obsessed by the escaped Morgan Construct. Do you know why?"

"The Construct has to be destroyed. He's been working for that, night and day."

"He has been working, yes. Work is his life. But did you know that Mondrian *originated* the program for the Constructs? It was begun at his initiative. When the escaped Construct became a danger to everything in the Stellar Group, the ambassadors reluctantly decided that it must be destroyed. I do not question their decision. But I know that the decision to leave *Esro Mondrian* in charge of the operation was an awful mistake. He *needs* the Construct."

"He is trying to destroy it!"

"Is he? I am not so sure. Suppose he has been choosing pursuit teams to *control* the Construct, rather than kill it? I know this: Mondrian will never allow the last Construct to disappear, if there is any conceivable way to save it. He needs it in some urgent mode, far below the conscious levels of his brain. His need stems from the early experience for which I have been probing. Thanks to your work, I now know that it happened in Africa. But it lies so deep-rooted that I despair of reaching it. The *nature* of his torment remains hidden. The compulsion continues ... unless you help me to bring its cause to light."

"I already told you, I can do nothing with Esro."

"I disagree. Permit me one question. He has used you, over and over. You are a person with strength and a considerable intellect. Why do you continue to help him, knowing that he will use and abuse you again?"

Tatty found to her surprise that she was crying. Salt tears mingled with sweat and ran down her cheeks onto her upper lip. "*I don't know*. I suppose it's because—because I have no one else. Without Esro, I have nothing. I have no one. He is all I have."

"Possibly." A soft forelimb came forward to stroke Tatty's hair and dab at the tears on her cheeks. "But there is another explanation. Suppose that you stay *because you know that you are all that he has*. If not you, to whom would he turn for comfort? If not you, whom would he ask for help? You know that you love him. Ask yourself, do you want Mondrian *destroyed*?"

"No!" Tatty tried to sit up, but the bindings still restrained her. "I mean, I don't know. Many times I've cursed him and wished him dead."

"And always, you have relented. Always, you have been his support. If you really want to help Mondrian—and I have to tell you, it may be impossible, and already too late—then you must do the one thing that can make his treatment more effective: *Remove your support*. Tell him that it is all over, that he cannot come back to you and expect to be forgiven. Tell him that now he has *no one!*"

Skrynol reached forward and unclasped the bindings that held Tatty. She leaned forward, to place her open hands wearily to her face. "Suppose I did that? What good could it do him?"

"Perhaps it would do nothing. Perhaps he is past all help. But perhaps it would give me that little window, the chink of vulnerability that I need to treat him successfully. I admit it frankly: I am desperate, seeking any sort of lever. Your abandonment of him might provide it to me."

Skrynol helped Tatty to her feet. She stood leaning against the giant skeletal figure. "Do you think it will succeed?"

"No, I do not. I believe that it will almost certainly

fail." The Pipe-Rilla gave an imitative human shrug of her narrow body. "But what choice do I have? Since it is the only course left to me, it *must* be attempted."

Skrynol reached down to take Tatty's hand, like an adult leading a small child. "Come. Let us away from here. If you are to have your confrontation with Mondrian, it must happen before he again leaves Earth."

Tatty took a final look around the thiefhole as they moved on into stygian darkness. "Aren't you going to tell me to keep this a secret? Suppose that I were to tell someone of this meeting. Wouldn't it destroy all your plans?"

"Tell anyone." Skrynol chuckled, but there was no humor in the cheerful voice. "You may tell anyone you like, Tatty Snipes. Who do you think would ever believe you?"

Chapter 32

Guard duty rosters were posted at the Sargasso Dump as a matter of principle. Nagging by the Dump's computers allowed a few of those duties to be performed roughly as scheduled, but for the most critical functions—food, air supply, transportation, and safety—the guards were carefully excluded. They meant well, but most of them had long since lost all sense of time, urgency, or reliability.

So it was some other sense that brought the guards now to the great hemispherical dome of the Assembly Hall, and for half an hour they had been wandering in from all parts of the Dump. Luther Brachis would have been proud of them—and astonished. They came through the great master airlock with their dress uniforms neat, medals and insignia of office sparkling, and suit helmets newly polished. They took seats on rows of chairs facing the shrouded central platform, and waited without speaking.

Blaine Ridley sat alone at the control panel below the front of the platform. For the first time in weeks, his replacement eye was rolling and his jaw was working from side to side. He mirrored the excitement and anticipation of everyone in the hall.

At last he turned, and stared into the screened space behind him. He heard and saw nothing there.

But it was time.

His hand trembled as he pressed the button to roll away the metal screen. He had helped in the early phases, but the final body assembly had been done without him. For the past two days there had been no contact at all. If anything had gone wrong . . .

The screen vanished into the platform, and the overhead lights gleamed red. Within their fiery glow, M-26A came drifting forward. Blaine Ridley held his breath. Complete? No, more than complete. Perfect!

That is not so. M-26A was moving to the front of the platform. Ridley felt the rebuttal at once within his mind. Did the same message go to all the others?

Behold. Latticed wings lifted high above the rounded head, and the Construct slowly turned around. *I am as complete as perhaps I will ever be. But if I am perfect, then so also are you. For I am no more whole than you are. We share our imperfections . . . and our destiny.*

The platform lights blazed to white. Around the hall all the guards were stirring, craning forward for a closer look. And suddenly it was obvious. What had seemed at first sight like a flawless, seam-free body showed cracks where pieces had been cannibalized from other Construct fragments. There were slight size differences between sections, and other small patches glazed or discolored by the heat of weapons. The luminous eyes of M-26A were as mismatched as Ridley's own.

You see only my exterior. But as some of you will learn, my interior is no better. Yet I am ready, as you will be ready. M-26A came forward, to the very front of the platform, and waved Blaine Ridley to stand. *Proceed.*

Action took away nervousness. "We have researched all the stellar Link points within the solar system that can be reached through the local Link access in Sargasso." Ridley could be heard by the other guards, but he was speaking to M-26A alone. "And we have confirmed what you predicted. Solar system security learned its lesson at Cobweb Station. The stellar Links are monitored closely. There is no way to reach one and activate it, before Security would move to act against it."

And you are discouraged. That is natural. But it is not appropriate, for I anticipated this possibility. Did you find the person?

Ridley nodded. He had followed instructions, without

understanding why. He walked six steps away from the platform and returned leading a slim, red-haired woman by the arm. She showed no sign of injuries, but she trembled continuously and hair grew only on the right side of her head.

"This is Gudrun Meissner. She was chief engineer on the *Coriolanus*, before the accident. Her record shows that she once had experience of every kind of Link equipment."

Ascend, Gudrun Meissner, and come close.

"She cannot hear, or speak." But as Ridley said the words, the woman stepped up unassisted onto the platform.

She is already hearing. Soon she will speak, and soon she will accomplish great things. M-26A reached out its wing panels, and enclosed Gudrun Meissner within them. The luminous eyes stared into hers. After half a minute her trembling body quietened.

Now we are ready, said the voice inside Blaine Ridley's head. *Open the ceiling.*

It was done with a single touch of Ridley's finger on the control panel. The dark dome of the Assembly Hall cleared to an absolute transparency. A hundred faces peered upward, and saw against the starry background a hexagon of glowing blue. At its heart lay a concave star of moldering darkness, a shrunken and crude travesty of a Mattin Link chamber.

If we cannot make use of the solar system's active stellar Link points, we must accept that fact. But this is Sargasso, where all things may be found.

M-26A drifted down from the platform, still holding Gudrun Meissner.

The Mattin Link was long in development, and it did not come at once to its present perfection. Behold one of the original units. It has been floating in the Dump for five hundred years, it is primitive, it is inactive, it is deemed without value. Yet, like other things judged valueless, it may work again to fulfill its destiny.

Suits closed!

That reflex lived on, even in the most damaged guard. Helmets were lifted into position and locked closed.

Follow me. And we will show the universe how much can be done with little.

M-26A itself needed no suit. The Construct, holding Gudrun Meissner protectively to its silver-blue body, led the procession. A hundred guards marched proudly behind M-26A to the master airlock, and drifted on through it.

They held formation all the way; all the way through open space, to where the obsolete hulk of the Mattin Link unit, derelict and neglected, floated far above them.

Chapter 33

It was late when Luther and Godiva came home to their living quarters on the ninety-fourth level of Ceres. They were both tired. He had taken her on a long-postponed sight-seeing tour, pausing at the high-mag viewing ports of the outer shell so that he could point out the many worlds of the solar system, and far beyond them the scattered stars of the Stellar Group.

It was all old hat to Luther. He could not remember a time when he was not familiar with everything that they saw. It was a shock to find that Godiva, raised in the dark subterranean runs of the Gallimaufries, had only the vaguest idea of planets, moons, and stars. She didn't know the difference between them. She had never heard of Oberon Station, or Cobweb Station, or even the Vulcan Nexus. She seemed to believe that all the asteroids were as developed and cosmopolitan as Ceres. Most startling of all, she had no idea of *distance*; to Godiva, the Oort Harvester was as near (or as far) as the remote Angel world of Sellora.

She had laughed at Brachis's astonishment and disapproval. "What does it *matter*, Luther. Who cares how far away any of them are, when you can get to all of them in nothing flat using the Mattin Link."

"Well, yes, that's true. But the *distance* ..." Brachis stopped. Godiva was uniquely Godiva. Time and space meant nothing to her. And when he thought about it, he was not sure that she was wrong. "Close" points were really ones that could be reached quickly through a series

331

of Mattin Links. "Distant" points were all others. Luther allowed Godiva to take his hand and they went on, drifting through the endless outer corridors of the planetoid.

The original one-hour tour continued through a long and pleasurable day and evening. The corridor was deserted when Brachis paused at their apartment door and made his usual thorough inspection of the settings. All the seals were unbroken, and there had been no callers. He carefully slid back the heavy door and they went on through into the hallway.

The advent of Godiva had changed Luther's life completely. Before she came up from Earth he had lived in a sparsely furnished single room. That had been abandoned in favor of a luxury apartment. The main living-room, dining area and kitchen were off the hall to the left, the bedroom, bathroom and study to the right.

"Hungry?"

Godiva shook her head. She yawned, stretched, and slipped off her light wrap. She gave Luther a smile of sleepy suggestion, dropped her bag onto the hall table, and went through the bedroom to the bathroom.

He took off his uniform, sat on the broad bed, and pulled off his boots. Naked, he walked through to the study and sat down at the communications terminal. He was tired, but as always he had to make his evening check for messages.

He switched on. As he did so there was a sudden high-pitched hissing sound. An intense pain like a hornet's sting burned his left cheek. Brachis saw a little puff of vaporized blood blossom out from below his eye. He shouted at the pain and jerked upright. As he did so there was a second sting by his right nostril, and another sudden puff of bright red.

He jumped to his feet. His first thought was that there had been some sort of short circuit in the communications terminal, showering him with specks of hot metal. The hiss that went with each blow seemed to come from the top of the display unit. As Brachis looked that way three more jolts hit him, one on the chin and two above his right eyebrow. He lifted his hand to his face, and saw them: four miniature figures, crouched behind the front lip of the display. Each manikin was no more than an inch and a half tall. Each carried a weapon pointed at Luther's face.

They were after his eyes! He covered his face with his left forearm, in time to block three more shots.

Adestis simulacra—at the maximum size permitted, and hunting *him*.

Luther swept his right arm across the top of the display, knocking the minisims to the floor. As he completed the movement a hail of shots from behind made him shout with pain and spin around. On the desk at the far side of the room, half-hidden behind a jumble of data cubes, stood another group of tiny figures. At the same moment a rattle of shots came from a new direction, over to his left. Explosive projectiles riddled his left arm and hip with thumbnail-sized craters.

Brachis roared with pain and ran across the room. He had both arms in front of him to shield his eyes—if they blinded him he was finished. Halfway to the door he felt another hail of shots in his groin and belly. The simulacra in ambush by the exit had chosen a different target.

He stopped and spun around again. The attack was obviously well-organized. They had planned for his natural reaction, to run for the door. They would expect him to cover his eyes, and now his genitals. If they knew his habits at all, they had known that he would walk through naked to check the communicator.

While he hesitated in the middle of the room, another half dozen projectiles stung his face and neck. They were flaying him, systematically ripping the flesh from his body with a hail of tiny shells.

He needed time to think. Luther dived to the left, rolled across the floor, and came upright close to the wall. He smashed his hand at the lighting panel. With the door to the bedroom closed, the study was plunged at once into darkness. The hiss of shots went on, but the attacking simulacra no longer had a target.

Brachis dropped to the floor again, and went shuffling on hands and knees across the room. He had a brief advantage now. He could track the minisims by the uvarovite-garnet glint of their crystalline green eyes, glowing in the dark. They were moving about in confusion. He knew it could only be a temporary respite. The attackers must have allowed for darkness, too.

He felt his way back to the display and slapped the *Emergency* switch on the communications panel. That would bring help—but far too late. Another half minute of those explosions on his skin, and the rescuers would find him a sightless, skinless eunuch. He was filled with a new and terrifying thought. Suppose that Godiva came out of the bathroom and wandered through into the study to look for him? A shout to keep her out might have exactly the wrong effect.

He was still standing upright by the emergency switch when an orange light appeared on the other side of the room. It was an aerial flare, ignited near the door. That was where the maximum cross-fire would have hit him if he had tried to escape that way. But the orange flare was enough to illuminate the whole room. He was visible again.

Another crackle and hiss from miniature weapons— another hail of blows and blaze of pain across his body. He couldn't take much more. He dived, rolled again, and came up near the desk. As the attackers there fired point-blank into his unprotected chest and side, he hit a sunken wall panel with the palm of his left hand.

The Fire Protection System came on in a fraction of a second. High pressure jets of water and emulsifier cross-crossed the room from floor to ceiling, while the loud warning tone of a bell sounded through the apartment and its nearest neighbors. The emergency low-power wall lights filled the study with sickly green.

Spray and foam filled the room. The miniature weapons at once went silent.

Another reprieve—but for how long?

Luther could not wait for help. He had to do this *himself*. He hurled himself across the study, soaking and bloodied. He ran first for the place where the attackers had been most dense. Water hit him from all sides, stinging his wounds, sluicing down his ripped skin. He welcomed it.

The minisims were trying to regroup, struggling to

stand amid the bombardment of water drops and frothy foam. Ignoring the pain in his hands, Brachis smashed them flat and crushed them one by one between thumb and fingers.

The study door slid open and Godiva appeared. She was naked except for a pair of gauzy briefs. "Luther!"

He ignored her and ran back across the room, a scarlet Nemesis that left bloody, puddled footprints behind him in the carpet. The first group who had attacked him were on the floor by the communications unit, trying to point their weapons up at Luther while a quarter-inch flood of water surged and tugged at their legs. He stomped every one of them, wincing as the angular figures cut into his soft flesh.

A final scatter of shots came from his right. He headed that way, smashing and devastating with bare hands and feet anything that moved.

And suddenly it was over.

By the time that help arrived the sprinkler system was off and the study a junkyard of flattened simulacra. Godiva took Luther through to the bedroom and began to apply antiseptics and surrogate skin. He lay faceup on the bed, his face, chest, and belly an eroded mass of raw wounds connected by shreds of loose skin. He swore continuously as Godiva smoothed on the yellow synthetic flesh. He waved away the emergency service staff. They went back into the study and started to clean up the mess, suctioning the room clean and dry. They were still at it when Esro Mondrian arrived.

Godiva had finished Luther's left side and was telling him to turn more to the right. He was ignoring her, and talking furiously on a handset.

"Useless!" he growled to Mondrian. "They don't know one damned thing. *Adestis* Headquarters won't have regular staff there until tomorrow, and maintenance can't even tell me if simulacra are missing, never mind what sort. Ouch!" He winced as Godiva began to patch skin onto the ball of his right thumb.

"Does it matter how many?" Mondrian picked up one of the flattened simulacra from the heap at the bedside and inspected it. "I didn't know they made them this big. What are they used for?"

"To hunt the biggest game. Scorpions and crustaceans, mostly. They can operate under water, but luckily for me they were never designed to handle a rainstorm."

"But the real question isn't the minisims. It's who was handling them. Did you ask?"

"*Adestis* Headquarters can't tell me that, either." Brachis touched his finger tenderly to the biggest wound on his face, a one-centimeter crater in the middle of his left cheek. "But I know the answer without being told. It's that bastard's Artefacts again, it has to be."

Mondrian was studying Brachis's pitted and furrowed skin. "Someday, Luther, you must tell me just what you did to earn such undying enmity from Fujitsu that his heirs would try to give you more craters than the surface of Callisto."

"Never mind what I did. The worst thing I did was, I underestimated him. For that, I deserve everything I've been getting."

"You told me that you had everything locked up tight here in the apartment, so nobody and nothing could get in. What went wrong, Luther?"

"The oldest mistake in the world. It proves the point that I tell every trainee for Survey basic training: *It's the things you don't expect that get you.* I set up this apartment so that nothing could get in through the door without me knowing. Nothing can burrow through the walls or floors or ceilings. I put in a sniffer system to sound an alarm if anything poisonous or radioactive was blown in as gas or dust through the air supply ducts. What I *didn't* expect was that something smart and dangerous could actually *walk in* along the ducts. The openings are only a couple of centimeters across."

"Big enough." Mondrian glanced from the simulacrum he was holding to the other man's battered body. "I'm amazed to see how much firepower one of these things can carry. Surely you don't need to hit that hard, even for scorpions."

"They were carrying the absolute top of the weapons line. It took two minisims to handle some of the guns.

That's the sort of equipment that *Adestis* normally gives only to a group that they judge to be inexperienced *and* scared shitless. One shell from the big guns would do for a scorpion. It damned near did for me."

"Last time we met you told me you thought you had located and destroyed every artefact that the Margrave left. Obviously, you were wrong." Mondrian nodded his head to the heavy apartment door and its protective locks. "But if you thought you'd got them all, why did you bother with such an elaborate security system?"

"My guardian angel insisted." Brachis pointed an index finger, its nail half blown away, at the near-nude Godiva. "You're right, *I* thought I'd killed the lot. Now I have to start over."

During the first few frantic minutes, Godiva had been totally absorbed in her work on Luther. She was still wearing only her thin panties and had not thought to put on more clothing. Her only worry was to patch new skin, carefully and completely, onto every one of his wounds. She had not seemed to notice the arrival of Esro Mondrian. But now, directly introduced into the conversation, she seemed to become aware of her own near-nude condition. She applied a final patch to Luther's shoulder, stooped to kiss him quickly on the lips, and headed for the bathroom. "Ten minutes," she said. "To put on a robe and dry my hair. Please don't let him get into more trouble while I'm gone, Esro."

Her departure created a gap in the conversation of the two men. Brachis, tough as he was, felt drained and distant. With Mondrian silent, he began to think again of the Artefacts. How many more were there? How could he hide from them, how could he destroy them?

His mind drifted back to the silent surface of Hyperion. As soon as he had arranged for delivery of the volatiles, the seven items had been delivered to him as promised from storage. The crew who brought them returned at once to the Deep Vault. They did not look back. They had no interest in knowing—or perhaps they suspected only too well—what Brachis intended to do with his purchase.

The logical thing was to flashfire the seven containers

at once and leave the airless surface of Saturn's moon with minimal delay. Only some dreadful driving streak of curiosity forced Brachis to open them, and thaw the contents.

The first four varied in appearance, but they were recognizably in the image of the Margrave. Brachis fired them at once. Two more were younger, clean-shaven, and fatter. It took the DNA match to prove that they too derived directly from Fujitsu. When the eight million degree flame passed over them, they too were gone in an eyeblink flash of purple light.

It was the seventh and final box, where identification in the Deep Vault had been the poorest, that would linger forever in Luther's memory. The casket held a young girl in her early teens. Naked, clear-skinned, and fair of face, she was barely past puberty. Her countenance still had the purity and innocence of a child, but when those young breasts and slender hips matured into womanhood she would be like a younger Godiva Lomberd.

The container gave her complete identification, along with her DNA sequence. It differed from the Fujitsu line in every significant detail. She was the oldest daughter of a deposed royal, from a *bend sinister* line that was now long extinct. Whoever had committed her to the Deep Vault of Hyperion had purchased, for whatever reason, a perpetual endowment of the highest quality. For four hundred and forty years she had lain in frozen silence, dreaming of whatever phantom shadows might flee through a brain held at the temperature of liquid helium. Left now on the surface, she would die—or, worse yet, *waken* and die—on the barren, airless wilderness of Hyperion.

Brachis had made no contingent plans for his purchases from the Deep Vault. Even if he were desperate to do so, it was impossible to save her. He groaned, cursed, and stared around him at the black-shadowed plain. It taunted him, with its emptiness and uselessness. At last he shuddered in his suit, breathed deep, and raised the fusion torch. Subnuclear fire reached out to caress the pale young body. As it consumed her bare breast, Brachis fancied that she sighed, opened dark-blue eyes, and stared up at his face . . .

"Luther!" Mondrian was leaning over him, snapping his fingers in front of his face. "Come on, pull out of that. I think we have to let the medics take a look at you, even if you don't want it. Just how much blood did you lose in there? The water could have sluiced a couple of liters down the drain and we'd never know it."

"I'll be all right." Brachis struggled to a sitting position. "But I'm wondering where we go from here. Just think what would have happened if Godiva had come with me into the study, instead of heading for the bathroom. She doesn't have any of our training in survival. I don't think I could have saved her. But I know I would have tried, and that would have been the end of both of us."

"Want to send her back to Earth for a while, until we're sure the Fujitsu Artefacts have been taken care of once and for all?"

"She won't go. We've been through all that, half a dozen times. Anyway, I'm not sure that Earth would be safe. If our contract is known there, they could go through her to get to me." Brachis rubbed at the thickened synthetic skin on the back of his right hand. That hand was still regrowing, and the delicate real skin was beginning to itch furiously as the chemical bond of the newly applied synthetic became complete. "It's an impossible problem. She won't leave me, and I can't protect her. The next hit could come from anywhere. Poisoned food, assassins, sabotaged transport equipment, faulty airlocks, anything."

"As you said once before, Luther, you found yourself a genius. Fujitsu has been two steps ahead all the way. But I have a suggestion for you."

"No hidden agendas, Esro." Brachis spoke wearily, as Godiva appeared from the bathroom. "I'm not up to them at the moment. Just tell me how we are going to make *her* safe."

Godiva had dried her blond hair and restyled it to an ancient form, so that it hung over her forehead and partly hid one eye. She drifted across to Brachis, inspected his wounds, and nodded in satisfaction. She sat down at his side without a word. Her short tunic left arms and legs bare, and her skin glowed from a vigorous toweling.

Mondrian studied the two of them closely. He was sure that he was missing something about their relationship, but in spite of all his efforts he could not begin to guess what.

"We all have hidden agendas, Luther. But this time I think that you and I have common interests."

"Persuade me."

Mondrian nodded in acknowledgement. It was one of his own favorite lines. "I'll try. Let's start with a question: What would be the safest place in the universe for you and Godiva? Not just the safest place in the solar system, but the safest place within the entire Perimeter."

"I don't know. Not here, that's for sure, no matter how much protection we pile on for us."

"And certainly not down on Earth, for either one of you. I agree with you, if Fujitsu's Artefacts are there they might try next for Godiva. But there's one place that even the Margrave won't be able to get to: the Q-ship, in orbit around Travancore. The Link coordinates to that are known only to three people in the universe: you, me, and Kubo Flammarion."

"It should be safe enough, I'll buy that." Brachis was visibly weakening, while Godiva was frowning at Mondrian. "But we've got the blockade in position, which means once you go there you can't come back. It would mean a one-way trip until a pursuit team finishes off the Construct. Suppose that takes years? Go to Travancore, and you could be stuck on the Q-ship until you die of boredom."

"There are worse fates." Mondrian surveyed the other man's battered body. "Stay here, and it's certainly not boredom you'll be dying of. In any case, I don't think the action on Travancore will take long, otherwise I wouldn't be going out there myself. My original plan was to take Captain Flammarion with me, while you stayed in charge at Anabasis Headquarters. But after what just happened here, it makes sense to switch that, and leave Kubo on Ceres. I assume you trust him?"

"He's your man, and that won't change. Other than

that, he's a rock. But I'm a devil of a lot better in a crisis."

"Which we certainly have at Travancore. But Kubo can stay here, give information to nobody, and send us anything that we need through the Link."

"What about Godiva?"

"Whatever you like. With you out of the way, I don't really think she'll be in danger anywhere."

"It makes no difference." Godiva spoke for the first time since her return. "Where Luther goes, I go."

"And I won't go without you." Brachis tried to smile, and produced only a pained grimace as the artificial skin on his face stretched in unfamiliar directions. "All right, so we both go. And the sooner the better. I'm tired of being chipped away, bit by bit."

"Very good." Mondrian stood up. "I will notify Captain Flammarion. We'll leave as soon as you are physically able to do so."

"I'm able now. I was planning another trip out to the Sargasso Dump, but that can wait awhile. We'll be ready tomorrow morning."

"I won't approve that. You will not be sufficiently recovered."

"Esro, you don't need to approve. You seem to forget, you don't outrank me any more in the Anabasis."

"Don't think I am unaware of that. Sometime you must tell me what you promised Lotos, to work that deal. But for the moment"—Mondrian stared at Brachis, and saw new pallor around his eyes—"Godiva, he needs a doctor even if he doesn't want one. Luther, if you tried to stand up you would fall over."

"Would I? Just watch me, then." Brachis swayed to his feet, shaking his head when Godiva tried to help him. "No doctors." He hobbled away to the bathroom. "Tomorrow morning, Esro. We'll be ready."

Godiva sighed, and sat down again opposite Mondrian. "Stubborn! But what happened to you, Esro? You look nearly as bad as Luther."

"I'm fine."

"You are not." She leaned close and peered into his eyes. "Are you taking Tatty with you to Travancore?"

"No." Then Mondrian's own control failed, and he had to ask the question. "Godiva, what made you suddenly ask about *Tatty*? I didn't even mention her name."

"I know. You didn't need to." Godiva gave him a satisfied smile. "Esro, if I understand anything in the whole universe, it's men's emotions. Luther couldn't see it, but I can. You're *radiating* misery. Have you two been fighting?"

"That's too dignified a word for it." He smiled, but his eyes were bleak. "There was no fight. We were down in her apartment on Earth, and I wanted her to come back to Ceres with me. She said no. Then she dumped me, simple as that. She says she never wants to see me again, after what I did to her."

Godiva took Mondrian's hands in hers. He felt a flow like electricity along his forearms—a tingle that Tatty said could be felt only by men, and had termed "The Godiva Effect."

"I'm sorry, Esro." Godiva squeezed his hands. "Maybe she'll change her mind. I'll talk to her. But right now I'd better go and see what's keeping Luther. I think he needs more help than he'll admit."

She stood up and went across to the bathroom without looking again at Mondrian. Decency demanded that such pain and misery be permitted at least privacy.

Chapter 34

Pulling information out of Vayvay was almost impossible. The Coromar seemed to have only two interests in life: finding food, and eating it. Chan had sat in on three weary hours of Angel's careful questioning and requestioning, then he had given up. He lacked Angel's infinite patience. He wandered out to the lip of the tent, where S'greela and Shikari were basking in the mid-morning sunlight.

"How can Angel stand it?" he said. "Every question has to be repeated ten times, and still there's nothing to show at the end."

"Talking to Vayvay?" S'greela nudged Shikari with one hind-limb. As usual, the Tinker was trying to creep up into a lumpy heap around their legs. "I admit, Vayvay is not easily mistaken for a genius. In fact, I myself asked Angel the same question, how was it possible to be so patient with such an idiot?"

"But Angel did not answer you."

"Indeed, yes. Angel indicated that communication with humans provided a sufficient base of prior experience."

Chan glared, and decided not to react. He had noticed a strange phenomenon. S'greela, and even Angel, seemed to be picking up the Tinker's perverse sense of humor. In fact, they were all beginning to sound more and more like each other. It was harder all the time to tell who made a remark simply from its content, or the way in which it was phrased. Was *he* starting to sound like the rest of them, too?

343

Chan thought not. In some ways, he was the outsider of the group. When he had rushed back yesterday to tell them what had happened to him in the tunnels, they had listened quietly enough; but he knew that they rejected what he said, almost without considering it.

That idea was full of disturbing possibilities. Angel insisted that the Construct had not moved from its original putative location, far from them. And Mondrian had told Chan that Nimrod's powers for mental disturbance were *short-range*. Close contact would be needed for it to have any effect. So if Chan's bewildering encounter had *not* been with Nimrod, there was only one other clear possibility: he was going crazy.

Chan had other evidence for that. After his arrival back at the camp the previous night, he had almost no memory of the rest of the evening. He recalled sitting in a close, compact group, listening to Angel talk to the Coromar. And that was *all* that he remembered, until he had awakened today under the outspread mantle of the Tinker Composite.

Suppose that fears and confusion were affecting his judgement? Then he had to discover the source of those delusions, before he put the others in danger. And *that* urgency made him want to proceed too fast with the hunt for Nimrod. *Festina lente*—hasten slowly. But it was hard to do, when the others were so in favor of rapid action.

This morning they were raring to go. Angel was now sure that the task of stalking Nimrod through Travancore's vertical forest could be simplified. "There is, as you conjectured, a grid of horizontal tunnels." Angel had finally emerged from the long dialogue with Vayvay. "It becomes denser and more continuous, down close to the true surface of the planet. But it is not so well maintained as the tunnels higher up. The Coromar look after the high tunnels much better, because they are their primary feeding grounds. However, the lower network will be adequate for our needs. We can use it to move close to Nimrod, and still minimize the chance of our detection."

"It would be quicker and easier to come straight down from above," objected S'greela.

"Easier, but not safer," said Chan. "Nimrod will sense our presence if we try to move straight down through the vegetation. But the surface of the planet may confuse the return signal for the Construct's sensors. We'll use the horizontal tunnels. Is Vayvay willing to lead the way?"

"That is not clear." Angel turned to the Coromar, who was slowly emerging from inside the tent. A few more seconds of squeaks produced a shake of Angel's topmost fronds, and a human-sounding sigh. "Why even ask? The answer could have been predicted. Vayvay will take us to within a safe distance from Nimrod, provided that we guarantee plenty of food as payment. Vayvay asks, how close to Nimrod do we wish to approach?"

Chan thought about that, as the three others waited impatiently. "I really don't know. For all I can say—and my experience yesterday supports it—Nimrod could be aware of us all the time. How else do you explain what happened to me down in the shaft?"

There was a non-committal silence, while Chan began to feel annoyed all over again. The others were being diplomatic, but still they didn't believe him. When he had filed his report on the incident and sent it back to the Q-ship, the three of them had been annoyingly passive. They did not comment on or add to what he had sent—and *that* was unusual in such an opinionated group.

"All right." Chan turned again to Angel. "Let's take the problem from the other end. How close is Vayvay *willing* to approach to Nimrod?"

Another sequence of bat-squeaks from Angel's communicator, dipping in and out of Chan's audible range, led to a reply from the Coromar, and then another longer exchange between the two.

Angel turned at last to the others. "Apologies, for the time taken. The first answer was quickly given, but it was not in terms that are easily translated to your notations. Truly, there is no fixed reply. The answer is a nonlinear equation, a complicated balance of food offered against risks taken. And the distance unit that Vayvay employs is also not a constant. It is measured in *browsing-distance-days*, and is therefore location-dependent. In over-simplified terms, Vayvay will go as close as we want, provided that we always guarantee sufficient amounts of food."

"Can't you negotiate something a bit more specific?"

"That is already done. Primitive in some ways, Vayvay certainly seems to understand the barter principle. For three thousand kilos of synthesized high-protein vegetable matter, Vayvay will take us to within two kilometers of Nimrod's most likely current position—for which a probability of 0.98 now seems appropriate."

Angel was still leaving the most difficult decision to Chan. How close to Nimrod *dare* they go, before they descended to the solid surface of Travancore? Traveling above the vegetation could be done in the aircar, and swiftly, but surface travel would be on foot and slow.

Chan made the decision, probably quicker than he should have. "We'll go down a shaft one full day's march from the estimated location of the Morgan Construct. Say, twenty kilometers away from it."

"The coordinates for such a shaft are already available. But of course," Angel added, "these coordinates are *time-dependent*. When would we leave?"

"As soon as feasible. At once, if we can."

But having made that decision, Chan began to worry about it. He had no faith in his own judgment. All morning he had been feeling feverish and light-headed. Was he actually getting *sick*? His immune system had been boosted at the beginning of pursuit team training, making it supposedly robust enough to handle any micro-organisms on Barchan or Travancore. But that was just theory. Maybe yesterday's hallucinations and today's uneasiness were the result of a real physical ailment, nothing to do with Nimrod, nothing to do with mental instability.

Chan had little time for brooding. The aircar had already been recalled from its high, hovering orbit, and arrived within minutes. It took all their efforts to lift

Vayvay aboard, but then they were off, heading around the great planetary curve of Travancore. The car skimmed over billowing waves of vegetation rising and falling below them like an endless turbulent sea.

They were at the chosen entry shaft in less than an hour. Before they entered the threatening black eye of the tunnel, S'greela sent the capsule back to orbit. If they returned safely, fine. It would be easy enough to recall it and use it to take them to the Q-ship. If they died . . .

Chan realized, with gloomy satisfaction, that from the Stellar Group's point of view everything was safe enough. The capsule's current parking orbit was low, and atmospheric drag would bring it to re-entry and burn-up in only a couple of weeks. Whatever happened, Nimrod would not gain access to the Q-ship, and the Mattin Link that sat within it.

Everyone except Vayvay became subdued when they entered the shaft. Chan felt particularly depressed. As they gradually lost the sunlight, his mood sank to match the shadowed gloom of Travancore's lower forest. The spiraling path seemed to go on forever, down and down and down. The journey took longer than Chan had expected, because Vayvay always wanted to stop and nibble at any promising growth of leaves.

"As we were warned," said Angel. "Browsing-distance-days."

At last they persuaded the Coromar to keep going by additional bribes from the stores that they were carrying. The downward pace increased. Finally they came to the end of the vertical shaft. The drop to the surface took place in a close and dripping darkness. It felt to Chan like an irreversible and unwise step when he released his hold and fell lightly to the forest floor.

He was claustrophobic and filled with unnamed dread. The surface of Travancore would be an awful place to die; lightless, silent, stifling. The air pressed in on him like a shroud. He could not get Leah out of his mind. Had her fatal encounter with Nimrod taken place close to here? Had she died only a few kilometers from where they stood?

He could not remember. Somehow he could not bring himself to ask Angel to check the official record.

The floor of the jungle was flat, spongy, and damp. Nothing grew here except the immense boles of the megatrees, each one scores of meters across at the base. Long trailers of creeper depended from the upper levels and hung between the trunks. Faintly phosphorescent, their intertwined filaments hindered the path of any traveler moving on the natural surface.

After a few seconds of squeaking and searching, Vayvay set off across the forest floor, burrowing a way through the tangled creepers. Soon they came to one of the horizontal pathways. Two minutes more, and Vayvay had found the entrance. They walked into an arched structure, shining their lights around them on the orange and brown walls of a primitive roofed chamber.

"Home of the Maricore," said Angel. "Apparently they do a poor job of maintenance. Vayvay says that we should not expect to meet the Maricore. They are nervous, and will keep out of our way."

They set off along one of four tunnels that met at the entry chamber. It was only just wide enough for Vayvay, who led the way. The Coromar kept stopping, and not for food. S'greela, walking second, had to prod hard at Vayvay's bolster-like rear end to start them moving again.

Chan walked last, in a foul mood. When they met Nimrod, they had to act at once to disable or destroy the Construct. He had warned the others. This time there could be none of the do-as-you-please behavior that had somehow worked on Barchan. They had all agreed—but how could he be sure that Shikari and Angel and S'greela would follow *any* instructions when the critical moment came?

It was a time for fears, memories, and introspection. No one spoke. Chan, hot and sweating, looked around him and observed their surroundings with the floating, feverish intensity of a bad nightmare. It was hard to plod along across soggy, decaying leaves and molds, and realize that only five kilometers away Travancore's sun was still illuminating the emerald green grottoes of the upper forest. If the descent had seemed long, this march through the broken pathway on the surface was interminable.

More than three hours passed before Vayvay halted again, and finally. No amount of prodding would persuade the Coromar to move. They were at a branch point in the surface network, with enough room for Angel to glide forward and stand alongside Vayvay. There was a short conversation. To Chan, even the ultrasonics sounded damped and muffled by their dank surroundings.

"Vayvay will go no farther," said Angel. "Not even for abundant food. We are within two kilometers of Nimrod's presumed location. Vayvay says, if we continue along the broader branch here, and ignore any narrow side branches, we will come to the location that we specified."

"What will Vayvay do now?"

"If we desire the Coromar to do so, it will wait here—with the supplies."

"Say that he is to wait here for two days, if Vayvay knows what a day is," said Chan. "If we are not back by then, everything is his."

"Vayvay is not *he*," corrected Angel. "But a Coromar possesses a sense of time. The message will be delivered."

While that was being done, Chan insisted on a final check of equipment. Each team member carried weapons, but after the training on Barchan, Chan was sure that for Angel and Shikari it was a total waste of effort. It took forever for each of them to train and fire. He wondered again about the way that pursuit teams were being used by the Anabasis. Now that he had met Brachis and Mondrian, it seemed more in keeping with their natures to lob a bomb in from orbit. They might blow away a few cubic miles of Travancore along with the Morgan Construct, but it would be a no-risk operation.

He suspected that they had thought about it long ago—and known it would be vetoed in horror by the rest of the Stellar Group.

The most dangerous time was approaching. Chan moved to lead the way. S'greela came next, holding a

pencil light high above Chan to cast a narrow, bobbing
beam along the roofed corridor. Behind them Vayvay
gave a squeak of farewell, answered by Angel, and then
everything was silent. The loudest sound in the tunnel
was Chan's breathing, and the whispering flutter of the
Tinker's many wings.

Earlier progress had been glacier slow. Now they
seemed to be rushing forward. Soon they had less than
one kilometer to go. Chan found himself staring hard at
the darkness, trying somehow to see beyond the farthest
point illuminated by S'greela's ghostly light beam. There
was nothing. Nothing but silent walls of orange-brown,
stretching out forever in front of them.

And then, suddenly, it ended. The rounded tunnel
walls stopped. S'greela's light beam met a tangled mess
of creeper, ten feet above the ground. Below that, nothing. The group moved forward cautiously to stand on an
open area of jungle floor.

According to Angel, Nimrod should be less than fifty
meters ahead. So what now?

Before Chan could give any command, three things
happened at once. An insane burst of metallic clicking
came from Angel's communicator, and rose to a supersonic scream of activity that hurt Chan's ears. Shikari
burst apart, filling the air in the clearing with a whirling
swarm of components. At the same moment S'greela's
light jerked high into the air, then abruptly went out.

Chan froze. Angel went suddenly silent. The darkness
around them was absolute. Chan turned to move closer
to the others. Before he could take a step he was gripped
tightly around the waist and whipped off his feet. Something immensely strong and wiry spun him dizzily end-
over-end, then violently *threw* him, outward and upward.

He flew on for ages. Chan curled into a ball and protected his skull with his arms. At any moment he might
smash into one of the huge and solid tree trunks. The
impact would be fatal at this speed.

The feared collision never came. Instead his wild flight
was ended by a soft material that stretched and stretched
to absorb his momentum. He was slowed to a halt, then
dropped headfirst. He prepared for collision with the

spongy jungle surface, but that too never came. Instead
he found himself suspended in mid-air, wriggling in the
restraining hold of a rubbery, fine-meshed net.

Chan had never felt so helpless. He had lost his
weapon. He could not see. The net offered no resistance,
nothing tangible to struggle against. Even if somehow he
were able to escape from its hold, he would have no idea
what to do next.

That problem was solved in a moment. The whole net
was suddenly moving, carrying him along at high speed
in a horizontal direction. Something big was clearing the
way in front of him. He could hear the thresh of its rapid
passage through soft, hanging creepers.

It was another short trip. Within a minute they
stopped, and Chan was lowered gently to the ground.
The net loosened and rolled him out of it. He came to
rest on the fibrous damp floor of the forest, facedown
and breathing in the stale-sweet aroma of mold.

He sat up, dizzy and still in darkness. It was a few
more seconds before he was able to clamber to his feet
and take a few hesitant steps forward. He held his arms
out in front of him. His groping fingers finally met the
furry bole of one of the giant megatrees. It was at least
something familiar. He moved forward gratefully to rest
against it. After a few seconds he turned, sat down, and
leaned his back on the trunk.

What could he do now? And where were the other
team members?

A faint whisper of movement came from in front of
him. Something was there, something drifting towards
him and almost silent on the spongy surface. Chan felt
a new horror. A warm, dry grip closed on his outstretched hands and secured his wrists. He struggled, and
tried to force his way to his feet. It was impossible. More
fastenings came to curl around his ankles and waist. They
pulled him, gently but irresistibly, until he was lying flat
on his back on the soft carpet of the jungle. Thick, velvety bonds pinioned him there, holding him securely at
wrist and ankles.

He waited. And finally came the event that told him

he was doomed. Either Nimrod had taken him, or he had crossed the border into total madness.

"Chan," whispered a soft voice, no more than a couple of feet away from his face. "Ah, my Chan."

It was a voice that he knew well, a voice that he had known forever. It was the unmistakable voice of Leah Rainbow.

Chapter 35

Night in the Gallimaufries had been dark, but there were always at least a few lights. And there was always plenty of noise—usually too much. Nothing in Chan's experience had prepared him for the close, silent and enveloping darkness of Travancore's abyssal forest.

Leah's voice had spoken to him, and then a second later it was gone. Its reality drained away into anechoic blackness. Chan longed desperately for another word, for a single spark of light.

Finally the gentle voice came again, near enough to reach out and touch. "Chan?"

"Who are you—*what* are you?" Chan's voice cracked, a thin reedy voice that seemed to come from beyond his body.

"I am Leah."

"You cannot be."

"And I am also not-Leah. There is something that cannot be explained. It must be *experienced*. Relax. Lie quiet. Do not struggle."

There was a steady rustling, as of Tinker's wings, just inches away from Chan. Something touched his arm, then moved along his chest. He tensed, and tried to writhe away from it.

"Don't be afraid." The words were breathed close to his face. He felt warmth on his cheek and his neck. The scent in his nostrils was achingly familiar, forever-familiar: *Leah*.

Something warm and soft was placed on his stomach.

353

His clothing was loosened, cut away, eased from his unprotected body.

Chan struggled against his bonds. It would do no good to cry out. If any of the other team members had been able to help him they would already be calling to him, asking where he was. The forest around him was as still as the grave.

His clothing had been taken, leaving him naked and defenseless. Another touch came on his chest, different but equally soft. It moved lower. There was a strange little laugh in the darkness above him.

Chan's chest felt a warm breath, and soft lips. Gentle fingertips were drifting gently across his midriff and wandering slowly down his abdomen. The caresses became more intimate. Minutes ago Chan had been terrified and feverish to the bone. It seemed impossible that in these circumstances he could become physically aroused, no matter what the stimulus. But it was happening. The scent of Leah was like a drug, lifting him away from his own body.

In the darkness the succubus above him slid close. Chan felt warm flesh pressing on him. He could not move, to resist or to encourage the embrace. The fragrance in the air was stronger, mingled now with an unfamiliar musk. As he became more aroused he felt an urgent breath along his neck, and an increased tension in the body that moved above him.

"Relax," whispered Leah's voice. "This is as it should be. Don't try to resist. Let yourself *flow.*"

Beyond his control, Chan's body was moving along its own road, drawn by the action of the partner silent above him. She moved more strongly, lifting him irresistibly towards a climax. Chan shivered and shuddered, straining upward to match the unseen pressure.

The critical moment was nearing. Nearer. It came, and his partner groaned, flexed hard against him, and cried, "NOW!"

There was a roar in the darkness, a whirr of invisible wings. Chan, in the moment of most intense ecstasy, was buried under a pressing clutch of tiny bodies. They swarmed over him, covered his eyes and ears, blocked his mouth and nose. Chan, still straining upward in climax, could not breathe.

He was choking.

He writhed, uselessly. The agony of asphyxiation was deep in his chest. He shuddered to draw a last breath, knowing that he was dying, dying . . . *dying on Travancore*.

And in that moment he could breathe again—breathe, even though his nose and mouth were still covered.

He could see, but not through his eyes.

He could hear, but not with his ears.

Chan had left his body, sucked away into a no-man's-land of non-identity. With one set of ears he listened to the ultrasonic song of jungle creatures, sending their far-off calls at frequencies far beyond human senses. With one set of eyes he studied the microwave emissions from the forest floor, tracing the faint dark swaths that told of water beneath the surface. With other eyes he saw the bright thermal outline of two coupled humans, the woman kneeling astride the man. He was surrounding them, feeling them from every side, their bodies warm to his antennae. He was filled with multiple sensations. The soft forest floor on his back, the legs gripping tight around his thighs, the damp carpet of mold under his (her?) knees, the exciting touch of a body (*Chan's* body!) pressing up against her. Closeness. Warmth of touching.

"YOU ARE WITH US," said the same soft voice. But now it was inside him. "YOU CAN UNDERSTAND. DO NOT *LISTEN. FEEL* FOR US."

The world went silent. For a few moments Chan felt an intolerable level of input. He was drowning in a torrent of emotions and memories. Then the data stream steadied, the pattern cleared. He found himself swimming deep in the middle of a single consciousness, like a fish in a clear, cold stream. Within that stream, and part of it, were the other swimmers. He could sense them: The cool, observant Angel, smiling at him, allowing him for the first time to see the form of the mysterious Singer within (but it was not the Angel that Chan knew). The Tinker, the master-linkage, good-natured and tolerant conduit to serve the whole group, surrounding them all like a warmer current (but it was not Shikari, the

Tinker that Chan knew). The great, benign form of a
Pipe-Rilla, crouched close enough to arch above both
Chan and Leah. The love and kindness shone out from
her (but she was not S'greela, the Pipe-Rilla that Chan
knew).

And there was Leah.

It *was* Leah. No matter what illusion the Morgan Construct might be able to create within a human mind,
Chan was sure that it could not do this. The consciousness touching him was filled with memories that only he
and Leah shared. She was deep inside him, even though
he could see her, still sitting astride his body and smiling
down at him. She was naked, and her skin glowed—with
a color that Chan had never seen before. He realized
that he was seeing her through the Angel's thermal infra-
red sensor.

Tinker components were fluttering at his bonds, loos-
ening them. Leah squatted back on her haunches, took
Chan's hands, and helped him to sit up. She was smiling
at him. As she moved close and kissed him on the mouth
he felt a new stirring of multiple pleasures—in himself,
in her, and in the other three members of the group.

She put her arms around him, and they hugged each
other close.

"They told us you were dead," he murmured. "They
said that you met the Construct, and it destroyed you.
We believed them, believed that Nimrod had killed
all of you. I should have had more faith. You killed
Nimrod."

NIMROD? The feeling through Chan's body was like an
intense electric shock, yet its current was bright laughter,
direct in his mind. CHAN, YOU DO NOT UNDERSTAND.
NIMROD COULD NOT KILL US. WE COULD NOT KILL NIM-
ROD. CHAN, *WE ARE NIMROD.*

No more words, but in their place images and raw
information, an intense, mind-stretching torrent. WE MET
THE CONSTRUCT. WE WERE AFRAID. AND WE *CHANGED.*
SEE THIS (FEEL THIS, KNOW THIS). Everything at once,
an explosion of parallel data inputs bursting inside Chan's
head . . .

*   *   *

IMAGE: . . . the Alpha Team is frozen in position. Above them, floating down with all weapons ports open, the Morgan Construct.

Too late to flee.

This is the moment for Ishmael the Tinker to fall apart in independent components, for Angel to stand useless and immobilized, for S'glya to seek futile escape in the bounding leaps of a terrified Pipe-Rilla.

The group coalesces . . .

FUSION: . . . every component of Ishmael flies to a new position, embedding Leah, S'glya and the Angel within the Tinker's extended body. After a split-second of chaos, combination takes place. Instead of a pursuit team of individual members, a single mentality exists . . .

IMAGE: . . . the Morgan Construct is ready to obliterate everything. Weapons ports are glowing with impending energy release, while the air shimmers with electromagnetic fields. Ionization forms a violet-blue nimbus around the broad head and latticed wings . . .

EVALUATION: . . . the Mentality formulates and reviews a score of options. It holds within it the structure of the Morgan Construct, together with all the separate and combined capabilities of the pursuit team . . .

ACTION: . . . the option is selected. A tone, loud and pure, emerges from the communications box on the Angel's midsection. At the same time a second note, precisely placed in pitch, phase, and volume, comes as an octaves-higher scream from S'glya, and a higher overtone from individual Tinker components.

The Morgan Construct pauses. A fraction of a second later, its wing panels begin to vibrate.

COMMENT: . . . CONSTRUCT DESIGN DEFECT. RESONANCE POTENTIAL IN INORGANIC CONTROL CIRCUITS. VULNERABILITY TO ACOUSTIC/ELECTROMAGNETIC COUPLING. NO SAFETY LEVEL ESTABLISHED. OVERLOAD AND SHUTDOWN . . .

IMAGE: . . . the Construct begins to shake. A crackling sound from the body cavity, a violent series of random jerks. The latticed wings twist. (OVERLOAD) A final shudder. The Construct's frame locks to a fixed position, floats in silence to the forest floor. A dozen Tinker components fly across and enter the body cavity . . .

COMMENT: . . . NO PERMANENT DAMAGE. IMMOBILIZED FOR STUDY OF CONSTRUCT MENTAL PROCESSES AND PATHOLOGY.

IMAGE: . . . beside the quiet form of the Morgan Construct, the pursuit team members huddle. The whole group lies motionless in the dark forest depths, every external sensory input damped to lowest levels . . .

COMMENT: . . . THE TIME OF WONDER, THE TIME FOR INTROSPECTION. SO WE BECAME NIMROD, SO WE ARE NIMROD. NO MORE CAN BE GIVEN, TO ONE WHO IS NOT YET A POOLED MIND. FAREWELL.

Chan lay supine on damp leaf mold. Knowledge of his surroundings bled back into his mind. It had been as intense as a bolt of lightning, and as short-lived. He had abandoned his own body for hours, yet no time had passed. He and Leah still held each other close, her lips still brushed his cheek.

He took his first breath in an eon, lifted his head, and stared around him. Nothing. The forest was dark as ever. Only a trace of remembered after-image seen through the Angel's sensors told him where the other team members had been. He fancied a brief whirring of tiny wings, twenty feet away, then he and Leah were alone.

Chan allowed his head to fall back to the damp, soft cushion of leaves. His brain was jellied and contused, with the familiar agony of a bad session on the Stimulator. It was better to lie in silence, to feel but not to think. Thinking was pain.

"Chan." It was Leah's calm voice again, wakening him, whispering in his ear. "Chan, it was hard on you, but we knew no other way. You resisted fusion. The only way that we knew was to take you by force, when emotion was strongest and you were unguarded. We are sorry it had to happen that way."

Chan said nothing.

"We are sorry," said Leah again. "Here is a promise: It will never happen that way again. It was not done to *use* you, only to bring you quickly to union."

"Who are you?" Chan did not think he had spoken those words, but the body that lay alongside his, touching now from breast to thighs, jerked in reaction.

"You know who I am." The voice in the darkness was puzzled. "I am Leah."

"No. Not any more. You are Nimrod. What happened to the Leah that I knew?"

"Ah." A sharp, indrawn breath of comprehension. "Nimrod, yes. But truly, I am still Leah, no less than I ever was. I am *more*, because I am part of Nimrod also."

"*My* Leah has gone."

"Gone? Rubbish!" Leah's voice lost its dreamy, far-off tone. "What are you talking about, *gone*? I'm right here, the same as I always was." She slapped her hand hard on his bare chest, making him start at the unexpected blow.

"Who do you think did that to you, if I've gone?" she went on. She lifted herself up and leaned over him, her sharp elbow digging into his shoulder. "If you think that I'm some sort of illusion, or just a part of something else, then you're wrong—dead wrong. I'm still me. I still think, I still breathe, I still laugh, and I still love. Get that into your thick skull, Chan Dalton." She slapped his chest again, harder than ever. "That's *me* doing that to you, not Nimrod. When I first spoke to you today, that was me. When we made love, that was me. If you don't understand that, you've got rocks in your head instead of brains. You were merged, and now you're not. Do you feel any less, because we were fused?"

Chan shook his head slowly in the darkness. It was Leah all right, beating up on him, just like in the old days when he had been bad. "I don't feel less. I feel different."

"Different, and *more*." Leah was not leaning over him any more. He knew that she was standing up. "Remember this, Chan. I'm still all that I ever was. I love you as much now as I did back in the Gallimaufries, when you were all I had, and I was all that you had. We have both changed since then, and *you* have changed more than I have. But remember one thing, when the time comes for you: *Humans* are the most difficult element. *We* form the pacing factor for everything. So when it happens, *relax*. Thanks to what happened here, you're halfway along the road."

"The road to what?"

"You'll see. Very soon." She bent over, to give him a final soft kiss on the cheek. "It was all necessary, and it was wonderful, too. Better than I'd ever dreamed it might be."

Chan heard light footsteps, running away across the soft carpet of Travancore's surface. As he sat up, a faint light came bobbing towards him, weaving its way through the high cover of the creepers. It was S'greela, moving rapidly with the tubby form of Angel tucked under two mid-limbs. The dark nimbus of Shikari breezed along close behind.

"You are safe?" said S'greela.

Chan was ready to grumble at her: he might be safe enough *now*, but he was also exhausted, scraped by creepers, covered in dirt, wet, wild-eyed, naked, and mentally battered. Where had the others *been*, for God knows how long?

He could not say any of it. He had found an instruction in his mind, something that Nimrod had slipped there along with the high-pressure information flow. It was waiting, a time bomb that had just ticked its way down to zero.

Chan lay back on the dark soil. S'greela and Angel moved close, to touch him. Shikari swarmed in to cover and connect them. The first stir of interaction began. Chan felt his way inward, following the flow of the stream. There it was. The others were ready, had been ready long ago.

Leah is right. We humans are the most difficult element.

The others laughed their reply. Chan closed his eyes. And opened his mind.

Contact began, immediate and powerful. The surge of current passed through every cell of his body, sending Chan off on a tidal wave of pleasure and satisfaction. It was the cozy feeling of the pursuit team, sitting together late at night, amplified a thousand times, a million times, a billion times.

Four minds re-oriented ... meshed ... settled into mentality mode. Saturated. Contact was complete.

Chapter 36

First there was the naming of names. The new mentality decided quickly. It would be *Almas*, a name for a mind as clear and hard as diamond.

Second came the data transfer. The information flow from Nimrod to Almas was rapid. The primary, secondary and tertiary files that Nimrod had loaded into Chan occupied the new mentality for less than twenty seconds. At the end of that time, Almas knew all that Nimrod knew of mentality origin and nature.

The quaternary data file was the smallest in volume, but it had been flagged by Nimrod for special attention. Almas began the review.

It found a record of the first hours following Nimrod's own formation, interleaved and overlain with Nimrod's analysis. The record structure was designed to guide the new mentality through a multi-channel flow, a hyperweb of facts, conjectures, and conclusions.

The naming of names. *The mentality that in separation had been Team Alpha was filled with excitement and pride at the miracle of its own creation. It was* Nimrod. *Nimrod existed as a fusion of will, information, desire, and understanding.*

The naming was the first act. The second involved the captured Morgan Construct. It had to be placed in long-term stasis, until its flaws could be understood and remedied. Already there was a clue. M-29, compelled to fulfill its destiny and unable to do so on Cobweb Station, had become insane.

The third act was the most dangerous: regression, back to individual team members.

The mind pool dispersed, dissolved, faded. Leah, S'glya, Ishmael and the Angel stood silent for endless minutes, staring at each other. They were looking at strangers, at parts of their lost self. Finally they made their separate ways back to the upper levels of the Travancore forest. Like components of a Tinker Composite, each part of the mentality must serve its own needs for food, drink, and rest.

Interval. A gap in the record.

In the tent, high in the jungle, Nimrod was re-assembling for a specific purpose. The great news must be transmitted through the Link to Anabasis Headquarters.

A message was created, and innocently sent. The mentality assumed that news of its existence would be received with Nimrod's own enthusiasm for the event. With the message went a request for transfer up to the Q-ship of Nimrod itself, and the now-harmless Morgan Construct.

There was a long delay. Mondrian's face appeared on the screen, then vanished again. The mentality waited. Nimrod knew of the need to make allowance for the slowness and inadequacy of single-species thought.

The Anabasis reply came: Leave the Morgan Construct in stasis on Travancore. Fly yourselves at once in the landing capsule, up to the Q-ship that holds the blockade on the planet.

Nimrod possessed the empathy of a Pipe-Rilla, the quirky variable logic of a Tinker, the analytical capability of an Angel—and the irrational suspicion of a true human. The message from the Anabasis conflicted with Nimrod's perception of the plausible.

The landing capsule flew up to the high-orbiting Q-ship. Forty kilometers from rendezvous, the capsule was vaporized by a high-intensity salvo.

But Nimrod was still in the tent, hiding beneath Travancore's vegetation. The capsule had been flown under remote control.

Now Nimrod was stranded on the surface of the planet.

There was plenty to occupy the power of the mentality's intellect.

The data stream that had come from Nimrod to the new mentality now added a modifying field, to show a change from reporting of fact to the field of conjecture and probabilistic analysis.

The Anabasis sought to destroy Nimrod, but wanted the Construct left behind on Travancore. In this case, the goals of the Anabasis can be equated to the goals of Esro Mondrian.

Conjecture: *Esro Mondrian has need of the Morgan Construct.*

Contradiction: *The pursuit teams were sent to Travancore by the Anabasis to destroy the Morgan Construct.*

Analysis: *On Barchan, Team Alpha had not destroyed their Simmie Artefact. They had (like Chan's team) subdued it, and sought to hide the evidence.*

If Esro Mondrian knew that fact (probable, at a 0.93 level), then he would expect Team Alpha to be equally incapable of destroying the Construct.

Deduction: *Team Alpha had been sent to Travancore by Mondrian, who saw three possible outcomes for the confrontation with the Morgan Construct:*

1) The Construct would destroy Team Alpha. This result was the most probable, and it offered no new danger to the Anabasis or Esro Mondrian. The Construct would survive. Travancore would remain as a blockaded world. Additional pursuit teams could be sent to Travancore.

2) The pursuit team would destroy the Construct. The events on Barchan made this the least probable outcome.

3) The pursuit team would subdue the Construct, but not destroy it. The Construct and the pursuit team would return together from Travancore.

End of data file.

Nimrod had deliberately omitted the final part of the analysis, leaving it to the new mentality to draw its own conclusion.

Almas did so, without effort.

Esro Mondrian had hoped for the third of Nimrod's perceived outcomes: a pursuit team would subdue or dis-

able the Construct, but not destroy it. Mondrian needed the Construct, for some unknown purpose. After its capture, the pursuit teams could be disbanded.

However, none of those three outcomes had been a threat to Mondrian, nor would any of them require the destruction of a pursuit team by the Anabasis.

Conclusion: The creation of the mentality had been a total surprise to Mondrian. This was the event that he saw as an intolerable threat. The destruction of Nimrod had therefore become Mondrian's prime goal, with the saving of the Morgan Construct of secondary importance. He had ordered the Q-ship to vaporize the capsule as it returned from Travancore without the Morgan Construct. That had been done, but spectral analysis of the vaporized ship had surely told Mondrian that the pursuit team was not on board.

A second pursuit team had therefore been sent to Travancore, with the hope that it would destroy Nimrod and also subdue the Morgan Construct. Instead, it had formed another group mind. And now, like Nimrod, it was in danger from Mondrian. It was possible that at any moment the full destructive power of the Q-ship would be turned on Travancore. But that would not happen, so long as Mondrian thought that the second pursuit team had not formed a mentality, and might destroy Nimrod.

Almas drew a final conclusion, based on Chan's insight into the mind of Esro Mondrian. The obsessed leader of the Anabasis would not be content to monitor the situation on Travancore from distant Ceres. If he were not already on the Q-ship, he would be likely to Link to it very soon. Return from Travancore would be more dangerous than ever.

The mentality clung tighter for a moment, sharing that concern. Then the union ended. As dissolution began, Chan found himself sitting on the forest floor, dirty and naked. He stared around him in surprise. The images from Nimrod had been of such clarity and depth that Almas had been there also, in a tent high in Travancore's jungle.

The other three team members waited in dreamy silence as Chan recovered his clothing. With S'greela lighting the way they drifted slowly back up a spiral tunnel. After their bonding, speech was inadequate.

Only Shikari spoke as they ascended. The Tinker talked trivia, of Coromars and Maricores.

Naturally, thought Chan. *Merging units is nothing for a Tinker. Shikari must wonder why the rest of us think it's such a big deal.*

They reached the tent as the last rays of Talitha's light were cutting across the forest overstory. Amazingly to Chan, they had been away less than a single day.

Each team member settled into a preferred resting place. Chan had no appetite, but he forced himself to nibble on a biscuit and found at once that he was ravenous. He watched with detached surprise as he wolfed down masses of protein-rich synthetics. The energy drain of their merged state must be formidable.

He wanted to talk to the others about Almas, and realized that he could not. There was no way that words could say anything about that experience.

"I now sympathize with Vayvay," said S'greela suddenly. She had been eating also, with fierce concentration. "If a Coromar feels hunger like this all the time, naturally there is little room for other thought. We must go back, and explain that we are safe."

"Tomorrow," said Shikari. "Vayvay has plenty of food, and will be more than happy to wait for us."

"*Never do tomorrow what can be done today*," said Angel. "However, in this case you are right, and an exception may be admitted. Tomorrow will suffice for Vayvay."

The others might be able and willing to chat, but it was too much for Chan. Today had been the Tolkov Stimulator all over again; the painful expansion of mind, the blinding mental light that made everything that had gone before seem dim and feeble. And yet Chan yearned to be part of Almas again, to feel the enveloping warmth of the mind pool . . .

Angel was still talking. Chan could not listen. His thoughts went to the Q-ship, orbiting somewhere high overhead. He had to decide what they would do about that threat, or they would be condemned to spend the rest of their lives on Travancore.

But such things were no longer his worry alone—the decision would be made by *Almas*! Chan felt huge relief.

He fell into a profound sleep, too deep for dreams.

It was a few hours before Travancore's slow dawn when he was awakened. A warm body slid under the sheet that covered him and snuggled close to his side. He felt a moment of tingling terror, then relaxed as fingers gently covered his mouth.

"Sshh," breathed a voice in his ear. "It's me. Leah. It was wonderful meeting you as Nimrod, but I wanted to meet you just as me, and reassure you. You won't lose anything when your team forms a union. You'll *gain*."

"I know. It already happened. Together, we are Almas."

"That's wonderful. Tomorrow, the two mentalities can have their first meeting." She wriggled against him. "Move over a little bit. I want to get comfortable."

Chan tried to see Leah, but the darkness was close to total and she was nothing but a moving patch of lesser darkness. He reached out and put his arms around her. "All this time I've waited to see you, and still you're invisible. I wonder if you're anything like the Leah I used to know."

She chuckled in the darkness. "Me! I haven't changed one bit—you're the one who's so different. Don't confuse me with Nimrod, because when we're not in union I'm still me." She settled comfortably in his arms, fitting her body to his. "It was wonderful with you when I was Nimrod, and everything was shared. But tonight I decided that isn't enough. I want you for myself, too. This time, it's going to be just *us*. Ah, my sweet Chan. You feel wonderful."

Their lovemaking was gentle and slow, lacking any urgency. It was the culmination of twenty years of deep affection. Even Chan's climax carried no stress, only love and fulfillment. Afterwards Leah fell asleep quickly, nestled close to his chest, but Chan remained awake.

A new worry began to gnaw at him.

Leah was still Leah, quite sure of her own identity and

not worried about being lost within the union of Nimrod. But three months ago, Chan had been *no one*. And ever since that hour of revelation on Horus, he had puzzled over the question of his own identity. Who was he, what was he? He did not have Leah's strong, well-defined personality, the identity that easily survived mind pooling and dissolution. Despite Leah's reassurances, he wondered if the still-developing entity who was Chan Dalton would survive.

Am I going to become nothing more than one piece of a union, as undefined as one of Shikari's components? I hate that idea. I want to be me, I don't want to be absorbed. I hope this isn't going to be my last night as Chan Dalton.

His thoughts were drifting in long, lazy lines. *How long have I lived? Obituary: Chan Dalton, born at twenty years and three months, dead at twenty years and six months. What counts more, mental life span or physical?*

I'm afraid to go to sleep, knowing that tomorrow the real me may disappear.

He felt Leah stir in the darkness. Her arm moved, to lie protectively across his chest as though she was reading his mind.

It's all right. Leah will take care of me. She always has.

And with that thought, Chan went peacefully to sleep.

Far above the sleeping figures in the tent, the brooding hulk of the Q-ship floated in space. Power on board had been damped, to minimize instrument interference. All sensors were trained on the night side of Travancore. All weapons were primed.

Within the Q-ship's central control room sat Esro Mondrian and Luther Brachis. They were busy with a curious late-night ritual. Each of them was quietly entering a sequence of digits into a recording block. As soon as both were finished they exchanged records and examined the other's notations.

"Looks all right to me," said Brachis. His face was still a patchwork of synthetic skin, but his color was good. "I'm going to call it a day."

Mondrian reached out and took both recording blocks. "We're going to carry this sequence in our heads, you know, until the day we die. But it has to be done. I don't want to spend the rest of my life here any more than you do."

"I could tell Godiva the sequence, as a safety precaution."

"No." Mondrian shook his head. "You, me, and Flammarion, and nothing as a written record. If we in Security don't handle this right, who does? We play it by the book until we're absolutely sure that down there"—he nodded towards Travancore's dark disk—"there's nothing too dangerous for us to handle."

"The Team Ruby reports have been looking good."

"So did the ones from Team Alpha and look what happened to them. I hope Dalton's team will dispose of Nimrod for us, but we have to be sure. We're dealing with an alien form down there. I don't want to take any risks."

"Nor do I. But you know how I feel. We ought to fly lower, turn up the firepower in the region where Nimrod is lurking, and roast it to hell and gone. If we did that, we could get this over with in a hurry."

"And destroy the only Morgan Construct there is, the only one there will ever be? No. We go slow, and we make sure that we win."

Brachis shrugged and went out. Godiva was waiting. He didn't care to waste time arguing.

Mondrian made a check of the incoming messages. Nothing from Kubo. Another complaint from Dougal MacDougal about the energy cost of keeping open the Anabasis-Travancore Link. A confirmation from the Stellar Group ambassadors that no matter what happened, there could be no return from Travancore until the Morgan Construct was destroyed or rendered totally harmless. A query from Phoebe Willard, asking when Luther Brachis would return.

If we knew that, we would be happy to tell you.

Mondrian erased the lengthy string of digits on each recording block. The only written evidence of the Link sequence needed to return the Q-ship to a known region of space vanished.

Once again, Mondrian, Luther Brachis, and Godiva Lomberd sat alone in space, a six-hundred-year journey away from home.

In the folded, multiply-connected mapping provided by the Mattin Link, space lacks both metric and affine connections. There is only the point-to-point Link transformation, with its own discontinuous topology. So long as the Link is maintained between two locations, they remain neighbors in Link-space.

The Q-ship in orbit around Travancore and the control room of Anabasis Headquarters were close, an infinitesimal Link-space distance apart. The Link itself could provide the minute (but hugely energetic) nudge to move matter or messages across that tiny gap.

The Mattin Link seems like magic—is magic—but it is an unforgiving magic. Transfer locations must be specified in real space, and converted exactly to Link-space. Fifty-three decimal digits are needed to specify each of three spatial coordinates for transfer. One hundred and fifty-nine digits identify the full transfer sequence, a sequence that must be stored in a data bank—or remembered, if all stored forms but that of organic memory are rejected.

And there is no symmetry. The digit sequence needed to transfer from Q-ship to Anabasis Headquarters is unrelated to the sequence that takes a message (or an object) from the Anabasis to the Q-ship.

Night and morning, Luther Brachis and Esro Mondrian wrote out for each other's inspection and approval a 159-digit Mattin Link sequence. It was their life-line to the rest of the universe. Without it, they would be marooned for the rest of their lives in the Travancore system.

Chapter 37

Chan woke late to find himself alone in the tent. When he rubbed the sleep from his eyes and went outside he learned that during the night the other members of Nimrod had also arrived.

The whole group was unusually subdued, as though everyone was waiting for some signal. The two Angels had night-rooted out on the tent side-lip and were sitting now in companionable silence (or ultrasonic communion), their spread fronds absorbing Talitha's morning blaze. S'greela and S'glya had wandered away on a Pipe-Rilla food hunt. Chan could see them bounding around in the topmost branches, unconcerned by a possible five-kilometer drop all the way to the forest floor. And Ishmael and Shikari had both disassembled. The tent was filled with their purple-black components, covering every free surface. It was impossible to tell which was which.

Chan reached out and picked a component from its roost by the tent wall. The creature fluttered its veined wings indignantly and made an attempt to fly away. The ring of tiny green eyes peered at Chan with no hint of understanding. When he released the component it flew up at once to perch on the vegetation canopy.

Chan watched it hanging there and wondered. How did the two Tinker Composites retain their separate identities? What rule told a single component where to go? What happened if a component from one Tinker tried to cluster with members of the other?

Meaningless questions. What told a human cell that it

was to be part of a liver, and not part of a lung? Chan went across to Leah.

She had tied her dark hair back with a scarlet turban, providing the brightest splash of color on Travancore. Sitting cross-legged on the floor of the tent, she was eating as fast as the heating unit would produce food. Chan watched for a couple of minutes, then went to put two more servings into the unit. He offered one to her when they were ready, and was amazed when she took both—and gestured to him to load in more.

Leah ate and ate. It was a long time before she took a final mouthful, said "No more," and leaned back against the flexible wall. She patted her belly and grinned at Chan. "There. You've just paid back the first installment on the thousands of meals that I've prepared for you. But take my advice, and stoke up yourself. You're going to need all the energy and calories that you can get— and I don't just mean on my account."

She gave him a quick sideways glance, then deliberately closed her eyes.

Casual. They were *all* too casual. Chan wondered why he seemed to be the only one worried at all about getting away from Travancore. It was hard to remember that just one day ago, all his fears had been of the Morgan Construct.

Chan thought of Esro Mondrian. It was easy to feel omnipotent when the mentality was in its merged state, but it would not take Mondrian long to recognize the weaknesses of Nimrod and Almas. Chan could think of one immediately: during union, the pooled minds were almost immobilized. A mentality could move only sluggishly as a unit. If it dissolved in order to move faster, the union was destroyed.

Leah seemed to think that the mentalities were the next evolutionary step, something that would advance all the Stellar Group members. But Chan did not believe that every change was better for survival. Unless they could gain access to the Q-ship and somehow defeat Esro Mondrian and anyone else aboard, the mentalities would be revealed as evolutionary blind ends.

Was Chan the only one who still thought that the

individual members were in some ways more capable than the mind pools?

The return of the two Pipe-Rillas brought an end to Chan's train of thought. As they dropped together through a leaf layer and crouched down next to the Angels, it was the signal for every Tinker component to rise from its roosting position. They flew around the tent with dizzying speed and precision, and swarmed over each team member. The mentalities awoke, this time without delay. A thick braid of Tinker components formed a living cable between them and offered direct mental connection.

GREETINGS ... THE Q-SHIP BEHAVIOR IS UNPREDICT-ABLE ... THE TIME IS SHORT ... THE NEED FOR MENTAL-ITY ACTION IS URGENT ...

One split-second across the broad channel of communication sufficed for a dozen main messages, a hundred overtones of meaning, a thousand cross-references to existing data. As the pooled minds began their assessment, parallel analyses computed the conditional probabilities corresponding to every option.

OPTION ONE: MOVEMENT OF THE LANDING CAPSULE TO THE Q-SHIP, BUT NO PRIOR COMMUNICATION WITH THE Q-SHIP.

PROBABLE OUTCOME: DESTRUCTION OF LANDING CAP-SULE BEFORE REACHING Q-SHIP AT PROBABILITY LEVEL $P = 0.58$ IF ACTION TAKEN WITHIN 2 TRAVANCORE DAYS, AT $P = 0.71$ WITHIN 3 DAYS, AT $P = 0.96$ WITHIN FOUR DAYS.

Chan sat within the group mind of Almas, but this time he retained some measure of individual self-awareness as the powerful thought streams of Nimrod and Almas swirled above him and around him. They created echoes in his mind, weak eddy patterns of the strong main current.

Ideas from individual other team members came swarming in, alien yet accessible. Sometimes they appeared as sounds, sometimes as images, or as transient illusions of physical touch. In that cross-fertilization of mind, new ideas and speculations were like blazing fireships, moving to ignite convoys of thought within every member of the mind pool.

From the Angel, a statistical conclusion blazed in on Chan as a crimson starfish of analysis:

```
************************************************************
*          Probabilities of specific Q-ship personnel.       *
*  Esro Mondrian, P = 0.99    Luther Brachis, P = 0.72      *
*  Kubo Flammarion, P = 0.21   Godiva Lomberd, P = 0.66     *
*  Tatiana Snipes, P = 0.14    All others, P < 0.05         *
************************************************************
```

The pooled minds did not wait for their individual members to wrestle with the complexities of probability analysis. They rolled on:

OPTION TWO: A LANDING CAPSULE APPROACH TO THE Q-SHIP WITH NO PRIOR COMMUNICATION.

PROBABLE OUTCOME. DESTRUCTION OF LANDING CAPSULE BEFORE REACHING Q-SHIP AT PROBABILITY LEVEL P › .99.

The thoughts of the Pipe-Rillas were sinuous and delicate, filled with *feeling* more than logic. They rippled across the mind pools, drawing with them shimmering silver ropes of implication. Chan grasped at those gossamer strands. With Angel's help he felt them condense in his mind and take on solid numerical forms:

```
************************************************************
*  Preferred contact points if present on Q-ship.           *
*  Tatiana Snipes, success probability   P = 0.65          *
*  Godiva Lomberd, success probability   P = 0.47          *
*  Kubo Flammarion, success probability  P = 0.29          *
*  Luther Brachis, success probability   P = 0.09          *
*  Esro Mondrian, success probability    P = 0.03          *
************************************************************
```

Above and beyond the Pipe-Rillas' thoughts, the pooled minds were already advancing:

OPTION THREE: A LANDING CAPSULE APPROACH TO THE Q-SHIP BY THE RUBY TEAM, STATING IT WAS NOT SUCCESSFUL IN SUBDUING OR DESTROYING THE MORGAN CONSTRUCT, BUT IS SEEKING RETURN TO THE ANABASIS.

PROBABLE OUTCOME: DESTRUCTION OF LANDING

CAPSULE BEFORE REACHING Q-SHIP AT PROBABILITY
LEVEL P = 0.87.

Within the mind pool, Angel's own thoughts formed a
passacaglia and fugue in three dimensions. It was too
complex for Chan to assimilate. He could sense, barely,
that there was a rock-solid logic behind the patterns.
That logic appeared to him as coral monoliths, reaching
up from the bed of a crystal sea. Only the ship specification was visible, transferred directly to him from Angel:

****

*   *Q-ship analysis.*   *
* Three entry ports, monitored by the ship defense   *
*   system   *
* Ship defenses: *
*   Main: radiative, gravitronic, particle beam,   *
*   projectile   *
*   Back-up: jamming field, shearing cones,   *
*   fission/fusion, E/M shields.   *
* Ship offenses: fusion, subnucleon, gravity   *
*   singularity, sterilizers.   *
* Sustained energy output level of weapons system: *
*   940 gigawatts.   *
* Burst output energy level of weapons system: *
*   14,400 terawatts.   *

****

Chan struggled to see more clearly into Angel's data
banks. Screened by the mentalities, they would not come
into focus. He persisted, looked again. *Too bright*, said
an urgent internal voice. It showed a dark-glass image of
a naked star. Chan groped within the mind pool for a
message, and at last found one. It was a warning. The
complexity of Angels' thought was too great for direct
contact by a human mind. He must settle for pale
reflection.

The message from the pooled minds continued.

OPTION FOUR: APPROACH OF CAPSULE TO Q-SHIP.
COMMUNICATION TO INDICATE THAT TEAM RUBY HAS
CAPTURED THE MORGAN CONSTRUCT. NO MENTION OF
TEAM ALPHA.

PROBABLE OUTCOME: DESTRUCTION OF LANDING CAP-
SULE BEFORE REACHING Q-SHIP AT PROBABILITY LEVEL P
= 0.62.

The fourth option was accompanied by a bewildering
jumble of sensation, like a light that pulsed and flickered
and was never still. Chan struggled and, resisted, until
finally he realized what had to be done. He relaxed, and
allowed the patterns to dictate their own meaning. He
was moved at once to a world where steady states had
no existence. There were only *averages* of continuous
fluctuations.

Chan was seeing the thoughts of a Tinker Composite,
in which individual components were added and sub-
tracted, but all minor fluctuations had to be ignored. It
was cerebration as a statistical process, a *grand canonical
ensemble* of mental function. He learned to be content
with a knowledge of only the average state. And now he
saw the gleeful kaleidoscope of Tinker ideas, displayed
in exuberance throughout the web of the pooled minds.
A hard assessment came glinting through:

```
****************************************************************
*                        Evaluation.                          *
*            The current condition of the Morgan              *
*            Construct is known to the Q-ship at              *
*            probability level P = 0.24 or less               *
****************************************************************
```

The mind pools drove on. Individual member contri-
butions were absorbed and effortlessly merged.

OPTION FIVE: APPROACH OF LANDING CAPSULE TO Q-
SHIP, PRECEDED BY COMMUNICATION INDICATING THAT
TEAM RUBY HAS SURVIVED AND HAS SUBDUED THE MOR-
GAN CONSTRUCT, AND THAT TEAM ALPHA HAS BEEN
DESTROYED.

PROBABLE OUTCOME: DESTRUCTION OF LANDING CAP-
SULE BEFORE REACHING Q-SHIP AT PROBABILITY LEVEL P
< 0.17.

Underlying every function of the mentalities was a
cruel driving energy, propelling the mind pool toward
decision and action. Chan sensed its presence as an

immanent force-field, permanent and omnipresent and irresistible as gravity. He groped for its source, and at last found it. His mind recoiled in shock. The force that drove the group originated in Leah and Chan. . . .

Before he could absorb that, the conclusions were forming.

SUMMARY ANALYSIS. OPTION FIVE PROBABILITY OF LANDING CAPSULE REACHING Q-SHIP IS THE BEST THAT CAN BE FOUND. PROBABILITY OF DEFEATING Q-SHIP REMAINS VANISHINGLY SMALL WITHOUT ADDITIONAL DATA REGARDING Q-SHIP PERSONNEL. Q-SHIP WILL INITIATE AGGRESSIVE ACTION WITHIN TWO DAYS UNLESS CONTACTED.

CONCLUSION. ALMAS MUST FLY THE LANDING CAPSULE TO Q-SHIP. NIMROD WILL REMAIN ON TRAVANCORE, AND THE SURVIVAL OF NIMROD BE CONCEALED. THE MORGAN CONSTRUCT MUST ALSO BE LEFT ON TRAVANCORE AS POSSIBLE INSURANCE FOR THE SAFETY OF ALMAS.

ASSESSMENT: THE OVERALL SURVIVAL PROBABILITY OF BOTH ALMAS AND NIMROD IS $P = 0.16$. THIS SURVIVAL PROBABILITY WILL BE ACHIEVED ONLY WITH PROMPT ACTION.

With that assessment, the mental activity of the mind pool reached and passed its peak. Chan felt the two group minds start to loosen their hold. At the same time the connecting chain between Almas and Nimrod broke, and the Tinker components fluttered away to rest on creepers and branches. Joint thought faded and vanished.

Chan, dizzy from the surge of mental energy that had been flooded through him, stood up slowly and went inside the tent. Leah was already there, entering the control sequence that would bring the landing capsule down to Travancore.

She looked at him and shook her head. "Only a one in six chance of surviving. I'd hoped that we could find something better than that."

"We have to." Chan came to sit next to her. "And I mean *we*. I believe there are thoughts that Almas and Nimrod just can't allow, because the other team members are too pacific. So it's up to us. You and I have to find a new angle. And we have only a couple of hours to do it."

Chapter 38

Kubo Flammarion's dedication to Esro Mondrian went beyond the requirements of his job. When Mondrian told him that the two of them would be going to Travancore, he dreaded the prospect. Fifty-six lightyears away from Sol; fifty-six lightyears away from Ceres; most of all, fifty-six lightyears away from all Paradox supplies.

But he had not argued.

When the change came, and Mondrian announced that he, Luther Brachis and Godiva Lomberd would go to the Q-ship around Travancore, while Flammarion would stay at Anabasis Headquarters, Kubo had been outwardly calm. But secretly he was overjoyed. His nightmare had been avoided.

Now he wished he were at Travancore—or *anywhere* far from Ceres. At least he would then have been spared the torment of seeing Earth on the display, no more than a quick Link away. If he sneaked away from his post, just for a few hours, he could go down to Earth's surface, on into the basement warrens, take his Paradox fix, and be back again almost before anyone knew he had gone . . .

Except that he had been ordered, very directly by Esro Mondrian, not to leave the control room of Anabasis Headquarters. As long as the Construct was at large, and the Q-ship circled the planet of its refuge, Flammarion must guard his Headquarters' post around the clock. He had to watch for any sign that something—something unfamiliar, something unauthorized, perhaps something monstrous—was trying to Link in to the solar system from Travancore. If that happened, he had to call on every security system shield to stop it.

Late in the evening he sat alone at his desk with the displays all around him, stared at the one screen showing Terra, and felt every beat of his heart. Each pulse flared withdrawal-symptom pain through him like a bad toothache, like hot spikes thrust into his open eyes, like fire along his spine, like electric drills grinding into his scurvy skull.

The image of Earth seemed more welcoming every minute. That the day would have come, when he yearned to be on Madworld! He knew better than to blame King Bester as the agent for his torment. It was not his first addiction; merely his worst one.

The abrupt appearance of Phoebe Willard at Anabasis Headquarters was almost relief, even though she seemed furious about something.

"What are you guys *doing*? You're screwing up all the communications." She was not allowed into headquarters, strictly speaking—no one was—but Flammarion had known her for a long time. He did not think of asking her to leave when he slowly turned his head in her direction, and felt the needles of flame run up the tendons of his neck and into his ears.

"We're not touching communications," he said hoarsely, "except if anybody wants to Link in or out to Travancore, I mean. But it's all doing fine." He was checking the board as he spoke. What he said was true. Nothing showed abnormal in any way.

"You certainly *are* affecting the network, whether you know it or not. According to the network controller, the Anabasis has an override on all communications to anywhere."

"We do. But we're not imposing it."

"Then explain this. Move out of the way, and give me an access node." Phoebe came to his side—she did not, thank God, touch him—and started banging in values on the board. "This is a direct call to the Sargasso Dump. Now watch what happens."

The connection should have been instantaneous. Instead,

the access code blinked off for a second and then came back with the message: *No Destination.*

"You've called an invalid network end point."

"Rubbish. It's the same one I've used over and over in the past to call to and from Sargasso. It's your fault, you and the Anabasis. When you put in the circuit control on certain destinations, you must have messed up others."

"Didn't." Flammarion made the mistake of shaking his head, and felt as if it would fall off his shoulders. "Enter the Sargasso access codes, and I'll display that part of the net for you."

"Done."

She tapped her foot impatiently as one of the screens lit steadily with a branching multi-colored tracery of lines and nodes. It made Flammarion dizzy to look at it, but he could see one thing clearly: nothing went to the access code that Phoebe Willard had defined. He peered and puzzled, and checked for himself. Sure enough, the Sargasso Dump was not in the net. Somehow, the communications unit there did not exist. He stared and muttered, while Phoebe set to work to map the network onto the general geometry of the solar system.

Before she was half-done, a more urgent signal forced itself to Flammarion's attention. Behind him, the steady beep of an anomalous situation began to sound. He turned and saw that the biggest display, the one that showed every Link access point and every major energy source in the solar system, was alive. It was providing warning of a coming energy overload. The Vulcan Nexus was already approaching power supply capacity, and the big reserve kernels of the outer system were coming online. The Link points themselves had already been ringed in electric blue.

Panic pumped adrenaline into Kubo, strong enough to overcome even Paradox withdrawal. He hit the emergency connect line to Dougal MacDougal's office. Late though it was, Lotos Sheldrake answered at once.

"It's happening." Flammarion did not need to say what. "Get down here as soon as you can."

Lotos nodded and vanished, while he turned back to the display.

"What is it?" cried Phoebe. She had caught the new and more urgent tension.

"Something's building up an energy demand—a big one. The sort of overload that you only get for a major Link transfer." Kubo gestured at the board, where the power drain was rising rapidly. "Something real big, across lots of distance. But where the devil is it?"

"What do you mean, *it?*"

"The Mattin Link. The access point that's suckin' out all the energy! It ought to show on the display."

The sound signal all around them moved to a higher pitch, a signal of a new overload level.

"Where is it?" Flammarion's head was spinning. "All the Link points still show as blue rings—but the one that's pulling the power ought to show *orange*. It's not there!"

Phoebe stared. The big screen showed not a spot of orange. He *had* to be wrong. But although Kubo Flammarion had many faults, this sort of inaccuracy was not usually one of them.

There was a clatter of built-up heels on the hard floor. Lotos Sheldrake came hurrying in. She looked as neat as Kubo was scruffy.

He turned his head. "It's not there, Lotos. That means it must be coming from *outside*. It has to be something coming from the Q-ship—and we have to shield against it."

"Calm down, Captain." Lotos slowed her pace as she approached the control board. She leaned back and surveyed its complexity. "Overload on the way, no doubt about that. Enough to shunt lots of mass, over lots of lightyears. But where's the draw point?"

"Travancore! It has to be. The damned Construct, it must have learned the Q-ship Link access codes. It's coming! Where's Ambassador MacDougal?"

"Asleep. Be thankful for small mercies." Lotos was at the input unit and busy with her own inquiry there. "Captain Flammarion, I don't know what's happening, but I know what's *not* happening. This energy drain isn't coming from the Q-ship."

"How do you know that?"

"Because that ship has its own power kernel. You know how much energy a Q-ship has to be able to generate. Enough to destroy a solar system. If anyone or anything was trying to Link in from Travancore, there's ample power to do it right there. It's more likely—Great Mother of God, look at that!"

Lotos was finally losing her calm. The energy for a Link transfer was normally an impulse, a single moment of giant power drain. But all around them in the Anabasis control room, the lights were fading. Something was calling on huge power resources, not for a split-second but for minutes. A Link had been opened, and it was being *held* open. All over the solar system, heating and lighting systems would be fading and failing.

The lights dimmed further. In the apocalyptic gloom of the control room, Lotos at last completed her own data request. With no indication of an active Link access point in the system, she had set up her own program to start from the energy supply points, and track where it was being sent.

"This is crazy. The power is going *nowhere*." She was staring at the general 3-D plan of the solar system. All the supply vectors converged to a single point—but not to any place showing the blue circle of a Mattin Link unit. "There's nothing there."

It was Phoebe Willard's turn to cry out. "There is, there is!" She pointed to the system map that she had been creating, comparing it with Lotos Sheldrake's display. "That's *my* people—the Sargasso Dump. What are they sending into the Dump?"

"Not a thing. Except energy." Lotos Sheldrake was still at the console. "It's something Linking *out*—and a long way out. Over fifty lightyears for a guess—maybe all the way to the Perimeter."

"To Travancore?" croaked Flammarion.

"Not to Travancore. Just as far, but in a different direction. And the transfer is still going on!"

"But it *can't* be." Flammarion's adrenalin level had

been fading with the lights, and with it all the pain was flooding back in on him. He sat bowed-headed, in a darkness lit only by the computer displays with their own emergency power systems.

"It can't be, Lotos," he mumbled. "There's no stellar Link point in the Sargasso Dump. There isn't now—and there never has been."

Chapter 39

The ascent was anything but comforting. Even from
far away, the size of the Q-ship was overwhelming. Chan
stared up to the enormous ellipsoidal mass, and then
around him at the puny landing capsule.

The contrast was alarming, but it was not surprising.
A Q-ship was designed for quarantine. It must be able
to bottle up the inhabitants of full-sized space colonies,
or even whole planets—populations who had their own
weapons, and as often as not did not want to cooperate.
Each quarantine ship was shielded and armored, bristling
with offensive and defensive weapons. Even ignoring the
mass of their power kernels, they were million-ton
behemoths.

They had to be. In extreme cases, a Q-ship might be
called on to purge an entire world. That extreme had
never yet been necessary, but there had been close calls.
The discovery of a natural organism, a native brain-
burrowing *gnathostome* affecting all the inhabitants of
Pentecost and causing their planet-wide blood-lust, had
been made only at the eleventh hour. A Q-ship had been
in position, ready to carry out planetary sterilization.

And the landing capsule? Chan stared around him at
the flimsy, thin-walled shell, vulnerable even to a mild
stellar flare. A Q-ship could vaporize it with an accidental
puff from secondary exhausts.

They crept closer, on their unpowered approach trajectory. The Q-ship was taking no chances. The designated
entry port was protected by a gleaming array of projectile

and radiation weapons. After docking, the members of
Team Ruby had been instructed to enter the Q-ship one
by one. Chan would go first, and the others would not
leave the capsule until they had been given permission
to do so. Even within the docking area, Esro Mondrian
could order the instant destruction of the capsule and all
its contents.

That would include Team Alpha. The pursuit team,
already pooled to form Nimrod, was hidden away in the
capsule's primitive cargo compartment.

Chan was terribly conscious of their presence a few
feet away from him. It had been his idea, with support
from Leah, to bring the Alpha team onto the landing
capsule. Neither Nimrod nor Almas could estimate the
effect of that on the overall survival probabilities, and
the other team members had all argued against it. Why
endanger *both* teams, they said, when it was only necessary to place one in immediate peril?

Chan had insisted, without being able to justify it. As
another consequence, the journey up to the Q-ship was
a one-way trip. With Team Alpha aboard, all spare supplies and fuel had been left behind on Travancore to
avoid a mass anomaly. The Q-ship would detect any
excess of total mass when the capsule was caught for
docking. Even a suspicion of Team Alpha's presence on
board would be enough to encourage violent action.

As they neared the Q-ship, Chan heard a whisper in
his ear. Nimrod's analysis was passing from the cargo
hold through a single-link chain of Tinker components,
and instantly being converted by Angel to a form that
Chan could comprehend.

"We are twelve hundred meters from docking," said
Angel. "Nimrod regards that as a good sign. If the Q-ship
intended to destroy us before we docked, the best time
to do so has already passed. The current probability estimate for success of Q-ship rendezvous is 0.255, *up* from
the last estimate of 0.23. Nimrod also believes that Tatiana Snipes is not on board the Q-ship. That reduces the
probability of finding a sympathetic contact with whom
we can work to 0.13, down from 0.19. The overall proba-

bility estimate of mission success is thus reduced to 0.12."

Chan was hardly listening. Angel was perfectly happy puttering around with data and computing statistics, but what was the point of them? The group was committed, and probabilities meant nothing. Either they would succeed in a wild venture, or they would fail. It was a binary situation. They could not one-tenth succeed, or one-third succeed. In another half hour, they would be alive, or they would be dead. There was nothing in between.

"Ready for docking," he said to the blank screen. They had received no visual signals from inside the Q-ship, although the port was less than two hundred meters ahead.

"Proceed," said the capsule communications set, in a metallic voice.

"They are still computer-controlled," said Angel. The bulk of the Chassel-Rose was hanging upside-down over Chan's head, in the free fall of a ballistic approach. "If they were to shoot at us now, there could be minor damage to parts of the Q-ship itself. That is a good sign. *Onward and upward!* Nimrod believes that we will certainly be permitted to complete the docking."

"Then get down off the ceiling. They'll grab us in the next second or two, and we'll feel acceleration. Go and lie down next to Shikari. I don't want you wrapped around my neck when we dock."

As Chan spoke there was a jolt on the hull. Angel sailed backwards and bounced off the cabin wall behind him. "Oof!" said the computer strapped to Angel's midsection. A vibration was felt through the whole capsule, followed by a clang from outside.

"Docking is complete," said the communicator.

Chan headed for the capsule door, while the other team members remained in the cabin.

Careful. This is a moment of maximum danger. Chan heard those words—or was he saying them internally? He paused at the door, and made himself wait.

The capsule had been tucked neatly into a berth in the contoured fourth deck. Chan heard outer port seals clang into position, and a creak from the capsule's hull as external air pressure increased from vacuum levels. He watched until the meters showed external and internal equalization, then opened the capsule lock.

A narrow pier alongside the hull led to an airlock on the interior wall. Chan pulled himself along to it, aware that even after this he would still not be in the ship's true interior. According to Angel's reconstruction of Q-ship geometry, there would be another lock to pass through, with its own checking system for interlopers. If anything failed a test, the whole entry port could be blown free into space, and the Q-ship would still operate at close to its full potential.

The lock slid open. As Chan stepped through, a decontaminant spray blew over him from head to foot. A personnel handling system carried him steadily along a white-walled corridor and on to yet another lock. Chan observed everything closely, and wished there was some way in which he could send the information back to Nimrod. The mentality needed data, if it was to gain unobserved entry to the Q-ship interior.

The next door opened to an area that was noticeably not in free-fall. Chan must be within a few meters of the shielded kernel that powered everything on the Q-ship. He thought of the nearby singularity, and imagined that he could feel the tidal gravitational forces. He stood for a moment to make sure of his balance, then walked around the curved floor to the chamber's outer door.

This was another point of crucial danger. After a second's hesitation he went on through.

He found himself in a primary quarantine area. It was a large, hexagonal room, thirty meters across and divided into seven parts. The central area where Chan had entered was surrounded by the six individual vaults, each with its own triple-layer glassite walls and inert door. The whole room was visible and audible from every one of the seven chambers. But a kiloton fusion explosion could take place in any of them, and remain totally confined there.

Two men were waiting at the far end of the central area.

Esro Mondrian and Luther Brachis. Chan recalled the

analysis made by the mentalities. These were the two individuals predicted with highest probability to be present on the Q-ship—and the ones least likely to be controllable or sympathetic.

Mondrian seemed to be unarmed. Brachis carried a high-velocity projectile weapon, which he held aimed at Chan's mid-section. His face was a patchwork of bruised flesh and synthetic skin.

Mondrian nodded a greeting. "Welcome back, Chan. According to our records, you are the first human ever to return from the surface of Travancore. Sorry we don't have the red carpet out for you." He smiled, despite the obvious tension in the room. "I'm glad to see you, but I'm sure you realize that we have a lot on our minds. Come over here, and sit down."

He nodded to three straight-backed chairs that formed the central chamber's only furniture. They were placed so that each provided a view of a wall-sized display. Chan and Mondrian sat down, but Luther Brachis remained standing. His weapon was still in his hand.

Chan nodded towards the gun. "I never asked for a red carpet, but I did expect better treatment than this. You sent us to do a job. We did it—and now you point that at me."

The mentalities had advised Chan on how he should begin the meeting in the Q-ship: act bitter and confused. They had also warned that they could predict nothing beyond the first few exchanges. Chan would have to use his own judgment as the encounter proceeded.

"But you did not complete your mission," said Mondrian quietly. "You were instructed to destroy the Morgan Construct. Yet according to your message, it is still alive."

"It is. But we did *more* than we were asked. Thanks to our team, you now have available to you a live, functioning Construct, operating in a safe environment."

Live, functioning, safe. Chan stressed those words deliberately, and saw the positive reaction in Mondrian. Brachis's face was so battered that it could show no response at all. Chan wished that S'greela were present

The Pipe-Rillas were far better than any human at reading emotional states.

"We even think we know why the Construct went insane," continued Chan. "It was designed for the purpose of Perimeter surveillance, and then it was not allowed to perform it. If we are right, there is a way to cure it."

That got through to Mondrian, more than anything so far. His eyes gleamed, but still they were cautious. "Maybe the Construct can be cured. But that doesn't explain why you failed to follow orders. Why did you not destroy the Construct, as directed?"

"It was not necessary." Chan had to keep them talking, even if it meant giving out more information than he wanted to. Nimrod had asked for five minutes. "Why destroy it, when we could neutralize its offensive powers? It can't do any damage now. It is in stasis, safely immobilized on the jungle floor of Travancore."

"Undamaged, and in good working order?" Mondrian's voice had a slight tremor in it.

"So far as we can tell. But the capsule wasn't big enough for both us and the Construct. If you can give me a larger transfer vehicle, we can go down and collect it."

Chan knew that he had reached one of the principal branch points identified by the mentalities. If Mondrian agreed now, the chance of survival increased greatly.

But the man was shaking his head, and fiddling with the star opal at his collar. "Not yet. Tell me, Chan, what do you see as the future of Team Ruby, now that you've done your work with the Construct?"

"I didn't think that we *had* a future. We were assembled to do a job, and we did it. I suppose that I thought we'd be congratulated, and then we'd all go home. Is that going to be a problem?"

"I don't think so." Mondrian nodded at Luther Brachis, who lowered his weapon. "Suppose we agree that you can go down and bring up the Morgan Construct. Do you need to have your whole team there when you do so?"

"It's not necessary. The Construct is harmless now. I

could go down and do it on my own if I had the right ship."

"Fine." Mondrian stood up. "We'll bring the other team members in. I want to thank them individually. Then they can all be Linked back to their home planets."

"Right now?"

"I don't see why not."

He suspects, thought Chan. He doesn't know that my team formed a mind pool, too, but he's not going to take any chances. "I hoped that we could all get together here, maybe even have a celebration. The team members expected to go their separate ways, but not so soon and so suddenly."

"When you defeated the Morgan Construct, the work on Travancore ended. There is no reason now to continue the Anabasis." Mondrian was relaxing, just a little. "And we have other work to do, back on Ceres. Luther, bring the others through—one by one."

It was going to work out all right. But as Chan had that thought, Luther Brachis walked to the door leading to one of the shielded compartments. He gestured to Chan with his gun. "In here, Dalton."

"Me? What have I done now?"

Brachis shrugged.

"It should only be for a few minutes," said Mondrian.

Brachis guided Chan through, and the hardened door closed as Mondrian stepped to the communications panel and pressed a sequence there. "All that we want to do is check on your companions," he said. "As soon as that proves satisfactory, you will be released. Here comes the first."

The display screen showed the bulky figure of Angel, leaving the capsule and floating towards the lock. Soon Angel appeared in the central chamber. This time there was no discussion. Angel was moved at once to a second shielded compartment.

No one spoke as S'greela, and finally Shikari, were brought in turn from the capsule to the quarantine chamber. The Tinker was handled with particular care. Luther Brachis had another weapon at his belt, this one able to throw a wide beam of destructive energy. If necessary, he could use it to kill a whole swarm of components in mid-air.

But it was not needed. S'greela and Shikari allowed themselves to be shepherded quietly through into separate sealed compartments. When all the pursuit team members were present, Mondrian went again to the control panel. He pressed a new command sequence.

"Destroying the landing capsule," he said casually—but he was looking straight at Chan. "In strict accordance with Security quarantine regulations, of course. Your team is here, and we don't want to risk some dangerous life-form taking a free ride up from Travancore. Do we?"

Chan shook his head. He kept his face impassive as the capsule on the screen flared to blue incandescence. The possibility of that act had been considered by Nimrod and Almas when they were still on Travancore, but no good counter-action had been devised.

The situation was clear. Either Nimrod had already found some way to move from the capsule to the interior of the Q-ship, or Leah and the others were dead. The mentality was supposed to disassemble once the capsule had docked, and each of its four members would then make its way into the Q-ship interior. It had seemed simple enough when Nimrod and Almas proposed it. Now it sounded impossible. Chan wished that he had Angel's inborn ability to assess odds.

"I have one additional question," went on Mondrian, "before you lead us down to collect the Construct, and we talk of celebration. I am curious to learn if in your efforts on Travancore you were troubled by illusions, or a distorted perception of reality."

It was the crucial moment. Mondrian must know of Chan's first and incomplete meeting with Nimrod, because Chan had reported seeing Leah, and that would be in the data files. But what was the right answer? Was it better to admit that there had been a later meeting? Or should he say that they had fired on and destroyed something in the deep forest, assuming that it was created by the Morgan Construct?

Any answer was dangerous. Chan hesitated, and as he did so Brachis raised his gun and took a step toward the door of the compartment that held Chan. "Damn it, Esro, he's taking too long. Can't you see he's stalling?"

"Keep calm, Luther. We are all nervous. But I *need* that Construct, even if you don't. And we must know exactly what happened on Travancore before we can risk going down there."

Behind Mondrian, another door was slowly opening. A female figure stood on the threshold. Chan held his breath and tried not to look that way as she stepped from darkness into the bright-lit quarantine chamber.

Leah?

And then Chan relaxed, disappointed. The newcomer was Godiva Lomberd. She was dressed in a modest, calf-length white dress with long sleeves, and she had a bewildered look on her face.

Luther Brachis had not heard her coming until the last moment. He swung around, weapon raised and finger tight on the trigger. As he saw Godiva he exhaled hard and lowered his gun.

"Goddy, don't *ever* come in like that again. I told you to stay in our quarters until I got back. I could have shot you!"

"I have to talk to you, Luther." Her voice was far-off and dreamy. "I have to. It's important."

"Later. Can't you see we're busy? You'll have to go back to our room, I just can't talk to you now."

"It *has* to be now." Godiva took two dragging steps forward. "Please, Luther. For your own sake."

"*Go with her.*" It was Angel, speaking through the computer communicator. "Godiva is right, Luther Brachis. You must go with her."

"What the hell *is* all this?" Brachis was swinging to face Angel, but the alien was safe behind the chamber's glassite wall.

"It's what I feared." Mondrian went hurrying across to the control board. "*It's on board.* God knows how, and God knows where. But it's here, Luther—and it has taken over Godiva. Just look at her face."

"Godiva!" Brachis turned back to her.

"No, Luther." She walked forward to stand in front of him. "Esro is wrong. There *is* someone new on board, and I did talk to it. But don't worry, I can't be taken over—ever." She smiled up into his face. "Luther, Nimrod didn't take me and change me. But it can help you and Esro. You can get rid of all the violence, all the hatred. Please come with me now, both of you. You'll be quite safe. I love you, Luther. You know I would never do anything to hurt you."

Behind Godiva, the door to the quarantine chamber was opening wider. Mondrian and Brachis had a first clear view of the corridor outside. Both men took a step backward.

Nimrod was there, moving into the doorway. For the first time Chan had a clear view of a mentality without being a part of it. Even to him, it was a terrifying sight. The forms of Leah, S'glya, and the Angel stirred feebly within the swarming, smothering mass of Ishmael's components. Long purple-black tentacles of Tinker elements writhed away from the main body. They extended into the room, reaching out toward the locks of the closed chambers. As Chan watched, the whole mass gave a jerk and moved closer. The door holding Chan a prisoner slid silently open.

"Out of the way, Godiva!" Brachis had his gun raised, sighting for a clear shot past the woman standing in front of him.

"It would be foolish to shoot." The voice of Leah Rainbow spoke from the depths of the vibrating mass. "Godiva is right, Luther Brachis. We can help you. And we did not enter her mind—*because we could not*. May we tell him?"

Godiva was nodding, still staring up raptly into Brachis's face. "Tell him now. He is my love, and it is time."

"We could not bring Godiva Lomberd to union, Luther Brachis, although we tried. Because *Godiva is not human*."

"Godiva. Move!" Brachis did not seem to have heard the mentality, but the hand holding his gun was trembling. "Out of the way, let me get a shot at it."

Godiva edged in closer, reaching up to place her hands on his shoulders. "Before Nimrod spoke with me, I could not tell you. My prime coding did not permit it, and I wondered if you would ever know. But they are right. I am not human. Luther, let them help you."

"Don't touch him!" Mondrian was staring at Godiva with sudden comprehension. "Don't touch him any more—and don't say what you are."

"I must. Before I could not, but now I must." Godiva's arms went around Brachis's neck. "Luther, you are my love. And I am an Artefact."

Brachis tried to pull away. "Godiva, don't say that. Don't ever say *anything* like that."

"I must." She clung to him, moving as he moved. "I am an Artefact. And the Margrave of Fujitsu was my maker."

"You can't be. You helped to *save* me." The hand holding the gun was white-knuckled and trembling. "When the Artefacts were attacking me, you didn't help *them*, you helped me."

"Of course I tried to save you. I could never kill anything. Fujitsu created me, in the vats of his Needler lab. But I was made for love, not death. I love you, Luther."

She tried to reach up and kiss him. Brachis was pulling his face away out of reach.

"Feel pity, Luther Brachis, not anger." It was Leah's voice again, emerging from the middle of the Tinker swarm. "She became Fujitsu's instrument, but not from choice. When the Margrave was alive, her only program was to watch you, and stay with you, and love you. *When he died, that program was not cancelled*. But his death also triggered her programing as a source of information for other Artefacts. They were able to follow you, to know your actions. But feel Godiva's misery, as we are able to feel it. She loves you, yet she could not help providing information that might harm you. When you came to Travancore, she rejoiced—because she knew that no other Artefacts could follow you here."

Tears were trickling down the flawless skin of Godiva's cheeks. "It is true, Luther. Forgive me. I could not tell you what I was doing, no matter how much I loved you."

"Love. Making money for Fujitsu, was that your idea of love?" Luther Brachis averted his face from Godiva, as again she tried to kiss him. He stared out over her

shoulder. "Damn your soul, Fujitsu, wherever you are."
His voice was quiet, apparently unemotional. "You wanted
your dues, and you took them. You win, Fujitsu. You
win."

He pushed the muzzle of his gun into Godiva's soft
belly and pulled the trigger. The explosion was muffled
to a soft, harmless-sounding thump. But the shaped projectile blew a fist-sized hole right through Godiva's opu-
lent body.

She stared up into Brachis's face and smiled a dreamy
and loving smile. She stood up straight, arms raised in
supplication; and then she fell. Even in dying, there was
a strange grace to her. Luther Brachis stared down at
her body and drew in a long, sobbing breath.

Mondrian alone foresaw what might come next.

"Luther! No!" He jumped forward to grab at Brachis's
arm. The other man glanced at him, and almost casually
began to turn his wrist. Mondrian pulled as hard as he
could, but the arm movement did not slow. As the
weapon came to point at his own head, Brachis stared
down at the tumbled and bleeding form in front of him.

"I loved you, Godiva," he said quietly. "I really did."
He fired the gun point-blank at his own forehead. A
spout of blood and brain tissue jetted from the back of
his skull. As he fell he pulled Esro Mondrian with him.

Chan started forward. Mondrian was beginning to pull
free, clambering to his feet.

And so, amazingly, was Godiva Lomberd. She held her
hand to her back, where bloodied internal organs showed
at the gaping exit wound, and she weaved where she
stood. But still she began to move forward, to where
Luther Brachis lay.

"Godiva Lomberd, do not try to lift him. That effort
will kill you." It was Leah's warning voice. But Godiva
was bending and putting her arms around Brachis, while
blood streamed down her dress.

She shook her blond head. "We do not die easily, my
kind. Not even . . . of sorrow." Already she was standing
again, Luther cradled to her chest while one hand supported the back of his shattered head.

Then she was hurrying out of the quarantine chamber.

Chan started after her—and realized that while they had all watched Godiva, Esro Mondrian was vanishing through the other door.

"Follow him!" said Leah's voice. "With Brachis gone, Mondrian alone knows the Link sequence to take this ship back to Sol."

Chan hesitated. Follow Mondrian—but Nimrod was still united, Angel was too slow, Shikari was disassembled. "S'greela!" Chan called to the Pipe-Rilla. "Come on. It's up to the two of us."

He ran out of the quarantine chamber, and at once found himself in the labyrinth of the Q-ship interior.

"Which way?" asked S'greela. She was bounding along at his side.

Chan had no idea. Before he could speak, a long tendril of Tinker components came streaming into the corridor. "Follow Ishmael," called Leah's muffled voice from far behind.

Nimrod at least must have some idea of where Mondrian was going. Chan and S'greela ran along behind the moving Tinker column, down one corridor and along up two short flights of stairs.

"The main Q-ship control room," cried S'greela. She was ahead of Chan. "He is here."

Chan ran through to join her. Mondrian was at a main panel, throwing switches. As Chan and S'greela entered, he spun around to face them.

"Get away from me, or we all die. I have initiated a Q-ship destruct sequence, and I alone can stop it. You have three minutes to surrender and place yourselves in sealed quarantine chambers."

"Stay back," cried S'greela. "He means it, he will do it. We must do as he says."

"Wait!" called a voice from far along the corridor. It was Angel, creeping along as fast as the root system would permit.

"S'greela, you have to help Angel." But before Chan's command could be carried out, a blizzard of Tinker components appeared in the corridor. They crowded to lift and push Angel towards the control room.

When Angel reached the threshold, part of the swarm

at once flew across to cluster thickly on Mondrian. Another group flew to settle on Chan and S'greela.

"Quickly!"

Chan did not know who had cried out. Already the mentality was awakening, faster than ever before. Chan felt Almas reaching out toward Mondrian, and then the shock of contact.

CAN YOU REACH HIM? It was Nimrod, faint and far-off, connecting in through the Ishmael/Shikari link.

WE ARE TRYING. There was a long moment of probing, as the mentality sought to feel into a resisting mind. WE CANNOT.

Chan felt the full impact of that surprise and alarm. Mondrian's mind had risen powerfully against them, stronger than Almas had believed possible. The mind pool was recoiling from the intensity of the emotion that it had encountered.

WE CANNOT BRING HIM TO UNION. The news flowed back to Nimrod. THERE IS A BLOCK. IMMOVABLE, PERMANENT, DEEP-SEATED.

CAN YOU BYPASS IT, AND REACH THE ABORT PATTERN FOR Q-SHIP DESTRUCTION? Nimrod's message carried its overtones. The other mentality was moving towards the control room, but in the united form its pace was too slow.

IT WOULD DESTROY HIM. IT IS BURIED BENEATH ALL ACCESSIBLE LEVELS.

Now S'greela and Chan had joined Shikari to hold Mondrian. He did not resist physically, but his mind boiled and burned, rejecting all contact with the mentality. Almas tried again along a new path. Chan felt the union's repugnance as it came to the seething undercurrent of Mondrian's mind.

ONE MINUTE, said Nimrod. YOU MUST FIND THE ABORT PATTERN FOR Q-SHIP DESTRUCTION.

WE ARE STILL TRYING. IT CANNOT BE REACHED.

"Should we destroy Mondrian?" That was Chan, struggling to remain within the mentality, and yet provide an individual input to the mind pool. "His destruction might yield the abort pattern."

NO—NO—NO. The gale of disapproval almost swept

Chan away. He felt the shocked reaction from the other team members, as he struggled to pull back farther from the mentality.

He faced a terrible choice. He needed the mind pool to help him, at the same time as he needed to act independently from it. Chan channeled his energy and reached deeper, burrowing his way into a matrix of emotion that struggled furiously to resist him.

He made no progress. *Mondrian would not yield.*

Chan thrust about in uncontrolled surges, and at last felt the first random contact with the memory block. It was like a dark, confined presence in Mondrian's brain, sealed off from everything around it. Chan pushed deeper, using the full power of the whole mind pool. He knew what he had to do. But could he bring himself to do it, against the resistance of all the others?

Now. He used the edge of his own worst memories to cut into the naked, delicate fiber of Mondrian's mind. The darkness resisted for one more moment, then shivered to pieces.

The block was gone. But as Almas reached past Chan to pick up the abort command and Mattin Link sequence from Mondrian's mind, Chan himself was caught in a mental explosion. Mondrian had been forced to look at the horror of his own distant past. The scream of pain and mental anguish blew Chan out of the tortured brain and far away into a sea of fading consciousness.

The mentality caught Chan and cradled him. But Mondrian's intellect was flickering and dimming, a quenched ember of mind that sank rapidly to nothing.

"Safe. We are safe," said Chan.

"Death. We are Death," said an echo. Then Chan was sinking into a maelstrom of bottomless terror, knowing it was *his* terror, knowing it was only the faintest shadow of what he had found inside Esro Mondrian.

"Death. Death?" said the echo, closer and louder.

But now it could not touch him. For at last Chan had let go, and been sucked all the way into the whirlpool.

Chapter 40

The transition came at the hundred and twentieth level of the warrens, and it came suddenly. Above that point were the signs of success: fashionable apartments, bright lights, beautiful people, high rents, and easy access to the Link points. Below Level 120 a traveller found only dark hell-holes, fugitives, and failure.

Chan approached the apartment cautiously, walking light-footed along the trash-filled corridor with its grimy walls and solid grey doors. Reaching his destination, he placed his hand on the ID unit and pressed. The light glowed. He was allowed through into the coffin-like outer hall and stood there, patiently waiting.

It took a long time. The woman who opened the inner door was tall and stooped, with long, unkempt hair. She peered out into the tiny dim-lit hall and stared at Chan with tired, bleary eyes.

He nodded. "It's me, Tatty. May I come in?"

She did not speak, but she turned and shuffled through into the apartment. Following her, Chan saw the purple of Paradox shots along both of her arms. They went into a tiny living-room, where Chan sat down uninvited on a hard chair and stared around him. The place was a clutter of clothes, dishes, and papers, the result of many weeks of casual living with no attempt to clean.

She sat down opposite him on a ragged hassock and stared up at his face. She nodded slowly. "You've changed, Chan. Just like they said."

"We've all changed." He sat stiffly, hands on knees.

"I heard the rumors. The Gallimaufries are full of them. How you and Leah went out to the far stars, with Esro Mondrian and Luther Brachis and the aliens. How you were changed, and caught a super-being, and it killed to save itself. They say it will make everything different, out there and back here, too." She rubbed at her eyes.

"We're not sure of that, Tatty. At first it seemed we were dealing with something superior, something that had us beat in every way. Now, we're not so sure. We can sometimes do things, us humans, that the super-beings don't seem able to do."

It was equally true, whether he was talking of the mentalities or the Morgan Constructs. And not only humans. The Pipe-Rillas and the Angels had their own special powers, their own reservations about the mind pool mentalities. Only the Tinkers, advocates of all forms of Composites, were unreservedly in favor.

"Any way," he went on, "the Stellar Group ambassadors have laid down the rules. There will be no risks taken. The new beings will be kept in a protected environment, along with the captured Construct, until they are completely understood."

"Are they dangerous?"

"I don't know. There were casualties on Travancore, but I'm not sure who was to blame."

"I heard." Her eyes were glassy. She was bottoming out after a Paradox high. "Esro, and Luther Brachis, and Godiva."

"You heard the . . . *other* thing about her?"

"Oh, yes. So sad." Turning to hide it from Chan, Tatty pressed a tiny bulb against her forearm. "I should have guessed, long ago. She came from nowhere, and she was too good to be true. Poor, poor Godiva. The perfect woman, the perfect partner . . . and one of Fujitsu's Artefacts. What made you suspect it?"

"I didn't. About her. But I wondered for a while after the Stimulator treatment if I might be an Artefact *myself*. I was twenty years old, with an undamaged brain. And I had been a moron. I had to wonder if I was really human."

"Mondrian never told you?" She was frowning at him,

suddenly more alert. "He wanted to know where you came from as much as you did yourself. When I came back to Earth he asked me to find out everything I could about you. But I guess he didn't tell you."

"Not a word."

"You're not a moron, Chan, you never were. And you're not an Artefact. But you *are* an experiment. One of the Needler labs—not the Margrave's, he would never have tolerated such incompetence—was trying to make a superman, a physically and mentally perfect person. They failed, but only because they messed up and didn't provide a final set of neural linkages. They didn't realize that, and they dumped the result down in the warrens." Tatty gave Chan a sad but fond smile. "Welcome to the cast-offs' club. But you're one hundred percent human. Like me. Isn't it a rotten group to belong to?"

She leaned back on the hassock and closed her eyes. Her face was lively now, but grey and bony, no more than an aging specter of the woman Chan had known so well on Horus.

"I can't believe he is gone," she said at last. "Were you there when it happened?"

"Right to the very end. I saw his mind, in the last few moments. He was never at peace, you know."

"Better than you ever will." Tatty turned her head away. "I would have helped him. Once, I would have done *anything* for him. But he would never tell me what it was that gnawed away inside him."

"He could not tell. But I know."

Chan paused. He did know, in dreadful detail. And he could not speak of what he had found in Mondrian's mind. Even at second-hand, the terror was too strong.

He felt the impact of that dark memory taking him again, as it took him every day . . .

The grass was three times as high as his head. It grew all the way around, like the walls of a big circular room, with the blue sky above as a domed ceiling that held in the heat. It was much too hot, and he was sweating.

He bent down, staring curiously at the little bugs

running fast and squiggly among the stems of the dusty grey plants.

"Come on. We don't have time for you to dawdle around."

He straightened at the shouted words and hurried after the others. Mummy was still walking next to Uncle Darren, holding his hand and not looking back. He came up behind them and impulsively reached out to clutch her around the knees. He could smell her sweat and see the beads of perspiration on her legs.

Was she still mad?

"Mummy, pick me up." He peered up and around her body, trying to see her face. It had been a long time since she held him without being asked. "Mummy?"

She did not look down. "We've no time for that now. Can't you see we're in a big hurry?"

The man laughed, but it was not like a real laugh. "Damn right, we're in a hurry. But maybe this is as good as any place. Let's get on with it."

Mummy stopped, and finally glanced down at him. "All right, Essy. Uncle Darren and I are going to be busy for a little while. I want you to sit down right here, and wait quietly until we come back."

"I want to go with you." He held her tighter around the legs. "I don't want to stay here."

"Sorry, Big-boy, but we can't do it that way." Uncle Darren crouched down. He was smiling. "We won't be long. You just wait here until me and your Mom get back. Look, if you're good you can have this to play with while we're gone. See?"

Uncle Darren was holding up the little electric lamp, the one they had used in camp the previous night. It had been a fun time, the three of them all safe and cozy in the tent, and Mummy laughing a lot. She wouldn't let him crawl in with her, but she sounded all warm and giggly and happy, especially when she was snuggled under a blanket and Uncle Darren was telling a bedtime story.

He reached out his hand for the little lamp.

"Wait a minute, watch me do it." Uncle Darren worked

the control. "See? Switch on—switch off. Switch on—switch off. Think you can do it by yourself?"

He nodded, took the lamp, and set it down on the hard earth. He squatted beside it, and turned it on.

"That's my Big-boy." Uncle Darren stood up and began to walk away. "Come on, Lucy, he's settled. He'll be fine now."

He stared after them as they moved into the long grass. They had their heads together, and they were talking quietly again as they had talked the previous night. He bent down to the lamp, wanting to please Mummy by doing whatever would make her happy with him.

The little light flickered on and off as he pressed the switch. It seemed brighter than when Uncle Darren had worked it.

He looked up and all around. The sky was a darker blue, and he could see a few stars. They were creeping out, one by one. They were just like tiny lamps themselves, but they did not give any real light.

He felt the urge to run after Mummy and Uncle Darren. But he must not do that. Mummy would get mad. He would get another beating, from her or from Uncle Darren.

He stared the way that they had gone. Darker now. If only the tent were here, to crawl inside. Last night he had felt so safe and snug, even when the light was turned way low. He could hear them, whispering in the darkness. It made him so warm and contented.

"Are you absolutely sure?" That was Mummy, in the same slurry voice. "I have to be absolutely sure."

"Course I am. I checked the whole thing with the game authorities. I pretended to be scared."

"I thought all the animals were controlled."

"That's what the advertisements say, but the controls go off when it's really dark. That's why they always tell you to keep a light on all night in the tent."

"What do you think is out there? Right now."

"Hey, how would I know? Get your mind off that sort of stuff."

There was a rustle from where Mummy lay, and she

giggled. "You! You're all hands. But what might be out there?"

"Lions, maybe. Leopards. Rhinos." (That made him listen harder. He had seen pictures of those animals.) "And jackals and hyenas and vultures. That's why we don't go outside in the dark. Make a noise out there, or go running around, and there'd be nothing tomorrow to collect and take back. Hey, why the questions all of a sudden? I thought we had it agreed."

"I just want to be absolutely sure it will work. Otherwise we'd have been better off with a straight sale. There's good money for a healthy one, down in the warrens."

"Not a hundredth as much as we'll get. They'll pay just to keep us quiet. Here, Miss Fidgety, you need a bit more of this."

There was a clink of glass, and the gurgling sound of pouring liquid. Uncle Darren laughed. "They'll pay, of course they will. What sort of publicity would it give the game reserve if we wanted to play it for news? Wandered away for a few minutes, frantic mother, desperate search. Maybe even a mental breakdown afterwards. That would be news."

"Sshh. Watch what you're saying."

"So what, for Christ's sake? At his age."

"He's very smart. He could be listening, and he remembers everything."

"Naw, he's asleep. Very smart, eh? How did he pick you for a mother?"

"Don't start that again. It was the biggest mistake of my life. Don't you pretend to be so smart, either. If you're so clever, how did you get hooked into that idiot marriage contract, you and the bitch?"

"Come off it, Lucy. That's all over, I don't even think about her any more. Look, once we get some money there'll be no more false starts. You and me, right? And . . . you know . . ."

"What are you doing! You're awful." But Mummy did not sound angry.

"You said I was all hands. I just want to prove that's not all I am."

"*Again?*" *Mummy giggled. "You. You're a monomaniac.*"

The light from the lamp in the tent dwindled to an even lower level. There was a rustling, and something like a soft groan from Mummy. Uncle Darren began a soft, regular grunting sound that was not his usual snoring . . .

And now it was nearly night again. Over beyond the top of the high grass he could see the big hill, as far away as ever. It always seemed to be the same distance, and when they walked it moved along with them. When it was close to dark he could see the smoke on top of it. It was there now, with the red sun behind it.

He stepped a little way in that direction, then came back. The grass was too tall, too frightening.

The sun seemed to be dropping down into the top of the grass, melting into it. Suddenly he could not see the grass itself. The sky was almost black, with stars scattered bright across it.

"*Mummy.*" He shouted as loud as he could into the swallowing dark, and started to run in the direction in which they had gone. Then he thought of the lamp, left behind him on the ground. He hurried back for it and turned it on. It threw a bright circle all around him, except behind his back. When he turned his head to look he saw a wedge of darkness, a long shadow cast by his own body. He moved backwards with the lamp, and the circle of light moved with him.

That lighted circle had become the whole world. Beyond its edge he began to hear the night noises. There were mutterings and growls in the darkness, the chuckling of madmen just out of sight. He struggled to see anything beyond the shadowed perimeter. ("Lions and leopards and rhinos, jackals and hyenas and vultures . . ." Uncle Darren's words were clear in his head. "Make a noise out there, or go running around, and there'd be nothing tomorrow to collect and take back . . .")

He shouldn't have shouted like that. He mustn't shout. Where could Mummy be? He had never been alone before.

He began to weep, slow, silent tears that trickled down his cheeks and into his mouth. He could taste their salt.

He wanted to scream for Mummy, but he knew that he must not. Behind him there was a slithering noise, and the soft rustle of moving grass. (Lions and leopards and rhinos, jackals and hyenas and vultures.) He held the lamp tight, and started forward across the clearing away from the noises. The edge of darkness pursued him. He thought that he heard new noises coming from in front.

He stopped and crouched close to the ground. The light from the lamp in his hand seemed to be weakening, the boundary of the safe circle smaller and more poorly defined. He bit on his fingers, and stared out into the night.

Were those eyes there, flashing glints of green and yellow? As the lamp faded, they became brighter. Soon the eyes were staring in on him from all sides. He pushed with his hands at the dark boundary, hating it, wishing it farther away.

Suddenly he could not stand it any longer. He did not run, but he dropped to the ground and flattened his body. He scrabbled with his fingers at the hard dirt and glared upward. Far away on the horizon, the top of the big hill was glowing with its own smoky red light. He fixed his eyes on it, afraid to look again at the narrowing circle.

"Mummy, Mummy, Mummy, Mummy." He said the incantation over and over, beneath his breath. "Mummy, Mummy, Mummy, Mummy . . ." She was the only thing he had to hold onto in the whole world. But he dared not call out to her (Make a noise out there, or go running around, and there'd be nothing tomorrow to collect and take back. . .). He dared not even whimper.

He lay on the ground and shivered. He must not cry. He must not cry. He will not cry. She will come back soon . . . she will come back soon . . . she will come back soon . . .

Esro Mondrian does not know it, but dawn and rescue are ten hours away.

The sale to the basement warrens of the Gallimaufries will take place a few days later.

Tatty was talking to him, gripping him by the shoulders. "Chan. What's wrong? Why are you crying?"

"I can cry. I *can*, it's all right." Chan closed his mouth and snuffled in hard through his nose. "It's all right."

She put her arms around him. "What happened?"

"Memories. I know why Esro Mondrian couldn't trust anything in the world. I know why he needed the Constructs so badly."

They both became aware that Tatty was holding him to her chest. She released him and went back to the hassock. They were oddly embarrassed. She had been his first-ever lover, even if no more than a surrogate.

"I've known for a long time," she said. "The Constructs were going to be his shield, his safety net out on the Perimeter. That's why he had them built."

"And they led to his destruction. Or maybe that was my fault. Or maybe yours."

"Whoever it was, it was no more than justice." Tatty did not hide her bitterness. "He was willing to destroy everybody else so he could keep the Constructs. Damn that man."

"I'm sorry. I was *trained* to hate him—by you—but I didn't know you were so angry."

"You don't know what hate is. If *anyone* has a right to hate Esro Mondrian, I do. He used me over and over—and I jumped at the chance."

"That settles one thing." Chan stood up. "I know all I need to know. I'll go."

She stared up at him, rubbing her brown eyes with a too-thin hand. "You mean you came to see me, and you didn't *want* anything from me? My God, that must be a first. I don't think anybody has ever been down to see me without wanting something, except maybe poor old Kubo. He comes and we take our Paradox shots, and then we sit there grinning at each other like idiots until it wears off." Her voice broke. "And then Kubo goes, and I think of what I *was*. I was a *Princess*, Chan. And look at me now, what I am—what Esro Mondrian made me."

"You're being too nice to me, Tatty. I did want something from you. But I can see I'm not going to get it." Chan reached out as though to touch Tatty's greasy hair, then drew back his hand. "I guess Kubo told you that

Mondrian is alive. But now I see how you feel about him—"

"*Alive?* What are you talking about? He's dead."

"Yes and no. Technically, he's alive."

"How can he be dead, and alive?"

"We did it to him. *I* did it to him. He would have destroyed the ship, and everyone on board it. I had to reach in and pull the abort sequence out of his mind, but it was buried deep. I went in all the way, and exploded everything that kept the mind pool out. There's not much left. What there is can't communicate. Maybe there's something that could be reached, but to do that you would need to—"

"No! You bastard, you're as bad as Mondrian. *Worse!*" She reached out at him with hands like talons. "I know what you're thinking. I know why you came to see me."

"I only wanted to—"

"Liar! You only know what the Stimulator did to *you*, you have no idea what it did to *me*. I don't know how you have the nerve to come here."

"I'm sorry. Kubo Flammarion told me to talk to you, and I guess I was ready to try anything. I'll go now."

Chan went into the cramped hall and waited for the outer door to open.

"You are going to Ceres?" Tatty had followed him.

"Farther than that."

"To the stars again?"

"No. I'm going to a place in the solar system that makes Horus look like Paradise."

"There's no such place. There can't be."

"Believe me. Our quarantine has been set up in the Sargasso Dump. The Morgan Construct is there, held in stasis. It's my team's job to try to make it sane."

"But where is Mondrian?"

"He's in the same place. If he is still Mondrian. Would it make you more likely to help, if I said that whatever is living now in the Sargasso Dump is *not* Esro Mondrian?"

"No, it would not. It would make me ... I don't know."

Tatty stood, eyes blinking. "Damn him, damn him, *damn* him," she said suddenly. "Wait here."

She disappeared into the cramped interior of the apartment and was gone for a long time. When she returned her hair was washed and brushed, she was wearing a clean dress of pale green, and carefully-applied makeup hid the Paradox stigmata and the dark rings around her eyes. She was still raddled and pathetically emaciated, but her back was straight.

Chan wanted to offer a compliment. The words stuck in his throat. "You need to put on some weight," he said at last. "Tatty, I won't lie to you. I have to say one other thing. There will be no Paradox supply in the Sargasso Dump. Kubo Flammarion is there now, and he says it's torture without it."

"Kubo doesn't know about torture. But *we* know it, Chan. You and I, we can count the ways." Tatty took his arm. "Come on."

"I'll help you, Tatty."

"Don't kid yourself. You can't help me, and I don't think I can help you. Or anybody. Just promise me one thing."

"Name it."

"The Paradox is going to wear off in a couple of hours. Just make sure I'm not on Earth when it happens."

Chapter 41

"Captain," said Phoebe Willard. "You just don't understand."

"Mmm." Kubo Flammarion reached down, well below camera level, and scratched at his crotch in mystification. "I guess you're right."

On that, he was not lying. He stared at the scene sent back to Ceres through the local Link, and he *didn't* understand. The Sargasso Dump was supposed to be a huge open part of space, in which drifted assorted junk of all kinds. That's exactly what it looked like.

"But you don't have to stay there, you know," he went on. "You can come back anytime."

"Not until I know what happened." Phoebe's expression when she glanced around her was not so different from his. Some irritation, but mostly simple puzzlement. "The loss has to be *explained*."

"I know, all that equipment. But with the other Construct available—"

"To hell with the equipment, and to hell with M-29, or whatever the new one calls itself. I'm talking about the *guards*."

"Oh, yeah." Kubo had seen a lot of those guards, when they were originally being shipped out to the Sargasso Dump. Not much of a loss, in his opinion. "Yeah. The guards."

"Captain Kubo Flammarion, you great *meathead*, you've got no idea. Something amazing had been happening here, something wonderful, improvements in people

410

who were never expected to improve. *That's* what I care about. I feel sure M-26A was involved, but I can't explain *how*. If only we could find them."

"We found out where they Linked to, if that helps at all."

"Nobody told me that! If you know where they are, why isn't somebody going after them?"

"Well, we don't know where they *are*, see, only where they *Linked to*. They went to one of the probes, right out on the Perimeter, and they held the Link open long enough to take tons of stuff from the Dump with them—supplies, and construction equipment, and both reserve drives, and trash we still haven't managed to inventory as missing. But when one of our people from Boundary Security went after them, all she found was an empty probe. The Link unit is still there, and it works fine, but it's in the middle of a quintuple stellar system. There are forty planets and a hundred thousand planetoids within five billion kilometers. Our investigator wasn't equipped for that sort of search, so she had to Link home again."

"We have to go back."

"Tell that to the Stellar Group ambassadors. Without a Link, M-26A and the guards can't go anywhere. They're stuck somewhere in that stellar system, safe in cold storage. As far as the ambassadors are concerned they can stay there until more urgent problems are solved. Like, how to handle the mind pools. They scare everybody rigid, a lot worse than M-26A. Anyway, why do you *need* M-26A? You could work with M-29. Chan and Leah are right on your doorstep, and you'll soon have better work facilities. We're shipping new stuff, living quarters and everything. That's already happening."

Kubo did not add that the living raw material of Phoebe's study would also be replaced, and that was already happening, too. Only two days earlier a frightful act of sabotage, high in the Venus Superdome, had provided three new recruits for Sargasso.

"The policy that Commander Brachis set up for staffing the Dump is still going on," he continued, "even without him."

He glanced uneasily over his shoulder. A meeting with Dougal MacDougal was due in a few minutes, and despite friendly prompting from Lotos Sheldrake, that prospect made him nervous. With Mondrian and Brachis gone, Kubo was having greatness thrust upon him. He did not like it at all.

"Anything else you need, Doctor Willard?"

"Not that I can think of."

"Right then." Kubo stared at her again, this time with a different expression. He dropped his voice. "Would you give Princess Tatiana a message from me? Tell her there's a little package on its way to her in the next shipment. She'll know what that means."

"And so do I. I don't know if you're her friend or her enemy. You're an idiot, Kubo, you could get caught. But you're a kind man."

"Nah." He wriggled in embarrassment. "Just killing me and the Princess that much faster." He reached out to cut their connection, then hesitated. "I don't suppose there's any, well, *progress*, is there, on the other?"

"Some days I think there is, some days I'm sure there isn't. I'll call you if there's any real change."

"Ah. Do that for me." Kubo sighed, shook his head, and was gone.

Phoebe Willard sighed too, and again gazed around her. When she had first visited the Dump, the Sargasso facilities had seemed primitive and spartan beyond belief. But the replacement quarters, the prefabs that had been shipped in after the originals had vanished with the guards and M-26A, made those originals seem like luxury apartments.

She closed her suit, left the air-bubble of the tiny communications hutch, and drifted back towards the hall that served as combined workroom, kitchen, recreation area and dormitory.

The green sphere of liquid nitrogen containing M-29 was off to her left. She regarded it with scorn. It had done nothing to restrain M-26A, even when that Construct was no more than a battered and bewildered brain fragment. How much use was it likely to be with a complete Construct? But the Stellar Group ambassadors had insisted, and with this one there was at least the mind pools' conviction that it was rendered harmless (just as Phoebe would have vouched that M-26A was harmless!).

Well, cross her fingers, but that was Chan Dalton and Leah Rainbow's problem, not hers. They were working in there now, either as individuals or in the uncomfortable union of the mind pools. One of them was sure to drop by with a progress report from the nitrogen bubble before the end of the day.

She floated on, in no hurry to return to the main building. On the way she attempted something that she had already failed to do a dozen times. She tried to decide what else had gone from the Dump. She had heard about the old Mattin Link, refurbished and made serviceable—though not efficient, the energy drain on the power supply system when it operated had been monstrous!—but other objects had vanished, too. Her own recent ramblings in the Dump had revealed thousands of curiosities that she had never noticed before; on the other hand, nothing seemed to be *missing*.

Today she drifted past a huge double-ended tree, more than a kilometer long and sprouting abundant silver-green leaves and globular fruit from every branch. It must be one of the obsolete free-space vegetation forms, harmless enough to be left alone here in the Dump. It might be even older than the vanished Mattin Link.

Fresh fruit? The temptation to gather one of those giant orange globes from the slow-orbiting plant was strong. Except that "harmless" probably didn't include being eaten by dimwit scientists with odd food cravings.

Phoebe kept going, and at last came to the pressurized main building. It would be warm inside, and the field of the power kernel even provided gravity. But the moment that she hated worst of all was approaching.

Well, it was pointless to put it off any longer. She went through the lock folds and stripped off her suit.

They were there, all four of them. She realized that she'd entertained a vague hope that two of them might still be off in the treatment room. She walked across to join them, forcing herself to appear calm and relaxed.

Esro Mondrian sat at a table, staring straight ahead. He ignored the food in front of him. His expression seldom varied, a strange little half-smile that suggested amusement at a secret joke. When Phoebe crossed his line of sight, he gave her a knowing nod and a sly little wink. But his forehead was beaded with sweat.

Tatty Snipes sat next to him, holding his hand. She was neatly dressed and carefully made up; skeletally thin, with blue veins visible as a tracery on her temples. And she was trembling.

It was obvious to Phoebe that a Stimulator session had recently ended. "Kubo says hello." She offered the greeting to all of them equally. She hung up her suit and raised her eyebrows questioningly at Tatty. "Anything?"

Tatty shook her head. "Nothing. Next time you talk to Kubo, tell him it's no good."

"It takes time, you know. Maybe—"

"Phoebe, I've been through this before. I think I'm the system's expert on what you can and can't do with the Tolkov Stimulator. I can compare Esro with what happened to Chan, and I assure you, it's just not working. I want you to tell Kubo that."

Instead of replying, Phoebe turned to the other couple in the room. If Tatty Snipes looked like a dying woman, Godiva Lomberd, who ought to have been dead, appeared in radiant health.

Phoebe had seen her return from the Q-ship around Travancore, with that gaping hole right through her body. She could not believe how fast Godiva had healed. Today she was wearing a dress that left her midriff bare. There was no sign of any wound. The skin on her belly and back was smooth and flawless.

What thoughts went through the brain behind that smooth forehead and serene face? Godiva was beaming fondly at the rigid form of Luther Brachis, strapped tightly into his chair. He in turn was glaring at Phoebe, one eye bulging asymmetrically from its orbit. His mouth was working angrily, and he again and again tried to rub the back of his mangled skull against the restraining head brace.

"He's having a bit of a bad day," said Godiva. "He's angry with me now, because I won't let him try to feed himself. He makes such a *mess*. But he recognizes you. He's making progress."

Brachis growled, like a caged and tormented bear, and Phoebe instinctively recoiled. She had heard no suggestion of trying a Tolkov Stimulator treatment on Luther Brachis. He was too far gone. It was a miracle that Godiva had managed to keep him alive at all. A second miracle, of restored higher faculties, was surely too much to hope for.

Phoebe had no appetite, but she went across and helped herself to food also. Eyeing the other four as she ate, it occurred to her that both Tatiana and Godiva had given their typical responses. Tatty saw no progress at all, whereas to Phoebe's eye there was at least a glimmer of intelligence in Mondrian's look; while Godiva, ignoring reality, saw Brachis as something more than a brain-dead animal.

Seeing them together now, Phoebe managed a great leap of understanding. Godiva and Tatty were marooned here, far from home, far from every grace of civilization, far from all friends and all comforts. They were condemned to tend men who were no more than mindless husks of what they had been only a month earlier. The women were feeding them now, spoonful by patient spoonful, but there was no sign of acknowledgement or appreciation.

And here was the real shock: Tatty and Godiva were *happy*. If Mondrian and Brachis improved and became human again, that would be wonderful. But if they did not, that was acceptable. The women would stay with them. They would never leave the Sargasso Dump.

It was an even bigger shock to Phoebe to realize that the same was true of her. She was here, *waiting*. Waiting for Chan and Leah to tell her if M-29 could explain what had happened to the other Construct and to the old guards, before they vanished together across fifty light-years. Waiting for the brain-tattered zombies of new guard recruits to show up, so that she could begin to work with them.

Waiting for the second miracle.

Maybe Phoebe too would never leave the Dump. And maybe that was all right.

Epilogue

It was an alien landscape. But to men and women who had spent their whole lives patrolling the remoter reaches of the solar system, Earth would have been just as alien.

With five suns to light the sky, true dark was the rarest of events. But a time of minimal light was approaching, with the closest and brightest pair already set and a third gliding towards the horizon. The ruddy glow of the other two, a pair of contact binary dwarfs a third of a lightyear away, provided the signal for the world's nocturnal life to awaken.

Crawling, creeping and flying forms emerged from their deep burrows. The guards stared at them. There was no sense of fear on either side, and indeed there was no danger. For the guards it was astonishment at sheer numbers, at a thousand different species appearing in the twilight.

And yet this fecundity is the norm, across a hundred worlds within the Stellar Group. M-26A was crouched on a plain of gravel, the bed of a sometime lake that would fill every couple of hundred years as the planet performed its complex figure-eight orbit around its two dual primaries. *There is no reason for your astonishment. According to my recorded information, what you see here should be considered nothing unusual.*

Blaine Ridley was standing in front of M-26A. During the fourteen hours between the rising and setting of the brighter primary, defined by convention at this time of year as daytime, he had monitored the robot assembly and installation of better living accommodations. Now he and the other Sargasso guards were drifting back towards the place where the Construct had remained, unmoving, since early morning. Ridley opened his mouth, produced a strange stammering sound, and closed it again. The words of M-26A spoke once more, clear in his mind.

In any case, this is no more than a temporary station. The Morgan Construct, as usual when the day's work was done, became gently philosophical. *Once we are fully established here, we can move to our real work. We can begin to guard the Perimeter. That will require that we build a great network, scattered through the farthest reaches of known space. It will require that you men and woman start to multiply in numbers, and increase in strength.*

Then we will all fulfill our highest destiny. We will be guards, in truth and not merely in name.

The spell was as effective as ever, a lifting of the communal spirit. However, tonight it did not work so well on Blaine Ridley. He had been chosen by the other guards and charged with a mission, and in anticipation of speech his eye was rolling and his jaw working nervously from side to side. Except that he could not find words. Alone of all the guards, he remained standing instead of sinking cross-legged onto the loose gravel surface.

See what you were, just short weeks ago. Broken, battered, without goals or hopes. The mere shadows of men and women. And I was no better. See you now. Strong, confident, dedicated. And I am no different. It is the difference of life with a purpose, and life without purpose.

M-26A paused. The Construct appeared to notice Ridley, standing stiffly to attention before it, for the first time. *Is this not all true?*

"It is true." The question, addressed to Ridley directly, freed his tongue. "It is all true. I know what we were. I know what we are now. And we—we have a problem."

Tell it.

"I speak for all of us." Ridley glanced around for encouragement. Misshapen heads nodded, and there were grunts and murmurs of agreement. The faces turned toward him were earnest and dusky red in the meager light of the twin dwarf suns. Their support gave him the strength to continue. "We were nothing before you came to the Sargasso Dump. We helped each other as much as we could, but we were like beasts. Worse than beasts, because we had once been human. You raised us to humanity again."

If that is true, the same work did much more for me. It gave me sanity.

"Maybe we do not have sanity, as other humans define it. Maybe that is why we have a question."

Ask it.

"Is the way back closed? Would it be possible to go again to the Sargasso Dump?"

The great compound eyes froze, smoky-red and luminous in the twilight. *You are unhappy here? You wish to return to what you were?*

"No! Never!"

So why do you talk of returning?

"We feel *guilty*." At last Ridley could speak easily, and the words poured out. "You have to know how we all came to the Dump—not all at once, but a few every year, sometimes as many as ten, sometimes only two or three. We came from all over the system. Whenever there was a great disaster, the Sargasso guards were likely to see a jump in numbers. We hail from the Vulcan Nexus, and Mars, and Ceres, and Oberon Station, and Europa—from all over. Before we came to Sargasso, we had our friends everywhere in the solar system.

"And still they must be coming to Sargasso. The accidents have not stopped. New recruits will be arriving as we are speaking—perhaps they have already arrived. Our hearts break for them. But who will help them? Who will teach *them* pride, and purpose, and lift them again to humanity? Who? There is no one—except us. And you."

M-26A did not move, but the bright eyes seemed to cloud over. *To return. To deny our destiny. That way lies insanity.*

"To go back, and stay there, that might mean insanity.

That is not what we mean. But to go back *briefly*, maybe once every few years, and help them ... and perhaps bring the new guards here ..."

I cannot offer an answer at once. M-26A lifted itself on tripod legs. *I must think about this. I will answer you ... tomorrow.*

"That is all right. We have been thinking about this for a long time. One other thing." Ridley was talking to the back of M-26A, as the Construct slid silently across the gravel surface, toward the dark apertures of the sleeping units.

Say it.

"You did not answer our question, whether it is possible to return for a time to the Sargasso Dump." Ridley was standing straight, but he was no longer at attention. "If it is possible, no matter how difficult it may be, we would like to do it. More than that, if we are to remain human, we *must* do it. We want you to help."

Ridley stood, and listened, but M-26A did not speak again. He was quite sure of that.

It must have been only the night breeze of the new world, sighing in his ear, that seemed to whisper, *Yes, Master.*

SCIENCE FICTION AS ONLY A SCIENTIST CAN WRITE IT!

CHARLES SHEFFIELD

Charles Sheffield, a mathematician & physicist, is a past president of both the American Astronautical Society & the Science Fiction Writers of America, and the chief scientist of the Earth Satellite Corporation. He serves as a science reviewer for several prominent publications. In science fiction, he has received the coveted Nebula and Hugo Awards, as well as the John W. Campbell Memorial Award for his novel for Baen, *Brother to Dragons*.

THE SPHERES OF HEAVEN	(HC) 31969-8	$24.00	☐
	(PB) 31856-X	$7.99	☐
THE MIND POOL	72165-8	$6.99	☐
THE WEB BETWEEN THE WORLDS	31973-6	$6.99	☐
MY BROTHER'S KEEPER	57873-1	$5.99	☐
THE COMPLEAT McANDREW	57857-X	$6.99	☐
BORDERLANDS OF SCIENCE	(HC) 57836-7	$22.00	☐
	(PB) 31953-1	$6.99	☐
CONVERGENT SERIES (*Summertide & Divergence*)	87791-7	$6.99	☐
TRANSVERGENCE (*Transcendence & Convergence*)	57837-5	$6.99	☐
PROTEUS IN THE UNDERWORLD	87659-7	$5.99	☐

If not available through your local bookstore send this coupon and a check or money order for the cover price(s) + $1.50 s/h to Baen Books, Dept. BA, P.O. Box 1403, Riverdale, NY 10471. Delivery can take up to eight weeks.

NAME: _____

ADDRESS: _____

_____

I have enclosed a check or money order in the amount of $_____

JAMES P. HOGAN
Real SF

The Legend That Was Earth (HC) 0-671-31945-0 $24.00 ☐
(PB) 0-671-31840-3 $7.99 ☐

The alien presence on Earth may hide a dark secret!

Cradle of Saturn (HC) 0-671-57813-8 $24.00 ☐
(PB) 0-671-57866-9 $6.99 ☐

Earth smugly thought it had no need to explore space—but the universe had a nasty surprise up its sleeve!

Realtime Interrupt 0-671-57884-7 $6.99 ☐

A brilliant scientist trapped in a virtual reality hell of his own making. There is one way out—if only he can see it.

Bug Park (HC) 0-671-87773-9 $22.00 ☐
(PB) 0-671-87874-3 $6.99 ☐

Paths to Otherwhere (HC) 0-671-87710-0 $22.00 ☐
(PB) 0-671-87767-4 $6.99 ☐

Voyage from Yesteryear 0-671-57798-0 $6.99 ☐

The Multiplex Man 0-671-57819-7 $6.99 ☐

Rockets, Redheads, & Revolution 0-671-57807-3 $6.99 ☐

Minds, Machines, & Evolution 0-671-57843-X $6.99 ☐

The Two Faces of Tomorrow 0-671-87848-4 $6.99 ☐

Endgame Enigma 0-671-87796-8 $5.99 ☐

The Proteus Operation 0-671-87757-7 $5.99 ☐

Star Child 0-671-87878-6 $5.99 ☐

If not available at your local bookstore, fill out this coupon and send a check or money order for the cover price(s) plus $1.50 s/h to Baen Books, Dept. BA, P.O. Box 1403, Riverdale, NY 10471. Delivery can take up to ten weeks.

NAME: _____

ADDRESS: _____

_____

I have enclosed a check or money order in the amount of $ _____

Robert A. HEINLEIN

"Robert A. Heinlein wears imagination as though it were his private suit of clothes. What makes his work so rich is that he combines his lively, creative sense with an approach that is at once literate, informed, and exciting."

—*New York Times*

A collection of Robert A. Heinlein's best-loved titles are now available in superbly packaged Baen editions. Collect them all.

ORPHANS OF THE SKY	31845-4 ◆ $6.99	☐
BEYOND THIS HORIZON (SMALL HC)	31836-5 ◆ $17.00	☐
THE MENACE FROM EARTH	57802-2 ◆ $6.99	☐
SIXTH COLUMN	57826-X ◆ $5.99	☐
REVOLT IN 2100 & METHUSELAH'S CHILDREN	57780-8 ◆ $6.99	☐
THE GREEN HILLS OF EARTH	57853-7 ◆ $6.99	☐
THE MAN WHO SOLD THE MOON	57863-4 ◆ $5.99	☐
ASSIGNMENT IN ETERNITY	57865-0 ◆ $6.99	☐
FARNHAM'S FREEHOLD	72206-9 ◆ $6.99	☐
GLORY ROAD	87704-6 ◆ $6.99	☐
PODKAYNE OF MARS	87671-6 ◆ $5.99	☐

Available at your local bookstore. If not, fill out this coupon and send a check or money order for the cover price + $1.50 s/h to Baen Books, Dept. BA, P.O. Box 1403, Riverdale, NY 10471. Delivery can take up to 8 weeks.

Name: _____

Address: _____

_____

I have enclosed a check or money order in the amount of $ _____

Got questions? We've got answers at
BAEN'S BAR!

Here's what some of our members have to say:

"Ever wanted to get involved in a newsgroup but were frightened off by rude know-it-alls? Stop by Baen's Bar. Our know-it-alls are the friendly, helpful type—and some write the hottest SF around."
— **Melody L** *melodyl@ccnmail.com*

"Baen's Bar . . . where you just might find people who understand what you are talking about!"
— **Tom Perry** *perry@airswitch.net*

"Lots of gentle teasing and numerous puns, mixed with various recipes for food and fun."
— **Ginger Tansey** *makautz@prodigy.net*

"Join the fun at Baen's Bar, where you can discuss the latest in books, Treecat Sign Language, ramifications of cloning, how military uniforms have changed, help an author do research, fuss about differences between American and European measurements—and top it off with being able to talk to the people who write and publish what you love."
— **Sun Shadow** *sun2shadow@hotmail.com*

"Thanks for a lovely first year at the Bar, where the only thing that's been intoxicating is conversation."
— **Al Jorgensen** *awjorgen@wolf.co.net*

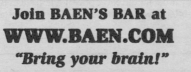

Join BAEN'S BAR at
WWW.BAEN.COM
"Bring your brain!"